The excit
bestselling
THE NEW JEDI ORDER,

a..ssly
fi.................................conquer the galaxy, and
Han Solo struggles with grief and anger at the
greatest loss of his life!

*We gather in memory of Chewbacca: honorable
son, beloved mate, devoted father, loyal friend and
comrade in arms, champion and clan uncle to all of
us in spirit . . .*

*In Chewbacca, the defiant flame burned brightest.
On Kashyyyk or farr afield on distant worlds, he was
never less than courageous and incorruptible—a
Wookiee with heart enough for ten and eagerr
strength enough forr fifty . . .*

*Now, in the same way the branches of the
wroshyr seek out and support one another,
Chewbacca's spirit merges with and gives sustenance to ourr own, strengthening us forr the challenges we have yet to confront . . .*

—from *Agents of Chaos I: HERO'S TRIAL,* by
James Luceno

Previously in The New Jedi Order series

By James Luceno

The ROBOTECH series
(as Jack McKinney, with Brian Daley)

THE BLACK HOLE TRAVEL AGENCY series
(as Jack McKinney, with Brian Daley)

A FEARFUL SYMMETRY
ILLEGAL ALIEN
THE BIG EMPTY
KADUNA MEMORIES

THE YOUNG INDIANA JONES CHRONICLES:
THE MATA HARI AFFAIR

THE SHADOW
THE MASK OF ZORRO
RIO PASION
RAINCHASER
ROCK BOTTOM

STAR WARS: CLOAK OF DECEPTION

STAR WARS: DARTH MAUL, SABOTEUR (e-book)

STAR WARS: THE NEW JEDI ORDER:
AGENTS OF CHAOS I: HERO'S TRIAL

STAR WARS: THE NEW JEDI ORDER:
AGENTS OF CHAOS II: JEDI ECLIPSE

STAR WARS: THE NEW JEDI ORDER:
THE UNIFYING FORCE

STAR WARS: LABYRINTH OF EVIL

STAR WARS

THE NEW JEDI ORDER

AGENTS OF CHAOS
HERO'S TRIAL

James Luceno

BALLANTINE BOOKS • NEW YORK

A Del Rey® Book
Published by The Random House Publishing Group

Copyright © 2000 by Lucasfilm Ltd. & ™.
All Rights Reserved. Used Under Authorization.

Excerpt from *Star Wars:* The New Jedi Order: *Balance Point* copyright © 2001 by Lucasfilm Ltd. ® or ™ where indicated. All Rights Reserved. Used under authorization.

Published in the United States by The Random House Publishing Group, a division of Random House, Inc., New York.

Del Rey is a registered trademark and the Del Rey colophon is a registered trademark of Random House, Inc.

www.starwars.com
www.delreybooks.com

ISBN 0-345-48038-4

Map design by Daniel Wallace
Map by Chris Barbieri

Manufactured in the United States of America

First Edition: August 2000
First Mass Market Special Edition: April 2005

OPM   9 8 7 6 5 4 3 2 1

DEDICATION

For my young son Jake,
and *The New Jedi Order*

ACKNOWLEDGMENTS

I want to extend heartfelt thanks to those who kept me on track and loaned a hand along the way: Dan Wallace, who knows the expanded universe better than anyone; Rob Brown, whose suggestions helped shape chapter 7; and Alex Newborn, who steered me to a new character for chapter 14. Thanks, too, to Mike Kogge, Matt Olsen, Eelia Goldsmith Henderscheid, Enrique Guerrero, and Kris Boldis for their keen commentaries; fellow authors Robert Salvatore, Mike Stackpole, and Kathy Tyers for their detail work; and Shelly Shapiro, Sue Rostoni, and Lucy Autrey Wilson, without whom *The New Jedi Order* would never have taken shape. Finally, infinite gratitude to my late friend and collaborator, Brian Daley.

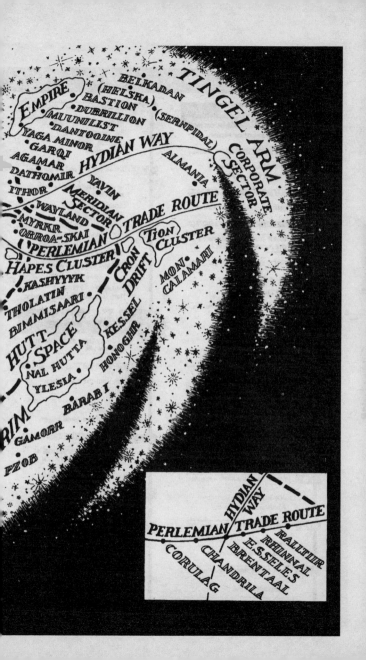

THE STAR WARS NOVELS TIMELINE

44 YEARS BEFORE STAR WARS: A New Hope

Jedi Apprentice series

33 YEARS BEFORE STAR WARS: A New Hope

Darth Maul: Saboteur
Cloak of Deception

32.5 YEARS BEFORE STAR WARS: A New Hope

Darth Maul: Shadow Hunter

32 YEARS BEFORE STAR WARS: A New Hope

**STAR WARS: EPISODE I
THE PHANTOM MENACE**

29 YEARS BEFORE STAR WARS: A New Hope

Rogue Planet
Jedi Quest series

22.5 YEARS BEFORE STAR WARS: A New Hope

The Approaching Storm

22 YEARS BEFORE STAR WARS: A New Hope

**STAR WARS: EPISODE II
ATTACK OF THE CLONES**

Star Wars Republic Commando:
Hard Contact

21.5 YEARS BEFORE STAR WARS: A New Hope

Shatterpoint

21 YEARS BEFORE STAR WARS: A New Hope

The Cestus Deception
The Hive*

20 YEARS BEFORE STAR WARS: A New Hope

Medstar I: Battle Surgeons
Medstar II: Jedi Healer

19.5 YEARS BEFORE STAR WARS: A New Hope

Jedi Trial
Yoda: Dark Rendezvous

19 YEARS BEFORE STAR WARS: A New Hope

Labyrinth of Evil
**STAR WARS: EPISODE III
REVENGE OF THE SITH**

10–0 YEARS BEFORE STAR WARS: A New Hope

The Han Solo Trilogy:
  The Paradise Snare
  The Hutt Gambit
  Rebel Dawn

5–2 YEARS BEFORE STAR WARS: A New Hope

The Adventures of Lando Calrissian:
  Lando Calrissian and the Mindharp of Sharu
  Lando Calrissian and the Flamewind of Oseon
  Lando Calrissian and the Starcave of ThonBoka

The Han Solo Adventures:
  Han Solo at Stars' End
  Han Solo's Revenge
  Han Solo and the Lost Legacy

STAR WARS: A New Hope YEAR 0

**STAR WARS: EPISODE IV
A NEW HOPE**

0–3 YEARS AFTER STAR WARS: A New Hope

Tales from the Mos Eisley Cantina
Star Wars: Galaxies: The Ruins of Dantooine
Splinter of the Mind's Eye

3 YEARS AFTER STAR WARS: A New Hope

**STAR WARS: EPISODE V
THE EMPIRE STRIKES BACK**

Tales of the Bounty Hunters

3.5 YEARS AFTER STAR WARS: A New Hope

Shadows of the Empire

4 YEARS AFTER STAR WARS: A New Hope

**STAR WARS: EPISODE VI
RETURN OF THE JEDI**

Tales from Jabba's Palace
The Bounty Hunter Wars:
  The Mandalorian Armor
  Slave Ship
  Hard Merchandise

The Truce at Bakura

6.5-7.5 YEARS AFTER STAR WARS: A New Hope

X-Wing:
Rogue Squadron
Wedge's Gamble
The Krytos Trap
The Bacta War
Wraith Squadron
Iron Fist
Solo Command

8 YEARS AFTER STAR WARS: A New Hope

The Courtship of Princess Leia
A Forest Apart*
Tatooine Ghost

9 YEARS AFTER STAR WARS: A New Hope

The Thrawn Trilogy:
Heir to the Empire
Dark Force Rising
The Last Command

X-Wing: Isard's Revenge

11 YEARS AFTER STAR WARS: A New Hope

I, Jedi

The Jedi Academy Trilogy:
Jedi Search
Dark Apprentice
Champions of the Force

12-13 YEARS AFTER STAR WARS: A New Hope

Children of the Jedi
Darksaber
Planet of Twilight
X-Wing: Starfighters of Adumar

14 YEARS AFTER STAR WARS: A New Hope

The Crystal Star

16-17 YEARS AFTER STAR WARS: A New Hope

The Black Fleet Crisis Trilogy:
Before the Storm
Shield of Lies
Tyrant's Test

17 YEARS AFTER STAR WARS: A New Hope

The New Rebellion

18 YEARS AFTER STAR WARS: A New Hope

The Corellian Trilogy:
Ambush at Corellia
Assault at Selonia
Showdown at Centerpoint

19 YEARS AFTER STAR WARS: A New Hope

The Hand of Thrawn Duology:
Specter of the Past
Vision of the Future

22 YEARS AFTER STAR WARS: A New Hope

Junior Jedi Knights series

Friendly Fire*
Survivor's Quest

23-24 YEARS AFTER STAR WARS: A New Hope

Young Jedi Knights series

25-30 YEARS AFTER STAR WARS: A New Hope

The New Jedi Order:
Vector Prime
Dark Tide I: Onslaught
Dark Tide II: Ruin
Agents of Chaos I: Hero's Trial
Agents of Chaos II: Jedi Eclipse
Balance Point
Recovery*
Edge of Victory I: Conquest
Edge of Victory II: Rebirth
Star by Star
Dark Journey
Enemy Lines I: Rebel Dream
Enemy Lines II: Rebel Stand
Traitor
Destiny's Way
Ylesia*
Force Heretic I: Remnant
Force Heretic II: Refugee
Force Heretic III: Reunion
The Final Prophecy
The Unifying Force

*An ebook novella

DRAMATIS PERSONAE

Nom Anor; executor (male Yuuzhan Vong)

Malik Carr; commander (male Yuuzhan Vong)

Reck Desh; Peace Brigade mercenary (male human)

Droma; spacer (male Ryn)

Elan; priestess (female Yuuzhan Vong)

Harrar; priest (male Yuuzhan Vong)

Belindi Kalenda; New Republic Intelligence (female human)

Raff; battle tactician (male Yuuzhan Vong)

Roa; captain, *Happy Dagger* (male human)

Major Showolter; New Republic Intelligence (male human)

Luke Skywalker; Jedi Master (male human)

Mara Jade Skywalker; Jedi Master (female human)

Anakin Solo; Jedi Knight (male human)

Han Solo; captain, *Millennium Falcon* (male human)

Leia Organa Solo; New Republic ambassador (female human)

Tla; commander (male Yuuzhan Vong)

Vergere; Elan's familiar (female Fosh)

ONE

If the system's primary was distressed by the events that had transpired on and about the fourth closest of its brood, it betrayed nothing to the naked eye. Saturating local space with golden radiance, the star was as unperturbed now as it was before the battle had begun. Only the conquered world had suffered, its punished surface revealed in the steady crawl of sunlight. Regions that had once been green, blue, or white appeared ash-gray or reddish-brown. Below banks of panicked clouds, smoke chimneyed from immolated cities and billowed from tracts of firestormed evergreen forests. Steam roiled from the superheated beds of glacier-fed lakes and shallow seas.

Deep within the planet's shroud of cinder and debris moved the warship most responsible for the devastation. The vessel was a massive ovoid of yorik coral, its scabrous black surface relieved in places by bands of smoother stuff, lustrous as volcanic glass. In the pits that dimpled the coarse stretches hid projectile launchers and plasma weapons. Other, more craterlike depressions housed the laser-gobbling dovin basals that both drove the vessel and shielded it from harm. From fore and aft extended bloodred and cobalt arms, to which asteroidlike fighters

1

clung like barnacles. Smaller craft buzzed around it, some effecting repairs to battle-damaged areas, others keen on recharging depleted weapons systems, a few delivering plunder from the planet's scorched crust.

Farther removed from the battle floated a smaller vessel, black, as well, but faceted and polished smooth as a gemstone. Light pulsed through the ship at intervals, exciting one facet, then another, as if data were being conveyed from sector to sector.

From a roost in the underside of its angular snout, a gaunt figure, cross-legged on cushions, scanned the flotsam and jetsam a quirk of a gravitational drift had borne close to his ship: pieces of New Republic capital ships and starfighters, space-suited bodies in eerie repose, undetonated projectiles, the holed fuselage of a noncombat craft whose legend identified it as the *Penga Rift*.

In the near distance hung the blackened skeleton of a defense platform. Off to one side a ruined cruiser rolled end over end in a decaying orbit, surrendering its contents to vacuum like a burst pod scattering fine seeds. Elsewhere a fleeing transport, snagged by the spike of a bloated capture vessel, was being tugged inexorably toward the bowels of the giant warship.

The seated figure beheld these sights without cheer or regret. Necessity had engineered the destruction. What had been done needed to be done.

An acolyte stood in the rear of the command roost, relaying updates as they were received by a slender, living device fastened to his right inner forearm by six insectile legs.

"Victory is ours, Eminence. Our air and ground forces have overwhelmed the principal population centers and a war coordinator has installed itself in the mantle." The acolyte glanced at the receiving villip on his arm, whose soft bioluminescent glow added appreciably to the roost's scant light. "Commander Tla's battle tactician is of the opinion that the astrogation charts and historical data stored here will prove valuable to our campaign."

The priest, Harrar, glanced at the warship. "Has the tactician made his feelings known to Commander Tla?"

The acolyte's hesitancy was answer enough, but Harrar suffered the verbal reply anyway.

"Our arrival does not please the commander, Eminence. He does not dismiss out of hand the need for sacrifice, but he asserts that the campaign has been successful thus far without the need for religious overseers. He fears that our presence will only confound his task."

"Commander Tla fails to grasp that we engage the enemy on different fronts," Harrar said. "Any opponent can be beaten into submission, but compliance is no guarantee that you have won him over to your beliefs."

"Shall I relay as much to the commander, Eminence?"

"It is not your place. Leave that to me."

Harrar, a male of middle years, rose and moved to the lip of the roost's polygonal transparency, where he stood with three-fingered hands clasped at the small of his back—the missing digits having been offered in dedication ceremonies and ritual sacrifices, as a means of escalating himself. His tall slender frame was draped in supple fabrics of muted tones. A head cloth, patterned and significantly knotted, bound his long black tresses. The back of his neck showed vibrant markings etched into skin stretched taut by prominent vertebrae.

The planet turned beneath him.

"What is this world called?"

"Obroa-skai, Eminence."

"Obroa-skai," Harrar mused aloud. "What does the name signify?"

"The meaning is unknown at present. Though no doubt some explanation can be found among the captured data."

Harrar's right hand gestured in dismissal. "It's a dead issue."

A flash of weapons drew his eye to Obroa-skai's terminator, where a yorik coral gunship was angling into the light, spewing rear fire at a quartet of snub-nosed starfighters that had evidently chased it from the planet's dark side. The little X-wings were closing fast, thrusters ablaze and wingtips lancing energy beams at the larger ship. Harrar had heard that the New Republic pilots had become adept at foiling the dovin basals by altering the frequency and intensity of the laser bolts the fighters discharged. These four pursued the gunship with a single-mindedness born of thorough self-possession. Such fierce confidence spoke to qualities the Yuuzhan Vong would need to keep solidly in mind as the invasion advanced. Largely oblivious to nuance, the warrior caste would have to be taught to appreciate that survival figured as strongly in the enemy's beliefs as death figured in the beliefs of the Yuuzhan Vong.

The gunship had changed vector and was climbing now, seemingly intent on availing itself of the protection offered by Commander Tla's warship. But the four fighters were determined to have it. Breaking formation, they accelerated, ensnaring the gunship at the center of their wrath.

The X-wing pilots executed their attack with impressive precision. Laser bolts and brilliant pink torpedoes rained from them, taxing the abilities of the gunship's dovin basals. For every bolt and torpedo engulfed by the gravitic collapses the dovin basals fashioned, another penetrated, searing fissures in the assault craft and sending hunks of reddish-black yorik coral exploding in all directions. Stunned by relentless strikes, the gunship huddled inside its shields, hoping for a moment's respite, but the starfighters refused to grant it any quarter. Bursts of livid energy assailed the ship, shaking it off course. The dovin basals began to falter. With defenses hopelessly compromised, the larger ship diverted power to weapons and counterattacked.

In a desperate show of force, vengeful golden fire erupted from a dozen gun emplacements. But the starfighters were simply too quick and agile. They made pass after pass, raking fire across the gunship's suddenly vulnerable hull. Gouts of slagged flesh fountained from deep wounds and lasered trenches. The destruction of a plasma launcher sent a chain of explosions marching down the starboard side. Molten yorik coral streamed from the ship like a vapor trail. Shafts of blinding light began to pour from the core. The ship rolled over on its belly, shedding velocity. Then, jolted by a final paroxysm, it disappeared in a short-lived globe of fire.

It looked as if the X-wings might attempt to take the fight to the warship itself, but at the last moment the pilots turned tail. Salvos from the warship's weapons crisscrossed nearby space, but no missiles found their mark.

His scarified face a deeply shadowed mask, Harrar glanced over his shoulder at the acolyte. "Suggest to

Commander Tla that his zealous gunners allow the little ones to escape," he said with incongruous composure. "After all, someone needs to live to speak of what happened here."

"The infidels fought well and died bravely," the acolyte risked remarking.

Harrar pivoted to face him fully, a bemused glint in his deeply set eyes. "Is that respect I hear?"

The acolyte nodded his head in deference. "Nothing more than an observation, Eminence. To earn my respect, they would have to embrace willingly the truth we bring them."

A herald of lesser station appeared in the roost, offering salute by snapping his fists to opposite shoulders. "*Belek tiu*, Eminence. I bring word that the captives have been gathered."

"How many?"

"Several hundred—of diverse aspect. Do you wish to oversee the selection for the sacrifice?"

Harrar squared his shoulders and adjusted the fall of his elegant robes. "I am most eager to do so."

The transport gullet's diaphanous seal opened on an immense hold, packed to the bulkheads with captives taken on and in the skies above Obroa-skai. Harrar's entourage of personal guards and attendants moved into the hold, followed by the priest himself, perched atop a levitated cushion, one leg folded beneath him, the other dangling over the edge. The throbbing heart-shaped dovin basal that kept the cushion aloft answered to Harrar's quiet prompts, attracting itself to the hold's vaulted ceiling when the priest called for greater eleva-

tion, drawing itself toward one or another distant bulkhead when Harrar wished to be borne forward, backward, or to either side.

Well illuminated by bioluminescent patches that rashed
the walls and ceiling, the hold had been sectioned off into
a score of separate inhibition fields, arranged in two parallel rows and maintained by larger dovin basals. Pressed
shoulder to shoulder in each field stood scholars and
researchers from a host of worlds, humans and others—
Bothans, Bith, Quarren, and Caamasi—all jabbering at
once in a welter of tongues, while black-clad wardens
armed with amphistaffs supervised the winnowing process. Meant for coralskipper sustenance rather than
living cargo, the immense space reeked of natural secre-
tions, blood, and sweat.

Mostly, though, fear was in the air.

Harrar hovered on the cushion, surveying the scene
with hooded eyes. His retainers fell back so that he could
proceed directly down the center aisle and inspect prisoners to both sides. In order to reach the first pair of
inhibition fields, however, the priest was obliged to cir-
cumvent a large access shaft that had been filled to over-
flowing with confiscated droids, hundreds of them, heaped
together in a mound of entangled limbs, appendages,
and other mechanical parts.

When Harrar ordered a halt alongside the small
mountain of machines, those droids that constituted
the summit began to tremble under his scrutiny. With a
whirring of strained servomotors, domed, rectangular,
and humaniform heads swiveled, audio sensors perked
up, and countless photoreceptors came into sharp focus.

A momentary avalanche sent several machines screeching and tumbling to the base of the pile, far belowdecks.

Harrar's intrigued gaze fell on a contorted protocol droid whose upper right arm boasted a band of colored cloth. He commanded the cushion to bring him within reach of the immobilized machine. "Why are some of these abominations affecting garments?" he asked his chief attendant.

"They appear to have functioned as research assistants, Eminence," the attendant explained. "Obroa-skai's libraries could be accessed only by those who had contracted with trained researchers. The symbol depicted on the machine's armband is that of the so-called Obroan Institute."

Harrar was aghast. "Do you mean to say that serious researchers consorted with these things as equals?"

The attendant nodded once. "Apparently so, Eminence."

Harrar's expression changed to one of contempt. "Allow a machine to think of itself as an equal and it will soon come to consider itself superior." He reached out, tore the armband from the droid's arm, and threw it to the deck. "Include a representative sampling of these monstrosities in the sacrifice," he ordered, "and incinerate the rest."

"We're done for," a muffled synthetic voice whined from deep within the pile.

Living arms of sundry lengths, colors, and textures reached imploringly for Harrar as the cushion carried him toward the closest inhibition field. Some of the prisoners begged for mercy, but most fell silent in stark apprehension. Harrar regarded them indifferently, until his eyes happened on a furred humanoid, from whose bulging brow emerged a pair of ringed, cone-shaped horns. Bare hands and feet were hardened by physical labor, but the calluses belied a deep intelligence evidenced in the creature's limpid eyes. The humanoid wore a sleeveless sacklike garment that fell raggedly to the knees and was cinched at the waist by a braided cord fashioned from natural fiber.

"What species are you?" Harrar asked in flawless Basic.

"I am Gotal."

Harrar indicated the belted sackcloth. "Your attire befits a penitent more than a scholar. Which are you?"

"I am both, and I am neither," the Gotal said with purposeful ambiguity. "I am an H'kig priest."

Harrar twisted spiritedly on the cushion to address his retinue. "Good fortune. We have a holy one in our midst." His gaze returned to the Gotal. "Tell me something of your religion, H'kig priest."

"What interest could you have in my beliefs?"

"Ah, but I, too, am a performer of rituals. As one priest to another, then."

"We H'kig believe in the value of simple living," the Gotal said plainly.

"Yes, but to what end? To ensure bountiful harvests, to escalate yourself, to secure a place in the afterlife?"

"Virtue is its own reward."

Harrar adopted a puzzled look. "Your gods have said as much?"

"It is simply our truth—one among many."

"One among many. And what of the truth the Yuuzhan Vong bring you? Aver that you recognize our gods and I may be inclined to spare your life."

The Gotal stared at him dispassionately. "Only a false god would thirst so for death and destruction."

"Then it's true: you fear death."

"I have no fear of a death suffered in the cause of truth, the alleviation of suffering, or the abolishment of evil."

"Suffering?" Harrar leaned menacingly toward him. "Let me tell you of suffering, priest. Misery is the mainstay of life. Those who accept this truth understand that death is the release from suffering. That's why we go willingly to our deaths, for we are the resigned ones." He scanned the captives and raised his voice. "We ask no more of you than we do ourselves: to repay the gods for the sacrifices they endured in creating the cosmos. We offer flesh and blood so that their work might endure."

"Our god demands no tribute other than good acts," the Gotal rejoined.

"Acts that raise calluses," Harrar said in disdain. "If this is all that is expected of you, it's no wonder your gods have abandoned you in your time of need."

"We have not been abandoned. We still have the Jedi."

Murmurs of fellowship moved through the throng of captives, reticently at first, then with mounting conviction.

Harrar regarded the disparate faces below him: the labrous and the thin-lipped, the rugose and the smooth, the hairless and the hirsute, the horned and the furrowed. In their home galaxy, the Yuuzhan Vong had attempted to eradicate such diversity, prompting wars that had raged for millennia and had claimed the lives of peoples and worlds too numerous to count. This time, though, the Yuuzhan Vong planned to be more circumspect, destroying only those peoples and worlds necessary to complete the cleansing.

"These Jedi are your gods?" Harrar asked at last.

The Gotal took a moment to answer. "The Jedi Knights are the trustees of peace and justice."

"And this 'Force' I have heard about—how would you describe it?"

The Gotal grinned faintly. "It is something you will never touch. Although if I didn't know better, I would swear you were sprung from its dark side."

Harrar's interest was piqued. "The Force contains both light and dark?"

"As do all things."

"And which are you with regard to us? Are you so sure you embody the light?"

"I know only what my heart teaches."

Harrar deliberated. "Then this struggle is more than some petty war. This is a contest of gods, in which you and I are but mere instruments."

The Gotal held his head high. "That may be so. But the final judgment is already decided."

Harrar sneered. "May that belief comfort you in your final hour, priest—which, I assure you, is close at hand." Again he addressed the multitudes. "Up until now your species have faced only Yuuzhan Vong warriors and politicians. As of today know that the true architects of your destiny have arrived."

He beckoned his entourage forward. "This Force is

a strange, stubborn faith," he said quietly as one of his attendants came alongside the dovin basal cushion. "If ever we're to rule here, we need to understand just how it binds these myriad beings together. And we need to vanquish the Jedi Knights, once and for all."

TWO

In a galaxy fraught with wonders, the convergence of columnar tree trunks and forking branches that supported the Wookiee city of Rwookrrorro enjoyed a place of special honor. Viewed from above against its backdrop of fathomless forest, the city appeared to have been rescued from the planet's harsh underworld and submitted to Kashyyyk's scudded sky as an example of nature and technology in consummate poise.

At the outskirts of the city, distant from the circular buildings that rose from its spongy floor and scaled the trunks of the giant trees themselves, atop a massive fallen branch that spanned several treetops, a ceremony was in progress, enacted in observance of nature's timeless cycle of life and death.

The participants, including two dozen Wookiees and humans of both sexes, were arranged in a loose circle around a wooden table that happened also to be circular. Some stood, others sat on their haunches or on the ground, but all wore solemn expressions, save for the group's only nonliving members, the droids C-3PO and R2-D2, whose alloy countenances remained, in all circumstances, essentially neutral.

C-3PO stood with his bulbous head tilted slightly to one side and his arms bent at angles rarely adopted by the life-form after which he had been modeled. To the droid the rigid posture seemed entirely natural, a consequence of the way he was put together and the ever-changing demands of the servomotors that permitted him to gesticulate and move about. Beside him, R2-D2 stood still as a fixture, locomotion struts planted firmly on the fallen wroshyr tree branch and center tread retracted.

In passing, C-3PO noted that the view from the fallen branch was really quite extraordinary. Fog was thick in the treetops, concealing the nearest of the Wookiee nursery rings and diffusing the morning light as might a prism. The view could even be said—though certainly not by him—to be *breathtaking*.

[We gather in memory of Chewbacca: honorable son, beloved mate, devoted father, loyal friend and comrade in arms, champion and clan uncle to all of us in spirit, if not in the traditional way.]

The Wookiee speaker was called Ralrracheen, though C-3PO had often heard him referred to simply as Ralrra. He was tall and aged, even for his arboreal species, but it wasn't the graying muzzle that distinguished him so much as his curious speech impediment. On any other occasion C-3PO would have been tasked to serve as translator and interpreter, but none of the humans present had need of his polyglot faculties that particular morning.

[In Chewbacca, the defiant flame burned brightest,] Ralrra went on, black nose twitching and long arms dangling at his sides. [On Kashyyyk or farr afield on distant worlds, he was never less than courageous and incorruptible—a Wookiee with heart enough for ten and eagerr strength enough forr fifty.]

Chewbacca had died six standard months earlier, during an ill-fated rescue attempt on the planet Sernpidal, after it had been targeted for destruction by the Yuuzhan Vong. The fact that it hadn't been possible to retrieve his body was a source of sorrow to all, for had Chewbacca been returned to Kashyyyk a funeral would have been held—though for honor family members only. What Wookiees did with their dead remained a closely guarded secret. Some experts speculated that the dead were cremated; others, that they were either buried within tree knots or lowered by kshyy vines into the murky depths from which the species had risen. Still others claimed that the dead were hacked to pieces with sacred ryyyk blades and scattered on select wroshyr branches to be carried off by predatory katarns or kroyie birds.

C-3PO understood that he may not have been allowed to attend the funeral, in any case. Everyone attending the memorial was a member of Chewbacca's extended family, but it was unlikely that the affiliation applied to him—much less to his counterpart, R2-D2. For all their espousal to machines, intelligent and otherwise, flesh and bloods could be extremely proprietary about matters of kinship and family.

Close to Ralrra squatted Chewbacca's father, Attichitcuk, along with Chewbacca's auburn-furred sister, Kallabow. Alongside them sat Chewbacca's widow, Mallatobuck, and their son, Lumpawarrump, who had taken the name Lumpawaroo—Waroo for short—on the successful completion of his rite of passage. Interspersed among the Wookiee contingent stood assorted friends, kin-brothers, cousins, nieces, and nephews—Lowbacca among the latter, a Jedi Knight.

The humans numbered only six: Master Luke, Mistress Leia, Master Han, and the three Solo offspring, Anakin, Jacen, and Jaina. Conspicuously absent was Lando Calrissian, who, much to Master Han's disquiet, had sent word that unexpected—and unspecified—developments would prevent his attending. Master Luke's wife, Mara, might have attended if a sudden relapse in her mysterious malady hadn't forced her to remain on Coruscant.

The exquisitely carved table at the center of the circle rested on a carpet of wroshyr tree leaves, its pedestal base entwined with dark-green kshyy vines and its round top strewn with kolvissh blossoms, wasaka berries, Orga root, and the glossy yellow petals of the syren plant. The cool air was redolent with the aroma of smoldering tree-resin incense.

[Here on Kashyyyk, Chewbacca's mettle made itself known at an early age,] Ralrra continued. [With his late friend Salporin]—he paused to glance at Salporin's widow, Gorrlyn—[Chewbacca left the nursery ring to venture down along the Rryatt Trail to the Well of the Dead, in the heart of the Shadow Forest. Armed only with a ryyyk blade, he braved mock shyrr, jaddyyk moss, needlebug, trap-spinnerr, and shadow-keeperr to harvest strands from the heart of the flesh-eating syren, thus earning the right to wearr a baldric, carry a weapon, and confirm the name he chose to be known by. Here, too,

Chewbacca ventured into the great Anarrad pit—not once or even twice, but five times, taking down the taloned katarn on three of those hunts and once receiving a wound from the beast in return.] Ralrra indicated a spot on his shaggy torso. [Here, on the left side of his chest.

[In preparation for his marriage, which took place atop this very branch, Chewbacca descended to the fifth level and there with bare hands captured a quillarat and presented it to Malla as an expression of his love. And when it came time for Waroo's initiation, Chewbacca was steadfast in his support and encouraging of his son's quest of the scuttle grazerr.]

While some of Chewbacca's accomplishments on his homeworld were familiar to C-3PO, his memory lacked anything in the way of corroborative data, so he summoned recollections of his own experiences with the Wookiee and was immediately inundated with a rapid-fire sequence of images, some of them dating back twenty-five standard years.

His first sight of Chewbacca, standing like a cinnamon-colored tower outside Docking Bay 94 in the Mos Eisley spaceport on Tatooine . . . Chewbacca as a sore loser in dejarik holoboard contests . . . Chewbacca on Bespin's Cloud City, incorrectly reattaching C-3PO's head after it had been used by Ugnaughts as a plaything in a game of Wookiee in the Middle . . . Master Han's assertion that Chewbacca was always thinking with his stomach . . . The many, many times Chewbacca was referred to as "flea-bitten furball," "overgrown mophead," "walking carpet," or "noisy brute," occasionally by

C-3PO himself—in imitation of humans, of course—and always with affection, given Chewbacca's scrupulous character and great size.

A sudden flutter gripped C-3PO, and he found that he was unable to summon additional recollections. An unnatural and most discomfiting heat surged through his circuitry, prompting him to run a diagnostic program, which ultimately left the source of the glitch unrevealed.

Ralrra woofed, brayed, and barked.

[Natural curiosity compelled Chewbacca to leave Kashyyyk at an early age, but like all of us he was soon enslaved by the Empire. Fortunately, Chewbacca regained his freedom at the hands of a man of like strength and honorr—ourr revered brotherr Han Solo. And in the company of Han Solo, to whom he had pledged his life, Chewbacca was to play a crucial role in the Rebellion, and in the events that led eventually to the downfall of Emperor Palpatine.]

C-3PO focused his photoreceptors on Master Han, whose eyes were red-rimmed and narrowed, and whose right hand Mistress Jaina had taken between her own. The dark-blue military-style trousers Master Han was wearing were similar to the tattered pair he had attempted to preserve for posterity, but which only the previous day had proved incapable of conforming to Master Han's slightly increased waistline and had torn irreparably. Present during the incident—the cause of no small measure of vexation to Master Han—C-3PO had assisted in affixing to the outside seams of the replacement trousers twin embellishments known as Corellian Bloodstripes.

Across from the father and daughter stood Master Jacen and Mistress Leia, her head resting on her elder son's shoulder and her cheeks glistening with tears. Near them squatted Master Anakin, brooding and withdrawn, along with Master Luke, certainly no stranger to death, having lost both his natural and adoptive parents, as well as Obi-Wan Kenobi and Yoda, two of his Jedi mentors.

[Chewbacca went on to become a soldierr in the New Republic,] Ralrra boomed and rumbled. [He aided in Kashyyyk's liberation afterr the Battle of Endorr. But he remained first and foremost devoted to Han Solo, as friend and indebted protectorr, and as guardian to Han Solo's spouse and three children.] Ralrra turned to Han. [It was Chewbacca's honorr to have been able to come to his friend's rescue on several occasions, even as recently as the crisis involving the Yevetha, when he freed Han Solo from imprisonment aboard a Yevethan warship.]

Once more C-3PO tightened the focus of his photoreceptors on Master Han, who lowered his head in abject grief, as Jaina stroked his shoulders. Master Han's relationship with Chewbacca was similar to C-3PO's with R2-D2, though it seemed at times that the two droids had been together even longer than had the human and the Wookiee.

R2-D2 must have been regarding Master Han, as well, for the astromech suddenly rotated his monocular receptor to C-3PO and warbled tremulously, almost as if he, too, had picked up an enigmatic flutter.

C-3PO changed the cant of his head.

The past several months had afforded ample opportunities to study humans in grief, but for all his observations he was no closer to understanding the process than he had been before Chewbacca's death on that dreadful world. All living beings eventually died, when not from the effects of age, then as the result of accidents or illnesses almost too myriad to catalog. Death was in some ways analogous to deactivation or memory erasure, but in fact it was something quite different, a total ceasing-to-be—the end to all adventuring, indeed. In the face of that revelation, C-3PO felt compelled to wonder if he hadn't been wrong all along about his lot in life. If, as he so often declared, droids were made to suffer, what then of flesh and bloods?

Perhaps it was better not to know.

As constructed, C-3PO was incapable of shedding tears or enduring heartbreak, as it was called, but his programming did allow him to experience sorrow of a sort, if not nearly to the depth experienced by humans and other living beings. And it was suddenly clear that sorrow was the source of the flutter that continued to plague him. Try as he might, he could not summon a sound thought, and with each glance at Master Han his dismay increased.

As the one closest to Chewbacca—and perhaps because he was a very *human* being—Master Han seemed to be suffering the most, alternating between anguish and rage, despondency and agitation. The man C-3PO had once dismissed as impossible was now deeply distraught, as unreachable as if he were encased in carbonite, and there seemed nothing C-3PO could do to put the matter right. Being fluent in millions of forms of communication did not guarantee an understanding of human behavior, let alone human emotions. C-3PO was only a droid, after all, and not very knowledgeable about such things.

There had been an incident during Master Han's courtship of then Princess Leia when Master Han had had occasion to place a hand on C-3PO's arm and say, "You're a good droid, Threepio. There's not many droids I like as much as I like you." He had gone on to ask C-3PO's advice on matters of the heart, and C-3PO had gladly provided a poem for Master Han to use as ammunition in his contest with Prince Isolder for the princess's hand.

But curse my metal body, C-3PO said to himself. Why hadn't his maker equipped him with the necessary programming to come to Master Han's aid now? Instead, all he could offer was mindless philosophizing!

[Adventure is as alluring and potentially dangerous a thing as the heart of the syren plant,] Ralrra roared plaintively. [But even Chewbacca's final act was one of sacrifice, giving his life to save someone dearr to him.] The aged Wookiee looked at young Anakin, then at Master Han and Mistress Leia. [And as everr he kept his claws retracted in battle. Now, in the same way the branches of the wroshyr seek out and support one anotherr, Chewbacca's spirit merges with and gives sustenance to ourr own, strengthening us forr the challenges we have yet to confront.]

Warfare had figured in C-3PO's existence for so long that a new invasion shouldn't have come as a surprise. But there was something different about the Yuuzhan Vong and the harrowing war they were waging on a galactic scale. It wasn't merely that they didn't distinguish among species or among worlds—New Republic, Imperial Remnant, or nonaligned—or even that their biotic warships and weapons packed such awesome destructive power. What worried C-3PO most was that this most recent conflict was one in which not even droids were spared. And that meant that, like it or not, he might yet arrive at a true understanding of grief and death.

The circular table was covered with foodstuffs—bowls of xachibik broth, barbecued trakkrrrn ribs, forest-honey cakes, salad garnished with rillrrnnn seeds, and flasks of wines, juices, and liquors. Humans and Wookiees were conversing in groups, recounting tales of Chewbacca's exploits that brought laughter, tears, or moments of sober reflection. The breeze had picked up, stirring leaves and enlivening wind chimes.

Han sat dejectedly on a short-legged wooden stool, resting his elbows on his knees. "Y'know, I never thought I'd hear myself say this, but I think I actually envy Threepio."

Jaina followed her father's gaze to where the droid was standing with his squat counterpart, looking completely at a loss. "It's better not to have a heart, you mean."

"At times like this, anyway." Han exhaled wearily and ran his right hand down over his face.

Jaina motioned to the table. "Let me get you something to eat, Dad. You must be starved."

He managed a smile. "Thanks, sweetie, but I'm not hungry."

"You should have something anyway," she said in a maternal way.

Han brightened slightly and reached for her hand. "You help yourself, I'm fine."

She frowned. "Are you sure?"

"Positive." He gestured with his chin. "Get going. Eat enough for the both of us."

Reluctantly, Jaina headed for the table. Han watched her for a long moment as she mingled with her siblings, Luke, and Lowbacca. Observing them, he wondered what he might do if he could use the Force the way the Jedi did. Would he remain on the light side, or would he avail himself of the sinister powers of the dark side to teach the Yuuzhan Vong a thing or two about vengeance? Violent and ghastly images blossomed in his mind like explosions, but he put a quick end to them. He had had months of such images already, and they had come to nothing. No amount of vengeful thinking was going to bring Chewie back.

He glanced at his hands and found them balled into fists. While he'd spent the past six months isolated and incapacitated, often in the dark or secreted inside a tap-caf on Coruscant, the Jedi had at least been taking the fight to the enemy, and that was exactly what he needed to do.

He berated himself silently, then took a deep breath and blew it out through pursed lips. Loosening his hands, he slapped his thighs in a gesture of finality and got to his feet. He was starting out for the table when Mallatobuck and several other members of Chewbacca's family approached him. Malla was cradling a meter-long wooden box.

[Han Solo,] she said, smiling down at him, [we want you to have this.]

Han's brows knitted. He set the box down on the stool and unlatched its finely wrought metal clasp. Inside, snug in a bed of cushioning material was a beautifully carved bowcaster, its marked and blemished skeleton stock polished to a deep brown gleam. An artfully disguised magnetic accelerator, the weapon propelled explosive quarrels at extremely high speeds. This one was equipped with a sighting scope and a recocking mechanism few human hands would be capable of operating.

"I recognize this," Han said, nodding. He compressed his lips to trap a moan fighting to escape him. "It's one of the first I ever saw him make."

Malla hooted. [Chewbacca fashioned it shortly after we married—while you were here. He fashioned better versions in his time, but this one retains the warmth and power of him.]

Han hefted the weapon. "I feel it." He turned and hugged Malla, his head barely reaching her chin. "I'll treasure it."

Waroo handed Han a carry pouch made of hide. [This also belonged to my father. I know he would have wanted you to have it.]

Han placed the curve-bottomed pouch over his shoulder, knowing full well that it would hang down past his knees. Malla, Waroo, Lowbacca, and the rest boomed their delight in earsplitting yowls. Jaina returned with a plate of food in time to join in the laughter.

"If Chewie could see you now," she said, grinning for the first time all day.

Han backhanded a tear from his left eye, smiled, and

put his arm around his daughter's waist. "The big lug would bust a gut."

Jowdrrl, Chewbacca's chestnut-colored female cousin, growled something to Malla that Han didn't catch. Seeing Han's inquisitive expression, Malla explained. [Jowdrrl is wondering when you and your family will be returning to Coruscant.]

Han and Jaina traded shrugs. "I hadn't thought about it," Han said. "Tomorrow sometime, I suppose."

Jowdrrl lowed in elaboration. [I ask only because Dryanta and I need a small measure of time to prepare.]

Han's features mirrored his bewilderment. "Prepare for what? Are you coming to Coruscant with us?"

Chewbacca's father, Attichitcuk, yaupped in a meaningful way. [Jowdrrl and Dryanta are arranging the feast for Waroo and Lowbacca's farewell.]

"Waroo and Lowbacca," Han said nervously.

[They will be assuming Chewbacca's life debt.]

Han's jaw came unhinged. He glanced from one Wookiee to the next in rising dismay. "But—but you can't. Chewie's dead. All debts are off."

Attichitcuk issued a sustained, bass-register growl. [Death may have extinguished my son's defiant flame, but our debt to you continues until yours is extinguished.]

Her lower lip between her teeth, Jaina placed a comforting hand on her father's arm, only to have it shrugged off. Han was shaking his head back and forth.

"No, no, I can't accept this. Chewie saved my life ten times over. He *died* saving Anakin's life." His agitation increased as he spoke. "Besides, I'm the one who owes all of you a life debt." He cut his eyes to the dark-brown son of Dewlannamapia. "Your mother was kinder to me than my own." He searched out Gorrlyn. "Your husband, Salporin, gave his life protecting Leia from Noghri assassins." He appealed to Jowdrrl and Dryanta. "Your cousin Shoran died aboard the *Pride of Yevetha* saving *me*!"

[As you would have died for them,] Attichitcuk rumbled, nearly showing his fangs. [A life debt is just that.]

Malla, too, was glowering at Han. [You would not defame Chewbacca's memory by refusing to allow his debt to be honored.]

Jaina swallowed audibly. "Dad doesn't mean any dishonor." She glanced at her father. "Right, Dad?"

Han stared at her, mouth still ajar. Malla's vibrato growl had summoned a memory of a day following the wedding when Han had tried to persuade Chewie into remaining behind with his bride rather than accompanying him back to Nar Shaddaa. He thought, too, of Groznik, a Wookiee who had attached himself to the Rogue Squadron pilot Elscol Loro, wife of a man named Throm to whom Groznik was life-debted.

"Right, right," he said at last, looking from Jaina to Malla. "I'd cut off my arm before I'd dishonor Chewie's memory in any way. You know that. It's just that . . ."

Everyone waited.

"It's just that I'm not ready." He shook his head as if to clear it, then looked up at Attichitcuk and the others. "Chewie's still alive for me. I can't just allow him to be . . . replaced. You've gotta understand that. He was more than a protector. He was my closest friend."

The Wookiees exchanged sympathetic looks and indecipherable brays.

[He clings to his memory of my husband,] Malla remarked sadly.

[He needs time,] Attichitcuk growled, somehow without making it sound menacing.

"That's it," Han said, grasping at straws. "I just need time."

After what seemed an eternity, Chewbacca's father nodded his huge head. [Then time we'll grant you. The life debt involves more than simply providing shelter from bodily harm. It succors the spirit, as well.]

Han saw the truth of it. "I want that to go on."

Malla put her huge paws on his shoulders. [Then it shall.]

THREE

Holographic images of star systems and entire galactic sectors pirouetted in a blue-gray shaft of projected light. Flashing overlays showed hyperspace lanes that linked far-flung regions of space. The pressure of a fingertip against a touch screen was sufficient to conjure information on individual worlds, stars, or lightspeed routes. Dots of artificial light expanded to reveal data on native species and cultures, planetary topography, population statistics, and in some cases defense capabilities.

"It disheartens me to have to subject you to inert technology, Eminence," Commander Tla's tactician apologized, "but we have yet to discover a way to separate the data from the metallic shells that sustain them. And until our villips have had a chance to absorb the captured information, we have no choice but to make do with some of the enemy's own machines. Each has been cleansed and purified, but I'm afraid there is simply no disguising their vacuity of spirit."

Though repulsed by the devices that had been conveyed to him, Harrar granted the tactician absolution. "To abhor a thing in ignorance is to fear it. A deeper understanding of machine nature will only firm my resolve to see machines exterminated." He waved his abbreviated hand. "Proceed."

The tactician, Raff, inclined his tattooed head in a bow, then raised a bony, gloved hand to the animated hologram. "As you can see, Eminence, we have here nothing less than a portrait of the galaxy. In broad strokes to be sure, and yet detailed enough to aid us in our push toward the Core."

His protected forefinger made contact with the touch screen, and a representation of the Obroa-skai and neighboring star systems took shape in the cone of light.

Scrawniness wasn't confined to the tactician's hands. Rail-thin wrists poked from the voluminous sleeves of his robe, and a spindly neck protruded like a baton from the robe's high and equally spacious collar. Pledged in service to Yun-Yammka, the god of war, Raff had a mouth that was a black-stained maw, featuring an outsize tooth that sometimes wreaked havoc with the clarity of his speech. But it was his powers of rumination and analysis that counted most. Frequent rapport with war coordinators and dovin basals kept him abreast of nearly all aspects of the war, from details on individual New Republic warships to combat casualty statistics. In keeping with his abilities, his hairless and distended cranium was adorned with etchings suggestive of the eddies and convolutions of the enhanced brain contained within.

"Unfortunately, the bulk of the liberated data is historical in nature and of dubious value. Obroa-skai dedicated itself to preserving cultural documents in the original languages and access formats." The tactician gestured toward a levitated pallet stacked with blood-smeared durasheet texts, data cards, and other storage contrivances, waiting to be slagged by holy fire. "Thus the need for such an endless array of decryption and translation devices. Even so, our assault on the library world was justified. Ultimately—and once rendered in villip speech—these documents will yield a wealth of information regarding the psychological makeup of many of these species, and that knowledge will be crucial to our maintaining control over conquered territories."

A male attendant, barefoot and sheathed in a long tunic, climbed the rough-hewn yorik coral steps of the command platform to place plates of food and a carafe of amber-colored liquid on the low table that separated the priest and the tactician. His pointed chin was etched in deep purple to suggest a beard, and the sacs under his closely set eyes were fully tattooed. His forehead sloped sharply back from a prominent brow and was in the same way covered with signs and designs.

At the base of the platform a lone figure waited patiently in the shadows. Harrar bade the attendant prepare libations for himself, the tactician, and the figure below. He sipped his drink while he considered the tactician's appraisal of the spoils of battle.

Generations of travel in intergalactic space had taken a toll on many Yuuzhan Vong vessels—warships and worldships alike. Where their interiors had once been warmed by sumptuous curtains and carpets, and the monotony of their decks balanced by rich mosaic inlays, an austere coldness now prevailed. The vaulted ceilings of communal spaces were still supported by ornamental columns, but their surfaces were grazed, marred, and cheerless. The bioluminescent growths that provided oxygen and light didn't thrive as they once had, and often flickered like guttering candles. Even the grotto-like spaces reserved for the elite had a forlorn aspect.

"What do the seized documents have to say about the Jedi?" Harrar asked after a moment.

"Curiously little, Eminence. One senses that data on the Jedi were either purposely withheld from the library or systematically purged."

Harrar set his drink down. "The distinction is significant. Which interpretation do you favor?"

"The latter. Since the libraries are replete with philosophical documents of all variety, why disallow studies on the Jedi?"

"Perhaps it is the Jedi who disallow such documentation," Harrar suggested. "Perhaps they are more secretive than we realize."

"That would explain the lack of iconography attached to them, along with the fact that the Force does not appear to be the manifestation of a supreme being."

"And yet you have reason to believe that the records were purged."

"Even if proscribed by law, Eminence, it's likely that a written or oral history would have been compiled—if not by a Jedi, then by someone outside the order, even someone who was opposed to it. A chronicle of Jedi deeds, biographies of prominent Jedi, that sort of thing."

"An order, you say."

Tactician Raff glanced at the unrevealed figure below, then nodded in affirmation. "The Jedi appear to have begun as an order devoted to the pursuit of philosophical and theological studies. It's unclear whether they were the first to discover the energy source they call the Force, or whether they were simply the first to discover ways of accessing it. In either case they seem to have evolved gradually from cloistered meditators to public servants, and for thousands of generations they served as the guardians of justice throughout this galaxy."

Harrar steepled his six fingers and tapped them against his tattooed lips. "That would have required an army."

"Precisely, Eminence."

"But no army of Jedi has been dispatched against our warriors. Battle reports indicate encounters with a mere handful." The priest smiled faintly in revelation. "Someone not only purged Obroa-skai's libraries but the Jedi order itself."

"That is my belief."

"But who?"

The tactician shrugged. "Advocates of the so-called dark side? Those whom the Jedi call Sith?"

Harrar leaned back against the cushions that propped him. "Then we may have allies in the galaxy."

"If any Sith remain, we may indeed."

Resolute footsteps trespassed on Harrar's reply. Their source was a young female of severe beauty, whose long, shimmering garment accentuated an already lean frame. A turban encased most of her raven hair, and iridescent insects shone from the borders of her robe. Long strides carried her boldly to the foot of the command platform, where she folded her arms under her breasts and inclined her head and shoulders in a deferential bow.

"Welcome, Elan," Harrar said pleasantly.

Elan lifted her head, which was neither as sloped as the priest's nor as asymmetrical as the tactician's. Wide across the cheekbones, her face tapered to a cleft chin.

Ice-blue, her eyes swam in a sea of lavender and maroon swirls, and her nose was wide and almost without a bridge.

"Your pleasure, Eminence?"

"For the moment, only that you join us." In invitation, and absent even a hint of condescension, Harrar patted the cushion adjacent to his own. "You've arrived in time to witness the sacrifice."

Elan glanced over her shoulder.

Accompanying her was a diminutive creature of motley countenance and a peculiar manner. Made piebald by an arrangement of short feathers, the trim torso supported two thin arms, each of which ended in graceful four-fingered hands. Willowy ears and twin antennae cork-screwed from an elongated, modestly disproportionate head, whose rear attenuated to a finely feathered ridge. The slightly concave face was slant-eyed, wide-mouthed, and delicately whiskered. A pair of reverse-articulated legs and splayed feet propelled the creature in agile leaps.

Harrar took note of Elan's hesitation. "Your familiar is also welcome to join us."

Elan glanced at the stranger standing nearby, then reached for her companion's right hand. "Come, Vergere." She climbed the stairs and sat, making room for Vergere, who settled in like a nesting avian. Then she looked at the priest. "Why have I been summoned, Eminence?"

Harrar feigned disappointment and motioned to the nearest attendant. "Let us observe the sacrifice."

The attendant bowed and voiced a command to a pair of artfully concealed receiving villips, which instantly fashioned an optical field. A sweeping view of local space resolved in midair, filling the entire forward portion of the compartment and eclipsing bulkheads and furnishings alike. It was as if that portion of the faceted ship had been rendered clear as transparisteel and the cosmos ushered aboard.

Obroa-skai's primary was a roiling cauldron at the center of the villip-choir field. Hurtling toward the star was a battered Gallofree transport that had been captured during the battle, its ablative shields just beginning to blush with heat. Inside the pod-shaped vessel, some two thousand captives and droids, cleansed by sound, purified by incense, and stacked like split firewood, lived out the remainder of their lives.

Harrar, his guests, and attendants fell silent and remained so as the rosiness the star had imparted to the nose of the transport began to spread aft, reddening alloy and liquefying superstructures. Parabolic dishes, sensor arrays, and shield generators melted like wax. The outer husk wrinkled and began to peel back from the frame. The hull blistered, buckled, and finally caved. The ship became a torch, a hyphen of flame, then vanished.

Harrar raised his hands to shoulder height and held them palms outward. "In praise of the Creator, Yun-Yuuzhan, and in humble gratitude for his actions in our behalf, accept these lives unworthy of life. May we find continued support for the challenge you have set before us, of bringing your light to this dark realm and of ridding it of ignorance and evil. We open ourselves to you . . ."

"May you find sustenance in our offerings," the others in the hold murmured.

"We lift up our hearts . . ."

"That you might prosper."

"We give ourselves freely . . ."

"Through you will we conquer."

Caught in the embrace of nuclear fire, the signal villip that had been tailing the transport was incinerated. As the visual field destabilized and faded, Harrar's attendants gradually resumed their duties.

"I will arrange for the images to be analyzed for portents," the tactician promised.

Harrar nodded. "See that the results are sent to Commander Tla. He may not place much stock in such things, but where omens are ignored and failure ensues, we have the makings of a convert."

The tactician bowed. "So be it."

Abruptly Harrar's cushion rose from the command platform and carried him out over the steps. "We will now speak to the matter at hand," he announced.

Elan made her eyes alert with interest and squeezed Vergere's hand.

"Thus far our campaign has been blessed with easy victories," the priest began. "Worlds crumble and populations fall at our feet. But while I've no doubt that we will someday rule these species, I fear we'll encounter great difficulties in altering the way they think. Something other than superior weaponry will be required to accomplish that."

He gazed at Elan. "Our chief impediment is a group that calls itself the Jedi. Think of them as a kind of moral police force—small in number but very influential."

Elan glanced briefly at Vergere and once more squeezed her hand. "What sort of gods do these Jedi worship?" she asked.

"None to speak of. Rather, they draw spiritual strength from a pervasive reservoir of energy known as the Force."

"And you have some strategy for subverting or nullifying this Force?"

"At the moment, no. However, there may be something we can do about the Jedi."

Harrar indicated the stranger at the foot of the stairs. "Elan, this is one of our field agents, Executor Nom Anor. Aside from being instrumental in helping secure a foothold in the Outer Rim, Nom Anor has managed to recruit agents from among the native populations and carry out many acts of sabotage and subversion. He is taking time out from his usual duties to oversee a project he and I have planned."

Elan leveled an appraising gaze at Nom Anor as he climbed the stairs to stand before her. Slender and of medium height, he was ordinary-looking, even with the facial markings and broken facial bones that attested to more than the usual sacrifices. Somewhere along the way, he had either lost or purposely surrendered an eye. Though the socket was a black aperture just now, Elan could discern that the bones had been reconfigured to house a plaeryin bol—the venom-spitting organ that resembled an eyeball.

"Dressed in an ooglith masquer, this one could easily pass for a human," she whispered to Vergere.

"He's an ambitious one, Mistress," Vergere whispered back. "Take care."

Nom Anor bowed to Harrar, though not as deeply as he might have.

"Before the invasion commenced, and as a means of testing what we were up against," Nom Anor said, "I seeded several worlds with a variety of illness-producing spores of my own design. One class of spores—a coomb variant—met with success, causing some one hundred individuals to fall ill and die, save for one—a human female Jedi Knight. Neither self-propagating nor contagious, the malady has not spread to the other Jedi."

Nom Anor scrutinized Elan. "By all accounts the human remains gravely ill, but she has thus far managed to survive, I assume by drawing on the Force. Her resistance, however, is a blessing in disguise, for I feel certain that we can make use of it to get close to the Jedi."

"Infiltrate them, you mean?" Elan said.

"Assassinate them," Harrar answered from his cushion. "Or at least, as many as possible."

Nom Anor nodded. "Such an event would prove demoralizing to countless populations. If even the Jedi could be brought down, what hope could there be for the rest? Confidence in the Jedi and the Force would be dealt an irreversible blow. Worlds would begin to capitulate without a fight. Supreme Overlord Shimrra could be apprised that our mission has been executed ahead of schedule, and that we await his coming."

Elan looked from Harrar to Nom Anor and back again. "What part am I to play in all this?"

The priest moved forward, until he was hovering before her. "One for which a priestess of the deception sect is uniquely suited."

FOUR

Han stood on the brink, with the tips of his knee-high black boots projecting over the edge of the natural bridge. The voices of his friends were distant enough to be indistinct. Fog that had clung to the giant trees all morning was falling like fat drops of rain. At once rank and perfumed, the breath of Kashyyyk's perilous and impenetrable underworld made his head swim. Nearby, a pair of kroyie birds rode updrafts in an oblique ray of sunlight.

With deliberate intent Han let go of a piece of wroshyr bark he had been turning about in his hands and watched it fall from sight. That section of the bridge lacked anything in the way of a railing, and nothing stood between him and the abyss.

"You'll want to watch that first step, flyboy," Leia said from behind him.

Han gave a start but didn't turn around. "Funny thing is, ground zero's always a lot closer than you think."

Leia's footsteps drew nearer. "Even if that's true, you might want to consider a sturdy pair of repulsor boots."

He aimed a skewed grin over his shoulder. Kashyyyk's humidity had fashioned a mane of Leia's long hair, and updrafts tugged at her flowing skirt and sleeveless blouse.

"No need to worry, sweetheart. I'm already down there."

Leia came alongside him and glanced warily over the edge. "And I thought the view from our apartment was unnerving . . ." She took gentle hold of Han's arm and eased him back from the edge. "You're making me nervous."

"That's gotta be a first." He forced a smile. "I'm fine."

Leia's brow furrowed. "Are you, Han? I heard about what happened with Malla and Waroo."

He shook his head in renewed agitation. "I have to put an end to this life-debt business once and for all."

"Just give it time. They'll understand. Remember when I couldn't even go to the 'fresher without Khabarakh or one of the other Noghri insisting on accompanying me?"

"Yeah, and you've still got the Noghri bodyguarding you. Not to take anything away from all they've done for you."

"I know what you're getting at."

Han shook his head. "Uh-uh, you don't know what I'm getting at. See, you could probably *command* the Noghri to stay away from you. But Wookiees are different. If you think that Lowbacca or Waroo are going to let this slide, you'd better think again."

Leia crossed her arms and grinned. "Okay. So as soon as we get back to Coruscant I'll have Cal Omas or someone propose legislation that limits the terms of a Wookiee life debt."

"And risk angering Councilor Triebakk? Forget it. I'll deal with this in my own way."

Chilled by Han's scowl, Leia straightened her smile. "I didn't mean to sound flippant, Han. I understand what you're feeling. Today couldn't have been easy for you."

He averted his gaze. "I wish I understood what I was feeling. I thought the ceremony would help put things to rest, but it's only made matters worse. Maybe if I'd been able to retrieve Chewie's body and there'd been some kind of funeral . . ." He allowed his words to trail off, then shook his head angrily. "What am I talking about? It's more than missing out on some ritual."

Leia waited for him to continue.

"I know I can't change what happened at Sernpidal, but I blame myself for getting us into that fix to begin with."

"You were trying to save lives, Han."

"And a lot of good it did anyone."

"Have you told Anakin that you've made your peace with not being able to save Chewie?" Leia asked cautiously.

Bitterness contorted Han's face. "That was my biggest mistake—putting him in the pilot's seat."

"Han—"

"I don't mean that it was Anakin's fault. But I know I wouldn't have made the same decisions he made." He snorted a bitter laugh. "We'd all be dead—Chewie, Anakin, me . . . And now this craziness about continuing the life debt." Han paced away, then whirled to face her. "There's no way I'm going to be responsible for the death of another member of the honor family, Leia."

"You weren't responsible."

"I was," he snapped. "Who knows what kind of life Chewie would have had if I hadn't dragged him all over the galaxy running spice and chak-root and whatever else we could smuggle."

Leia frowned. "Meaning what, Han? That you shouldn't have rescued him from slavery? For all you know, Chewie might have ended up dying in an Imperial labor camp or in some construction accident. You can't allow yourself to think that way. Besides, don't try to tell me that Chewie didn't enjoy gallivanting around with you—and that had nothing to do with a life debt. You heard what Ralrra said: Adventure was the reason Chewie left Kashyyyk to begin with. You and he were two of a kind."

Han firmed his lips. "I guess I know that. Still . . ." He shook his head mournfully.

Leia placed her fingers under Han's chin and turned his head. Positioning herself in his gaze, she smiled broadly. "You know what I remember most? The time Chewie strapped me to his chest and carried me across the underside of Rwookrrorro. Like I was a toddler."

Han snorted. "Consider yourself lucky. One time I had to ride in a quulaar slung from Tarkazza."

Leia clamped a hand over her mouth but laughed anyway. "Katara's father—the one with the silver stripe on his back?"

"That's the one." Han laughed with her, but only for a moment. Then he turned and gazed out over the treetops. "It gets easier for a moment, then I'm right back to remembering. How long does it take, Leia? Till you're past it?"

She sighed. "I don't know how to answer that without sounding trite. Life is all about change, Han. Look at this place: !uma-poles have begun to replace phosflea lanterns, repulsorlift vehicles are replacing banthas . . . Things have a strange way of reversing direction when you least expect them to. Enemies become friends, adversaries become confederates. The very Noghri who tried to kill me became my protectors. Gilad Pellaeon, who once came here to enslave Wookiees, fought with us at Ithor against the Yuuzhan Vong. Could anyone have predicted that?" Leia extended her hands to massage his shoulders. "Eventually the heartache fades."

Han's muscles bunched under her touch. "That's the problem. The heartache fades."

He sat down, letting his feet dangle over the edge of the bridge. Leia squatted behind him and wrapped her arms around him. They remained unmoving for a long moment.

"I'm losing him, Leia," he said despondently. "I know he's dead, but I used to be able to feel him alongside me, just outside the edge of my vision. It's like if I turned quickly enough, I'd catch sight of him. I could hear him, too, clear as day, laughing or complaining about something I'd done. I swear, I've had conversations with him that were as real as this one. But something's changed. I have to think long and hard to really see him, or hear him."

"You're getting on with your life, Han," Leia said softly.

He laughed shortly. "Getting on with my life? I don't think so. Not till I've found some way to make his death count for something."

"He saved Anakin," Leia reminded.

"That's not what I mean. I want the Yuuzhan Vong to

pay for what they did at Sernpidal—and for all that they're continuing to do."

Leia stiffened. "I can understand that coming from Anakin, Han, because he's young and hasn't figured things out. But please don't make me hear it from you."

He shrugged out of her hold. "What makes you think I know any more about life than Anakin knows?"

She dropped her hands by her sides and stood up. "That's something I hadn't considered, Han."

"Well, maybe you should," he rasped, without turning around.

Where moments earlier images of the sacrifice had played, twenty captives now huddled inside an inhibition field, raised and sustained by two small bloodred dovin basals. At the center of the mixed-species group stood the Gotal H'kig priest, whom Harrar had promised imminent death. The field's hemispherical outline shimmered like waves of rising heat.

With Harrar, Nom Anor, Raff, Elan, and her pet observing from the command platform, a youthful Yuuzhan Vong warrior wearing a wine-colored tunic entered the hold, paid obeisance to his elite audience, and approached the field.

"An assassin," Elan said to Vergere in hushed surprise.

"A mere apprentice," Harrar amended. "Said to show little promise—though the task he is about to execute will escalate him in the eyes of many."

Ripples played across the immaterial surface of the inhibition field as the warrior stepped through its one-way perimeter. Nearby guards raised their amphistaffs in anticipation of a desperate charge, but whether out of fear or curiosity none of the prisoners made a move against the intruder. Once inside, neither did the warrior move, except to turn slightly in the direction of the priest.

"Observe closely," Harrar said to Elan.

A subtle gesture of Harrar's right hand was the assassin's signal to begin. Swinging about, the youth emptied his lungs with a sibilant and protracted exhalation.

The effect on the captives was almost immediate. To a being they fell back in surprise, then in stunned realization, and finally in agony, clutching at their windpipes as if the inhibition field had been drained of breathable air. Smooth faces turned a ghastly shade of cyan; others lost color entirely or blackened, as if scorched by fire. Limbs and appendages spasmed, and tufts of fur wafted from the hirsute. Sudden blood mottled the flesh, then began to seep and mist from burst capillaries. Some of the prisoners fell to their knees and vomited blood; the more resilient staggered about, lurching into one another, until they fell writhing and gasping to the deck.

Only the assassin remained standing, but not for long. Knowing better than to draw a breath, he hurried for safety, only to find that the dovin basals maintaining the field were denying him egress. He spent a desperate moment moving along the perimeter, as if hoping to discover some gap, some oversight that would permit him to escape. Then the full awareness of his predicament dawned on him. Turning to Harrar, he drew himself up to his full height, snapped his closed fists to the opposite shoulders, and inhaled deeply. Blood began to stream from his nose and eyes. Torment warped his features into a macabre mask, but no sounds escaped him. His body trembled from head to foot, then he pitched forward to the deck.

All at once the inhibition field began to teem with hundreds of spontaneously generated life-forms no larger than phosfleas. In crazed motion they scuttled over the prostrate bodies and massed along the edges of the field, as keen on finding some way out as the warrior had been.

Harrar motioned one of his acolytes forward. "Capture a specimen and bring it here—quickly!"

The acolyte bowed and rushed to the field. Reaching a gloved hand through the invisible barrier, he pinched one of the scurrying critters between his thumb and index finger and ran it to the command platform. Even before he had reached the steps, the frenetic activity in the field began to abate, as if the swarm had suddenly expended its energy and was dying.

The acolyte delivered his tiny hostage to Harrar, who pinched the jittery thing between the three fingers of his right hand and held it up for Elan's inspection. Faintly opalescent, the creature was a flattened disk, from which sprouted three tiny pairs of articulated legs.

"Bo'tous," Harrar explained. "Both carrier and by-product of the toxin. Precipitated from the assassin's breath. They grow rapidly in the presence of abundant oxygen, but are extremely short-lived."

"Your weapon against the Jedi," Elan said knowingly.

"A skilled host can manage up to four bo'tous exhalations. But in a sealed environment, there is no defense—even for the host. Do you understand?"

"I understand that a host runs the risk of dying with his victims."

"The toxic effect of the exhalation is very brief," Nom

Anor added. "A host must be in close proximity to her target."

"*Her* target," Elan said.

Harrar held her in his gaze. "We would like to arrange for you to be captured by New Republic forces. Commander Tla—while not entirely enthusiastic—has even agreed to afford them a victory in the process. Once in their custody you would ask for political asylum."

Elan looked skeptical. "Why would they accept me?"

"Because we would convince them that you are a worthy prize," Nom Anor answered.

Harrar confirmed it with a nod. "You would provide them with valuable information. Information regarding why we have come to their galaxy and what we have left in our wake. You would also tell them of dissension among our ranks—of disputes that prompted your flight—as well as information of some strategic merit."

"Does Commander Tla know of all this?" Raff interjected uncertainly.

"Most of it," Harrar replied.

"Then I must protest, Eminence. I fear this will become too costly an enterprise."

"I will accept responsibility," Harrar said. "Let us not have genuine dissension, tactician."

Tactician Raff stood his ground. "Eminence, has not Executor Nom Anor just informed us that a Jedi Knight survived an earlier attempt at poisoning? Why, then, should bo'tous prove effective against any one of them, let alone a cadre of Jedi?" He glanced at Elan. "Notwithstanding the obvious sophistication of your designated delivery system."

Momentary doubt clouded Harrar's expression. "You do justice to your station, tactician. Your suggestions?"

Raff considered it. "At the very least, your infiltrator should be provided with accessory weapons—whatever Executor Nom Anor deems necessary to ensure success, should the bo'tous prove ineffectual."

Harrar looked at Nom Anor, who motioned in dismissal. "Unnecessary. But easily accomplished. There is a species of amphistaff that can be modified and implanted in the body for just such a purpose."

Satisfied, Harrar nodded. "Continue, Executor."

Nom Anor placed himself in Elan's view. "Unfortunately, I know of no accessories that will guarantee your success with New Republic Intelligence. That would depend on you. You would begin by claiming to have information regarding the coomb spores I introduced. You would, however, insist on delivering that information only to the Jedi. But be warned: the Jedi possess a kind of divining ability. They would be quick to discover deception—even in one trained since youth to beguile and mislead. Thus the need for a quick-acting toxin, carried by a quick-thinking host."

Harrar extended the pinched creature to Elan. "Quickly, Elan, take it in your palm and clench your hand around it."

Elan stared at him. "Should I do so, I am committed."

Harrar gazed back at her. "I will not command you to accept this charge, Elan. The choice is yours."

Elan looked to Vergere. "How would you counsel me?"

Vergere's oblique eyes clouded over with sadness. "I would counsel you to refuse, Mistress. And yet you have long desired to be tested. To be given a mission worthy of

your talents. Sadly, I know of no more unswerving path
to escalation."

Harrar glanced at the priestess's exotic pet. "Take her
along if it pleases you, Elan. She may even prove to be of
assistance."

Elan looked at Vergere once more. "You would accompany me?"

"When have I not?"

Elan took the minuscule creature into her hand and
closed her long fingers around it. When she relaxed her
hand, the thing had been absorbed.

"It will migrate to your lungs and there mature," Nom
Anor said, smiling. "You will know when the toxin has
reached maximum potency. Then you will loose your
four breaths against as many Jedi as you can arrange to
be gathered in one place."

Elan looked at Harrar. "What then, Eminence?"

"What's to become of you, you mean?" Harrar took
hold of her fine hand, examining the palm that had absorbed the carrier. "Nom Anor and I will do all we can to
monitor your whereabouts, but I cannot promise you
rescue, only exaltation. Should you succeed, you will either die with the Jedi or face execution afterwards."

Elan grinned faintly. "That choice is also mine."

Harrar patted her hand. "Look to the world beyond for
recompense, Elan. I envy you your imminent departure."

Cordoned off by kshyy vines and Wookiee security
guards, the *Millennium Falcon* sat on landing platform
Thiss, alongside the shuttle Luke, Jacen, Anakin, and
Lowbacca had flown to Kashyyyk. What remained of a
wroshyr limb horizontally pruned close to the trunk, the

fire-blackened platform at the edge of Rwookrrorro was large enough to accommodate passenger liners, but the *Falcon* and the sleek shuttle had the stage to themselves. Not since Chewbacca had piloted the *Falcon* to Kashyyyk during the Yevethan crisis had the city drawn so many well-wishers, tourists, and curiosity seekers. From Karryntora, Northaykk, the Wartaki Islands, and the distant Thikkiiana Peninsula they came, most in the hope of catching a glimpse of Luke, Han, or Leia, but many to have a look at the Corellian YT-1300 freighter Chewbacca and Han had made famous.

Like a taurill navigating a field of profligate shag ferns, Han edged his way through a throng of vociferous Wookiees intent on snapping his spine with backslapping blows or fracturing his ribs with crushing hugs. By the time he stumbled into the cordoned-off area surrounding the *Falcon* he looked as if he'd gone one too many rounds in a g-force simulator. Leia, Luke, the kids, and the droids were waiting at the foot of the extended boarding ramp.

"Dad, I thought we weren't leaving until tomorrow," Jaina said as Han approached.

"Change of plans," he muttered. "Did you do a preflight?"

"Yeah, but—"

"Then let's get everyone aboard and raise ship."

"Why the rush, Han?" Luke said, purposely stepping into his path. The cowl of his Jedi cloak was thrown back, and his lightsaber hung from the belt that cinched his black robes. "Are we running toward something or away from it?"

Han stopped short. Out of the corner of his eye he saw

Leia wince and turn to one side. "How's that again?" he asked Luke.

Luke's expression was unreadable. "Pressing concerns on Coruscant?"

Han worked his jaw. "Tomorrow, today, what difference does it make? But if you have to know, yeah, pressing concerns. A little matter called the Yuuzhan Vong and the fate of the galaxy."

"Han—"

"Don't!" Han interrupted. He bit back whatever he was going to say and began again in a more controlled voice. "Luke, it's just that I've had my fill of sympathy. So let's just drop it."

"If that's what you want, Han."

Han started up the ramp, then stopped and whirled. "You know, I don't know what's worse, everybody's fumbling attempts to make me feel better or your self-importance. You may think you have me figured out, pal, but you don't. Not by a long shot. Oh, I know you've lost friends and family, and now, with Mara being sick and all, but Chewie gave his life for my son, and that makes it different. You can't know about that, Luke."

"I don't pretend to know about that," Luke said calmly. "But as you say, I do know something about grief."

Han held up his hands. "Don't talk to me about the Force—not now. I told you a long time ago I don't believe in one power controlling everything, and maybe I was right, after all."

"After all we've been through?"

"What we've been through," Han said, pointing his

forefinger at Luke's face, "had a lot more to do with blasterfire than swordplay, and you know it."

"It was the Force that brought down the Empire."

"And just how does that help me?" Han glanced around at Leia, their three children, Lowbacca, C-3PO, and R2-D2, all of whom looked uncomfortable. "I don't have the abilities of a Jedi or the delete functions of a droid. I'm just a normal guy with normal feelings and maybe more than his share of shortcomings. I don't *see* Chewie, Luke. Not the way you claim to have seen Obi-Wan, Yoda, and your father. I don't have the Force at my back."

"But you do, Han. That's all I'm trying to tell you. Let go of your anger and bitterness and you will see Chewie."

Han opened his mouth and closed it. He spun on his heels and hurried up the ramp only to stop and reverse directions again. "I'm not ready to walk this plank," he grated as he passed Luke.

"Han!" Leia shouted.

He turned, but looked through her at Jaina. "Take the *Falcon* back to Coruscant."

Jaina's eyes widened. She swallowed hard and stammered, "But what about you?"

"I'll find my own way back," he yelled over his shoulder as he marched off.

In the command center of Harrar's faceted ship, a bio-engineered quadruped the size of an Ewok was meandering about the confines of the inhibition field, employing its long snout as a vacuum to rid the area of the carcasses of the carriers birthed by the assassin's toxic exhalation.

The dead captives—along with the body of their assassin—had yet to be removed.

Harrar and Nom Anor stood at the perimeter of the field, watching the creature at work. Elan and Vergere had left the compartment.

"Much hinges on the success of this plan," Harrar remarked.

"More than you know," Nom Anor agreed. "Ever since Prefect Da'Gara's failure at Helska, I am not held in the esteem I once was."

"I have faith in you, Executor."

Nom Anor inclined his head in thanks. "Do you think Elan will elect to die with the Jedi, or take her chances that the New Republic will spare her life?"

"I suspect she will die with the Jedi."

"And that doesn't trouble you? After all, her domain is very powerful. Her father has the ear of Supreme Overlord Shimrra, does he not?"

"He is a high priest," Harrar said, then sighed with purpose. "Only Elan can carry this task to fruition. I will lament her death. But it's often necessary to sacrifice the bait to ensnare the quarry."

FIVE

The *Millennium Falcon* put verdant Kashyyyk behind her. Jaina and Leia sat side by side in the outrigger cockpit, with C-3PO, quieter than usual, behind them in the navigator's chair. At Streen's unexpected request, Luke was taking everyone else to Yavin 4. Jaina might have gone along, but Leia had said she didn't want to pilot the *Falcon* home alone.

While the navicomputer calculated lightspeed coordinates for the jump to Coruscant, Jaina glanced at her mother, who looked small and fragile in the oversize seat Chewie had occupied for so many years. She had scarcely said a word since lifting off from platform Thiss.

"Not often I get to fly Dad's ship," Jaina said casually, hoping to open a conversation.

Leia reacted as if she had been yanked from a trance. "What?"

"I said I was surprised Dad asked me to fly the *Falcon* home."

Leia smiled at her. "Record holder at Lando's Folly . . . Rogue Squadron pilot . . . Your father thinks very highly of your skills."

Jaina was quiet for a moment. "I hope he gets home all right."

Leia laughed. "Don't worry, he'll hop a freighter or a trader's ship and probably beat us back to Coruscant. He doesn't need help in that area."

"Or any other area," Jaina said, frowning.

Leia made her lips a thin line and took her daughter's hand. "Don't confuse refusing help with not needing it."

"Why is he like that?"

"How much time do we have?" Leia joked. "The short answer is that your father wasn't raised the way you and I were. He didn't have the support of a family or the comfort of a stable home." She shook her head. "He's been so many things—a swoop racer, a pilot, an officer in the Imperial Navy, a smuggler—but all those occupations have one thing in common: they require extreme self-reliance and a certain amount of aloofness. He didn't grow up accustomed to getting help, so he's certainly not about to ask for it."

"But he's been acting like he's the only one who misses Chewie."

"He knows that isn't true, and he's aware of how he's been acting. When he and I returned to Sernpidal after Chewie died, he told me he suddenly felt that the world had become unsafe—that he'd always thought of our family and close friends as almost immune to tragedy, living in a kind of bubble. How all of us have managed to survive the things we've been through is nothing short of astonishing. But all the narrow escapes, the flirting with death, only made Han feel more invulnerable. Chewie's death changed that. Your father even included Mara's illness as evidence of how insecure and unpredictable everything has become."

Leia paused, recalling something. "It didn't occur to me until later on that I'd heard him express the same doubts once before—just after you and Jacen and Anakin had been kidnapped by Hethrir. Do you remember how protective he became?"

Jaina shook her head. "Not really."

"Well, you were pretty young. But trust me, your dad wouldn't let any of you kids out of his sight for months." Leia glanced at Jaina. "He'd like to have everyone believe he's a hardened skeptic, but the fact is, he runs on faith."

"Then why is he keeping such a distance from everyone?"

"Because giving in to his pain would require him to break down and really grieve, instead of shutting himself off from the world. And he's too slick for that."

"Is that how he got that nickname?"

Leia shook her head. "That's another story."

Jaina tortured her lower lip with her teeth. "Mom, he will come home, won't he? I mean, we're all he has right now, right?"

"Of course," Leia started to say, when C-3PO interjected, "I only hope it's enough."

Mif Kumas, Calibop sergeant at arms of the New Republic Senate for two terms running, spread his wings as he rose from his commodious seat on the dais of Coruscant's Grand Convocation Chamber.

"Senators, I would caution you to refrain from disrupting these proceedings with vocal displays or outbursts, warranted or otherwise." Kumas waited until everyone had fallen silent, then inclined his maned head toward the speaker's rostrum that stood opposite the dais on the polished stone floor of the great hall. "Director bel-dar-Nolek of the Obroan Institute has been recognized, and he deserves to be heard out."

Nodding curtly to Kumas in appreciation, bel-dar-Nolek resumed his tirade. "Furthermore, it is the Institute's contention that the New Republic has failed to honor its obligation to provide defense where needed."

A human of considerable girth, he affected custom-tailored suits and a walking cane hand-carved from greel wood. His jowls quivered as he spoke, and he frequently punctuated his remarks by stabbing the air with a chubby forefinger.

"It was clear to the members of this body that Obroa-skai was imperiled, but nothing was done to safeguard us from attack. The Yuuzhan Vong descended on us like velkers, picking our cities clean." He paused to clear his throat. "I was tending to business on Coruscant at the time, but I have seen the holo reports."

Hushed utterings, few of them flattering, spread through the hall, prompting Kumas to repeat his appeal for some measure of decorum. Gratified by the commotion his remarks had elicited, bel-dar-Nolek folded his stout arms and rested them on his ample abdomen.

Tiers of randomly positioned galleries, boxes, and balconies loomed on all sides, rising clear to the domed ceiling, with page, protocol, and interpreter droids moving along the ramps, bridges, and stairways that linked them. While placement was not an indication of rank, many of the senators seated in the upper levels represented worlds only recently admitted to the New Republic and were frequently regarded by the lower-tier delegates as audience members rather than participants. As an appeasement to them, there was talk of equipping some of the loftiest galleries with detachable hover platforms, such as had been used in the waning days of the Old Republic, but no one gave the rumors much credence.

From one of those galleries came the voice of Thuv Shinev, spokesperson for 175 inhabited planets in the outer reaches of the Tion Hegemony. Simultaneously, a life-size hologram of the human senator resolved from a projector well on the chamber floor between the speaker's rostrum and the advisory council's dais, with its tight arc of heterogeneous chairs. Anyone in doubt as to the senator's identity could access information on small displays built into the armrests of every chair in the hall.

"I submit to this body that a task force was deployed to protect Obroa-skai," Shinev argued, "and that all within reason was done."

Bel-dar-Nolek addressed Shinev's hologram. "A pair of reconditioned Golan Defense Platforms and a couple of antique warships hardly constitute a task force, Senator."

"That was all that could be spared, Director," Bothan Chief of State Borsk Fey'lya growled from his seat on the dais. His violet eyes flashed. "What's more, I find such recriminations reprehensible, in light of the enemy's erratic movements and often unpredictable strategies."

Bel-dar-Nolek spread his hands placatingly. "Chief Fey'lya, I'm simply trying to prevent further errors in judgment. It's one thing to ignore the pleas of Outer Rim worlds, but to allow a world of Obroa-skai's prominence to fall into enemy hands—"

"I object to the director's blatant chauvinism!" the senator from Agamar interrupted. "And by what right does Obroa-skai portray itself as a cynosure?"

Bel-dar-Nolek glowered at the human and flung his words with brutal carelessness. "Obroa-skai's dedication to the perpetuation of cultural diversity makes it more important than other worlds. I demand that something be done to rescue what remains of our historical documents before it's too late."

"Secretary Kumas," a deep and mellifluous female voice rang out, "I ask to be recognized."

Kumas spread his wings. "The senate recognizes Senator Viqi Shesh of Kuat."

A slender, handsome woman of indeterminate age, Shesh flipped radiant black hair over her shoulder as she rose from her balcony seat. Relatively new to politics, she had quickly become known as a clever deal maker, with a knack for keeping all sides happy. The media had taken an immediate interest in her, to the point where she had been the subject of countless news stories, and her face was almost as widely recognized as that of Chief of State Fey'lya.

"On the matter of rescuing data, Director, it is my understanding that shiploads of important documents were relocated to the Institute's facility on Coruscant well in advance of the attack on Obroa-skai. Was I misinformed?"

"A fraction of what we had hoped to save," bel-dar-Nolek countered nastily.

Shesh beetled her fine brows and nodded in a way that

combined gravity and conceit. "Forgive my saying so, but the past concerns me far less than the future. While the loss of Obroa-skai is a terrible blow, the New Republic military is hardly in a position to spare ships to retake a world when it is already overextended in defending so many others. The Yuuzhan Vong are widening their hold of key sectors in the Outer and Mid Rims, and unless their advance is thwarted, they could reach the Colonies or the Core in a standard year, leaving even Coruscant itself vulnerable to assault."

Bel-dar-Nolek studied her stonily. "I see through you, Senator. Obroa-skai was surrendered because it lacks strategic value. When Yuuzhan Vong warships begin to close on Kuat, Chandrila, or Bothawui, I doubt very much that the New Republic fleets will be otherwise engaged. The military was in force at Ithor. Even the Imperial Remnant."

"And Ithor was despoiled in spite of our efforts," Shesh said. "I sympathize, Director, but I certainly don't see what can be done now."

Bel-dar-Nolek slammed his fist into his open hand. "We can appeal to the Yuuzhan Vong to allow Obroa-skai to remain accessible to scholars."

Denunciations flew from every quarter. While Kumas was attempting to restore order, Borsk Fey'lya got to his feet, his cream-colored fur bristling. "It is not the policy of this body to bargain with aggressors," he pronounced, in a way that left little room for argument.

But bel-dar-Nolek was unmoved. "Then I'm afraid you leave the Obroan Institute no choice but to forge a separate peace with the Yuuzhan Vong."

"I strongly advise against that, Director," Shesh said.

"The most recent attempt at appealing to the Yuuzhan Vong's sense of fair play ended in the grisly murder of one of our own—Senator Elegos A'Kla."

"I hold Luke Skywalker and the Jedi accountable for the death of Senator A'Kla," bel-dar-Nolek said in disgust, "and all that has befallen us. Where were they when Obroa-skai fell? Anyone would think they would have been the first to protect a center of learning."

"Even the Jedi can't be everywhere at once," Fey'lya said.

"Still, I blame them. I blame the Jedi and the Bothans' own Admiral Traest Kre'fey, who has become a dangerous rogue!"

"I demand a retraction," Fey'lya fulminated. "Such remarks are blatantly inflammatory and provocative!"

"What information do we have about the genesis of this war?" the director said, playing to the audience. "We have only the word of the Jedi that the Yuuzhan Vong wiped out the ExGal outpost on Belkadan and attacked Dubrillion and Sernpidal. But who is to say that the Yuuzhan Vong weren't provoked to such actions by the Jedi themselves? Met with hostility, perhaps they simply responded in kind. Perhaps this conflict is nothing more than a perpetuation of that initial misunderstanding, fueled by the subsequent actions of the Jedi at Dantooine and Ithor, in league with certain elements of the military, including Admiral Kre'fey and Rogue Squadron, along with other hapless units that have been dragged into this struggle."

Bel-dar-Nolek paused dramatically and gestured broadly to the hall. "Where are the Jedi even now? Where is Ambassador Organa Solo? Wasn't it she, senators and representatives, who first brought the Yuuzhan Vong to your attention?"

Alderaanian councilor Cal Omas spoke up. "Ambassador Organa Solo is attending to personal business."

"And may I remind Director bel-dar-Nolek and other members of this assembly that she does not represent the Jedi Knights," Shesh added.

"Then just who does?" bel-dar-Nolek pressed. "Why are they permitted to take whatever actions they see fit, without having to answer to this body or to the Defense Force? We are alleged to be members of a New Republic, and yet it seems to me that we are weaker than the Old Republic, which at least had the Jedi under rein."

He looked around the hall. "I ask you, too, what are the Jedi waiting for? Do they fear the Yuuzhan Vong, or is it that they harbor secret designs of their own? I suggest that you put an end to their reckless conduct, and that you open negotiations with the Yuuzhan Vong, without using the Jedi—or anyone with ties to the Jedi, like Elegos A'Kla had—as intermediaries."

Viqi Shesh was the first to speak when the hall had quieted sufficiently for anyone to be heard. "Senators, if nothing else, I think we can all take some consolation in the fact that Director bel-dar-Nolek is neither a politician nor a military strategist." She waited for the laughter and applause to subside. "We must not allow ourselves to be undermined by divisiveness, nor should we allow the fall of Ithor and now Obroa-skai to undermine our confidence in the Jedi. I know that you will agree with me when I say that by weakening the Jedi Knights, we only weaken ourselves."

SIX

Mara rose from the couch to greet Luke as he came through the doorway of their suite on Coruscant. He met her halfway with open arms.

"It's about time," she said, shutting her eyes and holding him close.

R2-D2 trailed Luke into the room, toodled a greeting to Mara, and immediately headed for the suite's recharge station.

"I would've been back sooner if Streen hadn't asked me to go to Yavin 4."

"Trouble?"

"Could be. Now that the Yuuzhan Vong have occupied Obroa-skai, they could discover the academy. If that happens, we have to think about relocating the younger Jedi. In the meantime, Streen, Kam, and Tionne are watching over things."

They had been separated for only a standard week, but Luke was alarmed at how delicate Mara felt to his touch. He considered trying to feel her through the Force, but feared she would detect him and resent the intrusion. Instead he luxuriated in her embrace for a moment longer, then backed away to hold her at arm's length. "Let me look at you."

"If you must," she said with elaborate sufferance.

Her face was pale and her eyes were underscored by dark circles, but some of the sheen had returned to her red-gold hair, and her green eyes sparked to life under his gaze.

"What's the verdict, doctor?"

Luke pretended not to hear the quaver in her voice, but Mara saw through his pretense. There wasn't much they could hide from each other, though one of the more devastating aspects of Mara's illness had been its detrimental effect on the depth and intensity of their bond.

"You tell me."

"It hasn't been my best week." She smiled fraily, then compressed her lips in annoyance. "But I don't know how I ever let you talk me into coming here—and don't say you got me at a weak moment."

"I wasn't going to."

Months earlier, Mara had determined that the best way to fight the illness was to remain active and fully attuned to the Force. But after the brutal murder of Elegos A'Kla and the devastation visited on Ithor her condition had worsened. If all of Luke's and Mara's instincts were wrong and the illness wasn't linked to something the Yuuzhan Vong had introduced to the galaxy, her vitality at least appeared to wax and wane in accordance with the invasion. Where following the minor victories at Helska and Dantooine she had emerged strong, Ithor had constituted a new low, not only for Mara but for everyone.

Luke slipped out of his cloak, and the two of them

moved arm in arm into the suite's modestly furnished sitting room, his black trousers and shirt in stark contrast to Mara's white sheath. Mara lowered herself into a corner of the couch, her taut legs tucked beneath her. She gathered her long hair in one hand and twirled it behind her head, then spent a moment staring out the window at passing traffic. The apartment wasn't far from the Grand Convocation Center, but sonic-cancellation glass kept the noise from intruding.

"Did you meet with Dr. Oolos?" Luke asked at last.

She turned to him. "I did."

"And?"

"He told me the same thing Cilghal and Tomla El told me seven months ago. The illness isn't like anything he's ever seen, and there's nothing he can do. But I could have told you that—and saved both of us the trouble of coming here. Oolos wouldn't come right out and say that the Force is the only thing keeping me alive, but he implied as much."

"There's the one other . . . case," Luke started to say.

Mara shook her head. "He died. Just after you left for Kashyyyk."

Luke allowed his disappointment to show. A Ho'Din, Ism Oolos was not only a noted physician, but also a researcher of some celebrity, as a result of his investigations into the Death Seed plague that had swept through the Meridian sector twelve years earlier.

"Did he have anything to say about the beetle?"

"The infamous Belkadan beetle," Mara said jocularly, then shook her head. "Other than that it's also like nothing he's ever seen. But the tests he ran didn't show any evidence that my illness is connected to the thing."

Luke grew introspective. Many years earlier, the Mon Calamari Jedi Cilghal had employed the Force to heal then Chief of State Mon Mothma of an assassin-induced nano-destroyer virus. So how was it that she and Oolos and the Ithorian healer Tomla El could all remain powerless against the molecular disorder that had assailed Mara? It could only have come from the Yuuzhan Vong, Luke told himself. In the midst of an all-embracing conflict, he and Mara were waging their own private struggle.

"Was the memorial difficult?" Mara said, clearly eager to talk about something other than the state of her health.

Luke looked up and took a breath. "Not for Chewbacca's immediate family. Wookiees are very accepting of death. But I am worried about Han."

Mara frowned sympathetically. "Your sister might be Han's soul mate, but Chewbacca was his first mate. It's going to take time."

"I didn't help matters any. When I tried to suggest that he open himself up to the Force, he made a point of reminding me that he isn't a Jedi."

"Which is another reason he and Chewbacca were so close," Mara said. "He's surrounded on all sides." She grew quiet, then surfaced from her thoughts and looked at Luke. "I was just remembering a time I saw your father hurl someone against a bulkhead for showing a lack of respect for the Force."

"I don't think that's the right approach to take with Han," Luke said wryly.

"But it's exactly the approach the Jedi are expected to take with the Yuuzhan Vong."

"Yes. By the same people who fear us taking over the galaxy or succumbing to the dark side."

Mara smiled wanly. "Things haven't exactly turned out as planned, have they? Even after the peace accord, I never doubted that we'd face challenges and go through the usual ups and downs. But I truly believed we'd be able to send any enemies of the New Republic running for cover. Now I'm not so sure."

Luke nodded, wondering if Mara was referring obliquely to her own enemy. If so, her words suggested that she was losing confidence in her ability to prevail.

"Mon Mothma once asked me if I thought my students would eventually set themselves up as an elite priesthood or as a band of champions. Would the Jedi choose to insulate themselves or act in the service of those in need? Would we be a part of the citizenry or outside it?" He narrowed his eyes in recollection. "She envisioned Jedi who would be willing to get their hands dirty, Jedi in all walks of life—medicine, law, politics, and the military. She saw it as my duty to set an example, to become a genuine leader rather than a mere figurehead."

"And she'd be the first to admit that her concerns were unfounded."

"Would she? Obi-Wan and Yoda never talked about what the distant future held for me. Maybe if I hadn't spent the past few years trying to learn how to overcome ysalamiri and tune my lightsaber to cleave cortosis ore, I'd know what course the Jedi should take now. It's the dark side that calls constantly for aggression and revenge—even against the Yuuzhan Vong. The stronger you become, the more you're tempted." Luke gazed at his wife. "Maybe Jacen's right about there being alternatives to fighting."

"He certainly didn't get that from his father."

"His coming to it on his own makes it all the more significant. He thinks I've paid too much attention to the Force as power, at the expense of understanding a more unifying Force."

"Jacen is still a young man."

"He's young, but he's a deep thinker. What's more, he's right. I've always been more concerned with events in the here and now than the future. I don't have the long view, so I miss the big picture. I've had a harder time fighting myself than I had fighting my clone."

Luke stood up and moved to the window. "The Jedi have always been peacemakers. They've never been mercenaries. That's why I've tried to protect our independence and keep us from swearing allegiance to the New Republic. We aren't an arm of their military, and we never will be."

Mara waited until she was certain he was finished. "You're starting to sound like that Fallanassi woman who took you on a wild yunax chase looking for your mother."

"Akanah Norand Pell," Luke supplied. "I wish I knew where her people went."

Mara snorted. "Even if you found them, I don't think the Yuuzhan Vong are going to be as susceptible to Fallanassi-created illusions as the Yevetha were."

"Not judging by what we've seen."

An ironic laugh escaped Mara. "Akanah. Akanah, Gaeriel Captison, Callista . . . Luke Skywalker's lost loves. Not to mention that one on Folor . . ."

"Fondor," Luke corrected. "And I was never in love with Tanith Shire."

"Just the same, you met each of them during a time of crisis."

"When haven't we been in crisis?"

"That's what I'm getting at. Should I be worried that someone new will cross your path this time?"

Luke went to her. "Our crisis is the one that concerns me most," he said earnestly. "We need a victory."

"You want to talk about irony? My father told me a story that happened right here in the Meridian sector, maybe twelve standard years ago."

Captain Skent Graff—human and proud of it, with broad shoulders and a face that turned heads—was half perched on the com-scan integrator console of the *Soothfast*'s cramped bridge, one high-booted leg extended to the floor. His captive audience, slouched at sundry duty stations, were the half dozen who made up the light cruiser's bridge crew. The stations chirped and chimed intermittently, and the ship's Damorian power plant thrummed. The sloping viewports of the ingot-shaped vessel looked out on cloud-blanketed Exodo II and its poor excuse for a moon, and some light-years distant, the luminous dust clouds of the Spangled Veil Nebula.

"He's stationed aboard the *Corbantis*, out of Durren Orbital, when the ship's tasked to investigate reports of a pirate attack on Ampliquen. Actually, nobody knew for sure whether it was pirates or forces from Budpock violating a truce accord, but in fact the whole thing turned out to be a ruse engineered by Loronar Corp, a contingent of Imperials, and a guy named Ashgad, who was trying to spread a plague through this entire sector."

"The Death Seed plague," the young female Sullustan at the navicomputer said.

"Give the lady a glitterstim spliff," Graff said good-naturedly. "She knows her history. Anyway, the *Corbantis* never makes it to Ampliquen. It's quilled by a flock of Loronar's smart missiles and left for dead in an ice chasm on Damonite Yors-B—not too far from here as the mynock flies. But then along comes Han Solo and his Wookiee pal—"

"Who just happened to be in the neighborhood?" the communications officer asked.

"Actually they were searching for Chief of State Leia Organa Solo, who'd gone missing, but that's beside the point." Graff rested his elbow on a deactivated R series droid fastened to the bulkhead. "Solo and the Wookiee investigate the *Corbantis* and find seventeen severely rad-burned survivors—one of which was my father—and they take them to the sector medical facility at Bagsho on Nim Drovis. At the time the place was being run by some well-known Ho'Din physician—I can't remember his name, Oolups or Ooploss, something like that—and Ooploss does everything he can for his patients. The problem was that the med facility was so overcrowded that some of the survivors had to be relocated to bacta wards in the annex. And what do you think happens?"

"They come down with the Death Seed plague," the navigator ventured.

Graff nodded. "They come down with the Death Seed plague. Which just goes to show you that even when you figure you've cheated the odds, you're still a statistic waiting to happen."

"And now here you are, all these years later," the navigator said, "right back where your father was, making local space safe for Drovis's zwil packers."

"Zwil?" the Twi'lek enlisted-rating at the threat-assessment station said.

"Some sort of narcotic," Graff said.

The navigator's recurved mouth quirked a smile. "For those with membrane-lined breathing tubes wide enough to—"

"Captain," the comm officer interrupted. "Durren reports that their hyperspace orbiter has picked up a Cronau radiation event in our sector. Confidence is high that a large ship has reverted to realspace. Interrogators are awaiting a telesponder return."

Graff leapt to his feet and hurried to his swivel-mounted chair. "Do we have visual contact?"

"Not yet, sir. The event is well outside our sensor range."

Graff turned to the comsec officer. "Scramble Gauntlet squadron and go to general quarters."

Sirens blared throughout the ship, and garnet light began to suffuse the bridge.

The comsec officer looked over his shoulder at Graff. "Sir, forward tech station reports countermeasures enabled, shields up and fully charged."

"Data on the event coming in," the enlisted-rating said. "Ship is an unknown quantity. Radar and laser-imaging computers are compiling a portrait."

Graff swung to face the holo-imager, where the ghostly

likeness of an enormous, faceted polyhedron, black as onyx, was already taking shape.

"Yuuzhan Vong?"

"Unknown, sir," the enlisted-rating said. "It doesn't match anything in our data banks."

"Move us out of stationary orbit."

"Sir, drive profiles of the intruder match those of a vessel in the enemy flotilla that attacked Obroa-skai."

"Gauntlet squadron is out the door, moving to recon position."

"Any chatter from the Yuuzhan Vong vessel?" Graff asked.

"Negative, sir. No, wait. Scanners now show two ships."

Again, Graff swiveled to face the holo-imager, where a second, smaller polyhedron was forming alongside the original. "Is that thing a new arrival, or are we observing some sort of mitosis?"

"It appears to be a component of the larger vessel, sir. Vessel one is changing course, bearing for Durren Orbital Station. Module is accelerating to intercept our starfighters. Gauntlet is breaking formation, splitting up into attack elements."

"Patch me through to Gauntlet leader," Graff ordered the comm officer.

"Gauntlet leader is patched through," the woman said.

"Gauntlet One, can you show us what you're seeing?"

Relayed over the command net annunciator, the squadron leader's voice was thin sounding and disrupted by bursts of static. "Transmitting. Looks like the galaxy's biggest decoder ring lost its stone."

"Will you look at that thing," someone on the bridge remarked as a real-time image replaced the holosimulation.

"Sir, bio-energy massing in the smaller ship. They have us in target lock."

Graff engaged the chair's safety harness. "Brace for impact."

Effulgent golden light filled the *Soothfast*'s forward viewports. The ship shook as if snatched and shaken by a giant hand.

"Plasma energy," the enlisted-rating reported. "Consistent with Yuuzhan Vong–ranged weapons. No damage to vital systems. Shields are holding."

"Range?"

"Secondary vessel is moving within striking distance, sir."

Graff gave his command cap a downward tug. "Tell Gauntlet squadron to steer clear. Starboard main batteries, stand by to return fire."

A retrofitted *Proficient*-class ship of Corellian design, the *Soothfast* was 850 meters long, but with only ten heavy turbolasers and twenty ion cannons it was wanting in firepower. Some of the compartmentalization that had originally reinforced the cruiser's hull had been removed to create a docking bay for starfighters, but even with the fighters the sharp-nosed ship remained an ancillary weapon.

"Gauntlet is clear, sir."

Graff nodded. "Ready proton torpedoes. Set for detonation at the first hint of gravitic anomalies."

"Sir, torpedoes are armed as dictated by new protocol."

"Ready starboard turbolasers," Graff ordered.

"Sir, turbolasers enabled."

Graff looked at the weapons officer. "If that 'stone' operates true to form, it'll vacuum the torpedoes, but the lasers stand a good chance of scoring."

"Understood, Captain."

Graff pivoted his chair. "Main batteries, commence fire."

Blinding projectiles streaked into space, followed by lances of blue-green light, converging far in the distance with radiant, strobing flashes.

"Direct hit."

"Fire," Graff repeated.

Again, torpedoes and coherent light streamed from the ship and explosions wreathed the enemy ship, vying with the stars for brilliance.

"Cease fire." Graff glanced at his executive officer. "Let's hope that softened things up. Commander, tell Gauntlet to begin their run."

The XO relayed the order over the command net. On the bridge's main display screen, magnified views showed T-65A3 X-wings and E2 B-wings commencing attack runs against the lapidary ship. Bursts of scarlet laserfire spewed from the snubfighters' wingtip cannons, and proton torpedoes loosed by the B-wings blazed radiant pink trails through space. But the enemy ship merely consumed the energy and answered the attack with geysers of molten rock. Resembling shards of mirrored glass, individual hull facets flared to life, then winked out, becoming black as the ship's background.

"*Soothfast*, this thing's going after our shields," Gauntlet One reported a moment later.

"Gauntlet One, order your fighters to expand the field of the inertial compensators and switch over to new scan and targeting protocols. And keep an eye out for coralskippers."

"Already done, *Soothfast*. But shields can't be expanded enough to compensate for the warship's drawing power."

"Shields down," another voice said. "Breaking off."

"Stay with your wingmates," Gauntlet One shouted. "Keep your lasers quadded up on rapid cycle."

"Compensator is in failure. Aborting attack run."

"Watch your tail, Gauntlet Eight!"

"Captain, energy massing in the Yuuzhan Vong vessel."

Graff swiveled to his XO. "Instruct Gauntlet to abort."

"Enemy vessel is firing."

On the main screen, real-time holo showed three starfighters vanish in fleeting explosions. A sense of urgency punctuated Gauntlet One's words over the net.

"We're taking casualties—Two, Four, and Five. Still can't get a fix on dovin basal or weapons emplacements."

"What's he talking about?" Graff asked brusquely.

The Twi'lek enlisted-rating flipped his head-tails over his shoulders and studied console displays. "Battle analysis computer is working on it, sir. Enemy weapons and singularity projectors appear to be mobile. Sir, it's like the entire hull is capable of delivering fire and creating gravitic anomalies."

"Captain, module has drawn another bead on us."

No sooner had the words left the comm officer's mouth than the cruiser was jarred by a powerful strike. Bridge illumination diminished, then brightened, and blue electricity danced over one of the consoles. Vibrated free of its magnetic hold on the bulkhead, the R-series droid tipped forward to the deck. Fans clicked on, exhausting smoke from the area.

"Damage assessment coming in from forward technical station. Number-two power generator is down. Deflector shields are marginal."

"Order Gauntlet to regroup and pull back," Graff said quickly. "Alert crash and recovery crews to make ready. Fire control: stand by to coordinate forward turbolasers and ion cannons. I want a sustained burst to rake that ship pole to pole." A glance at the display screen showed him what remained of Gauntlet squadron fleeing for their lives. "Fire!"

Once more, energy streaked from the ship, but no telltale flashes followed.

Graff studied the display screen. "Did we miss?" he asked in disbelief.

"Negative, sir. Enemy vessel appears to have absorbed the energy."

"All guns," Graff said. "Fire!"

Light painted local space with such intensity that everyone on the bridge had to turn from the viewports. It was as if the *Soothfast* had been clipped on the jaw by a heavy fist and was seeing stars.

"Enemy ship is altering course, taking evasive action."

"All guns, fire!" Graff barked.

"Multiple direct hits. Evidence of debris. Enemy is altering course again, speed is diminishing."

Graff twisted to the navigator. "Maintain pursuit. Stay on it!"

Then, without warning, an enormous explosion erupted in the distance, saturating the display screens with white light. When Graff could, he stared out the viewport, but could see no sign of the Yuuzhan Vong ship.

"Where did it go? Did it jump?"

"Negative, sir," the enlisted-rating told him. "Debris is consistent with an all-out kill."

A spontaneous cheer rose from the bridge crew.

"Quiet!" Graff shouted. "Did we just get lucky, or did we discover a weak spot?"

"Unknown, sir, but the vessel is completely destroyed. We must have overwhelmed it. The ship that generated the module is bearing away from Durren Orbital Station, all speed."

Graff removed his hat and scratched his head. "I don't get it."

"Captain, Gauntlet leader reports that the destroyed vessel jettisoned an escape pod. The pod should come into visual range any moment."

Graff turned to the display screen. "Full magnification."

The navigator pointed to a fast-moving glimmer of light. "There it is, sir."

Graff saw what looked like a cylindrical asteroid, far from home, a small portion of its aft surface faceted. "What's its course?"

"Bearing for Exodo II."

"Wouldn't be my first choice," Graff remarked.

"Present heading will bring it just in range of number-two tractor beam."

Graff glanced at his XO.

"Could be a trap, sir. Some kind of sleeper bomb."

Graff nodded grimly. "Engage the tractor beam, but only to hold that thing at bay. Commander, alert Gauntlet. Tell them to scan for any evidence of weapons, but to keep their distance. Even if it turns out to be harmless, I don't want it anywhere near this ship. And patch me through to fleet office."

A new voice crackled from the annunciator.

"*Soothfast,* this is Gauntlet Three. It's definitely an escape pod, probably yorik coral. Negative for armaments, but registering life readings. No bigger than a landspeeder. Rudimentary dovin basal retros and attitude control. Faceted but transparent canopy. Like a sheet of mica. Request permission to investigate at close range."

Graff mulled it over for a moment, then said, "Gauntlet Three, you are green to investigate. But stay sharp."

"Affirmative, *Soothfast,* staying sharp."

No one spoke for a long moment. Then the speaker crackled back to life.

"*Soothfast,* I got a peek at the interior. Looks to be two, repeat, two occupants. One appears to be female. The other . . . Well, sir, the other is anyone's guess."

SEVEN

On Coruscant, Han stepped apprehensively into Eastport's Docking Bay 3733 and palmed the wall-mounted illuminator bar. A glow ring concentric to the interior rim of the docking bay's iris dome powered up, washing the *Millennium Falcon* in harsh light. Umbilicaled to sundry diagnostic and monitoring devices, the ship looked as if it were a patient on life support. The glow ring hummed loudly, and the air smelled faintly of ozone. The floor was a canvas of lubricant spills, scorch marks, and paint overspray.

Bay 3733 was leased to one Vyyk Drago, but in spite of Han's attempts to keep a low profile, almost everyone in Coruscant's administrative district knew that the *Falcon* was berthed there. In setting the ship down a week earlier, Jaina had bull's-eyed the permacrete's faded red landing circle. After what had happened on Kashyyyk, it had taken Han that long to marshal the nerve to visit. Three days aboard a dilapidated freighter hadn't helped any.

Approaching the *Falcon* head-on, her boxy mandibles aimed at him, he recalled his first glimpse of the ship on the Hutt world of Nar Shaddaa almost thirty years earlier. She had then been the property of Lando, who had won her—so the story went—in a sabacc game in Bespin's Cloud City. Though he had seen countless Corellian YT-1300s, it was love at first sight for Han, for there was something singular about the *Falcon*. Aside from promising amazing speed and maneuverability, the ship was built for adventure and proud of its obviously checkered past. Han had resolved that she would be his, one way or another.

Ironically, the chance came in Cloud City, during a four-day-long elimination-round sabacc tournament that ultimately found Lando and Han pitted against each other, with Han holding a pure sabacc hand to Lando's bluff of a winning idiot's array. Short on credits Lando had offered a marker—good for any ship on his lot—which Han had eagerly accepted. Dismayed by Han's win, Lando had tried to maneuver him into selecting a newer-model light stock YT-2400, but Han had chosen the *Falcon*.

He still savored memories of his first moments in the pilot's seat, awed by the power of her sublight engines and the response of her military-grade hyperdrive. She had speed, all right, but she needed muscle and stealth. So had begun a process of retrofitting and upgrading that would continue for twenty years. To Han the *Falcon* was a work in progress, a work of art, never to be completed.

Throughout those years he had protected her with his life, worrying about her as only a parent would, missing her as only a spouse could. There was the time Egome Fass and J'uoch had made off with her on Dellalt; the time the *Falcon* had clung to the aft command tower of the Star Destroyer *Avenger*; the time Lando and Nien Nunb had flown her against the second Death Star . . .

Mara's tasking her cherished *Jade's Fire* to crash into a fortress on Nirauan some years back was a decision he would never understand.

Circling the ship now, Han could still identify signs of some of the modifications he and others had made. At Shug Ninx's spacebarn in the Corellian section of Nar Shaddaa, Han and Chewie had installed a military-grade rectenna, a ventral quad laser cannon, and concussion missile launchers between the mandibles. Shug had macrofused to the hull just aft of the starboard docking arm a small sheet of armor plating from the Star Destroyer *Liquidator*.

Thanks to a group of outlaw techs who operated in the Corporate Sector, the *Falcon* was soon sporting augmented defensive shields, heavy-duty acceleration compensators, oversize thruster ports, and a late-model sensor suite, as well. Back then, the ship had had the distinction of violating the Corporate Sector Authority's performance-profile Waivers List in more ways than any ship of its class.

While the *Falcon* was on Kashyyyk during the Yevethan crisis, Jowdrrl had retrofit a quartet of transparent optical transducer panels to enhance port and aft visibility. Chewie's cousin had also designed the cockpit's auto-tracking fire controllers for the gun turrets.

More recently, as hostilities with remnant Imperial factions had begun to wane—and through no fault of Han's—the *Falcon* had slowly become a kinder, gentler ship. Routine maintenance at the hands of a well-meaning but bumbling shipyard boss on Coruscant had resulted in a near restoration. Cables had been tagged and bundled, mechanicals shock-mounted, electricals grounded and pulse-shielded. A Sienar Systems augmenter had been added to the drive matrix, a Mark 7 generator to the tractor beam array, a Series 401 motivator to the hyperdrive. Sensor lenses had been replaced, dings hammered out, holds recarpeted . . . Han had nearly gone berserk.

He liked that the ship wore all the bumps and bruises that had shaped her, much as he might have worn, had it not been for bacta treatments and synthflesh. He sometimes wondered what he might look like if he'd let all the wounds scar like the one on his chin, the result of a knife slash received in another lifetime.

The ultimate damage to the *Falcon* had been done a mere six months ago, however, with Chewie's death. What she lacked now, and what was likely to keep her grounded for an indeterminate time, no modification could offset.

Overcome by sudden grief, Han stood motionless below the starboard hexagonal docking ring, lost in time. The *Falcon* was so laden with memories, such a chronicle of his and Chewie's adventures and misadventures, that he could scarcely bring himself to look at her, much less board her. But after a moment he entered an authorization code into a handheld remote, and the ship's ramp lowered toward him, as if daring him to enter.

When he did so, he was like a man relearning to walk.

The ramp led directly to the ship's circular ring corridor. Han stopped at the intersection and ran his hand over the corridor's now unblemished padding. In the past five years, the *Falcon* had become such a spiffy ship. The floor grating had been replated, the interior lights worked, and there was always food in the galley and something fragrant in the air. Once utilized to conceal loads of spice or personnel, the shielded smuggling compartments just forward of the passageway to the ladder well had of late housed luggage for family outings, or pieces of folk art Leia had purchased for their home on Coruscant.

Han moved past the outrigger cockpit connector and deeper into the ship. A year back, thinking vaguely about returning the *Falcon* to stock, he had made a start on stripping her of many of the add-ons. The YT-1300 was a classic, after all, nearly as valuable a collector's item as the J-type 327 Nubian. And for all her rattles, squeaks, and carbon-scoring, she was in fine shape—not to mention of considerable historical interest.

One of the first things to go had been the concussion missile launchers in the jaws, which had always interfered with the operation of the cargo-loading mandibles. But that, of course, was before the Yuuzhan Vong had appeared out of nowhere to present the galaxy with a terrible new threat. Who could say how many besides Chewie would have died in the Outer Rim had he removed the quad lasers.

Han stepped down into the main forward hold and sat dejectedly in the engineering console's swivel chair. Flashy new carpeting covered both the smooth metal deck plates and port-side grating—another accommodation to family travel. It was from here that he had watched Luke practice lightsaber technique against a stinging remote. He swiveled to face the dejarik holo-game board, at which Chewie had spent countless hours, and around which—only a few years earlier—Leia, Admiral Pellaeon, and the late Elegos A'Kla had sat talking about peace.

Han drew his hand down his face, as if to erase the memories that came to mind unbidden, then he pushed himself up, crossed the hold, and stepped up into the circuitry/maintenance bay. Here, he and Leia had shared their first kiss, only to be rudely interrupted by C-3PO, announcing that he had located the reverse power flux coupling or some blasted thing.

A million years ago, Han told himself.

Worming his way aft, he emerged from the bay into the port-side ring corridor, opposite the bunk room where Luke had recuperated after losing his hand to his father's lightsaber.

The corridor passed under the power core ducting and exhaust vents into the main rear hold, which had seen more alterations than any other portion of the ship. Reduced in size to accommodate the hyperdrive, the hold had been partitioned in any number of arrangements. A would-be slaver named Zlarb had come to a grim end back here.

The location of the escape pods hadn't changed since the Corporate Sector days, but the original capsule-shaped pods—entered by way of hinged grates—had been replaced by spherical ones equipped with snazzy iris hatches.

Entering the starboard aft corridor and moving forward, Han passed the bunk room he'd often used as his personal quarters, and within which he had nearly had a showdown with Gallandro, then the galaxy's fastest gun.

Dead now, like so many others from the glory days.

Han spread his arms in a hatchway in the interior wall and leaned into the galley. Laughing to himself, he recalled preparing pudding in cora shells and spiced aric tongue for Leia, when he'd spirited her off to Dathomir during his very wrongheaded courtship of her.

A few more steps brought him full circle to the docking arm. But instead of exiting, Han continued on to the cockpit pod and reluctantly entered. Stepping between the pair of rear chairs, he leaned stiff-armed on the console and gazed through the fan-shaped viewport at the spare-parts shelves he and Chewie had erected on the docking bay wall only the year before.

Ultimately he dropped himself into the outsize co-pilot's seat and sat for a long while with his eyes closed and his thoughts shut down.

A month earlier, Chewie had still seemed so alive to him that he could almost hear the sound of the Wookiee's angry yaups or happy foghorn laughs reverberating in the docking bay. Sitting in the pilot's seat, Han would glance to his right, and there Chewie would be, regarding him sardonically with arms folded across his chest or paws linked behind his head.

Chewie wasn't the only alien he'd flown with—there'd been the Togorian Muuurgh in the Ylesia years—but the Wookiee had been his only real partner, and he couldn't imagine piloting the *Falcon* with anyone else. So he could either mothball her, as he had his BlasTech sidearm, or donate her to the Alliance War Museum on Coruscant, as persistent curators had been urging him to do for fifteen years.

A museum was probably where he belonged, as well,

Han told himself. Like the *Falcon*, he was part of the past and of little use to anyone now.

He sighed heavily. Life was like a game of sabacc: the cards could change at random, and what you were sure was a winning hand could end up losing you the pot.

Instinctively, he reached under the control console for the metallic flask of vacuum-distilled jet juice he and Chewie had often kept secreted there, but it was gone—placed elsewhere by one of the kids or swiped by some disreputable mechanic.

His minor disappointment quickly turned to bitter anger, and he slammed the edge of his right fist repeatedly on the console until his hand went numb. Then he lowered his head to his folded arms and let his tears flow.

"Ah, Chewie," he said out loud.

Han was on his way to Eastport's transport center when a voice behind him yelled, "Slick!"

Without slowing his pace, he glanced over his shoulder, then came to a dead stop on the beltway and spun around, grinning ear to ear. "Now that's a name I haven't heard in a long time," he said to the stocky, gray-haired human who was hurrying to catch up with him.

The man grasped Han's proffered hand and tugged him into a backslapping embrace. When they separated, Han was still smiling broadly.

"What's it been, Roa—thirty years?"

"I couldn't tell you exactly when, but I can tell you where. Departure terminal of Roonadan Spaceport in the Corporate Sector. You and a lovely, dark-haired young woman were waiting to board the *Lady of Mindor* to Ammuud, I believe."

"Fiolla of Lorrd," Han said, as if snatching the name from thin air. He gestured with his chin toward Roa. "You had on a white business suit, with some kind of rainbow sash . . ."

"And you, my young friend, were wearing an especially wary look." Roa's rheumy blue eyes glinted. "You told me you were out of the business, running a collection agency. Han Solo Associated, wasn't it? The next thing I hear, you've won the Battle of Yavin single-handed."

"Not true," Han said, "I had help."

Roa stroked his clean-shaven jaw. "Let's see, then I heard that you'd had yourself encased in carbonite—for posterity, I assumed at the time."

Han narrowed his eyes. "Actually, I was thinking of marketing molds of myself."

Roa laughed, then showed him a look of mild rebuke. "I warned you about working with the Hutts."

"You should have warned Jabba about working with me."

Han appraised Roa's Askajian suit, chromasheath ankle boots, and the rings that sparkled on the pinkies of his plump hands. Roa was already the grand old man of the smuggling trade when the late Mako Spince had introduced Han to him on Nar Shaddaa. Honorable, good-natured, and generous to a fault, Roa had launched many a young outlaw into the business, including Han, whom Roa had brought through his first Kessel Run. Han had even worked for him for a time, and along with Chewie, Lando, Salla Zend, and a couple of the other Nar Shaddaa regulars, had attended Roa's wedding, after which the old man had retired from smuggling, at his wife's insistence.

"So, you still in import-export?"

"Sold everything—almost ten years ago now."

Han studied him some more. "Roa, you don't look like you've aged a day since Roonadan."

"Nor do you," Roa said, almost convincingly.

Han smiled lopsidedly and tapped his forefinger against his front teeth. "Regrown." He touched his nose. "Broken and repaired so many times there's hardly any original tissue left. Plus, my face is all out of whack. This eye's higher than the other one."

"And you think I come by my youthful appearance naturally?" Roa asked theatrically.

"Don't tell me, you're a clone, right?"

Roa laughed. "Next best thing: rejuvenation therapy, coupled with some daily myostim." He displayed a noble profile. "I instructed the cosmeds to leave just enough age to keep me looking distinguished."

"And you do, you old scoundrel."

"Besides, the treatments were Lwyll's idea—mostly."

Han had an image of Roa's rich-voiced, blond-haired, elegant wife. "How is she?"

Roa smiled weakly. "She died a few months back."

Han's lips became a thin line. "I'm sorry to hear that, Roa."

Roa didn't respond immediately. "And I was sorry to hear about Chewbacca, Han. I actually tried to obtain authorization to visit Kashyyyk for the memorial, but you know how Wookiees can be about granting permission to humans."

Han nodded. "They've got a long memory for what the Empire did to them."

"Who doesn't."

Han was quiet for a moment. "So what brings you to Coruscant? I thought you liked wide open space."

Roa's eyes darted. "To tell you the truth, Han—you. You're the reason I'm here."

Han felt a shiver pass through him. Because of a series of unexpected encounters with Roa over the years, in out-of-the-way places like Nar Shaddaa and Roonadan, the old man had become one of those people who made Han wonder if the galaxy wasn't a lot smaller than he'd been led to believe, regardless of his own far-ranging journeys.

"Somehow I expected you to say that," he said at last.

Roa put his hands on Han's shoulders. "What do you say we go someplace where we can talk?"

Han nodded. "There's a restaurant in the transport center."

They rode the beltway indoors, talking about old friends—Vonzel, Tregga, Sonniod, the Briil twins—and familiar places, though Han was clearly preoccupied. All these years later he could still recite Roa's Rules—never ignore a call for help; take only from those who are richer than yourself; don't play sabacc unless you're prepared to lose; don't pilot a ship under the influence; and always be prepared to make a quick getaway—but that didn't mean he trusted Roa unconditionally.

At the Spacer's Lounge, a courtesy droid showed them to a table on the patio, where a group of Duros and Gotals were watching a shock-ball match on the HoloNet. Bland renditions of twenty-year-old jizz classics wafted from unseen emitters. For old times' sake Han and Roa ordered flagons of ebla beer—a Bonadan export. Halfway through their first, Han asked to know the purpose of Roa's seeking him out.

"Fair enough," Roa said, setting the flagon down on the table and patting his mouth dry. "Do you remember a smuggler from the old days named Reck Desh?"

Han thought for a moment and grinned. "Tall, sinewy guy. Fond of body markings, piercings, electrum jewelry. Chewbacca and I partnered with him on a small job for you, running R'alla mineral water into Rampa." His grin broadened. "The *Falcon* was being worked on by Doc Vandangante, so you loaned us your ship—the *Wayfarer*. Reck claimed she was faster than the *Falcon*, and after the Rampa Rapids run, we raced for fifty cases of Gizer ale."

"Which you and the Wook won, hands down."

Han nodded. "Reck was a decent navigator, but he never impressed me as a pilot."

Roa took a drink and licked his lips. "Sometimes you only know a soldier when he becomes an officer."

"Meaning what?"

"Reck's gone over."

"Gone over to who?"

"To the enemy, Han," Roa said, leaning forward. "Or at least to a group of mercenaries working for the Yuuzhan Vong."

"That can't be right. Reck wasn't the traitor type. Besides, he and Chewie got along great. No way Reck would have anything to do with the Vong after what they did to Chewie."

"Maybe he didn't hear about Chewie. Or maybe the credits are too good." Roa paused briefly. "The group Reck's fallen in with call themselves the Peace Brigade.

Word is they're stirring up anti-Jedi sentiment and scouting out worlds where the Yuuzhan Vong can repeat what they did at Sernpidal."

Han's eyes narrowed in irritation. "Why are you telling me this, Roa?"

Roa lowered his gaze. "Because Lwyll died on one of the worlds the Peace Brigade softened up for the kill."

Han's voice deserted him. He stared at his old friend.

"If we had left a day sooner," Roa went on, without looking at Han. "But I had to take care of some business." He laughed shortly and ruefully, then looked at Han, his eyes moist. "Always business. Lwyll died in the first Yuuzhan Vong wave. I was one of a handful who made it out alive."

Han squeezed his eyes shut and struck the table with the edge of his hand. But when he raised his eyes to Roa, his anger was muted by realization. "So your coming here—this is as much between you and Reck as it is between you and me."

Roa held Han's polar gaze. "I don't want anyone else to suffer because of what Reck and his cohorts are doing. The Yuuzhan Vong are masterful enough at causing tragedies without the Peace Brigade's help. If I could deal with Reck on my own, I would, but I'm more frail than I look, Han."

"Yeah, and who better to help you than me, huh? A guy who just lost his partner."

"To put it bluntly: yes."

Han snorted. "Never ignore a call for help, right, Roa?" He got to his feet and walked to the tall windows that overlooked the spaceport's liftoff zones. There wasn't a moment when some ship wasn't leaving for somewhere. When he returned to the table, he spun the chair around and straddled it.

"Where are Reck and his crew now?" he asked in a low voice.

"I don't know, Han. But I know where we could go to find out. First stop would be—"

Han threw up his hands. "Don't say anything. If I don't know where we're going, then I can't tell anyone."

"We'd have to leave while the scent is fresh," Roa said.

Han tugged at his lower lip and thought for a moment. "Your ship's here?"

Roa looked surprised. "Of course. But you want *me* to pilot *you*? Now that's a switch."

"Yes or no, Roa?"

Roa made a placating gesture. "Don't get me wrong, son, I'm more than happy to oblige. I just naturally figured you'd want to take the *Falcon*."

Han shook his head. "As an occasionally smart-mouthed droid I know once said, the *Falcon*'s better configured for running away than engagement. And besides, she's become a ghost ship."

EIGHT

"Aggressive postures are somewhat problematic when you haven't the slightest notion of your enemy's battle plan," Colonel Ixidro Legorburu told the commanders of the New Republic Defense Force and a melange of high-ranking officers. "Only now, with the fall of thirty planetary systems, the destruction of Helska, Sernpidal, and Ithor, and the more recent loss of Obroa-skai, are we beginning to have some sense of the path the Yuuzhan Vong are intent on cutting through the galaxy."

Legorburu's upbringing on agrarian M'haeli belied a shrewd intellect and urbane wit. A former intelligence officer, he had served as a tactical aide during the Yevethan crisis and had since been promoted to director of the Home Fleet's Battle Assessment Division.

"Let me emphasize, though, that the strategy underlying their incursion remains as much a mystery as their ultimate objective."

Exigency had dictated that the briefing be held on Kuat rather than Coruscant, though several officers and specialists were participating via real-time hologram from the New Republic capital and a host of other worlds.

"What have we been able to conclude regarding their

origin?" Admiral Sien Sovv asked. Fulcrum of the Defense Force command staff, the Sullustan sat at a data console adapted to his smallish hands and capable of filtering background noise, which might otherwise have proved irritating to his keen hearing.

"As you know, the first world to fall to the Yuuzhan Vong—to be razed by them, I should say—was Belkadan, where the ExGal Society had a listening post." Legorburu manipulated a parabolic holoprojector to fashion a 3-D view of the galaxy's Tingel Arm. "However, despite talk of an extragalactic arrival, our initial supposition was that they were native to some unknown stellar system, here, in the central Tingel, midway between the Corporate Sector and Imperial Remnant space."

"Does that hypothesis remain viable?" Brigadier General Etahn A'baht asked. Former commander of the Fifth Fleet, A'baht had also been involved in the Yevethan crisis. A Dornean, A'baht had tough aubergine skin and eyefolds that swelled and fanned out.

Legorburu looked to the representative from the Institute for Sentient Studies, headquartered on Baraboo. But before the Ithorian could respond, Sovv rose to his feet.

"I know I speak for everyone here in expressing my extreme sorrow at what has befallen your homeworld," the admiral said. "The galaxy is greatly diminished."

Tamaab Moolis acknowledged Sovv's sentiments with a motion of his long, upward curving head. "I thank the admiral," he said out of both mouths.

Attentiveness replaced the sadness in his widely spaced eyes. "Pursuant to the supposition that the Yuuzhan Vong originated in the Tingel Arm, we conducted a thorough search of our databases, but were unable to discover corroborating evidence. A protocol droid at Dubrillion stated that the Yuuzhan Vong language is reminiscent of Janguine, but that trail has led nowhere. We are continuing to investigate the possibility that the Yuuzhan Vong are a long-vanished race indigenous to our galaxy that has suddenly reappeared."

"Was that area of the Tingel Arm once populated?" Sovv asked.

The Ithorian deferred to the virtual presence of Been L'toth of the Astrographic Survey Institute. Another Dornean, Been was the son of Kiles L'toth, who had assumed command of the Fifth Fleet after his friend Etahn A'baht had been relieved of duty.

"We reject the possibility that a species as powerful as the Yuuzhan Vong could have originated there," L'toth's hologram began. "Given the extent of their resources and the size of their war fleet, they would be in control of hundreds of worlds, if not systems, and would certainly have come to our attention by now. At the very least, we would have heard about them from the Trianii or some other species that inhabits that area of the Tingel.

"Granted, however, the Tingel Arm has yet to be thoroughly mapped. The original explorations were terminated by the outbreak of the Clone Wars. That was one of the reasons Emperor Palpatine granted the Corporate Sector Authority free reign in their corner of the Tingel. Our thinking now is that the Yuuzhan Vong are indeed from outside our galaxy." L'toth paused. "Not merely from a nearby star cluster, as was the case with the Ssi-ruuk, but from another galaxy entirely."

A'baht huffed. "Any species capable of crossing intergalactic space would have to be considerably more advanced than any of us—on the order of a hundred generations more advanced. And yet the Yuuzhan Vong ships have been utilizing the same hyperspace entry points and egresses used by our own vessels."

"But suppose they have been in *transit* for hundreds of generations," Legorburu said. "Imagine if you will, a fleet of vessels plying the void, comparable to the Ithorian herd ships, only many times their size."

A'baht waved a hand. "I'm interested in facts, not poetry."

Legorburu gained control of himself. "At present we're trying to determine if Emperor Palpatine had any knowledge of the Yuuzhan Vong, as he did the Ssi-ruuk. Thanks to the generosity of Moff Ephin Sarreti, we've been given access to Imperial records relevant to the Outbound Flight Project."

Funded by the senate at the behest of Jedi Master Jorus C'baoth, the Outbound Flight Project had constituted a failed attempt to peer past the edge of the galaxy.

Transmitted from Bastion, in the distant Imperial Remnant, Sarreti's life-size hologram was almost colorless, and disrupted by diagonal lines of interference. A technician boosted the audio gain.

". . . Imperial records do not contain any mention of the Yuuzhan Vong—although it is now understood that Emperor Palpatine returned Chiss Grand Admiral Thrawn to the Unknown Regions on learning that the Chiss had been fortifying their systems against the threat of invasion by an unknown aggressor."

Sovv and his fellow commanders took a moment to

confer. "Are you suggesting that the Yuuzhan Vong might be that aggressor?" Sovv asked at last.

"If we could establish direct contact with the Chiss, we might know for certain," Sarreti said. "But Jag Fel has no interest in serving as a liaison, and all attempts at communications with Nirauan have gone unanswered."

"Have you tried dispatching a ship?" A'baht asked.

Sarreti smiled. "Have you, General?" When A'baht grimaced, the moff added, "We have no desire to intrude on Chiss space and risk having to wage wars on two fronts."

"Understood, Moff Sarreti," Sovv said, nodding glumly. He looked at Legorburu. "Continue with your briefing, Colonel."

Legorburu brought a close-up of the Tingel Arm to the light table. "The Yuuzhan Vong are using the central Tingel as a rendezvous point and staging area. Reconnaissance forces sent to adjoining sectors—both here, in the Trianii colonies, and here, at Dathomir—have detected a buildup of significantly larger ships."

"I want numbers," A'baht said.

Legorburu nodded to the Tammarian Ayddar Nylykerka, chief analyst for asset tracking during the Yevethan crisis and now director of Fleet Intelligence. "Based on available data, we are now estimating Yuuzhan Vong naval strength at one thousand capital ships, deployed in task forces and flotillas, comprising anywhere from twenty-five to seventy-five vessels."

Sovv and the others exchanged looks of astonishment.

"It may please the general staff to know," Nylykerka added quickly, "that the senate has ratified the Universal Conscription bill, and that the Kuat, Bilbringi, Sluis Van, and Fondor shipyards expect to double their production of heavy cruisers by the end of next year."

"Next year," Sovv repeated. "The Yuuzhan Vong could be in our laps by then."

"Yes, sir, but with our present stock of Mon Calamari *Mediator*-class battle cruisers, Bothan Assault Cruisers, and Corellian *Viscount*-class Star Defenders, we have sufficient firepower to engage the Yuuzhan Vong in multiple theaters."

Sovv nodded tentatively. "How do the enemy ships compare to our signature ships?"

Nylykerka glanced at durasheet notes. "Rated by size and armament, the fleet is comprised of warship analogs, cruisers, destroyers, troop carriers, frigates, corvettes, and gunboats, along with starfighter analogs known as coralskippers. Reconnaissance reports indicate that the more recently arrived Yuuzhan Vong vessels are comparable in size and firepower to *Super*-class Star Destroyers."

A Yuuzhan Vong warship took shape above the light table. "The command ship at Obroa-skai," Nylykerka said. "Myriad areas of its yorik coral surface are capable of unleashing destructive energy on the order of that delivered by our most powerful turbolaser and ion cannons. The vessel does not so much erect shields as employ gravitic anomalies to engulf or deflect anything directed against it. The anomalies are engineered by organic devices called dovin basals, which also combine the functions of repulsorlift, sublight, and hyperspace drives."

Nylykerka used a laser pointer to indicate the slender projections that emanated from the command ship's bow and stern. "The arms are also equipped with plasma launchers, sealed at the tips by organic, trefoil valves. What's more, each carries the equivalent of a wing of coralskippers, which are similarly shielded and capable of firing projectiles or plasma. It was initially believed that the coralskippers were remotes, like the old Trade Federation droid starfighters or Loronar Corporation's CCIRs, but in fact they are individually piloted—or at least to a certain extent. By that I mean that combat tactics seem to be directed by a creature known as a yam-mosk, or war coordinator, which serves as a kind of biotic battle analysis computer."

The laser pointer called attention to irregularities on the command ship's hull. "We have not been able to determine why some portions of the ship are smooth. However, certain markings observed on the smooth areas suggest similarities to the symbols and glyphs often seen on the ovoid vessels of the Aing-Tii monks. We believe that they might serve as indicators of lineage or status rather than military rank."

Legorburu broke the stunned silence of the commanders.

"Since entering the Tingel Arm, the Yuuzhan Vong have been moving oblique to the Core. The attack on Obroa-skai may mark the beginning of a push into the Mid Rim, but it would be premature to speculate at this point."

"Well, someone had better start speculating," A'baht growled. "We can't remain on the defensive indefinitely."

Legorburu wedged a finger into the collar of his uniform and continued. "Should the Yuuzhan Vong adhere to their current heading, without significant deviation from the ecliptic, they will pass outward of the Hapes Cluster, and perhaps Kashyyyk. But the Meridian sector, Hutt space, Bothawui, Rodia, and Ryloth lie almost directly in their path."

A'baht's swelling eyes took in the room. "Does anyone here actually believe that the Yuuzhan Vong are merely passing through, destroying worlds and sacrificing populations on a whim?" When no one answered, he added, "What are our options if they swing toward the Core?"

Nylykerka directed the holoprojector to display a disposition of the main fleets. "Admiral Pellaeon has returned the ships under his command to the Imperial Remnant to safeguard it from invasion. Elements of the Third and Fourth Fleets are spread along the Hydian Way and the Perlemian Trade Route. Most of the Second Fleet is positioned Coreward of the Hapes Cluster, near Borleias. Elements of the First and Fifth are deployed at Coruscant, Kuat, Chandrila, Commenor, and Fondor."

"Fleet strength and disposition get us only so far," Sovv said after a moment. "It's more important that we achieve some understanding of the Yuuzhan Vong as a species. Exactly what sort of beings are we dealing with?"

Legorburu scanned faces in the console displays. "Uh, Dr. Eicroth, perhaps you'd care to shed some light on the admiral's question."

Joi Eicroth's hologram did justice to her fair-haired allure. Briefly married to Admiral Drayson, she still worked with him as an operative in Alpha Blue, a covert branch of New Republic Intelligence. One of the first to have a look at a Qella recovered on Maltha Obex some years earlier, she was currently a member of the xeno-biology team tasked with compiling a profile on the Yuuzhan Vong.

"Essentially we are dealing with a near-human species," Eicroth said, "both externally and internally—excepting, for the moment, the semisentient reptoid proxy troops the Yuuzhan Vong deployed at Dantooine, Garqi, and Ithor. This is borne out by the fact that Jedi Master Luke Skywalker suffered no ill effects after donning both a Yuuzhan Vong coralskipper cognition hood and an organic breathing apparatus. However, the examples we've autopsied present some intriguing puzzles."

Holographic representations of three Yuuzhan Vong appeared above the light table, rotating slowly while Eicroth continued.

"The distinctions you see—this one's curiously elongated head, this one's auxiliary ribs, the deep patterns etched into the torso of this one—may indicate the existence of separate lineage groups among the Yuuzhan Vong. What is clear is that they undergo what must be excruciating physical alterations in service to some religious or warrior ideal. In any case, the uniformity of the disfigurements and markings suggests a complex social hierarchy.

"This is fully consistent with the nature of Yuuzhan Vong applied science, which, from what we've been able to determine, is based exclusively on a form of animated technology. The use of bioreactors, neuroengines, and biological weapons is indicative of a species that places great importance on organic rather than artificial innovation. Where we invent machines, they create life-forms that serve the same function as machines."

"Can they be brought down?" A'baht asked above the murmur of several separate conversations.

"They are taller and heavier than most humans," Eicroth said. "They are strong on an individual basis and in some instances enhanced or encased by living armor. However, they can be killed by conventional weapons and apparently by Jedi lightsabers. Bafforr tree pollen shows promise as an allergen that affects the armor, but it will be some time before the pollen can be synthesized in the amounts needed to serve as an effective deterrent or biological agent. Still, each encounter has furnished us with additional data as to their weak points—psychological, anatomical, and social."

Silence prevailed until Commodore Brand, former commander of the Fifth Fleet cruiser *Indomitable* and the most curmudgeonly of the cardinal commanders, drummed his thick fingers loudly on the console.

"All the while I've been sitting here listening to these reports I've been asking myself one question: What is it they ultimately want from us? Is this war about territory, resources, religion, some injustice committed by one of us so far in the past we don't even have a record of it? Do the Yuuzhan Vong consider us vermin like the Yevethan Duskhan League did, or do they want our life energies as the Ssi-ruuk did?"

Anyone who might have been formulating a reply was interrupted by the communications technician. "Sirs," he said, addressing Sovv and his peers, "I have Director Scaur with an urgent message he says should be heard by all of you."

Sovv muttered a curse. "All right. Activate isolation and patch him through."

A half-size hologram of the director of New Republic Intelligence resolved within the sonic containment field that sequestered the commanders.

"Admiral, I just received word of an incident that occurred in the Meridian sector early yesterday, standard time," the cadaverous Scaur began. "The good news is that the light cruiser *Soothfast* engaged and destroyed an enemy vessel near Exodo II. The better news is that two Yuuzhan Vong who jettisoned in an escape pod were captured alive. But the intriguing news is that the captives have requested political asylum."

His round black eyes even glassier than normal, Sovv reclined in his seat and glanced in astonishment at A'baht and Brand. "Well, gentlemen, it seems we may be about to learn what the Yuuzhan Vong want after all."

NINE

"I always knew you had a soft spot for the high life," Roa remarked as he and Han climbed from the repulsor cab that had delivered them to the skyway balcony of the Solo residence, in one of the administrative district's most exclusive neighborhoods.

"Don't kid yourself," Han said. "It's smaller inside than it looks."

Roa went to the balcony railing and glanced down, then up. Though the elegant apartment was well located, there was almost as much building above as below it. "Why, you're scarcely three hundred meters from the top. Practically the penthouse." He smiled roguishly at Han. "You should be proud of your accomplishments. I can't think of another pupil of mine who's done nearly as well."

"Thank my wife," Han muttered in embarrassment. "Her job comes with a lot of fringe benefits."

"Always nice to know what my taxes are paying for."

The door recognized Han and opened. Arms not quite akimbo on his webbed midriff and head tilted to one side, C-3PO was standing in the tile-floored atrium.

"Why, it's Master Solo—and a guest. Welcome home,

sir." To Roa, he added, "I am See-Threepio, human-cyborg relations."

Taking in the domed entryway, Roa whistled softly. "How long before I hear the echo?"

"Cut it out, will you," Han said out of the corner of his mouth. "Besides, we used to have a smaller place in the Orowood Tower, but once the kids started spreading out . . ."

Roa stopped him. "You need never rationalize luxury for my sake. I wouldn't live on Coruscant for all the credits in the New Republic Bank, but if you've got to be here, the high life is the way to go."

Han frowned and turned to C-3PO. "Where's Leia?"

"In the master suite, sir. I was just engaged in helping her pack when she sent me downstairs to fetch this." C-3PO held out a shimmersilk scarf Han had purchased for her on their most recent trip to Bimmisaari.

"Pack? Where's she going?"

"Actually, sir, I have yet to be informed of the destination."

"Must make it difficult to select a wardrobe," Roa commented.

C-3PO turned to him. Had he the necessary parts, his brightly illuminated photoreceptors might have blinked. "Sir?"

Roa merely smiled.

Han glanced at Roa. "You'd better wait down here while I handle this."

Roa nodded. "I agree wholeheartedly."

"Master Solo, sir, it seems that I am to accompany Mistress Leia."

"What of it?" Han asked as he headed for the winding staircase.

"Well, sir, knowing as you do my attitude toward space travel, I thought you might be able to put in a word for me."

Han laughed shortly. "I really feel for you, Threepio."

C-3PO tilted his head in a gesture of pleasant surprise, Han's sarcasm entirely lost on him. "Why, thank you, sir. Compassion may not rescue me from my responsibilities, but it is refreshing to note that at least one person cares enough to say so. It has long been my contention that you are the most human of humans. In fact, only last week I was saying . . ."

The droid's extemporaneous chatter pursued Han all the way to the master suite, where he found Leia laying out items of clothing on the bed. Barefoot, she wore a delft shimmersilk robe. Her hair was clipped behind her head, but loose strands dangled at her cheeks.

"Seems like every time I come up here lately, you're getting ready to leave. Maybe you should just keep a bag packed."

She froze on seeing him. "Where have you been? I've been trying to reach you all morning."

Han rubbed his nose. "Memory Lane. Anyway, I had my comlink switched off." He gestured to the open suitcase. "Threepio tells me you two are going somewhere."

Leia sat down on the edge of the large bed and curled a strand of hair behind her ear. "Ord Mantell, of all places. The refugee problem has become overwhelming, Han. Food shortages, disease, families separated . . . On top of everything else, there's widespread suspicion of the New Republic's motives in helping out. The advisory council asked me to meet with the heads of state of several Mid and Inner Rim worlds to discuss possible solutions."

"Suspicion about what?"

"A lot of people feel that the New Republic will be in a position to annex hundreds of worlds and systems once we've dealt with the Yuuzhan Vong."

"Not if things keep going like they're going."

"I know," Leia said in a troubled voice.

Han cut his eyes to the suitcase once more. "Don't you ever get tired of mercy missions?"

"Mercy begins at home," C-3PO interrupted, then amended, "No, wait. I do believe the phrase is 'altruism begins at home.' Why, I must have picked up a flutter. The anxiety of packing for a space voyage—"

"Threepio!" Han said, thrusting a cautionary index finger at him.

Human body language being among the millions of others with which he was conversant, C-3PO immediately silenced himself.

Leia looked from the droid to Han. " 'Mercy missions' are what I do. I'm trying to help any way I can."

Han nodded nonchalantly. "Actually, the timing couldn't be better, because I'll be away for a while myself."

Leia stared at him. "Away where?"

"I'm not sure."

Leia raised her eyebrows. "You're not sure?"

"It's a fact," Han said, glancing down into the foyer, where Roa was appraising a crystal statue Leia had picked up on Vortex.

Leia followed his gaze. "Who's that?"

"An old friend."

"Does he have a name?"

"Roa."

"Well, that's a start," Leia said facetiously. "I don't know where you're going, but at least I know who you'll be with—just in case I need to reach you." She paused. "Are you taking the *Falcon*?"

Han shook his head. "Feel free to take her out for a spin whenever you want."

Leia studied him. "Han, what's all this about?"

"We're just going to check up on a mutual friend."

"And you have to leave immediately?"

Han shot her a look. "Now or never, Leia. It's that simple." He grabbed a travel pack from the closet and began to stuff clothes into it.

Leia watched him for a long moment. "Can you at least stay until Anakin gets home? You've been avoiding him all week."

Han kept his back to her. "You can tell him good-bye for me."

Leia moved deliberately into his view. "You two have more to say to each other than good-bye. He's confused, Han. You tell him he shouldn't feel responsible for what happened on Sernpidal, but your silence and anger send the opposite message. You have to help him through this."

Han looked at her. "What's he need me for? He's got the Force." His eyes narrowed. "What was it Luke said to me? Something like, because the kids are Jedi, I won't be able to keep up with them much longer. Well, that's exactly what's happened. They've grown beyond me."

"Luke didn't mean that the way you're taking it." Leia approached him. "Han, listen to me. Anakin's need to avenge Chewie has as much to do with pleasing you as absolving himself. He needs your understanding and your support. He needs your love, Han. Even the Force can't grant him that."

Han blew out his breath. "If you're trying to make me feel guilty, award yourself a medal."

"I'm not trying to make you feel guilty. I'm only trying to—" She stopped herself and let her shoulders sink. "Forget it, Han. You know what? Maybe it'll be good for you to get away for a while."

Without comment, Han went to the wall unit and began to rummage through one of the drawers. In a moment he had hold of his thirty-year-old BlasTech DL-44. He ran his thumb over the nub of the front sight blade, then he slipped the weapon into its holster, purposely cut to expose the blaster's trigger guard.

Leia watched him place the handgun in his pack. "Promise me that's for a quick-draw contest," she said worriedly.

At first glance the attaché case dangling from the hand of the fair-complected human in the inexpensive trousers looked to be an ordinary valise, something the snatch-and-run thieves who worked the Bagsho terminal on Nim Drovis wouldn't have been interested in. The firmness of the man's grip might have persuaded some that the case was more valuable than it seemed, but the man himself was enough to give even the most desperate thief pause. His walk was entirely too confident and his loose-fitting jacket didn't fully disguise the width of his shoulders. More important, he was trying a bit too hard to appear nondescript.

He cleared immigration without incident and followed a routing line for the pubtrans flitter that would take him to the Sector Medical Facility.

Nim Drovis had changed since the days Ism Oolos had run the facility. In amends for what the Death Seed plague had wrought during Seti Ashgad's reign on nearby Nam Chorios, the New Republic had financed a weather station to regulate the teeming rain that had been a quotidian event, and the Jedi Knights had negotiated an accord between the Drovians and the Gopso'o tribes. The opportunistic molds and fungi that had reproduced so exuberantly had been brought under control, and even the canals of Old Town weren't the fetid swamps they once were. Slug ranching had become big business.

Arriving at the renovated medical center, the man with the attaché case took secret delight in the number of armed Drovian guards roaming the grounds, blaster rifles cradled in tentacles or clenched in pincers. Submitting to a routine scan at the entrance, he was admitted to a spacious reception area staffed by Drovians and humans, some of whom may well have been descendants of Nim Drovis's original Alderaanian colonists.

The man proceeded to the Drovian female receptionist at the front desk. "I have an appointment with Dr. Saychel."

"Your name?" she asked, around the quid of zwil lodged in her cheek.

"Cof Yoly."

She motioned him to a seat. Moments later, she motioned him back to the desk, where a human voice addressed him through an intercom.

"This is Dr. Saychel. You asked for me?"

"Yes. I believe I contracted a case of trichinitis on Ampliquen."

"Why didn't you have it treated there?"

"The med center refused to honor my insurance."

Saychel fell silent for a moment. "Take the door to the left of the desk and follow the routing lines to the lab."

The routing lines took him past examination rooms and primitive operating theaters, in and out of wooden buildings, and finally through a maze of dimly lighted corridors that ended at the isolation ward, where victims of the Death Seed plague had been quarantined twelve years earlier. Saychel, the station chief of Nim Drovis, was wearing a partially sealed anticontamination suit and macrolens goggles.

"Welcome to Bagsho, Major Showolter," Saychel said warmly. "I didn't figure someone of your stature would come all this way."

"Actually, I won the coin toss," Showolter said.

"I guess I can understand everyone's interest."

Showolter and Saychel knew each other from Coruscant, where they had worked together in an Intelligence safe house in the bowels of the governmental district, and had occasionally hobnobbed with the likes of Luke Skywalker, Han Solo, and Lando Calrissian. Saychel's thick blond hair had since become a yellow-white helmet, and his cheeks were reddened by patches of burst capillaries.

"I'm certain it's you," Saychel said, "but I'd prefer to double-check."

Showolter nodded and spread his arms for the scanner Saychel produced from one of the biohazard suit's pouch pockets. "That's what we pay you for, Professor."

The scanner quickly located the implant Showolter wore in his right biceps and verified his identity.

"So where are our two prizes?" Showolter asked.

Saychel led him through a retinal-print-secured door to a large, one-way transparisteel window in the rear wall of the lab. Dressed in hospital robes, the two alleged defectors were seated on separate cots in the room behind the window, quietly conversing in what Showolter assumed was their own language. The room also contained a table, chairs, and a portable refresher unit.

Falling on the Yuuzhan Vong female, Showolter's brown eyes widened with interest. "I didn't think the enemy was capable of producing anything so attractive."

"Yes," Saychel agreed, peering through the transparisteel, "she is a handsome specimen."

"And the other is, what—pet or partner?"

"A little of both, I think. They're inseparable, in any case. And the 'pet,' for lack of a better word, seems every bit as intelligent as her mistress."

"Her?"

"Indisputably. Perhaps of a species indigenous to the Yuuzhan Vong's home galaxy or vat grown—genetically engineered."

"Any problems with the transfer?"

Saychel shook his head. "Don't ask me where they got it, but the team from the *Soothfast* brought them down the well in an energy cage. We moved them in here after we completed our initial scans and tests."

"I read the reports. Any surprises?"

"None to speak of."

"What about with the escape pod?"

"Similar to the Yuuzhan Vong fighters, though lacking weaponry. Composed of a type of black coral and propelled by a dovin basal—which unfortunately was dead on arrival." Saychel indicated a nearby countertop, where a meter-wide, blue-spiked, heart-shaped mass floated in a large flask of preservative.

"More interesting than your standard repulsor engine."

"Quite," Saychel said humorlessly.

Showolter switched his gaze to a second, smaller flask, which held a brownish pod, about the size of a human head and crowned by a nubby ridge. "What's that thing?"

Saychel moved to the flask. "It fits the description of a villip—an organic communicator."

"Is it alive?"

"It seems to be."

"Has it . . . said anything?"

"No. But then I didn't think to pose it any questions."

Showolter frowned, unconsciously massaging his right biceps, then turned to regard the captives. "Have they been fed?"

"Routinely. In fact, the little one has quite an appetite for our foodstuffs."

"Maybe that's the way we win this war: with food."

"I've heard crazier suggestions."

"Have you been able to talk to them?"

"The Yuuzhan Vong female—her name is Elan, by the way—speaks Basic. She says she learned it as part of her training."

"As what?"

Saychel grinned. "Are you ready for this? A priestess."

Showolter's thick brows beetled. "You're kidding." He glanced at Elan. "I wonder if they're celibate."

"I didn't think to ask," Saychel said. "But she sounds sincere about wanting political asylum. I ran a voice-stress analysis just for fun, and the test results back me up."

"Have they asked for anything else?"

"To meet with the Jedi. Elan claims to have information about a spore-borne illness the Yuuzhan Vong let loose before they launched their invasion."

Showolter scratched his head. "The pet likes our food; the priestess speaks Basic, knows about the Jedi, and wants sanctuary . . . Next thing you'll tell me they have a bet down on the smashball finals." He sighed with purpose. "Director Scaur wants them transported to Wayland for a preliminary debriefing. Discreetly, of course. Our Noghri agents there have already been apprised."

"You'll be handling the relocation?"

Showolter nodded.

"It's obviously a trap," Saychel said. "These two, I mean."

"Of course it is. But this could be our only chance to interrogate one of them, and we're in no position to pass that up. Even if we do have to arrange a meeting with the Jedi."

"Welcome aboard," Roa said as he and Han reached the top of the SoroSuub 3000's carpeted passenger ramp.

A quick look around, and it was Han's turn to whistle. Even stock models of the sleek, arrowhead-shaped craft were considered luxury yachts, but the *Happy Dagger* raised the ante. From walkways to bulkheads, what wasn't furniture-grade wood was made to appear so, and in every nook and niche stood a valuable work of art or costly hologram. A nearby acceleration couch was up-holstered in crosh-hide and shimmersilk.

"Is this Fijisi?" Han asked in disbelief, squatting to run his fingers over a section of parquet.

"Actually it's uwa," Roa said. "Got it out of a sal-vaged Alderaanian pleasure craft. Pirates had stripped the thing of practically everything else."

Han roamed about, inspecting details and shaking his head. "You know who used to fly one of these? Lando Calrissian. But even his didn't measure up to this."

"Unless Lando's changed since I knew him, he probably spent more on tracking devices and weapons than it cost me to outfit the entire ship."

"Maybe, maybe." Han grinned at Roa, grateful for the opportunity to get back at him for the ribbing he'd taken at home. "So, what do you do, rent out cabin space to traveling jizz orchestras?"

Roa laughed shortly. "I make no secret of the fact that the tax-and-tariff agents I employed on Bonadan made me a wealthy man. But now this ship is all I have."

He clapped Han on the shoulder and steered him toward the main forward hold, where a burnished silver protocol droid stepped from a forward compartment to intercept them. "Pardon me, Master Roa, but a stranger is approaching the ship."

"Han, meet Void," Roa said. "He escaped destruction at the hands of some antidroid zealots on Rhommamool, but the incident was so traumatizing he had to undergo a memory wipe. I picked him up for a song, but it cost me five hundred Coruscant credits to get him up to speed."

Roa instructed Void to show him the stranger the security scanners had zeroed in on in the docking bay. A console screen instantly displayed video of a slight, brown-haired, blue-eyed teenager wearing an off-white, rough-weave tunic over brown leggings.

"You recognize him?" Roa asked.

Han's eyes narrowed. "My younger son."

Anakin was already at the foot of the *Happy Dagger's* ramp by the time Han appeared. The scanners had captured the boy's agitation. Now the disquiet turned to wariness. "Hey, Dad," he said carefully.

Han stormed down the ramp and planted his hands on his hips, thumbs backward. "How'd you track me down?"

Anakin took a step back. "Mom said you were traveling with someone named Roa, and that you weren't taking the *Falcon*. Wasn't all that hard to locate the right docking bay."

Han's expression hardened. "I hope she didn't send you here to find out where I'm going, because it's like I told her, I don't know yet."

Anakin frowned. "She didn't send me. I came on my own."

"Oh," Han said softly and awkwardly. "So . . ."

"I—I have something for you." Anakin unclipped a small leather case from the belt that cinched his tunic. "Consider it a going-away present."

The lightweight cylinder Han prized from the case was shorter than his hand and no more than four fingers wide. Scored along its length, it appeared to be made of some sort of shape-memory alloy.

"I give up," he said at last. "What is it?"

"A survival tool." Brightening slightly, Anakin took

back the device and ran through procedures for accessing a score of miniature utensils, including knife blades, spanners, a luma, and the like. The tool even featured a macrofuser and a miniature transpirator.

For a moment, Han didn't know what to say. "Look, kid, it's a clever piece of hardware, but I don't have any hiking trips planned for the near future."

"Chewie made it for me," Anakin said evenly.

Han's face fell. "All the more reason I can't take it, if he made it for you."

Anakin placed it in Han's hand nevertheless. "I want you to have it, Dad." His eyes darted nervously.

Han started to protest but thought better of it. The tool was a peace offering, and refusing to accept it would only widen the rift that had separated them since Sernpidal.

"First, Chewie's bowcaster and shoulder bag, now a survival tool. I usually don't do this well at birthdays." He forced a smile and turned the tool about in his hands. "Who knows, maybe it'll come in handy."

"I hope it does," Anakin muttered.

Han lifted an eyebrow. "Why's that sound like some cryptic remark your uncle would make?"

"I only meant that Chewie would get a kick out of your using something he made."

"Yeah, he probably would at that," Han said, averting his gaze. "Thanks, kid."

Anakin was about to speak when Roa called down to Han from the top of the ramp.

"We're cleared for liftoff."

Han turned to Anakin. "Time to go."

"Sure, Dad. Take care."

They embraced, stiffly and briefly. Han started for the *Happy Dagger* but stopped halfway up the ramp and swung back to Anakin. "It's going to be all right, you know."

Anakin stared at him, blinking back tears. "What is— the war, my feeling terrible about Chewie, or your taking off without letting anyone know where you're going?"

TEN

Imposing in size, coloration, and carriage, Commander Tla paced back and forth at the foot of the rough-hewn command platform at the heart of Harrar's ship. Dangling from the points of his broad shoulders, the commander's long campaign cloak swished as he swung to face the priest and Nom Anor.

"Destroying the spawn ship was a profligate act," Tla bellowed. "You should have found some other way to place Elan in their hands."

"Other stratagems might have proved even more costly in the long run," Harrar countered. "As it was, the crew of the spawn ship went willingly to their deaths, content to be ennobled by the importance of the sacrifice."

Tla cast an angry glance at his tactician. Promoted in the wake of Shedao Shai's death on Ithor, Tla wore his rank like a scowl.

"All respects, Eminence Harrar," Raff said, "but this isn't some game that can be decided by cleverness. We're waging a holy war."

"Ah, but any war is always a game of sorts. We needed to make certain that Elan's flight from us appeared credible."

Tla scoffed. "You're newly arrived in this arena, priest. You don't give the infidels enough credit. They will lay your artifice bare before long."

"Indeed? Would it surprise you to learn that Elan has already been taken into protective custody?"

Tactician Raff showed Harrar a dubious look. "I would advise you not read too much into that, Eminence. Elan is the first of us they have managed to capture alive."

"Of course. But the point is that I know where she is, and I know where she is to be taken next."

Tla turned skeptically to Nom Anor. "Is this the doing of your dupes and agents, Executor?"

Nom Anor smiled faintly, but shook his head. "Unfortunately, no, Commander."

"Then how do you know?" Tla demanded.

Harrar motioned to one of his acolytes, who carried forward, as one might a newborn, a light-brown and slightly oblate villip. Carefully, Harrar took the villip into his hands, then cradled it in his left arm.

"Elan's captors were beguiled enough to bring this little one's twin along with Elan. It has been most dutiful in reporting back to us." Harrar stroked the villip's ridge with his three-fingered right hand. "Come, little one, repeat what you told me earlier."

Commander Tla and the tactician moved closer in interest.

The puckered tissue at the center of the nubby ridge expanded, and the villip began to turn inside out. Fully everted, the creature did its best to mimic Elan's comely features.

"Way-land," the creature said. "Way-llland."

* * *

Slowed by braking thrusters, the civilian shuttle *Segue* coursed above the craggy northeastern uplands of Wayland's principal continent. Dense, canopied forest cloaked the southern slopes of now truncated Mount Tantiss, but to the east lay vast areas denuded by the seismic explosion that had destroyed Emperor Palpatine's storehouse more than fifteen years earlier.

One of three passengers in the shuttle, Belindi Kalenda, NRI's deputy director of operations, pressed her face to the window to soak in as much of the view as possible. As the shuttle continued to descend, a small city came into view at the base of the mountain.

"I'm shocked," Kalenda remarked to her seatmate. "I was picturing New Nystao as little more than a hamlet." Slim and dark-complected, with widely spaced eyes and a husky voice, she had been with NRI for only twelve years, but her success in foiling a dangerous conspiracy in the Corellian system had resulted in rapid advancement.

Xenobiologist Joi Eicroth leaned toward the window to have a look. "It started out that way. Now there are close to ten thousand living in the immediate area. Myneyrshi, Psadans, and humans, in addition to the five hundred or so Noghri that founded the place."

"And everyone gets along?"

"So far."

Kalenda laughed, mostly to herself. "The Noghri despise anything related to Palpatine, but they're fine living on a world he named."

"It has never been documented that Wayland was Palpatine's code name for the planet," Dr. Yintal said from the seat behind the two women. "I submit that human colonists conceived the appellation long before the Emperor decided to use Mount Tantiss as a treasure vault."

An analyst for Fleet Intelligence, Yintal was a small pensive man, and the suddenness of his outburst prompted Kalenda and Eicroth to exchange secret smiles of amusement.

"And where else would the Noghri get to pile dirt on anything that belonged to Palpatine, right, Doc?" Eicroth asked over her shoulder.

"That's certainly a contributing factor to their contentment with the arrangements," he observed coolly.

The shuttle circled, then settled down on a landing pad in the center of New Nystao. The three passengers gathered their belongings and waited at the hatchway. Wayland greeted them with resplendent light and crisp, sweet-smelling air.

A hodgepodge of wattle huts, wooden buildings, and stone mansions, the burgeoning city reflected its mix of cultures. Perplexing, however, was the profusion of hotels and ethnic restaurants that surrounded the landing pad. Kalenda was about to quiz Eicroth when Major Showolter arrived on the scene perched atop an old SoroSuub Corvair landspeeder. Out of passenger compartments missing their folding access panels climbed two Noghri.

Showolter was sporting tinted driver's goggles and a locally purchased poncho. He saluted Kalenda and shook hands with Eicroth and Yintal. Then he introduced everyone to Mobvekhar and Khakraim of clan Hakh'khar, who were attached to NRI's safe house. The pleasant sunshine did little to soften the savage brawn and vampiric hideousness of the gnomish gray beings.

Kalenda peered dubiously into the passenger compartment of the battered landspeeder. "Is there room for all of us in this thing?"

"I thought we'd walk," Showolter said, making it sound like a question. "It's not far."

Kalenda made an ushering motion with her hand. "Lead on, Major."

The Noghri insisted on carrying the bags. The narrow pressbonded lanes were crowded with spindly Myneyrshi, armored Psadans, humans, and Noghri, but interspersed among them were small groups of Bimms, Falleen, Bothans, and other species, lingering in front of hotels or sipping drinks at streetside café tables.

Baffled, Kalenda finally asked about it.

"A serendipitous result of the Debble Agreement," Showolter said while they walked. "The agreement stipulates that any works of art—formerly the property of Palpatine—found in or around Mount Tantiss can be reclaimed by the cultures that produced them. Ever since it was put into effect, curators and acquisition types from hundreds of worlds have been coming here to retrieve artifacts that survived the explosion and have since been discovered in the course of New Nystao's expansion. Off-worlders need to be housed and fed, of course, so hotels and restaurants started springing up, which in turn has led to the growth of the town."

"And to the discovery of yet more cultural artifacts," Yintal added.

Showolter nodded. "Treasure hunters have become as common as vine snakes."

As the NRI team neared the Noghri section of the settlement, the primitive dwellings of the Myneyrshi and the rock fortresses of the Psadans gave way to basic but well-constructed huts of lumber and stone. The village had been transplanted from Honoghr after the official razing of Mount Tantiss had commenced.

A short but steep uphill walk brought them to an inconspicuous Noghri-style dwelling nestled against the mountainside and shaded by flowering trees. Mobvekhar and Khakraim stationed themselves outside, while Showolter escorted everyone else into a sparsely furnished, windowless front room.

"The back door opens onto one of the tunnels that honeycomb Tantiss," the major explained. "About as hardened a site as you'll find between Wayland and Borleias." He gestured to a side room. "Our would-be defector's in here. We've got the other one—the pet—stashed downstairs."

"Is that her term or yours?" Eicroth asked.

Showolter turned to her. "What she actually said was 'familiar.' "

The four operatives entered the side room, where the Yuuzhan Vong female was sitting in a meditative posture on a pillow she'd borrowed from the cot. In place of the exotic garb she was wearing in the 2-D opticals Kalenda had seen, Elan was now attired in drawstring trousers and a hooded overshirt. Though outlandishly tattooed, she was even more striking and statuesque in person than she looked in the photos.

Her oblique eyes—a vivid blue—snapped open and darted from face to face.

"Elan, these are some of my associates," Showolter said smoothly.

She glared at him. "Where is Vergere?"

"Downstairs—eating, when I last saw her."

"You've deliberately separated us."

"Just for the time being."

"What is Vergere to you, Elan?" Eicroth said, moving to the cot and sitting down.

"She is my familiar."

Kalenda and Eicroth traded brief glances. "We understand the term, but perhaps in a different context. Do you mean that Vergere is something more than a companion?" Kalenda asked.

"She is that, as well."

"So, an aide and a comrade."

"She is not a comrade. She is a familiar." Elan rearranged herself on the pillow. "You've come to test me further?"

Kalenda sat down alongside Eicroth. "Just a few questions."

"Questions your despicable scanners and analyzers failed to answer?" Elan smiled maliciously. "How can machines be expected to communicate with a living being?"

Kalenda forced a smile. "Suppose we consider this a means of getting acquainted."

"We Yuuzhan Vong have no such protocols. We know who others are. We wear who we are." She ran her fingertips across her patterned cheeks. "What you see reflects what is inside. You are fools to suspect that I am other than what my face and body declare me to be. Why do you refuse to grant me political asylum?"

"The Yuuzhan Vong would accept one of us without question?" Yintal countered.

Elan looked hard at him. "Where doubt or suspicion exist, we have the breaking."

"What is the breaking?" Yintal asked, clearly intrigued.

"An expedient way of arriving at the truth."

Eicroth waited for Elan to go on, but instead Elan fell silent. "You say that you wear who you are. Are you referring to your body markings?"

"Markings?" Elan repeated with unconcealed revulsion. "I am a priestess of Yun-Harla." She touched her broad forehead, then her cleft chin. "This is Yun-Harla's forehead; this is her chin. These are not markings. I am elite."

"Why would an elite desert her people?" Yintal asked bluntly.

Elan narrowed her eyes in apparent deliberation. "There is dissension. Not all Yuuzhan Vong believe that we should have journeyed across the void to come here. As many believe that this war is not one the gods wish. Because I am a priestess of the high arts, I would have you see the light in other ways."

"You don't condone the mass murder and sacrifices that have characterized your campaign so far?" Kalenda said.

Elan turned to her. "Sacrifice is essential to existence. We Yuuzhan Vong sacrifice ourselves as often as we do infidels. Whether or not your galaxy is the chosen land, it must be purified to be made habitable." She paused briefly. "Death is not what we wish for you, however. Only that you accept the truth."

"The truth as revealed by your gods," Eicroth said leadingly.

"*The* gods," Elan corrected her.

Yintal made a sound of disdain. "You're not a priestess. You're an espionage agent—a pretender. The ship you jettisoned from was destroyed much too easily."

Elan's eyes flashed. "Vergere and I had already concealed ourselves in the escape pod when the battle began. We didn't know the ship would be destroyed. Our launch was . . . fortuitous."

"Even if that's true, why would your military leaders deploy such a small warship against our own, when a much larger ship was in the vicinity?"

Elan sneered at him. "Should I judge you by size, little man? The smaller ship was the more well armed of the two. Why else would the larger have fled with the destruction of its spawn?"

Yintal looked at Kalenda and Eicroth. "She's lying."

Elan sighed wearily. "You are a suspicious species. I've come to do good."

"In what way, Elan?" Kalenda asked.

"You must take me to the Jedi. I can supply information about the malady."

Yintal stepped closer to Elan and appraised her openly. "What does a priestess know about disease?"

She shook her head. "It is not a disease. It is a reaction to the coomb spores. The Jedi will know."

"Why can't you simply tell us?" Kalenda said. "Why is it so important that you meet with the Jedi?"

Elan sharpened her gaze. "Tell them what I have told you and they will understand."

Yintal paced away from her, then whirled. "We need proof that you've come as a benefactor and not as a spy."

Elan spread her arms wide. "You see me. What more proof can I offer?"

Yintal tightened his lips and squatted before her. "Military data."

Elan's face clouded over with perplexity. "Is that what you wish?"

"Give us something we can take to our superiors," Kalenda urged. "If what you give us can be corroborated, we might be able to do as you request and arrange a meeting with the Jedi."

Elan considered it for a moment. "My order works closely with the warriors to assure that the auguries are advantageous. We forecast which tactics to employ . . ."

"Then tell us where your fleet will strike next," Yintal demanded. "Name the world."

Elan had her mouth open to respond when a crashing sound issued from the front room, followed by muffled shouting, in Basic and Honoghran.

While Kalenda and Eicroth were rising from the cot, a tall, powerfully built man slammed into the doorjamb and fell to the floor, but quickly regained his footing. Dressed in spacer's garb, he stood swaying in the doorway for a moment, taking in the room. Blood seeped through rips in his jumpsuit and ran from slashes that crisscrossed his face. Eyes fixed on Elan, he wedged the forefinger of his right hand into the crease aside his right nostril and launched a blood-curdling, Yuuzhan Vong scream to the ceiling.

"Do-ro'ik vong pratte!"

Then several things happened at once.

As if possessed of a will of its own, the man's skin peeled back from his face, revealing a macabre, misshapen mask of whorls and undulating lines. Undercurrent to his scream, ripping and popping sounds emanated from beneath his clothing; then two torrents of gelatinous muck poured from his pants legs, consolidated into one mass, and streaked away like an animated oil slick.

Elan leapt to her feet and reared back against the wall, hissing and snarling at the intruder and curving her long fingers into claws.

"Assassin!" she shrieked through bared teeth. "They've found me!"

Yintal swung around and stepped in front of the assassin, only to take a backhand to the face that snapped his neck like a twig. The small man flew clear across the room, colliding with Showolter and dropping him to the floor.

The assassin was preparing to throw himself at Elan when he was suddenly attacked from behind by Mobvekhar and Khakraim, their sinewy limbs and lumpy craniums displaying scarlet bruises and wounds. The two Noghri drove the Yuuzhan Vong forward into the side wall of the hut, narrowly missing Elan, who ducked at the last moment and rolled herself under the cot.

The Yuuzhan Vong met the wall facefirst with bone-shattering force, and for a moment it seemed that he would succumb to the Noghri's slashing assault. All at once, however, he straightened, propelling the two commandos off him with such power that they sailed to the far sides of the room, crashing into opposite walls and collapsing to the floor.

The Yuuzhan Vong whipped around, flinging blood in

all directions, his closely set eyes searching the room. Barreling between Kalenda and Eicroth, whom he toppled like rag dolls, he overturned the cot with one hand and grabbed hold of Elan with the other. His fingers vised around the priestess's long neck, and he lifted her off her feet and pressed her to the wall.

At the same instant, Mobvekhar regained consciousness. Powerful legs launching him off the floor, he caught the assassin around the waist and sank his teeth into the enemy's back.

The Yuuzhan Vong howled. Swinging a flailing Elan to one side, he used his free fist to rain hammer blows on the Noghri fastened to him. Mobvekhar grunted and moaned as the air was driven from his lungs, but he clung tenaciously to his prey.

Dazed, Kalenda struggled to her feet, gave her head a clearing shake, then leapt onto the assassin's pumping arm, which she rode up and down for a moment, until the Yuuzhan Vong hurled her aside like some minor inconvenience. Her head struck something solid, and she blacked out. Bright shapes punctuated the momentary darkness; then, contorted in a corner of the room, she had an upside-down view of Showolter, his poncho twisted around his neck, crawling out from under Yintal and drawing a small blaster from a shoulder holster.

From a prone position—and careful to miss Mobvekhar, who had been driven to the floor—the major fired, catching the Yuuzhan Vong between the shoulder blades. Smells of ozone and burned flesh mingled in the air, but the assassin barely reacted. Showolter fired again, catching the Yuuzhan Vong in the back of the neck and setting his hair on fire.

Showolter fired a final time.

The assassin stiffened and crumpled to the floor in a scorched heap, his left hand still clasped to Elan's throat. Bleeding from her nose and eyes, the priestess pried open his thick fingers and slid down the wall, gasping for air.

Gracelessly, Kalenda somersaulted, and was bellying forward to help Elan when the hut was rocked by a powerful explosion. Showolter's comlink chimed, and he fumbled it out of his pocket.

"Yuuzhan Vong coralskippers," someone reported over the link. "Maybe half a dozen, executing strafing runs over New Nystao. *Soothfast* has been alerted. Starfighters are on their way."

Showolter clamped his hand around Kalenda's forearm. "Move her into the hardened area," he rasped, coughing up blood. "Now!"

At the cold edge of the star system in which Wayland orbited, a solitary Yuuzhan Vong gunboat lurked. On the bridge, Nom Anor stood before a visual field fashioned by distant signal villips, observing coralskippers and New Republic starfighters exchanging fire in the skies over New Nystao.

"Don't try too hard," he said aloud to the pilots who manned the coralskippers. "Just enough to convince them."

ELEVEN

Through the *Happy Dagger*'s wraparound slit of cockpit viewport, Han gazed queasily at the mottled indifference of hyperspace. Alongside him Roa dozed in the pilot's seat, snoring softly, and behind him one of the ship's droids was monitoring the navicomputer.

If only time were as easily outraced as light, Han thought. Then he might jump forward to a point where Sernpidal was a distant memory, or perhaps backward to a point before that harrowing day on the planet, so that he might restructure the events and put things right.

As it was, he was trapped in a tragic moment, compelled to relive it over and again . . .

The *Falcon*, taking on evacuees, hovering just above the bucking surface of Sernpidal. The small moon called Dobido caught in the grip of a Yuuzhan Vong monstrosity and descending.

Chewie on the ground with a kid under each massive arm, the wind tearing at his coat. Then Chewie and Anakin using blaster bolts and the Force to free a downed shuttle of rubble that held it fast.

The *Falcon* holding its own in a deafening wind, as

Chewie rescued another child, thrusting him up into Han's arms as he dangled from the extended ramp.

Sernpidal heaving and breaking apart.

Chewie lifting Anakin in his arms. His resigned expression as he tossed Anakin to Han. The frightful wail of the *Falcon*'s repulsorlift engines; the ship drifting up and to one side as Han, a group of evacuees holding him by the legs, reached desperately for Chewie.

The pitching surface carrying Chewie away.

Anakin hurrying to the bridge, weaving the upended *Falcon* through quickly narrowing alleys and around collapsing buildings. A fleeting view of Chewie, his back to the *Falcon* and his long arms upraised to Dobido, a plummeting streak of fire.

The arrival of Tosi-karu.

A searing wind that burned Han's face and hands and sent Chewie flying and buildings toppling. The *Falcon*'s shields groaning in protest.

Chewie once more, his blood-matted coat . . . regaining his footing . . . standing high on a pile of rubble, roaring defiantly at the seized moon, as if to hurl it back where it belonged.

The *Falcon*, still in Anakin's hands, clawing for space, abandoning Chewie to fate.

Han's first utterance to his son: "*You left him.*"

The memory of those words as heartrending, as piercing, as Chewie's death. A condemnation uttered in grief, and impossible all these months later to rescind.

Hollowed by anguish, Han squeezed his eyes shut and balled his hands. How long might he remain thus: still dangling from the *Falcon*'s ramp, arms extended to Chewie—

Beside him, Roa stirred, yawned loudly, and stretched his arms over his head. He blinked and swiveled to the droid at the navicomputer.

"Are we nearly there?"

"The ship will shortly revert to realspace, Master Roa."

Roa grinned at Han. "Like old times, isn't it, you and me on a run?"

Han forced himself from harsh reflection, his blood rushing like acid through his veins. "I remember that first Kessel Run like it was yesterday."

Roa's smile became enigmatic. "Speaking of Kessel, I've been meaning to ask you something. Now, granted, stories can change quite a bit in traveling from Tatooine to Bonadan. But the way I heard it, you claimed to have made the Kessel Run in less than twelve parsecs."

Han said nothing in a blank-faced definite way.

"Well?" Roa pressed.

"Ancient history, Roa. And that was always my worst subject."

"Think hard. I'll grade you on a curve."

Han showed the palms of his hands. "Look, Jabba was breathing down my neck for dumping a load of spice. Chewie and I needed the work, and sometimes you do or say whatever you have to."

"But it's true—you actually made it under twelve?"

Han brought his fingertips to his chest. "Would I make up something like that? When I brag, I mean every word of it."

Roa regarded him for a moment, then burst out laughing. "Ah, Han, whatever became of those days? Whatever became of chasing fortune and glory?"

"There's no future in it." Han gave his head a quick shake. "Still, the idea that decent guys like Reck would willingly throw in with the enemy ... The Yuuzhan Vong make the Hutts seem like schoolyard bullies. They make Palpatine seem like an enlightened despot."

"Perhaps. But the winning side is paying better," Roa said soberly. "Besides, credits don't have to come from clean hands to be appreciated by Reck and his ilk."

Han smiled. "You've become quite the philosopher in your old age."

Roa's shoulders heaved in a shrug. "When your partner dies, you suddenly have a lot of time to think." He looked at Han. "You've probably found that out."

Han said nothing.

The navicomputer chimed.

"Master Roa, we are emerging from hyperspace," the droid announced.

Roa and Han swiveled to the control console to prepare the *Happy Dagger* for sublight.

"Sublight engaged," Roa said shortly.

Han flipped a final switch. "Shields are enabled."

Elongated, blue-shifted light tunneled them into realspace. Abruptly, the lines collapsed to pinpoints, rotating slightly before coalescing into a star field, each distant sun like a piercing to an alternate reality. Save for a brief shudder, the ship executed the transition smoothly.

"Entering the Anobis system," the droid reported.

"Anobis?" Han said in surprise. "This place is the back end of nowhere. I can't see even Reck wanting to hide out here."

Roa was shaking his head when Han looked at him. "Anobis is only a side-door entry to our final destina-

tion. A direct jump might have landed us in the midst of
an enemy flotilla or an Imperial Remnant patrol." He
aimed a thick finger out the starboard viewport. "Take a
look at that."

Han swiveled to the right. Almost close enough to
touch floated the holed and battle-scorched remains of a
Star Destroyer. Listed to port and nimbused by debris,
the great ship's command tower and pointed bow had
been blown away. Her once-gleaming aft plating was
pockmarked by immense blackened craters. Power
cables and ducting trailed from her ruptured innards.
Han thought back to the attack on Yuuzhan Vong–held
Helska 4 and the Star Destroyer *Rejuvenator* that had
gone down with nearly all hands aboard.

"Do we have a fighting chance against these thugs?"
Roa asked.

"The Yuuzhan Vong wouldn't have it any other way."
Han swung from the view. "So just where are we going,
Roa?"

Roa tapped his forefinger on a star chart he called up
on a display screen. "Ord Mantell."

Han's mouth fell open a bit, then he threw his head
back and launched an explosive laugh at the ceiling.

Roa regarded him quizzically. "Worried about running into someone from your past?"

"Someone from the here and now," Han muttered.
"My wife."

Ord Mantell was still the same undistinguished sphere
Han remembered from previous visits, which had been
many over the years, some intentional, more by misad-
venture. But something new had been added since Han's

stint as grand marshal of the Blockade Runners Derby: a small space station of outmoded ring design, pieced together from salvaged and Hutt-supplied parts by a consortium of Mid Rim engineering companies. Parts of the station—two of its spokes and perhaps ten degrees of the outer ring—were still incomplete, and were likely to remain that way for some time to come, since construction crews had abandoned the project after the destruction of Ithor.

The *Jubilee Wheel*, Roa called it.

"Except for the gravitation debt, the station doesn't have much to do with Ord Mantell," he told Han from the pilot's seat of the *Happy Dagger*. "It was a free port. A highly successful one, until the Yuuzhan Vong invasion put a damper on trade. Now it's a transit point, filled with some of the most desperate types you're ever likely to meet."

"Long as our business doesn't take us down the well, I'm ready for anything," Han said. "It's Ord Mantell that's been bad luck for me."

Roa nodded. "Then we'll have to do our best to keep our feet from touching the ground."

Awaiting docking assignments, ships of all types were queued up around the station. Some were empty freighters and barges with nowhere to go—their home ports occupied by the Yuuzhan Vong or their holding companies bankrupted by the war—filled with half-starved spacers caught in a political no-man's-land. Others were fifty-year-old crimson-red diplomatic cruisers, and warships recently recommissioned from mothballed fleets. Then there were the passenger transports—including several shallow bowl-shaped Ithorian herd ships—crammed with displaced beings from conquered or immolated worlds, also in search of some planet to call home, even temporarily. And catering to the needs of those refugees with credits to spend were aged scows and tenders, crewed by pirates selling dreams of a new life to the blindly optimistic.

Waiting for clearance, Roa and Han passed the time running checks on the SoroSuub 3000's security systems and generally battening down the hatches. The crowded and filthy docking bay the ship was finally allocated had been salvaged from an MC80 cruiser and, in fact, still bore some of the original Mon Calamari markings.

First down the ramp, while Roa saw to lockdown procedures, Han was confronted by a group of five aliens of a species he had never encountered.

"You need perhaps someone to watch over your ship?" their spokesman asked above the din, in whistling, heavily accented Basic.

Han eyed the alien up and down. "I need perhaps someone to watch over you."

The alien—clearly a male—took a moment to catch on, then laughed loudly, a hearty, basso laugh that almost made Han smile.

A head shorter than Han, he was a biped with muscular legs and a slender yet useful-looking tail. Those parts of him left unconcealed by a colorful vest and strategically slit culottes were covered with short, smoke-colored fuzz, save for the backs of his forearms and tail, where the hair was darker in hue, stiff as slender rods, and possibly capable of inflicting damage.

Like the two other males in the group, the one who approached Han had a soft snow-white mustache that drooped past his pointed chin, and a fright wig of matching white hair. His front-facing eyes were large and bright; his nose was a chitinous beak that curved down over a thin-lipped mouth and was perforated like a musical instrument.

Slightly smaller than the males, the two women of the group were about the same size, with shapely curves to their compact bodies and splashes of vibrant color highlighting velvety, taupe coats. They lacked the drooping mustachios, and in place of crests had lustrous slicked-back hair that fell to the shoulders. The tips of their smooth tails looked as if they had been dipped in sky-blue paint. Jewelry of a sort hung in loops from their long necks, accented their small ears and five-fingered hands, and studded their nostrils.

"All right, all right," their mouthpiece was saying, "you perhaps prefer to have someone clean and detail the ship?"

Han put his hands on his hips and laughed. He was still sniggering when Roa came down the ramp followed by two of the *Happy Dagger*'s crew—Void and an EV supervisor droid, whose head resembled the curving bill of a large, fruit-eating avian.

"Roa, you want to hire this bunch to sonic the carpets and clean the 'freshers?"

Roa regarded the aliens with keen interest. "That's what the droids are for," he told the spokesman.

"Then we watch over the ship. Lots of thieves about."

"I do appreciate the offer," Roa said congenially, "but no thanks. Some other time, perhaps."

The aliens exchanged words in their melodic native language, nodded to Han and Roa, and moved off toward the neighboring ship in the bay, an old Sienar *Marauder*-class corvette.

"It's like somebody tossed a manka cat and a woola-mander into a blender," Han said, watching the aliens.

"Ryn," Roa said, identifying the species. "I used to run into them occasionally on out-of-the-way worlds in the CorpSec—Ession, Ninn, Matra VI. They're nomads—that is, when they're not being hunted or en-slaved, chased from one place to another, or made the scapegoat for someone else's crimes or misdemeanors. They've a reputation for thievery and confidence games, but I've never had a problem with them. They work hard, at just about any trade, from ship salvaging to jew-elry making. And I'll tell you, Han, they perform the most exhilarating music I've ever heard—music you can't help but dance to."

"I'm sure I could stop myself," Han said.

"No, not even you could. I'm not talking about jizz or any of the new music. I mean fiery, passionate music."

Han gave them another look. "Where's their home-world?"

Roa shook his head. "No one's ever been able to tell me."

Han laughed through his nose. "Just when you think you've seen it all."

Leaving the droids in charge, they headed for immi-gration and customs, where long lines of mixed species were undergoing document checks and security scans.

Han showed his documents, which identified him as Roaky Laamu, a freelance laser-welder. He had con-sidered wearing a disguise—synthskin, prosthetics, a beard—but in the end had opted for simply changing his hairstyle and leaving his face undepilated. He had often used the same approach when traveling with Leia and the kids, and it had usually served him well. After all, most circulated images of him depicted a youthful Alliance leader, with bright eyes, sideburns, and a mop of shiny brown hair.

Things didn't go awry until he reached the scanners.

"Open your pack," the young agent ordered in response to a prompt from the droid he was partnered with.

Han unsealed the pack, and the agent quickly located the blaster, its large scope and conically shaped flash suppressor stowed in a separate case.

"Is this a DL-44?" he asked incredulously.

"More or less," Han said. "I've made some special modifications—"

The agent laughed and got the attention of a human coworker. "Boz, does this classify as a weapon or an antique?"

"Antique," Boz answered around a broad smile.

"Laugh it up, fellas," Han said, refraining from boasting about the blaster's capabilities.

The agent glanced at Han's identity documents. "Either way, Laamu, I've got to drain the power pack."

Han put his tongue in his cheek, then shrugged. "Long as you've done that with the other weapons that have come through."

"All the ones we've discovered," the agent said.

"That's comforting."

"We're looking for the Bet's Off?" Roa asked while the agent was fitting a depletor to the power pack.

"Assuming you two have normal-spectrum vision,

Red route to the Yellow tram to White Two, then all the way down the Shaft. You can't miss it."

"What do you tell the color-blind?" Han said nastily.

The agent placed the depleted blaster in the travel pack and resealed it. "I tell them to take a cab."

Roa insisted on taking a cab. Their Sullustan driver was a former ambassador to Ithor, marooned on the *Jubilee Wheel* waiting for transit documents to arrive from his homeworld.

"It's the same story over and over," Roa told Han when the cab had dropped them off in White Two. "Some trying to get home, some fleeing their homes, some without homes—and rarely the required documentation to get them off station, let alone transport to their desired destinations. So you find diplomats working as drivers, university professors tending bar, important types from you-name-it waiting tables or risking their savings on sabacc games—most of which are rigged."

In the Shaft, they made their way through a mixed-species crowd of hopeless folks—Ithorians, Saheelindeeli, Brigians, Ruurians, Bimms, Dellaltians—refugees from up and down the Hydian Way, clutching meager possessions to their torsos or holding tight to their children, shuffling aimlessly, in search of the miracle that was going to get them off the *Wheel*, as many referred to the station. People huddled in the shadows, hungry, trapped, and wary. Elsewhere prowled the ones the war had elevated: uniformed soldiers, reclamation and salvage experts, document forgers, scavengers, scammers, relief flyers, and the rest.

Han recalled what Leia had said about the refugee

situation, about the lack of food and shelter, the diseases, the separation of families, and it began to dawn on him that he wasn't the only one in a bad way.

He was still mulling it over a short time later, while he and Roa sipped Gizers in the Bet's Off, a crowded and somewhat elegant tapcaf, with a back room devoted to sabacc and other games of chance.

"Time I started making some inquiries," Roa announced when he'd finished his drink. He stood up and squared his shoulders. "I won't be long."

Han watched him move off in the direction of the circular bar, then returned his attention to the pale-blue ale. Movement caught his eye, however, and when he glanced up, two Ryn males were standing at the table, darker and better dressed than the ones he had met in the docking bay.

"You'll pardon the intrusion," the taller one said in a trilling voice, "but you're off the recently arrived Soro-Suub 3000?"

Han extended his arms over the backs of the chairs adjacent to his. "Word gets around fast. What of it?"

"Well, kind sir," the other took over, "we were wondering—that is, Cisgat and myself—if your onward travels might be taking you in the vicinity of Rhinnal, or perhaps if you could be induced, for an equitable sum, to carry some passengers there."

"Sorry, boys, but we're not Core bound."

The two exchanged concerned glances.

"Perhaps if we explained," Cisgat said. "You see, this is a matter of some urgency. We were to rendezvous here with other members of our extended family, but there seems to have been a problem, and they have not arrived."

"Our contingency plan called for us to meet on Rhinnal," the other added, "but, as is the case with so many on the *Wheel*, we find ourselves marooned here, with dwindling resources and little hope of securing onward transportation."

"We fear our clanmates may move on from Rhinnal without being able to get word to us."

Han folded his arms over his chest. "I'm sorry to hear that your family's scattered, but it's like I told you—"

"We can pay you well."

"We won't cause you any problems."

"Hold it," Han said loudly. "I said I'm sorry. But I'm out of the rescue business, you understand?"

The pair fell silent for a long moment. "We, too, are sorry to hear that," the tall one remarked.

Han angrily drained his drink as the Ryn walked off. No sooner did he set the glass down than Roa returned.

"What did they want?"

"A ride to Rhinnal."

Roa frowned and sat down. "As I said, everyone's desperate."

"D'you learn anything?"

Roa nodded his chin toward a rangy, red-haired spacer who was approaching from the bar with a drink in hand. "Roaky Laamu, meet Fasgo," he said as the man took a chair and extended his hand to Han. "Just make sure to count your fingers when you're done shaking."

Fasgo grinned broadly, showing stained teeth, and took a long swallow from the ale Roa had obviously paid for.

"Fasgo was one of my best tax-and-tariff boys," Roa

continued. "Just ask him and he'll tell you. Since he left my employ, he's had occasion to work with Reck Desh."

Han watched Fasgo's smile collapse.

"Any idea where Reck can be found?" Roa asked pleasantly.

Fasgo swallowed hard. "Look, Roa, I appreciate your buying me a drink, but—"

"Roaky and I know all about Reck's new employers," Roa cut him off, "so there's no need to feed us a tale."

Fasgo licked his lips and forced a short laugh. "You know Reck, Roa, he follows the credits."

Han put his elbows on the table. "If the pay's all that good, how come you're not still with him?"

"Not my style," Fasgo said, shaking his head. "I'm no traitor."

Han and Roa glanced at each other. "So what about Reck?" Roa said.

Fasgo shook his head once more. "I don't know where he is now." Gauging the look in Han's eyes, he added, "I'm being straight with you guys, I don't know." He glanced around and leaned forward conspiratorially. "There is someone on station who can probably tell you. He runs things around here—the underground things. They call him Boss B."

"And just where do we find this Boss B?" Roa said.

Fasgo made his voice a whisper. "Ask around for him and he'll find you."

As the spacer was about to rise, Han laid a restraining hand on his shoulder. "Who's running Reck's enterprise? Who's his control?"

The color drained from Fasgo's face. "You don't want

to meet them, Roaky. They're nasty as they come, and then some."

"Give me a name?"

"I never learned any names—honest." Fasgo swallowed whatever else he was about to say and riveted his gaze on something over Han's shoulder.

Han twisted around to see three Trandoshans moving toward the table, armed with Merr-Sonn and BlasTech blasters and wearing knee-length climate-control coveralls. While two came to a halt on either side of his chair, the largest of the saurian trio—older, by the look of his graying skin—circled the table twice, never taking his black-pupiled, red eyes from Han. Eventually, he took up a position directly across from him.

"Now, you look very familiar," he rasped. His long tongue emerged from a lipless mouth and wriggled in the air for a moment. "And you taste even more familiar."

Han forced himself to relax. While the Trandoshan had clearly recognized him, Han wasn't sure if he and the alien had ever crossed paths. Native to a world in the same star system as Kashyyyk, the brackish-smelling Trandoshans had been instrumental in persuading the Empire to enslave the Wookiees and had often worked as slavers themselves.

"Last time I saw a tongue like that it was hanging in a meat market collecting stink-flies," Han said.

The Trandoshan's death trap of a mouth approximated a baleful smile, and he planted his triple-clawed hands on the table. "Now, the human you resemble has since become a very important person, but when I knew him he was just a second-rate smuggler, running spice for

Jabba the Hutt and anyone else witless enough to employ him."

Bossk? Han wondered. Could it possibly be . . . "Ah, you must have been the cutest little egg at the time," he goaded.

Conversation at surrounding tables was quieting, as patrons tried to determine if they should stay seated for the rest of the show or seek cover as quickly as possible.

"Among other dishonorable acts, this piece of human filth once interfered with a legitimate slaver operation on Gandolo IV."

Roa shifted in his seat and spoke up. "What's past is past, big guy. Or is it that you're so short on hunter's points you've got to disturb a couple of old friends sharing drinks?"

The Trandoshan glowered at Roa, then Han. "I don't know this fat one, but I do know you—Han Solo."

"Solo?" Fasgo said in astonishment.

Han held the Trandoshan's gaze. It had to be Bossk. He could only hope that the E-11A1 the alien wore on his hip had been drained at customs.

"Tell me, Solo, are you still sticking your twisted beak in the business of others?"

Han smiled lopsidedly. "Only when there's the chance of wrecking someone's starship and humilating her captain while I'm at it."

The Trandoshan straightened to his full and considerable height. "I heard you lost the Wookiee, Solo. Rumor has it you let a moon come crashing down on him. Which is just what I'd do if I had a Wookiee following me around."

Much to the alien's delight, Han had nearly come out

of his seat when Roa threw an arm across his chest. "What's the use, Han? They'll only regenerate anything we break off them."

The Trandoshan grinned malevolently. "But what's one flea-bitten Wookiee or another," he continued with elaborate casualness. "Why not just go out and get yourself another one?"

Han threw the punch that started it all.

TWELVE

"I spent time in a bacta tank during the jump to Coruscant," Belindi Kalenda told the six members of the Security and Intelligence Council, by way of explaining why she looked better than she felt.

"Your efforts are beyond the call of duty, Colonel," Diamalan Senator Porolo Miatamia said from the far end of the long wooden table, his leathery face radiating genuine concern. "You should have remained on Wayland. We could have arranged for a holoconference."

Kalenda smiled faintly. "Wayland hardly has the technology for a holoconference, Senator."

"Then let's come to the point, shall we?" Senator Krall Praget said from the chair closest to Kalenda. Never one to mince words, Praget, representing Edatha, had sought to remove Leia Solo from office during the Yevethan crisis.

Between Praget and Miatamia sat senators Gron Marrab of Mon Calamari, Tolik Yar of Oolidi, Ab'el Bogen of Ralltiir, and Viqi Shesh of Kuat. Also present was Luke Skywalker, curiously silent and all but shrouded by his Jedi robe, and his saturnine teenage nephew, Anakin Solo.

Kalenda addressed them. "Thank you for coming, Master Skywalker and Jedi Solo."

Skywalker offered a nod of acknowledgment and nothing more.

"To begin with," Kalenda said, rising with obvious effort from her chair, "the enemy raid on Wayland justifies the precautions we took in moving the defectors there. The air strike inflicted significant damage to New Nystao, but fatalities were minimal—which wouldn't have been the case had we relocated them to Bilbringi or some other more populous world."

She took a pained breath. "One of the fatalities was Dr. Yintal of Fleet Intelligence, though he died as a result of injuries sustained in the direct attack on Elan— the Yuuzhan Vong priestess. Dr. Joi Eicroth of Alpha Blue also sustained injuries, but she is well on her way to a full recovery, as is Major Showolter, who suffered several broken ribs and a punctured lung. Our two Noghri agents were already back on their feet when I left Wayland."

"Where are the defectors now?" Senator Shesh asked.

"They've been relocated to Myrkr for safekeeping until we decide just what to do with them."

"Colonel," Praget interjected, "it is my understanding that one of the defectors is not thought to be Yuuzhan Vong, that some question remains as to what she actually is."

"That's true. We have yet to determine if Vergere is of a species native to the Yuuzhan Vong home galaxy or if she's a product of their genetic engineering."

"Were you able to gain any further insight into what

compelled the enemy to invade the Outer Rim to begin with?" Miatamia asked.

Kalenda shook her head. "The assassin's attack occurred shortly into the interview. Up to that point, Elan reiterated much of what we already know about the motives of the Yuuzhan Vong. At the behest of their gods, they are determined to cleanse our galaxy and/or convert us to their religion. Elan contends that they would much rather convert than exterminate us. Recordings of the debriefing—such as it was—are available for your review."

She took a breath. "What I've come to tell you, however, is that, following the attack, Elan provided us with intelligence of a highly sensitive and potentially invaluable nature. Should it bear out, Director Scaur and I will be seeking authorization to relocate the defectors here, to Coruscant."

Senator Shesh's honeyed voice cut through the resultant murmur. "Is that wise, considering what happened on Wayland? As it is, New Nystao is demanding reparations."

"In part, we chose Coruscant precisely because it is not easily targeted. I'll be the first to admit that appropriate precautions weren't exercised in moving the defectors from Nim Drovis to Wayland, but that won't happen again. The plan we've worked out takes advantage of the current chaos in the Mid Rim, by effectively losing Elan and Vergere among the crowds of displaced peoples and jumping them to Coruscant via a circuitous route. At the same time, multiple decoy teams will be dispatched to confuse anyone with designs on sabotaging the operation."

Kalenda stopped to pass out durasheet documents, color-coded for most-secret data. "The route will take Elan and Vergere through Bilbringi, Jagga-Two, and Chandrila—assuming, of course, that nothing untoward occurs—and precluding the advent of any intelligence suggesting that such a move poses a threat to New Republic security."

"I fail to see the purpose of bringing them here," Bogen said, shaking his head almost hard enough to muss his meticulously styled blond hair. "Your point that the Yuuzhan Vong attack attests to the status of the defectors is well taken. But that attack might have been a ploy aimed at nothing more than convincing us of Elan's usefulness."

With utmost care, Kalenda resumed her seat at the table. "Again, Senator, the plan is contingent on corroboration of the intelligence Elan furnished." She paused briefly. "I'm as suspicious as anyone here—we all are—but I am also convinced that Elan could prove crucial to our efforts, even if she is part of a ruse. Not only does she claim to know the whereabouts of Yuuzhan Vong operatives who have infiltrated New Republic worlds, but also the identity of many of the agents they have recruited from among cells of smugglers, mercenaries, pirates, and the like.

"In fact, we have reason to believe that one such cell, which calls itself the Peace Brigade, may have been responsible for apprising the Yuuzhan Vong that Elan and Vergere were relocated to Wayland." Kalenda passed out additional durasheets, bearing the mercenary cell's insignia of two clasped hands: one that could have been human; the other, fully tattooed. "These contain dossiers on the members of the Peace Brigade, along with a brief summary of their suspected acts of subversion." She glanced at Luke Skywalker. "Stirring anti-Jedi sentiment is apparently one of their specialties."

Skywalker nodded.

"I hope Intelligence is keeping a watchful eye on this group," Shesh said, lifting her eyes from the durasheet.

"Read on," Kalenda said pleasantly.

Bogen cleared his throat loudly. "About the importance of this Elan . . ."

Kalenda turned to him. "Aside from being able to identify agents, Elan knows how the Yuuzhan Vong tacticians think—No, it goes beyond that. She knows the auguries and omens they look for in plotting their attacks. She may even be able to lead us to worlds where war coordinators have been entrenched."

"Just a moment," Tolik Yar broke in, one hand entering a flurry of commands into a datapad. "One report—I can't locate it just now—suggests that these war coordinators have telepathic abilities." Yar stopped doing input to glance at Kalenda. "Suppose this putative defector is telepathically linked to the creatures and is busy sending *them* intelligence about *us*?"

"The report you refer to was filed by an ExGal scientist who spent a brief time in Yuuzhan Vong captivity," Kalenda supplied. "In any case, the possibility of a link between the defectors and the Yuuzhan Vong—whether telepathic or otherwise—is the reason we've been keeping them essentially blind. They've been kept isolated from anything that could be of strategic value to the enemy. Even if the Yuuzhan Vong somehow manage to reclaim them, they'll have nothing vital to present."

"Why are these two so eager to defect?" Senator Shesh asked.

"Elan hinted at dissension among the Yuuzhan Vong ranks. Some disagreement as to the legitimacy of the invasion. Seemingly, she wants to help us."

"In return for what—wealth, a new identity, a hiding place? I'm not convinced that she doesn't have some ulterior motive. Even a vornskr that loses its teeth doesn't necessarily lose its nature."

Kalenda's eyes narrowed. "Elan does have one request." She looked pointedly at Skywalker. "She wishes to meet with the Jedi Knights."

Skywalker gave the disclosure his full attention. Even Anakin perked up. "Did she say why?" Skywalker asked.

"She said it has to do with some sort of illness the Yuuzhan Vong introduced in advance of the arrival of their worldships. She refused to elaborate. She said the Jedi would understand."

Skywalker and his nephew traded astonished glances. "Nothing more?" the elder Jedi said, clearly intrigued.

Kalenda shook her head. "As I told Senator Miatamia, feel free to review the recordings of the debriefing. In fact, I'd welcome your comments. Maybe you can pick up on something we missed."

"Master Skywalker," Gron Marrab interrupted, one bulging eye fixed on the Jedi while the other continued to regard Kalenda. "This probably doesn't need to be stated, but I want it made clear that you should feel under no obligation in this matter."

"Of course not," Senator Praget added, with a twisted grin. "After all, it's not as if the Jedi were in service to the New Republic."

"That was uncalled for, Senator," Shesh said in rebuke.

But Skywalker appeared indifferent to Praget's remark. "We will discuss it," he said at last. "Personally, though, I can say that I'm eager to meet with the priestess."

Everyone fell silent for a moment, then Shesh spoke up once more. "Colonel Kalenda, what is the nature of the intelligence Elan furnished?"

"The Yuuzhan Vong's next target—Ord Mantell."

With her back to the gentle sea that washed Worlport's sand-fringed southern coast, Leia took a moment to gaze at the buttes that soared from the smog-blanketed northern wastes, out past the expansive junkyards, all the way to Ten Mile Plateau. Her view from the transparisteel crown of Ord Mantell's Government House—site of the Conclave on the Plight of the Refugees—encompassed much of the vertiginous capital city as well, with its once grand examples of Corellian classic-revival architecture. However, most of the ornate spires, great sweeping colonnades, and huge rotundas, with their tall round-topped arches, monolithic lintels, and carved entablatures, were now engulfed by a sprawl of ersatz rococo domes and obelisks, which catered to the banal tastes of the gamblers and hedonists who frequented the planet in droves, and the whole of it was fissured by a labyrinth of narrow stairways, curving ramps, sheltered bridges, and dank tunnels.

Easy to lose your way in that maze, Leia told herself, as indeed she had lost her way some twenty-five years earlier at the end of her tenure as princess and diplomat but before Hoth and Endor, and long before marriage and children. Mentally, she tried to trace a route from

Government House down to the brown plains far below, a game to occupy the moment, to keep her from wondering about the kids, or where Han might be—

"Ambassador Organa Solo," the representative from Balmorra intruded, "is something wrong?"

Leia surfaced from her ruminations and steered a contrite smile across the table. "Excuse me. You were saying . . ."

"I was saying that you haven't answered my question," the slender, starched human said in a miffed tone. "How does the New Republic justify such a request, when countless habitable worlds exist where refugees might be sheltered, without the danger of their jeopardizing the economic well-being of native populations?"

Leia fought to maintain diplomatic aplomb. "Of course we have the means to transport tens of millions of refugees to any number of planets in outlying sectors. But our aim is not simply to rid ourselves of an inconvenience. We're talking about peoples who contribute significantly to the stability and prosperity of the New Republic, and who have lost everything—homes, livelihood, in many cases family members or entire kin groups."

"What good are such groups without worlds," someone at the table scoffed.

"Precisely the point," Leia said. "What the Senate Select Committee for Refugees requires are worlds with intact infrastructures—not only with habitable land, but also planetary defenses, spaceports, surface transportation networks, and dependable communication with Coruscant and the Core Worlds."

Alsakan's ringlet-haired representative sniffed. "A very laudable ideal, Ambassador, but who's going to feed and clothe these displaced billions? Who's going to construct the shelters and install the irradiators to ensure that the native populations are protected against whatever diseases the refugees might be harboring?"

"The senate has already allocated funds to address those very concerns."

"But for how long?" the twin-horned envoy from Devaron asked. "Should the New Republic renege on its promises—or be forced to by circumstance—economic responsibilities will fall to the host worlds, which by then will hardly be in a position to banish the groups they accepted in all good faith. The result could be economic catastrophe."

Leia allowed some of her frustration to show. "Need I remind you that we are in the midst of a war that threatens the very existence of that economy—not to mention the freedoms all of us have enjoyed since the defeat of the Empire?"

When she was certain she had their attention, she went on. "We have the capacity to move populations from the Outer Rim to worlds closer to the Core. Where necessary—and where they can be spared—we will make use of bulk transports and freighters to relocate tens of thousands at a time. But before that can happen, some of you are going to have to volunteer to accept these peoples, as Mon Calamari did with the displaced Ithorians, and as Bimmisaari has recently done with those who fled Obroa-skai.

"Our goal is to create self-sufficient enclaves, to be managed by appropriate individuals selected from within the refugee populations—administrators, physicians, teachers, technicians. However, these enclaves will serve as temporary facilities only. Little by little, we will relocate specific groups or species to suitable worlds, or perhaps introduce populations to currently uninhabited worlds."

"Individual enclaves for each species?" Jagga-Two's delegate asked.

"Where possible," Leia said. "Otherwise, we plan to place compatible groups together."

"And see to the diverse needs of those groups?"

"Of course."

"And what happens when antagonistic groups are required to share the same enclave?" the representative from a repopulated world in the Koornacht Cluster asked.

"We'll deal with those problems as they arise."

"How—by providing security forces?"

"Some forces will be necessary, yes."

The Balmorran loosed an incredulous laugh. "You use the word *enclaves*, but what you mean to say is containment camps."

The Devaronian glared at Leia. "What if additional worlds should fall to the Yuuzhan Vong? How many refugees will we be asked to accept? Is there a limit, or does the New Republic plan to squeeze the populations of thousands of worlds onto hundreds?"

"We will limit the number," Leia replied. She turned to Ord Mantell's representative. "Ord Mantell could inaugurate the plan by allowing people stranded on the *Jubilee Wheel* to settle in temporary camps north of the city."

The planet's button-nosed female representative looked aghast. "I'm afraid that's impossible, Ambassador. Why, for one thing, the area around Ten Mile Plateau is one of our most important tourist attractions."

"Tourist attractions?" Leia said in disbelief. "Ord Mantell lies practically on the edge of contested space. How many tourists do you expect to receive in the coming months?"

The woman made her face long. "Ord Mantell appears to have been spared the horrors. We anticipate an upswing in tourism very soon."

Leia took a calming breath. "Farther to the west, then," she suggested.

The woman ridiculed the proposal with a condescending laugh. "I'm very sorry, but those lands have been set aside as reserves for the Mantellian savrip. Hunters come from great distances for the honor of stalking the beasts."

Leia exhaled in exasperation. "Is there no one here who will step forward?"

The representative of Gyndine and the Circarpous system spoke up. "Gyndine will accept some of those stranded on the *Jubilee Wheel*."

"Thank you," Leia said.

"As will Ruan," delegate Borert Harbright of Salliche Ag announced proudly. "House Harbright will do whatever it can for the cause."

Leia smiled appreciatively, but she had to force it. A powerful and wealthy corporation, Salliche Ag controlled a string of worlds on the fringe of the Deep Core, with Ruan and a host of similar worlds ideally suited to relocation centers. But there was something about the supercilious Count Harbright that put her instantly on guard. Duplicity seemed to shine from his coal-black eyes and lurk behind his obliging smile.

But Leia thanked him anyway. "On behalf of the thousands whose lives your generosity will save, the Advisory Council applauds you." Her gaze swept the table. "Now, perhaps some of the rest of you can be persuaded to follow the count's lead."

When the meeting adjourned for lunch, Leia hurried to exit the circular room before anyone had a chance to get her ear. Olmahk, one of her Noghri bodyguards, was waiting in the hallway, along with C-3PO.

"I do hope the meeting went well, Mistress Leia," C-3PO said, hurrying to match her pace.

"As well as could be expected," Leia muttered.

They made their way to a turbolift and descended to Government House's spacious and ostentatious lobby, where every droid in sight appeared to be moving with uncommon haste toward the building's several exits.

"What's all this about?" Leia stopped to ask.

"I can scarcely imagine," C-3PO answered. "But I'll do my best to find out."

C-3PO angled across the lobby, placing himself directly in the path of an administrative droid, whose head was shaped like an inverted test tube. The 3D-4X was forced to come to a skittering halt on the polished floor. In an impossibly rapid exchange, the pair traded information like two insects meeting on a forage trail.

A moment later, C-3PO whirled and headed back

toward Leia, stiff-backed and arms pumping in a way she had come to associate with trouble.

"Mistress Leia, I have just received the most distressing news," C-3PO sputtered. "It seems that Ord Mantell has been targeted for attack by the Yuuzhan Vong!"

THIRTEEN

"The brute might have killed you, mistress," Vergere remarked in the secret tongue of the deception sect, while she ministered to the injuries Elan had received at the hands of the assassin.

The priestess moved Vergere aside so she could regard her image in the mirror Showolter had provided. "I never feared for my life. I feared only for the development of the bo'tous. The fool's blows might have damaged the carriers or retarded their growth."

Vergere sat back on her reverse-articulated legs, and her long ears pricked up. "Do you think they survived?"

Elan ran her hand over her lower chest and smiled maliciously. "I can feel them ripening, Vergere. They whisper to me. They await the four breaths that will liberate them. I can feel their eagerness."

"Theirs or yours?"

Elan turned from the mirror to regard her familiar. "For loosing their deadly toxin, my reward will be great. Word may well reach the ear of Supreme Overlord Shimrra."

"Without question," Vergere assured. "Although it will be the members of your domain who profit."

Elan continued to regard her. "You have so little faith that Harrar will be able to retrieve us after I have dispensed with the Jedi?"

Misgiving narrowed Vergere's slanted eyes and ruffled the short feathers at the back of her neck. "I trust that Harrar will do all in his power to find you. But our movements won't be easily monitored from this point on. Not after the assassin's attack. Showolter will jump us about until we're so deeply entrenched in New Republic space that even Nom Anor won't be able to reach us."

His injuries notwithstanding, the ever attentive Major Showolter had been careful not to identify the world to which they had been moved, though by all appearances it was even more remote and primitive than the last. On arriving, Elan had had the briefest view of impenetrable forests of peculiar trees. From snatches of overheard conversation it was clear that the planet boasted at least one small city, but also clear that Elan, Vergere, and the Intelligence operatives were far removed from it.

Elan stroked Vergere's downy back. "If my duties demand that I die, then so be it, my pet. My domain will prosper. My father will be escalated to the rank of most-high priest."

"And the determined Harrar will prosper."

"That is not our concern."

Vergere folded her arms and bowed her elongated head. "I will remain by your side, mistress."

Gingerly, Elan examined the raw bruises the assassin's powerful fingers had left on her neck. "I know the one Harrar sent," she said after a moment. "He apprenticed under the Shai."

Vergere pressed her hands to her eyes and applied some of her tears to Elan's abraded flesh. "The same sect that spawned Commander Shedao Domain Shai."

"The very same. Those of Domain Shai delight in inflicting pain for pain's own sake—to themselves or to others unfortunate enough to stray into their reach. To the Shai, there is no higher calling than torment, the 'embrace of pain.' Pain is the beginning and the end." Elan sighed relievedly. "Your tears refresh, my pet."

Vergere continued to minister to her. "Harrar's aim was to convince our captors of your importance, and in that he chose wisely. Better the New Republic thinks the Yuuzhan Vong intractable than reasonable."

Elan nodded, without comment.

Though Vergere might have been born of the Yuuzhan Vong's masterful talent for genetic manipulation, the exotic creature had in fact been transported to the main fleet two generations earlier by one of the first teams to reconnoiter the galaxy that had produced the Jedi. The scouting party had returned dozens of specimens to the worldships, including humans, Verpine, Talz, and others. After extensive experiments, some had expired and others had been sacrificed, but a few had been awarded as pets to children of select elite, such as Elan, youngest daughter of an adviser to Supreme Overlord Shimrra. Vergere's uniqueness was thought by some to be sacred. Through the long years of negotiating the intergalactic void, through the long years of Elan's rigorous training in the deception sect, Vergere had been her constant companion, confidante, friend, even tutor.

"Does it cheer you to be back among your own kind?" Elan asked carefully.

"Hardly my own kind, mistress."

"Among your home species, then?"

Vergere's large eyes smiled. "We Fosh were never at home among them. We were too few in number. Humankind had filled all the evolutionary gaps, bringing about the extinction of species like mine, which were merely holding a place, a niche in the continuum."

"But you are delighted with the food."

"Ah, the food," Vergere said, laughing. "That is another matter."

Elan grew serious. "You could reveal the truth to Showolter and escape back into your own realm."

Vergere reached for Elan's patterned hand and caressed it. "I am your familiar. Were it not for you, I would have been sacrificed or disposed of. We are linked until one of us dies."

Elan exhaled with intent. "Despite what you say or what you choose to reveal, you know these species better than anyone else—even Nom Anor."

Vergere shook her head. "The executor has made it his mission to study them—to know them better than they know themselves. We Fosh were more devoted to concealing ourselves."

"From what little you know, then, are Showolter and the women who visited us taken in?"

"Were I privy to the debriefing I might be able to answer with certainty. Undoubtedly the assassin's dedication to duty has helped to allay some of Showolter's initial misgivings."

Elan's expression changed. "He is most accommodating, that one."

"Because you have charmed him—as you do all."

"Of course you would say that. Then you believe they will provide me with an opportunity to meet with the Jedi?"

"It is too soon to tell, mistress. Should Commander Tla deem it wise to furnish the New Republic with a victory to support the data you provided, you may yet meet with them."

Elan considered it in silence. "Did you know of them in your time here?"

"As I say, the Fosh moved discreetly, but of course we knew of the Jedi. They were manifold. I was surprised to learn that they are now few." She paused briefly. "I thank you for revealing nothing of my past to Harrar, mistress."

Elan merely smiled. "Did you ever witness the Jedi employ the Force?"

"The Jedi consider the Force to be all around us, permeating all living things. So in that regard, I'm certain I witnessed the Force at work."

"Perhaps it would benefit the Yuuzhan Vong to learn how to use it."

Vergere took a moment to respond. "The Force is a sword with two edges, mistress. Cut one way and vanquish. But be careless on the backswing, or allow your mind to wander, and you risk undoing all you've accomplished." She gazed at Elan. "Indeed, it might befit the Yuuzhan Vong to become aware of the Force, but it is not for all to employ. Such power should be reserved for those with the strength to heft the sword and the wisdom to know when to wield it."

*   *   *

Squadrons of T-65A3 X-wings, E-wings, and TIE interceptors dropped from the forward launch bay of the *Erinnic*, an *Imperial II*-class Star Destroyer parked between Ord Mantell's like-sized and close-quartered moons.

"Fighter groups are away," an enlisted-rating reported from one of the crew pits below the overbridge's command walkway. "Dispersing to assigned coordinates."

"May the Force be with you," Vice Admiral Ark Poinard sent over the command net.

Out of the corner of his eye he saw a wry smile take shape on the deeply lined face of General Yald Sutel, onetime adversary turned ally in the war against the Yuuzhan Vong. "Problem, General?" Poinard asked, raising one bushy white eyebrow as he turned to Sutel.

Sutel shook his blockish head but kept smiling. "It's just that I'm still not used to hearing you say it."

Poinard snorted. "Believe it or not, I used to say it to myself even when this ship carried only TIE fighters."

"I don't believe that for a moment," Sutel said.

"Despite appearances, I always held the Force in high esteem." Hands clasped behind their backs, the two elderly veterans continued to advance on the bridge's semicircular expanse of triangular windows. As an accommodation to both the New Republic and the Imperial Remnant, Poinard had retained his honorific as captain of the flagship, while Sutel had been designated task force commander.

Of the sixteen vessels that comprised the group, some flew escort to the *Erinnic*, but most—including a *Mediator*-class Mon Calamari battle cruiser, two *Quasar Fire*-class cruiser-carriers, three escort frigates, and five

Ranger-class gunships—had taken up positions above the bright side of the star system's fifth planet. Since any ships jumping from Yuuzhan Vong–held space would have to enter the Bright Jewel Cluster Rimward of the planet, it was hoped that concealment would further enhance the element of surprise.

Poinard paused above the most forward of the crew pits. "Any signs of activity?" he asked a technician standing at one of the consoles.

"Negative, sir." The woman glanced at a readout, then up at the two commanders. "Forward elements report all quiet."

"Looks like Admiral Sovv's tacticians have us misdirecting our efforts," Poinard told Sutel in confidence.

"This came down from Intelligence," Sutel said.

"Even worse. Ord Mantell has little strategic value."

Sutel cut his eyes from the starfield to Poinard. "Did Ithor? Did Obroa-skai? The Yuuzhan Vong are waging a psychological war. You of all people should understand. Didn't your brother once command an AT-AT division?"

"Walkers had their place."

"As prodigal terror weapons," Sutel said. "The Yuuzhan Vong obviously mean to terrorize us in the same way—to break us by demoralizing us."

"But Ord Mantell," Poinard said dubiously. "Gamblers and tourists are the only ones they'll demoralize."

"Admiral Poinard," the woman in the crew pit interrupted. "Forward elements report enemy vessels emerging from hyperspace and shedding velocity. Performance and drive profiles confirm Yuuzhan Vong warships."

Poinard swung to the crew in the pit on the opposite

side of the walkway, as banks of threat assessors began to talk to one another in machine code.

"Go to full alert status. All nonessentials are confined to quarters. Engage sublight drives and pull us tight to number-two moon." He turned back to the female tech in the first pit. "How many vessels?"

"Sir, two corvette analogs, five frigate analogs, three light cruiser analogs, one warship analog."

Someone behind Poinard and Sutel spoke up. "Sirs, wing commander reports from target approach point that fighter deployment is complete. Awaiting authorization to engage. Tactical bridge reports the call board as clear and all systems enabled."

A holoprojection of the theater resolved above a light table in the forward pit. Poinard and Sutel studied it in silence.

"Looks like we're evenly matched for once," the general commented after a moment.

"Save for one advantage," Poinard pointed out. "They don't know we're here."

FOURTEEN

Han leaned his right shoulder against the pitted bars of the cramped jail cell and gently massaged the swollen knuckle of his left ring finger. "Good fight," he said. "I really enjoyed it."

Fasgo and Roa were seated on the squalid floor, backs against an equally fouled wall, the former with a comically swollen right ear, the latter looking remarkably unscathed.

"Some mess," Roa said around a grin.

Fasgo gently fingered the tip of his nose. "Feels broken," he muttered.

Roa clapped his former tax-and-tariff agent on the shoulder. "Next time remember that keeping out of range is often the best defense."

"I'm only sorry the big one didn't die," Fasgo said.

"Give him time," Han said loudly, gazing deliberately at the three Trandoshans in the cell directly across from theirs.

Fasgo held his thumb and forefinger close together. "The chair missed him by that much."

"Tough break for that poor Bith at the next table," Han said.

"We're lucky he thought one of the Trandoshans threw it," Roa interjected.

Fasgo nodded. "Having that group of balloon heads on our side definitely helped."

"Keep your voice down," Roa advised quietly. "They're only two cells down the corridor."

Fasgo waved a hand. "Half the crowd in the Bet's Off is in here." He glanced at Han and laughed. "We really started something."

"Yeah, and security finished it." Han chuckled. "No wonder the *Wheel* doesn't allow armed blasters."

A gate in desperate need of lubricant slid open down the corridor, and in short order a burly security guard in a gray uniform strode into view.

"All right, old-timers," the guard announced churlishly, "you're free to go."

Han, Roa, and Fasgo exchanged mystified glances. "I thought we couldn't post bail until the arraignment?" Roa said.

"You're not being arraigned," the guard said. "You must have some friends in high places."

Roa looked at Han. "I think you've been made, 'Roaky Laamu.' The Trandoshan certainly had no trouble recognizing you."

Han saw the sense of it. The word was out, and someone had contacted Leia.

The cell door slid aside, and the three of them filed out. Han stopped at the Trandoshans' cell, careful to remain just out of their clawed reach. "We'll have to do this again real soon," he said, smiling.

"Count on it, Solo," Bossk rasped.

The guard led them out of the confinement zone, returned their belongings, and pointed them to the exit. "Turn up here again and, friends or no, you'll be sorry," the man warned.

"Charming fellow," Roa muttered.

Han agreed. "Probably works for Vessel Registration on his days off."

No sooner had they stepped into the passageway than a surprisingly well-mannered Aqualish approached them. "Roa, Fasgo, Roaky Laamu," the alien began in somewhat garbled Basic, courtesy of his inward-turning tusks. "My employer requests the pleasure of your company."

"Boss B," Roa reminded Han quietly. "The information broker."

Fasgo gulped.

"Did we ask around?" Han asked theatrically. "I don't recall us asking around."

The Aqualish—a Quara—showed the palms of fingered hands. "Come now, gentlemen. Surely you can spare a few moments for the person who arranged for your release."

The sprung trio traded surprised glances. "Well, in that case," Han said, "lead on."

A repulsor limousine conveyed them ninety degrees around the *Wheel*, at times maneuvering through knots of stranded and despondent refugees. The swank hatchway to Boss B's lair was flanked by pug-nosed and prognathous Gamorrean sentinels, and the plush anteroom was filled with an assortment of toadies, sycophants, and camp followers. Stroking their long head-tails, two Twi'lek women in mesh bodysuits sprawled seductively in conform loungers. Elsewhere, a Rodian, a Kubaz, a Whiphid, and two Weequays were engaged in a desultory game of laro, while a bored Bith ran musical scales on a slender horn.

The Aqualish showed Han and the others to over-stuffed armchairs in the main room and offered them drinks. Han remained standing.

"Save the Gizers for the Bet's Off," a disembodied baritone voice suggested. "Have a tumbler of Whyren's Reserve instead."

"Now, that I won't turn down," Fasgo said, beaming.

"Make it two," Roa told the Aqualish.

"Three," Han said hesitantly, trying to discern the source of the resonant voice. One entire wall of the room was devoted to flatscreen displays, showing frequently shifting views of different sectors of the *Wheel*. On one monitor, Han recognized the immigration station where his blaster had been drained.

"Sit, please," the voice rumbled.

Han consented to the request when the amber-colored Corellian whiskey arrived. "Cheers," he said, setting his travel pack on the floor and lifting his glass in the air to their unrevealed host.

"More of the same," Roa said, joining Han in the toast.

"Your reputation precedes you, gentlemen," the voice said.

Fasgo ran the back of his hand over his mouth. "If you mean the damage to the Bet's Off, the Trandoshans were responsible for most of it—"

"You can blame me for that," Boss B interrupted. "I put them up to it."

"You? Why?" Han demanded.

"How else could I have ensured that you would accept my hospitality, except by arranging for you to be released from incarceration?"

"I don't get it," Han said.

Boss B laughed. "I am personally informed when individuals of honorable or disreputable distinction arrive on the *Jubilee Wheel*. Such was the case with you, Roa. But imagine my surprise when, after a bit of machine-assisted scrutiny, I discovered your traveling partner to be none other than Han Solo."

On hearing the name, the Bith ceased his noodling and the Twi'lek women and the cardplayers turned in unison. Han drained the glass in one gulp and set it down roughly.

Boss B laughed boomingly. "I have to say, Solo, I expected a younger man."

"Yeah, well, I used to be one."

"As did I," Boss B conceded. "In any event, after I learned that you were bound for the Bet's Off—where I already knew Bossk and his comrades to be—I simply relayed word to the Trandoshan that an old rival of his had turned up. It wasn't difficult to predict where things would go from there."

"That's your idea of hospitality, huh?" Han said.

"Come, Solo, you said yourself that you enjoyed the fight."

Han snorted. "You planning to show yourself or are we going to have to play 'name that voice'?"

Not three meters in front of Han, a shroud field dissipated, revealing what might have been the outcome of a Hutt and human mating. Though the lavender-hued humanoid managed to get around on two tree-trunk-thick legs—possibly with the assistance of repulsorcoil implants—he had the girth of a young Hutt and a head too large to fit through an ordinary hatchway. His round face was symmetrical and possessed the usual human features, but each was so outsized that they vied with one another for prominence. Shiny and slightly protruding, his eyes were the size of small saucers, his nose was a large flattened disk, and a thick, bristly gray mustache covered almost all of his labrose mouth. Disheveled, slate-colored hair crowned his head like an abandoned avian's nest, and enormous pink ears flapped against his skull like wings. In the reddish-stained fingers of one huge hand he held a fat, chak-root cigarra.

Han nearly fell out of his chair. "Big Bunji?"

The giant humanoid guffawed in merriment, laughing his mouth empty of aromatic smoke. "Boss Bunji, Han."

Roa smiled broadly. "It's amazing that you and I never met, considering all the mutual friends we had on Etti IV and other haunts in the Corporate Sector. A pleasure after all these years." He gestured to Fasgo and introduced him.

Bunji regarded the red-haired spacer. "Yes, Fasgo's petty scams aboard the *Wheel* have not escaped our notice."

Fasgo swallowed hard, but said nothing.

Han was still shaking his head in incredulity. "I figure I must be dying, because I keep seeing my life flashing before my eyes." He grinned at Bunji. "If Ploovo Two-For-One shows up right about now, I'm folding my hand."

"Were Ploovo to show up, Han, I can assure you he would be less than courteous. Even after extensive reconstruction surgery, he never quite got over the damage done to his proboscis by the dinko you so cleverly sicced on him in the Free Flight Dance Dome. For a time, in fact, he paid well for anyone who brought him a dinko— dead or alive. Taxidermied specimens of the vicious things were everywhere on display in his homes, his offices, aboard his ships. He even took to wearing a charm bracelet composed entirely of dinko fangs and the serrated spurs of their hind legs. I do believe he brought the species to the edge of extinction."

Han frowned. "I'm sorry to hear that, but I never cared much for people who tried to cheat me out of what was mine."

Bunji guffawed once more, all but rattling the bulkheads with his laugh. "As I myself learned."

"You're not still sore about my strafing your pressure dome on that asteroid—"

"Not at all," Bunji said. "I deserved it for trying to get the better of you on those chak-root runs to Gaurick."

"You took the words right out of my mouth." Han laughed. "You fix up the *Falcon* for what happened to her on Gaurick, then you go and deduct the costs from what you owe me. That's what sent me to Ploovo for a loan to begin with."

Bunji's sigh was a warm wind. "We live and learn, Han, we live and learn. But surely you knew I'd forgiven you. The fact is, I owe you a huge debt of gratitude for what you accomplished on Tatooine." He gestured broadly. "You could say that much of this station owes to your efforts."

Han jabbed himself in the chest. "What *I* did on Tatooine?"

Bunji puffed on his cigarra and grinned. "To be more

precise, what your wife did. You see, Han, I had attempted to relocate my business enterprise to Tatooine, only to be run off by Jabba. Not content to have done that, the Hutt all but crippled my cash flow for the next few years. His death, however, presented me with an opportunity to rebuild my power base, though I had to contend with the likes of Lady Valarian and a few others. Nevertheless, a few shrewd deals made during the Thrawn years and I was back on my feet. Then, just a year ago, I had the *Wheel* assembled in a nearby system and towed here, to Ord Mantell."

"This is yours?" Han said.

"Most of it. Borga the Hutt has a small stake in it. Now, if the New Republic would only do something about the Yuuzhan Vong."

Han's smile straightened. "Some of us are trying to do just that, Bunji."

"Is that what has brought you here—under a false identity, no less?"

"Han and I are trying to hunt down a former associate," Roa answered.

Bunji inclined his head in interest. "Hunt down?"

"Or just locate," Han said. "That all depends on what he says when we find him."

"Which former associate?"

"His name's Reck Desh."

Bunji fell silent for a long moment. He inhaled on the cigarra and launched a jumbo smoke ring toward the ceiling. "What do you want with him?"

"It's a long story," Han said, "even longer than yours."

Bunji nodded. "If I were you, Han, I wouldn't be so quick to catch up with Reck Desh."

Han leaned forward, resting his forearms on his knees. "Why's that?"

"Things have changed since the old days. Folks are engaged in activities now that wouldn't have been tolerated then—even by riffraff like Bossk."

"What sort of activities?"

"Such as providing information about planetary defenses, or pirating shiploads of refugees and delivering them into Yuuzhan Vong hands for sacrifices."

The muscles in Han's jaw bunched. Bunji continued. "Reck and the gang he runs with—they call themselves the Peace Brigade—have been colluding with Yuuzhan Vong operatives by helping to spread anti-Jedi sentiment and destabilize planetary systems in advance of invasion. In some cases, they've persuaded worlds to capitulate to the Yuuzhan Vong beforehand."

"You wouldn't happen to know where Reck is currently?" Roa asked judiciously.

"At last report, the Peace Brigade was operating in Hutt space," Bunji said, "much to Borga's dismay. If you'd like, I could make a few inquiries."

Han showed him a skeptical look. "Why would you be willing to do that for us?"

Bunji shrugged. "As I say, I owe you. If that isn't reason enough, then I'm doing it for the Wook. It near broke my hearts to hear that he had died. I'd have given anything to have had a partner like Chewbacca."

Before Han could respond, sirens began to blare and the illumination in Bunji's well-appointed enclave flickered. Without warning, the *Jubilee Wheel* shuddered as if it had been poked by the finger of a colossal hand. One of Bunji's henchmen rushed to a nearby terminal and called up data on a display screen.

"Yuuzhan Vong attack!" he blurted.

Humans and others leapt to their feet, running every which way for exits, shelter, and the antique sideboard that held the Whyren's Reserve and similarly exceptional libations. Directly in the path of a panicked Whiphid, Han and Fasgo were knocked to the floor.

Roa wedged his hands under Han's arms and yanked him upright. Bunji and the more important members of his coterie were already disappearing through a gaping hatchway in the cabin's rear wall. Han threw his pack over his shoulder and stumbled forward, only to hear the hatch lock solidly as he reached it.

"To the *Happy Dagger*," Roa said from the anteroom. "I've no intention of being on this wheel when the Yuuzhan Vong decide to roll it downhill!"

FIFTEEN

Ord Mantell's yellow star at its back, the New Republic task force emerged from behind the system's fifth planet with weapons blazing. Simultaneously from around the jagged edges of the planet's large moon, fighter squadrons raced forward to engage the invaders, the radiance of their ion drives dwindling in the night.

Batteries on the Mon Calamari battle cruiser and the escort frigates ranged toward distant targets and fired. Laser beams slashed outward, visible in vacuum as wrathful hyphens of energy. Strikes registered in the remote blackness. Overlapping spheres of brilliance flared in darkness, blossoming thicker than a meadow of wildflowers.

The Yuuzhan Vong vessels—pitted yorik coral and facet-hulled—withstood the initial barrage. Fashioned by dovin basals, defensive singularities formed around the enemy ships, guzzling countless ergs of energy. Answering bursts from fearsomely powerful arrays streaked toward the task force as spiraling golden projectiles, grotesquely beautiful against the starfield.

Diverting energy to their shields, the New Republic ships held their own, then returned fire. Laser light and nova-bright missiles gridded the night as the two flotillas continued to trade volleys.

X-wings, B-wings, E-wings, and TIE interceptors arrived from the defenders' precinct and began to distract, harass, and sting the vanguard Yuuzhan Vong vessels with narrow-beam fire. Dazed by the battle cruiser's initial volley, a corvette-size pyramid of yorik coral dropped its guard momentarily. Slipping through vulnerable spots in the ship's defenses, carefully placed proton torpedoes from a quartet of B-wings detonated against the carbon-black hull. Chunks of scabrous flesh large as starfighters blazed fiery trails through local space.

Centerpiece of the task force, the battle cruiser altered course, intent on steering the battle away from Ord Mantell and the many civilian vessels anchored there and in close proximity to the *Jubilee Wheel*. Turbolaser batteries and ion cannons swiveled and traversed. Light tore from already superheated alloy barrels, and blinding flashes strobed in the distance.

A second Yuuzhan Vong corvette tried unsuccessfully to evade the barrage. Sieved by laser spears, it disappeared in an effulgent globe of fire.

Asteroidlike coralskippers, varying in size, shape, and color, advanced in an unstoppable cloud, forging through the intense hail and swarming into the midst of the starfighter groups. Well-maintained formations broke apart as crafts peeled away to all sides, barrel- and snap-rolling into furious engagements with their quarries. In a bloodbath of swirling combat, coralskipper preyed on starfighter and starfighter on coralskipper.

Wingmates fought to remain together, but were more

often separated by furious blasts and forced into one-on-one contests. Dovin basals pillaged the New Republic fighters of their shields and assailed them with streams of molten rock gushed from cone-shaped weapons emplacements. Rendered defenseless, X-wings and E-wings were slaughtered by the dozen. Locked into fierce, pitched battles, opponents jinked and looped through evasive maneuvers.

Counterfire from the Yuuzhan Vong's largest ship silenced the battle cruiser temporarily. Retreating behind its shields, the Mon Calamari vessel endured storm after storm of projectile and plasma barrage, as frenzied electricity danced and coruscated at the boundaries of the great ship's invisible barriers.

Biding its time, the cruiser waited until the Yuuzhan Vong warship paused to repower, then it opened fire with all guns. Still stronger laser beams sliced through the night, some to be swallowed by gravitic anomalies, while others chipped away at the enemy ship's yorik coral hull.

Two *Ranger*-class gunships moved in, determined to outflank the warship. Pounding discharges from their main batteries vaporized dozens of coralskippers and escort craft at a burst. Desperate ploys saved some of the Yuuzhan Vong fighters, but most were outwitted, disintegrated, or transformed into short-lived comets.

The flotillas began to close ranks, saturating space with flaming missiles and harnessed light. Caught up in friendly fire, a trio of TIEs vanished without a trace.

Laser beams from a New Republic escort frigate skewered another Yuuzhan Vong corvette through its long axis, coral, weapons, and the rest disappearing in a cloud of fire. As if in riposte, a pack of coralskippers isolated and surrounded a lone gunship, leaching it of its shields, then battering it with projectiles, kindling a deadly inferno that quickly engulfed the ship.

Elsewhere, juking through whirling hunks of debris, a squadron of E-wings converged on a maimed Yuuzhan Vong ship and began to nip at it mercilessly. Proton torpedoes punched through its imperiled defenses and slammed into the bow. Stratified layers began to peel away from the ship, rubble exploding outward, rocketing from sight. A second, smaller craft, similarly lanced by laser fire, also blew to pieces, showering nearby space with briefly glowing motes.

Close to Ord Mantell's outermost moon, a chaotic melee raged as coralskippers, X-wings, and TIEs mixed it up, ferociously and with grim resolve. The starfighters came out of smooth rolls, inverted dives, and predatory banks to go to guns with their prey, riding them until they were annihilated. Other ships revectored, racing through fragment clouds to escape the carnage or form up for reengagement, sometimes slewing wildly out of control.

In midsystem the battle cruiser and warship advanced on each other, now trading fusillades and broadsides. Localized storms of blue lightning enveloped both ships as their extended energy defenses made contact. The Yuuzhan Vong vessel poured its most lethal fire into the larger ship, and the cruiser replied with volley after volley of directed light. Caught between the two, an escort took a direct hit, sending scorched and misshapen pieces of wreckage spinning off into space.

As if angered by the loss, the cruiser upped the ante with escalating fire. Boulder-size blocks of mirror-finish coral flew from the warship, but it was not about to be humbled. Plasma streamed from the tips of the enemy ship's forward arms, raising blistering explosions along the cruiser's port armor plate.

Weapons blazed and flared. Fire fountaining from the cruiser's aft hull, the ship began to founder, tipping to one side with main guns still discharging and sensor arrays in flames. Projectiles continued to penetrate her armor until the hull surrendered integrity and precious atmosphere began to stream outward. With artificial gravity disabled, hatches and seals, turrets, and sensor pods blew. Then vacuum played its hole card, tugging crew and contents into the polar night.

X-wings and E-wings rushed dauntlessly to the cruiser's support. Proton torpedoes found soft spots in the warship's tattered defenses, bursting against the superstructural arms and command ridge, and loosing geysers of spindrift coral.

But the starfighters' efforts came too late.

A hellish explosion pushed outward from a rift in the hull of the Mon Calamari vessel, splitting it in half. Escape pods launched, vectoring toward Ord Mantell like drops of radioactive rain, while the battle cruiser became a ballooning sphere of roiling incandescence, then exploded brilliantly.

The Star Destroyer emerged from between Ord Mantell's moons with main and auxiliary thrust nozzles flaring. Throwing itself headlong into the fray, it fired repeatedly as its pointed bow swung in the direction of the warship. Thread-fine against its enormous bulk, blue lines of energy from aft turbolasers and ion cannons stabbed unrelentingly at the black ship.

The *Erinnic* braced for return fire, but the plasma and projectiles never arrived.

Abruptly the warship changed course, accelerated, and began to unleash its fury on Ord Mantell, cutting loose with all forward guns. Blinding missiles streaked toward the planet's surface, burning seething tunnels through the atmosphere. Detonations on the ground lighted the undersides of ragged clouds.

Then, from a dark orifice in the bow, the warship extruded an enormous hose that was more living monstrosity than machine. The blunt nose of the stipple-skinned gargantuan caught the scent of the nearby *Jubilee Wheel* and, elongating, began to close on the small orbital station, weaving its way through the *Wheel*'s flock of freighters, barges, and passenger ships.

A trailing wedge of X-wings and TIEs launched from the cruiser-carrier *Thurse* attacked the herpetoid terror weapon like ravenous birds of prey, but to no avail. Still attached to the warship and shielded by dovin basals, the outsize creature struck at the *Wheel* like a venomous serpent. As if intent on yanking it from orbit, the creature recoiled and struck again, this time sinking its mawlike mouth into the rim, clamping down on the *Wheel* as if it were a piece of ring pastry, and shaking it back and forth.

In the florid haze of emergency illumination, and with blaring warning sirens making it almost impossible to hear one another, Han, Roa, and Fasgo raced down a curving stretch of corridor, hoping to reach the *Happy Dagger* before whatever had the *Wheel* in its grip decided to shake it apart.

Concussions from the battle raging outside the space

station heaved them to and fro as they ran, sometimes into sections of padded bulkhead, but too often into unyielding objects wrenched loose by the intense paroxysms.

Most of the panicked tide was going against them, but Roa maintained that he was following the shortest route to the docking bay. Each violent tremor sent crowds of people slipping, sliding, or hurtling through the passageways, many to be slammed into bulkheads or crushed under the weight of bodies massed in alcoves and junctions. Folk in repulsor cabs fared no better, as vehicles careened into walls or one another, frequently overturning and spilling riders across the deck.

With Han and Fasgo on his heels, Roa jinked left into one of the *Wheel*'s spokes, hurrying down a frozen stairway into a narrow, twisting corridor whose walls were in places caved in or crumpled. Sparks rained down from ruptured power ducts and exploded energy mains.

They weren't ten meters into the corridor when the station suffered another powerful jolt that temporarily disabled the artificial gravity generators. One moment Han and the others were snaking through the damage and the next they were airborne, drifting toward the partially collapsed ceiling like divers swimming for the surface of the sea. Then, just as suddenly, the gravity system reenabled, and they were jerked facefirst to the hard deck.

"Not much future in this," Roa shouted as he picked himself up and began to stagger forward once more.

"The future's what you make it," Han hollered back, somehow managing to hold on to his pack and keep his balance through a violent quake that brought down what remained of overhead tiles and ducting.

Ahead of them a heavy metal curtain dropped, sealing off the way and forcing them to detour back to the station's outer rim. Reaching a central passageway, they were immediately swept up in a mixed-species mob that was fighting its way toward the launch bays.

All at once the station sustained a strike of unprecedented force. Earsplitting, nerve-grating sounds of rending alloy filled the corridor as a huge arc of exterior bulkhead was simply ripped away.

And toward that dark breach the crowd was inexorably pulled.

Screams overwhelmed the metallic stridency. Waging a losing battle, people clawed at walls, deck plating, and one another in an effort to keep from being sucked into the maw.

Pressed to the inner wall of the curve, Han, Fasgo, and Roa managed to grab hold of the twisted remains of a hand railing. But even as they struggled to secure themselves—bodies lifted parallel to the deck by the vacuuming force—the railing tore away from the bulkhead.

The three of them were sucked forward several meters before the railing snagged on a section of floor grating wedged into a stairwell, but the force of the sudden stop dislodged them. Flags snapping in an incessant wind, they latched on to whatever handholds they could find, as people and droids flew past them into the breach and atmosphere roared out like an angry river.

An airborne, shoebox-size MSE-6 droid caught Fasgo square in the head and carried him shrieking into the current. Han watched him sail toward the breach, arms outstretched and flailing, as if plummeting from a great height.

Han tore his gaze away before Fasgo vanished.

"Looks like we took a wrong turn," he shouted to Roa, who was just out of reach to Han's left, plump fingertips curled around the slightest of ledges in the wrinkled section of bulkhead.

Roa twisted his head around. "Too bad the rejuvenation techs didn't equip me with the strength of a young man in addition to the good looks."

"Hang on, Roa!"

"How I wish I could. But I think I hear Lwyll calling me."

"Don't say that! Just hang on till I get there!"

Roa grunted in effort. "Bad luck creeps in through the hatch you leave open, Han. Fortune smiles, then betrays."

Han spit a curse. "All right, keep talking if you have to. But just hang on."

"I can't, Han. I'm sorry. I just don't have it in me." Roa's face betrayed the struggle. "Take care, old friend. Finish our business with Reck." Smiling resignedly, he submitted to the flow.

"Roa, no!" Han screamed, daring to extend one arm and nearly allowing himself to be carried away.

Han shut his eyes, hung his head for a moment, then screamed in anger until his throat hurt.

When his breath returned, he secured the travel pack to his back and began to pick his way toward a rib left exposed by flayed bulkhead sheets. He had no sooner wrapped his arms around the structural member when someone hurtled past his face a hair's breadth away and latched desperately onto his outstretched legs.

Han's backbone stretched like a rubber band and groaned in protest. When the shock abated, he peered down the length of himself and saw that his unsolicited hanger-on was a male Ryn, arms clutched around Han's knees and legs thrashing. This one was sporting a soft, brimless cap of bright red and blue squares, worn at a rakish angle.

"Mind if I rest here a moment?" the alien asked in melodic Basic. "If I'm too heavy, I'll toss the cap."

Han scowled at him. "Long as your head's in it."

"So you'd rather I let go."

"If you make sure to close the door on your way out."

"That isn't vacuum out there," the Ryn said, nodding toward the breach. "There's a mouth on the other side of that hole."

"A *mouth*?"

"The mouth of a Yuuzhan Vong dread weapon. For taking captives."

Han instantly saw the logic of it. The people, droids, and objects zipping past him weren't victims of compromised gravity; they were effectively being *inhaled* by whatever it was that had taken a giant-size bite out of the *Wheel*'s rim.

"So how do we gag that thing?" Han said.

The Ryn shook his head, long mustachios whipping about. "I don't think we can. But there might be a way to stifle it."

Han followed the Ryn's gaze to a seam in the corridor ceiling, between them and the maw.

"A blast shield!"

The problem was that the mushroom-shaped button that could lower the shield was located on the corridor wall, some five meters closer to the breach.

"There's a support strut just beyond me," the Ryn

said. "If I release my grip on you, I may be able to grab hold of it. But I still won't be able to reach the shield activation button."

"Finish your thought," Han said, trying to ignore a sinking feeling.

"Then you'll have to let go and catch hold of me. That should put you close enough to tap the button with your foot."

"Assuming I manage to catch hold of you!"

The Ryn snickered. "Assuming also that I manage to catch hold of the strut. If I miss, well, I suppose it's a matter of how long you think you can hold on. Otherwise . . ."

"Otherwise what?"

The Ryn grinned. "Otherwise, I'll see you in hell."

Han regarded him quizzically for a moment, then nodded grimly. "You've got yourself a deal. Good luck."

The velvet-coated Ryn eased himself down Han's legs until he was dangling from Han's ankles, then disengaged. Han heard rather than saw him make harsh contact with the strut.

"You all right?" he called.

"Your turn," the Ryn yelled shortly.

Han took a steadying breath. Carefully unwrapping himself from the alloy rib, he let fly. The current was even stronger than he expected. In a split second he was rushing past the Ryn, but when he reached out wildly to arrest his motion he hugged only air.

He was already imagining himself inside the Yuuzhan Vong dread weapon when something wrapped itself around his chest under his arms, yanking him to a halt. It took Han a moment to grasp that the Ryn had snagged him with his tail.

"Kick the button, kick the button!" the alien squealed in a pained voice. "Or plan on taking part of me with you into that creature!"

Han looked to his right and spied the mushroom-button, almost within reach of his right foot. "Swing me to the right!" he yelled.

The Ryn's muscular tail spasmed just enough to set Han swaying and bring him within reach of the corridor wall. He extended his foot and caught the button with the toe of his boot.

The blast shield dropped rapidly, hitting the grooved deck with a loud and reassuring thud. At once, Han, the Ryn, and everyone left in the corridor followed suit, falling to the floor like stones.

While Han was fighting to regain his wind, the Ryn sprang to his feet and tugged his cap down on his forehead. Han took in the rest of the alien's brightly colored outfit of vest, culottes, and ankle boots.

"What time do they switch you on?" he asked between breaths.

The Ryn laughed. "Round about your bedtime. Now what?"

Han stood up, clapping grit from his hands. "We get off this station before that thing decides it's still hungry."

"The launch bays are this way," the two of them said at the same time, although rushing off in opposite directions.

"Trust me," the Ryn said before Han could speak.

Han stared at him stonily, then waved him on and fell in behind.

Powerful spasms continued to rock the *Wheel*, throwing them from side to side. Han stopped t collect a pair of crying Bimm children who had become separated from their families. Other children and adults began to attach themselves to Han and the Ryn, if for no other reason than the two at least appeared to know where they were going.

"You'd better be right," Han warned as he ran.

"Don't worry," the Ryn called over his shoulder. "I'm too young to die."

"Yeah, and I'm too well-known."

Ahead, the corridor swept broadly to the right, and Han began to recognize where he was. The docking bays were only a short distance away.

"Can you pilot a ship?" the Ryn asked breathlessly.

Han grinned smugly. "Don't worry—"

"You know a few maneuvers."

Han's nostrils flared. "You're some conversationalist, pal."

"Try to stay awake, anyway."

The Ryn skidded to a halt at the first docking bay door and tapped the entry switch repeatedly. "Security lock," he announced.

Han shoved him aside to study the lock's control touchpad.

"Hurry!" someone in their crowd of distressed followers said. "We've got to get out of here!"

Han spun angrily from the mechanism and had his mouth open to respond when the Ryn said, "He's working on it, he's working on it."

Han thrust a silencing forefinger at the Ryn, then whirled and entered an override code on the touchpad.

The hatch remained closed. He tried another code, then a third. "What I'd give for a loaded blaster right about now," he mused.

"Would an R-series droid do?" the Ryn asked.

"If we *had* one." Han shot him a sarcastic glance. "Unless, of course, you've got a droid summoner tucked away in that suit of lights."

He had returned his attention to the touchpad, figuring to give it one final try, when from the edge of the crowd he heard the characteristic chirps, toodles, twitters, and warbles of an R2 unit. Swinging around in elated surprise, though, he saw that the sounds were coming from the Ryn, who was fingering the perforations in his chitinous beak as if it were a flute.

Han regarded the alien open-mouthed, then shook his head in a flustered way. "Do you sing and dance, too?"

"Only for credits." The Ryn smiled in elaborate self-satisfaction. "Sometimes I amaze even myself."

Han took a menacing step toward the alien. "Now, listen you—"

A mellifluous cascade of genuine hoots and whistles interrupted him as a red-domed R2 unit wheeled onto the scene.

"It wants to know how it can be of assistance," the Ryn translated.

Han gazed from the alien to the droid in disbelief, then silently indicated the hatch's security lock.

The droid extended a manipulator arm from a compartment high up on its cylindrical body, inserted it into an access port above the lock, and quickly sliced the code. The hatch raised and the crowd surged forward, almost flattening Han in the process.

"I'm certain they'll all thank you later on," the Ryn said as he brushed past.

Waiting on one of the docking bay launch pads was a bullet-shaped civilian shuttle, just spacious enough to accommodate everyone. Han hurried for the cockpit while the Ryn supervised the boarding; then the Ryn joined Han at the cockpit controls, slipping comfortably into the copilot's seat and buckling into the safety harness, despite his long tail.

Han flicked the switch that enabled the repulsorlift generators and raised the ship. Rotating it through a 180-degree turn, he maneuvered the shuttle through the docking bay door and out into the launch bay.

Local space was thick with fighters and lighted by flashes of explosive light. A band of coralskippers raced past the bay's magnetic containment window, pursued by twice their number of X-wings and TIE interceptors, lasers firing steadily.

"We're not out of this yet," Han said, gritting his teeth as he aimed the shuttle for the aperture.

SIXTEEN

The shuttle veered left and right, as Han wove a jagged course among the hundreds of ships moored in the *Wheel*'s shadow. Most of the barges and freighters remained at anchor, but some were every bit as bent on escape as Han was, and were moving out at all speed, in whatever direction seemed best.

Han twisted the shuttle to port, hugging the curve of the station's outer rim, ascending or descending as necessary to avoid debris yanked from the interior by the Yuuzhan Vong dread weapon that had struck it. A quarter of the way around the *Wheel* an enormous enemy warship came into view, black as night and made more hideous by pairs of branching yorik coral arms. Retracting into an orifice in the bow was the colossal serpentine creature obviously responsible for the trio of erose breaches along the outer face of that part of the station's rim.

"That's gotta be the thing that swallowed Roa and Fasgo," Han growled to the Ryn. ".You and I might have been inside it right now." Firewalling the shuttle's throttle, he accelerated straight for the creature, oblivious to his copilot's wide-eyed distress.

"What are you doing?" the Ryn screamed.

Han gestured with his stubbled chin out the viewport. "My friends are imprisoned in that thing."

The Ryn's voice abandoned him momentarily, then he exclaimed, "You can't just break them out!"

"You just watch me," Han said out of the corner of his mouth.

"You're demented!"

"Tell me something I don't know."

"Okay, how about, *we're unarmed*!"

Han suddenly grasped that he wasn't aboard the *Falcon*, and he cursed to himself. If he was alone, or even if it was just him and the Ryn, he might have risked attacking the dread weapon anyway. But the shuttle's passenger compartment was filled with scores of innocents who were already on the run from the war, and who definitely didn't deserve to be taken into battle by a madman at the controls of a weaponless and unshielded craft.

It also dawned on Han that he was in the same position Anakin had found himself in on Sernpidal, forced to choose between the lives of a shipload of strangers and the life of one friend. The realization pierced Han's heart like a vibroblade, and he swore to himself that if he made it home in one piece, he would put things right with his estranged son.

Still, Han couldn't resist harassing the creature with a flyby. When the nose of the thing loomed all but close enough to touch—and the Ryn was half out of his seat in naked alarm—Han slewed the shuttle hard to port, hoping the slithering aberration would get a good taste of the ship's ion exhaust.

The fact that the creature suddenly shot from the

warship, nearly snagging the shuttle with its vacuuming mouth, suggested that Han's wish had been realized.

"Nice going!" the Ryn fairly shrieked. "You certainly managed to get its attention!"

A bit wide-eyed himself, Han took the shuttle through a power climb, then a series of evasive loops and rolls while the creature continued to snap at it.

"Blasted thing's as temperamental as a space slug!"

"Yeah, and we're the mynock who riled it!" the Ryn said.

Han tightened his grip on the controls. Firing the braking thrusters, he shoved the etheric rudder hard to the right at the same time, then executed a nosedive that took the shuttle corkscrewing around the neck of the enraged creature and ultimately under the bow of the enemy warship.

"Who's going to clean up the passenger cabin?" the Ryn asked when he'd swallowed his gorge.

"We'll worry about that later."

For the sake of the passengers, Han dialed up the gain on the inertial compensator and trimmed back their speed. The shuttle was just emerging on the far side of the bow when the instrument panel began to scream.

Han's mouth fell open.

"What?" the Ryn asked nervously. "What?" He glanced at the indicators. "Why are you slowing down?"

Han fought with the controls. "A dovin basal has us! The ship's drawing us back!"

The Ryn sat up in his seat and reached for the auxiliary controls. While Han struggled with the stick, the Ryn opened up the engines, rocketing the shuttle through a steep hull-hugging climb that carried them over the top of the warship and down along the opposite side into an inverted dive.

"Good thinking," Han remarked as the shuttle shot for what looked to be clear space. "Glad to be away from that thing—"

Another outburst from the Ryn erased Han's words. Four coralskippers had launched from the underside of the ship and were already opening fire with projectile launchers.

Han broke right, angling away from the skips and soaring through a series of evasive maneuvers.

"You had to go and scare their pet!" the Ryn hollered while fiery missiles streaked past the shuttle to both sides.

Dead ahead a veritable swarm of coralskippers were making for the warship, with New Republic starfighters in hot pursuit. Han throttled down and banked, only to see the pointed bow of a Star Destroyer edge into view from behind the closest of Ord Mantell's moons. Angry blue hyphens of energy lanced from the fortresses' forward gun turrets, assailing the fleeing skips and very nearly impaling the shuttle. Then the Yuuzhan Vong warship responded with plasma, as blinding and wrathful as stellar prominences.

All caution forgotten, Han engaged the thrusters and veered from the thick of the firefight. But the four skips they had encountered earlier were still glued to the shuttle's tail.

"No doubt about it," Han muttered, "my past is definitely catching up with me."

The Ryn glanced at him. "Then you're not running fast enough!"

Han tightened his lips. "We'll see about that. Plot a course for the *Wheel*."

"We're going back?"

"You heard me."

"Would it help any to deny it?"

"Stop your squawking," Han barked. "Give me everything the thrusters have."

The Ryn set himself to the task, grumbling all the while. "I don't know why your past has to catch up with *me*."

"I think it has something to do with your hat," Han said. "Besides, who asked you to latch on to me?"

"You're right. Next time I'll pick someone else to hang with."

Han took the shuttle straight for the outer rim of the *Wheel*, but at the last moment he climbed over the top, then dived sharply and shot between two of the station's tubular spokes. The four skips followed, but only three succeeded in matching the precarious maneuvers. The pilot in the trailing craft failed to swerve at the right moment and flew head-on into one of the spokes, pulverizing himself.

Out from the *Wheel*, Han leveled the shuttle out, then made a dash for empty space.

"Projectiles coming in fast!" the Ryn warned.

Engaging the braking thrusters, Han slammed the control stick hard to one side, then punched the throttle and dived, spinning the ship 180 degrees and vectoring back toward the *Wheel*. The trio of coralskippers didn't bother attempting to mimic the maneuver, and by the time they were coming out of their wide turns, the shuttle was closing once more on the orbital station's outer rim.

Han jerked the control stick back, then forward, whipping the ship over the top of the rim. But this time, just short of the hub, he juked hard to starboard and dived, racing under one of the radiating spokes, then curved around to port, lifting the shuttle's nose to climb over the top of the next one. While the skip pilots tried to follow—losing another of their teammates in the process—Han threw the shuttle into an inverted dive and, reversing his course, made a figure eight of the maneuver.

Emerging out from under the rim, however, Han and his copilot found themselves back where they had started, twining their way through clusters of closely anchored ships.

"Any sign of those skips?" Han asked when he could.

The Ryn studied the display screens. "Only two left. But they're sticking with us."

Han coaxed the shuttle through a tight turn while the Ryn kept the retrothrusters from stalling. They were aimed back toward the ring when a lavender-and-red TaggeCo luxury yacht suddenly blasted from one of the launch bays, not only making straight for the shuttle but opening fire to boot, intent on clearing a path.

Han howled and twisted the ship up on end, narrowly avoiding laser beams and what would have been a sure collision. Lifting his eyes as the yacht tore past them, he caught a quick glimpse of the occupants of the cockpit and slammed his fist on the console.

"I'll bet anything that was Big Bunji's ship!"

"What are friends for," the Ryn remarked.

But just then, one of the pursuing coralskippers took a

laser bolt from the yacht and exploded. "Well, there you go," Han said, shaking his head in wonderment.

"That still leaves one," the Ryn reminded.

"Wanna bet?"

The shuttle leapt toward the *Wheel*, but Han didn't trust that he could outfly the surviving Yuuzhan Vong pilot with more over-and-under maneuvers. Instead he angled for the uncompleted portion of the outer rim, where construction gantries, hover platforms, and a scattering of inert drone ships created a kind of obstacle course.

Clasping both hands around the control stick, he threw the shuttle into a vertical swoop to dodge a platform, then rolled out to port to bring the shuttle beneath the longest of the open-framework gantries. Halfway along, however, a plasma discharge from the coralskipper slagged the gantry, forcing Han to veer sharply for the hub. Along the way, he came close to losing a wing to a rectenna projecting from the underside of one of the spokes, but the real problem was the enemy pilot himself, who was as accurate with his weapons as he was skillful with his craft.

With console indicators screaming and flashing, Han powered the shuttle through a circle concentric to the hub, cheating the turn tighter and tighter yet, then vectored outward, accelerating back toward the skeletal arc of the outer rim.

Tugging himself upright, the Ryn leaned toward the viewport in obvious misgiving. "You can't be serious!" he stammered.

Han studied the skinless rim, and the exposed ribs and structural members through which he planned to steer the shuttle. "There's no skin on the far side, either," he said in the most reassuring tone he could muster. "I checked."

"You *checked*? When?"

"Earlier," Han said nonchalantly. "Trust me, there's clear space on the other side. Just hang on."

The shuttle's instruments went into a panic, screeching and blinking warnings of impending doom, but Han did his best to ignore them. With the coralskipper pasted to the shuttle's tail, he increased speed. Then, just short of the rim, he feinted a climb by goosing the forward attitude adjustment jets. The skip pilot took the bait and soared upward. Realizing his error, the Yuuzhan Vong tried to increase the angle of his ascent and execute a backward loop, but he was too close to the rim. The skip clipped girder after girder, losing pieces of itself with each impact, then careened off to one side and smashed into a curve of unyielding hull where spoke and rim met.

Five degrees to port, committed to his original plan, Han took the shuttle straight into the rim, slaloming through a forest of reinforcing ribs, beams, stanchions, and struts. But just as he had surmised, the outer face of the rim had yet to be walled in, and clear space was only a heartbeat away.

"See, that wasn't so bad," he started to say, when something slammed deafeningly into the transparisteel viewport.

Han's and the Ryn's arms flew to their faces. Han was certain the ship had sustained major damage, but when he looked he found only a protocol droid, spread-eagled on the viewport and hanging on for dear life.

"Hitchhiker," the Ryn said.

Several options presented themselves for dislodging the droid, but Han didn't act on any of them. "Where's the harm," he said.

He held the shuttle to an unswerving course until they were some distance from the *Wheel*, then banked through a long, descending curve. The area was free of coral-skippers, and the Yuuzhan Vong warship was beginning to move off, its dovin basals devouring most of what the Star Destroyer and a pack of starfighters were hurling at it.

"Plot us a course to Ord Mantell," Han said at last. Out of the corner of his eye, he saw the Ryn nodding approvingly.

Han grinned. "I—" he started to say and stopped himself.

The Ryn stared at him questioningly.

"—have my moments," Han completed quietly, but by rote and absent any emotion.

In fact, it wasn't at all like old times. Roa and Fasgo were either captive or dead, and the hand Han had clamped about the shuttle's control stick was trembling uncontrollably.

From the overbridge of the *Erinnic*, Vice Admiral Poinard and General Sutel watched a projectile-shaped shuttle wend through debris surrounding the *Jubilee Wheel* and make haste for Ord Mantell. Out beyond the planet's moons, what remained of the Yuuzhan Vong flotilla was in full retreat.

"Sirs, technical command reports that shields have been badly damaged," an enlisted-rating said from the starboard crew pit, "and does not, repeat not, advise pursuit."

"Affirmative," Poinard said. "Tell technical command that we will stand pat. Secure from general quarters."

"Maybe it's for the best," Sutel remarked. "Seeing their forces limping home might give the Yuuzhan Vong pause."

Eyes riveted on the withdrawing ships, Poinard didn't respond.

"Sirs, after-action reports coming in," the same crewmember said. "In addition to the cruiser, we lost one escort frigate and three gunboats." She paused briefly. "Battle assessment estimates enemy losses as significantly higher. The *Jubilee Wheel* is rattled but holding together. Ord Mantell describes extensive damage to some inland population centers, but adds that shields protected the coastal cities from the worst of it and that fires are under control."

Sutel turned to his comrade in arms. "That has to cheer you some, Admiral."

Poinard grunted noncommittally, then swung away from the observation bay. "Advise headquarters that their intelligence was not unfounded," he instructed his adjutant. "I'm not certain how, but we managed to chase them off."

SEVENTEEN

Moving with cocky assurance, Reck Desh, black-haired, streamlined, and newly tattooed, stepped into the Nebula Orchid and took in the room at a glance. Patrons in the popular Kuat City eatery included the usual boisterous mix of human and nonhuman technicians, engineers, and shipfitters, many on surface leave from Kuat Drive Yards' orbital starship construction facilities, along with a dozen or so civilians. Among the latter were three veiled telbuns in heavy purple-and-red robes and tall cylindrical hats—mates-in-training for the spoiled daughters of the Kuati elite. Flesh-and-blood and droid waiters dashed about, taking orders and delivering over-priced platters of artistically styled meals.

"Where are you supposed to wait?" the larger of Reck's two cohorts asked.

Reck nodded his lantern jaw toward the booths that lined the back of the room. "Number six."

The big man counted the booths out loud, head bobbing as he moved left to right from tall windows that overlooked the street. "Six is empty."

"Then we're off to a good start," Reck remarked.

"You and Ven grab seats where you can keep an eye on me. But stay put. Don't do anything unless I give a sign."

"Got it," Wotson said as he and his partner headed for an unoccupied table in the center of the room.

Reck hitched up baggy trousers, crossed the room, and folded himself into booth six. Booth five was also empty, but in seven sat a lone telbun whose facial veil covered all but his eyes. Reck settled back against the padded seat to wait for his mystery contact to turn up. He was about to hail a waiter when the telbun sitting back-to-back with him spoke up.

"Don't turn around, Reck," the Kuati ordered in the neutered tone typical of a high-priced voice scrambler.

Reck barely managed to sit still. In his mind's eye he replayed his brief look at the telbun, and he reassessed the conclusions he'd naturally drawn. The rich robes and tall hat could conceal a being of any of a wide variety of species, and the voice scrambler made it impossible to know if the speaker was male or female.

"You the genuine article, or are you just on your way to a masquerade?" he asked after a moment.

The stranger ignored the sarcasm. "Signal your associates that everything is in order, Reck."

Reck leaned his head back, almost touching the telbun's. "What's to stop me from calling them over here and ripping that veil off your face?"

"Not a thing. But you'd be a fool to think I'd come here without backup."

Reck's hazel eyes leapt about, searching for likely candidates. Bluff or no bluff, there was little harm in hearing the telbun out. He turned partway in the booth and waved an okay to Ven and Wotson.

"Nicely done," the telbun said. "As I mentioned when we spoke by comlink, I have some information for you."

"Good for you," Reck said. "But first I want to know how you knew where to reach me."

"The simple explanation is that the activities and current whereabouts of the Peace Brigade are known to more people than you might imagine."

Reck blew his breath out sharply and gave his head a mournful shake. "That either means we're working for the same people or you have access to sensitive data. And since I doubt we're on the same team, you're either military security or New Republic Intelligence."

"You don't need to know that just now."

"Maybe yes, maybe no, but I came all the way from Nar Shaddaa for this meeting."

"And I'm sure you're already homesick for the Hutts."

"All I'm saying is that you'd better have something worthwhile."

The telbun took a moment to respond. "You run with the Peace Brigade, but you answer to Yuuzhan Vong operatives."

Reck took a moment, as well. "You already know that or you wouldn't have asked me to come here."

"Correct response. I'm something of a stickler for honesty."

"Get to the point," Reck hissed. "What information do you have?"

"I know a way to put you in good stead with your bosses."

"Yeah, so you said when you made contact. But what makes you think I'm not in good standing?"

"You showed up here. I wasn't sure where you stood

when I comlinked you, but I know now. You're ambitious and you're intrigued."

Reck snorted again. "I'll let you know when I hear the rest of what you have to say."

"The New Republic has a Yuuzhan Vong defector in custody. She's an elite—a priestess of some sort. She jettisoned from an enemy ship destroyed in the Meridian sector. The Yuuzhan Vong have already made an attempt at retrieving her, and after what just happened at Ord Mantell I suspect they'll double their efforts."

Reck's brows knitted. "What happened at Ord Mantell?"

"Based on intelligence provided by the defector, a New Republic task force thwarted a Yuuzhan Vong attack."

Reck loosed a surprised whistle. "So this priestess is now a hot property."

"She's traveling with a mascot. The two are being transferred from the Mid Rim to Coruscant for safekeeping. I know the route they're taking."

Reck checked an impulse to turn around. "I'm not sure I follow you."

"Think about it. Whoever returns the defector to the fold will be doing the Yuuzhan Vong a tremendous favor."

"Now I get it. I make everyone happy, and maybe earn myself a reward. But what's your payoff in this? You want a piece of the action, right?"

"Wrong. In exchange, you keep me apprised of the Peace Brigade's future dealings with the Yuuzhan Vong."

"And if I refuse to keep my side of the bargain?"

"I'll bring everyone down on you—military and New Republic Intelligence. After the stunts you've pulled, you'll be lucky to get a life sentence on Fodurant."

"Cards on the table, huh? So why do you want to see this defector returned?"

The telbun laughed shortly. "Did you throw in with the enemy only for the credits, Reck?"

"Credits scammed are twice as sweet as credits earned."

"That's cute, but I don't accept it. Doubtless, credits figured into your decision, but you know as well as I that there are larger issues at stake."

"What larger issues?"

"The New Republic is going to lose this war, and there's nothing to be gained by being on the losing side. Play this right, Reck, and both of us will come out winners."

"I'd be lying if I said it wasn't a tempting offer," Reck said tentatively. "But since you had no trouble getting to me, that must mean that NRI already has the Peace Brigade under surveillance."

"You leave that to me."

"To you . . . And when do I get to know who you are?"

"When the time's right—and I make that decision."

Reck took a slow breath. "All right," he said at last. "I'm willing to give this a shot."

"You won't be sorry." The telbun paused briefly. "The defector and her companion are being relocated to Bilbringi aboard an old starliner called *Queen of Empire*. I'll furnish you with their travel plans and keep you updated on additional details as I learn them. But I suggest you grab them before they reach Bilbringi."

"You leave that to me," Reck said, glad for the chance to even the score.

"One more thing: you keep quiet about where you received this information—even with your Yuuzhan Vong controllers. For the time being, this is strictly between you and me, and your two cronies."

"I can do that—on a trial basis anyway."

"I know you won't disappoint me, Reck."

A hand touched Reck's shoulder. Then, with a rustling of fabric, the telbun stood.

"I'll be in touch. Don't attempt to follow me."

Reck stayed put but his eyes swept the room for signs of the telbun's accomplices. When no one rose to follow the robed figure out the restaurant's back entrance, he swung to Ven and Wotson.

"Quick—after him!"

Reck was one step beyond the pair as they plowed through the rear doors, only to confront a sunken courtyard filled wall to wall with identically attired telbuns.

Warbling sirens signaled an all-clear as C-3PO hurried past the open-air launch pads of Ord Mantell's primary spaceport. Defense shields had protected the city from aerial bombardment, but to the north—in the direction of the planet's renowned junkyards—thick columns of oily black smoke climbed into a smudged sky.

"Thank the maker," C-3PO muttered as he walked. "Thank the maker."

Secreted with her vigilant Noghri bodyguard, Mistress Leia had tasked C-3PO with assuring that their spacecraft hadn't suffered damage during the Yuuzhan Vong attack, and indeed that had proved to be the case. But several ships had been caught unawares, and the sight of their scorched and punctured hulls had given C-3PO an unshakable flutter.

He shuddered to think what might have been his fate

had the New Republic task force failed to foil the enemy attack. Why, he might well have ended up in a scrap heap or, worse yet, at the bottom of a pit filled with incinerated droids, such as he had witnessed on Rhommamool, after a brief but disquieting encounter with the late Nom Anor.

"Your existence offends me," the political troublemaker had told him, with a minatory look that was permanently burned into C-3PO's memory core.

It was one thing to be shunned by Gotals, whose impressionable sensory organs tended to become overloaded by the energy output of droids, but it was quite another to be singled out for deactivation or annihilation. Of course, there had been cases where a droid was actually responsible for instigating antidroid sentiment, such as when a MerenData EV supervisor droid serving under Lando Calrissian on Bespin had destroyed one-quarter of Cloud City's droid population. But EV-9D9's ignominious acts were hardly typical of droid behavior.

More to the point, what could droids, or a single droid, have possibly done to fill Nom Anor with such hatred? In searching for precedents, C-3PO could recall instances of droid enmity coming from humans forced to wear artificial parts. But many humans were perfectly comfortable with harboring nonliving parts. C-3PO couldn't recall a single instance of Master Luke railing against his replacement hand.

It was all so baffling!

C-3PO had had more than his share of personal brushes with annihilation. An arm torn off by Tusken Raiders, traumatic dismemberment by Imperials on Cloud City and rioters on Bothawui, an eye yanked out by Jabba the Hutt's Kowakian monkey-lizard ... But only to be reassembled after each calamity, defragged and degaussed, bathed in oil—a droid's bacta tank—and polished back to his auric splendor.

Those periodic resurrections made actual deactivation inconceivable, or at the very least, challenging to contemplate. In effect, ceasing-to-be was shutting down permanently—eternally. But how could that be? And how torturous it must be to suffer forced deactivation at the hands of adversaries!

"We're *all* doomed," C-3PO muttered aloud. "It's the lot of all sentient beings, metal and otherwise, to suffer."

But exactly why was deactivation such a frightening prospect to ponder?

Did the fear owe to a desperate desire to remain activated, to sustain awareness indefinitely and at all costs? Or did it owe to an unnatural attachment to existence? An attachment that, if surrendered, would take with it all fears of ceasing-to-be—

The revelation discombobulated him momentarily, and he came to so sudden a halt on the permacrete landing field that a protocol droid not entirely unlike himself rear-ended him.

"*E chu ta* to you!" C-3PO said, throwing the droid's rude expletive right back at him.

The nerve, he told himself as he resumed his pace. To disrespect one who had seen so much in his time, who had traveled so widely, who had amassed so much knowledge since his first job of programming binary loadlifters—

Quite unexpectedly his photoreceptors zeroed in on

Master Solo. Conversing with a . . . why, a Ryn, of all species.

As C-3PO hastened toward them he couldn't help but note that Master Han and the Ryn looked somewhat the worse for wear, as did the shuttle they had obviously exited, accompanied by a mixed lot of woebegone beings and a red-capped R2 unit. And, in fact, Master Solo and the Ryn weren't so much conversing as *arguing*.

"See you around," the Ryn was concluding as C-3PO neared.

"Not if I can help it, partner," Han said, in a manner that held little sympathy.

"Master Solo!" C-3PO called, waving an arm over his head. "Master Solo!"

Han turned and saw him, then snorted a laugh—not at all as surprised as C-3PO might have expected him to be. But then, he had been made aware of Mistress Leia and C-3PO's impending visit to Ord Mantell. So perhaps he had come looking for them.

"Master Solo, you're injured," C-3PO exclaimed, on seeing dried blood on his hands and face.

"Could've been a lot worse," Han replied with his usual penchant for understatement. "Where's Leia, Threepio?"

"Why, she's at the Hotel Grand as we speak, sir."

Han thought for a minute, eyes narrowing as he glanced at C-3PO. "I don't suppose there's any chance of your not mentioning you ran into me?"

C-3PO inclined his head in perplexity.

"No, I suppose not," Han said, answering for himself. He blew out his breath. "In that case, I guess you'd better lead me to her."

EIGHTEEN

"I still can't believe you're here," Leia said as she applied a transdermal bacta patch to a nasty abrasion above Han's right eyebrow. Han was seated at the vanity in Leia's elegant hotel room, with Leia leaning over him and C-3PO standing silently in the background. Olmahk and Basbakhan had posted themselves at the door. "Where's your friend Roa?"

Han spoke through gritted teeth. "That's an excellent question, Leia. He got sucked into some sort of Yuuzhan Vong snakeship that latched on to the *Jubilee Wheel*."

Leia placed her hands on his shoulders. "Oh, Han, no."

"Maybe he's only been captured," Han vented. "But that's even worse." He clenched his jaw and shook his head back and forth.

"Did you two accomplish what you set out to do?" Leia asked guardedly.

Han's eyes found hers in the vanity mirror. "The enemy interrupted us."

"I'm sorry to hear that." Leia averted her gaze and returned to smoothing the bacta patch. "What will you do now?"

Abruptly Han stood up and paced away from the

vanity, combing his hair back from his face with his fingers. "I don't know. Look for him, I guess."

Leia regarded him with disbelief. "Look for him? How do you intend to do that?"

Han shook his head. "I don't know yet." He glanced at Leia and scowled. "What do you expect me to do—pretend it never happened?"

"Of course not. I only meant—"

Han waved his hand at her. "Ah, how could I expect you to understand?"

Leia folded her arms and squinted. "You think I don't know what it's like to lose a friend?"

Han held up a hand. "I don't need you reminding me about Alderaan or Elegos A'Kla—"

Leia's eyes flashed. "Have you completely lost your mind? How dare you say that?"

Han met her gaze. "Careful, Leia," he advised, "I'm not in the best mood."

Leia clutched her neck in elaborate concern. "And I certainly wouldn't want my name added to the list of people who have crossed the infamous Han Solo."

Han pivoted slightly to throw C-3PO a wry glance. "Great little fighter for her weight, don't you think, Threepio?"

C-3PO stared at him. "Pardon me for asking, sir, but—"

"Are you coming back to Coruscant with us?" Leia asked, planting her fists on her hips.

Han shook his head. "It's like I told you, Roa and I were interrupted."

"And you've no intention of telling me what this is about."

Han shrugged.

"What happened to the man who preferred a straight fight to sneaking around?"

Han's brow furrowed and his jaw dropped a bit. "Who's sneaking around?"

She frowned in disappointment. "You've changed, Han."

"What are you talking about?" he protested. "I'm the same as ever. Timeproof, weatherproof, rust resistant."

"You think so?" Leia took him by the shoulders and swung him around to face the mirror. "Take a good look."

Han fell silent for a moment. "That's not the years, it's the parsecs."

Leia exhaled wearily. "You can be so exasperating."

He snorted. "Yeah, I guess you wish you'd married some pro zoneball player instead of a smuggler, huh?"

Leia firmed her lips in anger. "That's not it at all." She gestured to the window. "It's reckless of you to be roaming about out there. For all you know, the Yuuzhan Vong have some kind of dossier on you. There might even be a price on your head."

"I'm not exactly 'roaming about,' Leia."

"Then tell me what you're doing."

Han started to say something but stopped himself and began again. "I knew it would be a mistake to come here," he mumbled.

Leia stepped back in genuine dismay. Now she stopped Han when he started to speak. "You know what I think, Han? I think that you should plot a course around Coruscant until you've worked this out. I mean it."

Han nodded, tight-lipped. "Maybe you're right, Leia. Maybe that's for the best."

She made no attempt to restrain him as he snatched his travel pack from the floor and let himself out. But no sooner did the door seal than she sank to the bed, as if stunned.

"Well, that certainly wasn't in the plans," she said flatly to C-3PO.

"The plans, Mistress?"

She looked at him askance. "It's an expression, Threepio. I didn't really have any plans."

C-3PO appeared to slouch. Leia smiled in spite of herself. "Human thinking isn't all it's prized to be, Threepio. In fact, sometimes it's better *not* to know what's on someone else's mind."

Han placed his hand over the top of the squarish glass to prevent the four-armed bartender from refilling it.

"Alcohol isn't the answer," he said.

The Codru-Ji studied him from behind the counter. "What's the question?"

"How do you change the past?"

"Simple. By changing the way you remember it."

"Yeah, I suppose I could get my memory wiped."

The bartender nodded in understanding. "Another whiskey and you'd be well on your way."

Han ran his hand over his stubbled jaw, then shook his head. "To nowhere."

The bartender shrugged. "Suit yourself, pal."

The bar at the Lady Fate Casino was almost empty, but the gaming tables were crowded with people celebrating their good fortune in escaping immolation—

perhaps the longest shot any oddsmaker had ever posted. Han figured he, too, would have been in a ...ood to revel, if not for what had happened to Roa and Fasgo.

But what sense was there in dragging Leia down with him? She wasn't to blame for their disappearance any more than Anakin was responsible for Chewie's death—perhaps any more than Reck Desh was. So maybe it was time to forget about searching for Roa or the so-called Peace Brigade and return to Coruscant, where he might even be able to engage in something constructive.

He paid for the drink, tipped the Codru-Ji generously, and was headed for the exit when Big Bunji's Aqualish lieutenant intercepted him.

"I see you made it off the *Wheel* in one piece," Han said with elaborate disappointment.

"Good to see you, too, Solo. Boss B thought you might be found here."

"Tell Bunji I want to thank him for leaving us behind."

"He sends his apologies. In the haste of the moment, he completely forgot that he had guests."

Han's upper lip twitched. "I'll be sure to tell that to Roa and Fasgo—assuming they survive whatever the Yuuzhan Vong have planned for them."

The Aqualish nodded inscrutably. "Perhaps this will help, Solo. The boss has learned that the human you were asking about—the one called Reck Desh—has an operation planned for Bilbringi."

Han's expression went from anger to wary interest. "What sort of operation?"

"Unknown. Only that it involves the entire Peace Brigade."

"When?"

"Imminently."

"Bilbringi, you say."

"That much is known."

Han pushed his hair from his forehead and loosed a slow exhale. "Okay, tell Bunji thanks."

The Aqualish gestured farewell and moved off, and Han returned to the bar to think. Presumably, the *Happy Dagger* was still docked on the *Wheel*, but there would be no way of knowing whether it had survived the attack without returning upside. The alternative was to find public transport to Bilbringi and nose around for clues as to what Reck was up to. Leia could probably pull the necessary strings to get him aboard a ship, but he couldn't ask her without coming clean, and he wasn't ready to risk that. Not yet, anyway.

But C-3PO . . . C-3PO could arrange for his passage on a Bilbringi-bound vessel.

As per Han's discreetly relayed request, C-3PO rendezvoused with him at the entrance to the Ord Mantell spaceport.

"Nothing better than a prompt droid," Han said smiling.

"I must confess, Master Solo," C-3PO responded anxiously, "that I feel less than right about this—especially about mimicking Leia's voice to arrange for your passage."

"Come on, Threepio. You've done it before. You did it to fool Grand Admiral Thrawn's forces."

"That's not very reassuring, sir. What's more, that was a matter of protecting the princess from assassins. This is a matter of protecting you from . . . I'm not quite sure what, Master Solo."

"I'm not asking you to lie, Threepio," Han said, dragging the final word out. "I'm only asking you to overlook. If Leia doesn't ask you about me, then there's no need for you to say where I've gone."

"But surely she will ask about you, sir."

"Okay, but she might not ask directly if you have any idea where I went, or where I am."

"But, sir, what if she does?"

Han considered it. "If she does, you tell her." He regarded the droid for a moment. "You'd have to, wouldn't you?"

C-3PO grew jittery. "It's beyond logic."

"Exactly," Han said. "It's beyond logic. You know, sometimes people are better off not knowing certain things."

"Sir?"

"Sometimes it's more painful to know the truth than not to know it."

C-3PO paid close attention. "Put that way, it doesn't sound so bad," he started to say, then made a flustered gesture. "But this matter of stretching the truth is as confusing as ceasing-to-be!"

Han raised an eyebrow. "Ceasing-to-be? What's a droid doing thinking about death? You can't die."

"Perhaps not the way a human can, sir. But I can be deactivated. And what will become of my memories, then—the memories of all I've accomplished and all I've been through?"

Han stared at him. "Did somebody loosen your motivator or something? If that's all you're worried about, we can download your memory to a data storage facility." He narrowed his gaze with clear intent. "In fact, I just might be willing to arrange for that, Threepio—especially if you'll agree not to say anything to Leia about Bilbringi."

C-3PO tipped his head to one side.

"Immortality, Threepio," Han said enticingly.

"But, sir—"

"It'll be like having a clone on ice. Your mind winds up in a different body, but you don't even know you were gone."

"Oh, I'm confident I could adjust to a new body, sir. After all, I am a mind more than I am a body."

"That's the spirit, kid."

"That's the spirit," C-3PO repeated excitedly, then came back to himself. "But, Master Solo, sir, about this ship on which you have passage. There's something you should know—"

"It's bound for Bilbringi?"

"Yes, sir, but—"

"Then that's all that matters. Where's it leave from?"

"Tenders and boarding shuttles are scheduled to depart from Launch Bay 4061 at thirteen hundred hours, local time. But, sir, if you'd just give me a moment to explain—"

"No time, Threepio," Han said, glancing at a nearby time display. "And thanks—for everything. You won't regret this."

C-3PO raised both hands above his head in agitation. "But, sir," he called out as Han was hurrying off, "it's the *Queen of Empire*—a jinxed vessel if ever there was one!"

NINETEEN

Showolter grimaced as he watched the ooglith masquer captured on Wayland envelop and attach itself to Elan, extruding microscopic hooks and tentacles that inserted themselves into pores, sweat ducts, wrinkles, and folds. Naked, Elan had her back turned to him, but he could tell by her contortions and the involuntary flexing of her shipshape muscles that the process of donning the living mantle was excruciating—*exquisitely so,* according to Elan.

Alert to his curiosity, she had asked him to watch, in a manner that had managed to mix indifference with a hint of flirtation. He could endure only so much of her agonized moaning, however, and turned away to gaze out the safe house's sole window at a stand of trees, whose high metal content made that part of Myrkr a challenge for transceivers and other communication arrays.

"All finished," Elan announced stoically, and Showolter turned again to find her clothed not only in the Yuuzhan Vong second-skin but also in the robe he had originally handed her. She looked more human than ever.

Elan massaged her cheeks, forehead, and chin, as one might smooth away creases. "You see, Showolter? No trace of my markings, no evidence of who and what I truly am."

Showolter realized he'd been holding his breath, and he let it out. "One size cloaker fits all, huh?"

"Why, are you interested in trying it on?"

"No," he replied quickly. "Just wondering whether there are male and female versions."

"Why should there be?"

He scratched his head. "Well, not every Yuuzhan Vong could have your shape."

Elan glanced at Vergere, squatting nearby, and the two traded cryptic smiles. Vergere's disguise amounted to no more than a loose-fitting garment that concealed her feathered torso and reverse-articulated legs. There wasn't much that could be done about her exotic face, but with so many folks displaced from the Outer Rim, immigration and customs officials were getting used to seeing new species every day.

"Is there something wrong with my shape, Showolter?" Elan asked at last.

"Quite the opposite." He laughed awkwardly.

"But surely you object to my facial and torso markings."

"Frosting," he said, trying to make it sound like a joke.

She tipped her head and regarded him frankly. "Perhaps you have the makings of a Yuuzhan Vong—despite your reluctance to assume the ooglith masquer."

"I doubt it. Though I might go as far as getting myself tattooed."

Her smile straightened. "If you think that the Yuuzhan Vong process is less painful, you're dead wrong."

He shrugged nonchalantly. "Sacrifices have to be made."

"Oh, indeed they do, Showolter." She let the remark

hang in the air for a moment, then added, "But I'm afraid my breath might offend you. .'s somewhat contaminated—"

"From the food," Vergere interrupted. "We're not accustomed to eating so much processed nourishment."

Showolter glanced at her. "Sorry, but there's nothing I can do about that." He appraised the concealing abilities of the ooglith masquer and gave his head a bemused shake. "A nerf in taopari's clothing," he muttered.

Elan's fine brows beetled.

"A play on a saying," he explained. "A taopari in nerf's clothing—a beast disguised as a grazer to infiltrate the herd."

Elan's eyes brightened in revelation. "So I'm a grazer in beast's clothing."

"I was thinking of the assassin your people sent."

"Of course you were."

Showolter cleared his throat and handed her undergarments, a simple dress, a jacket, and shoes. "Anyway, here's your outfit."

Elan examined the items one by one. "Who am I supposed to be, Showolter?"

"My wife. We're refugees, displaced from a planet called Sernpidal, traveling with our servant."

"That would be me," Vergere said, "as ever."

Elan looked from Vergere to Showolter. "I've no training in wifely duties."

"No one expects you to live the part. Just play it. We'll go over the details before we leave."

"It will be just the three of us?" Elan asked.

"We'll be met by backup on the ship."

"Are we going to a more populated world?"

He nodded.

"You will show me the sights?"

"That might take some doing. But, yes, eventually."

"How delightful."

Showolter left her to dress and went into the adjoining room to check on the two three-member decoy teams. The two female agents, faces painted in swirls and whorls and already attired in outfits identical to the one he'd given Elan, bore enough of a superficial resemblance to the Yuuzhan Vong priestess to pass for her. But Showolter was less confident about the Mrlssi and the Bimm operatives chosen to pass for Vergere.

"Maybe we'd have been better off employing a couple of Drall," he commented as he appraised the two costumed aliens.

"What about me, Showolter?" one of the women asked playfully. "Do I fit the bill as Miss Defector?" She struck a theatrically alluring pose and batted her eyelashes at him. " 'You will show me the sights?' " she said, aping Elan's voice.

Everyone but Showolter laughed. Instead, he began distributing weapons and last-minute instructions written on self-destruct durasheet.

"Let yourselves be seen in Hyllyard City," he told the members of the first team, "but don't overplay things. If there are Yuuzhan Vong operatives about, they're not going to be easily fooled." He handed them travel vouchers. "You'll be departing Myrkr for Gyndine, then traveling on to Thyferra."

Another set of vouchers went to the male member of the second team. "Myrkr to Bimmisaari to Kessel."

He slipped a blaster into his shoulder holster. "Everyone stays in touch with HQ through channels. Once our informants have reached Coruscant, you'll be notified to drop the charade and report in."

"What's your bet, Major?" team one's leader asked.

Showolter pulled down the corners of his mouth and shook his head. "After the recent setback at Ord Mantell, the Yuuzhan Vong might just avoid that sector. Besides," he added, buttoning his jacket over the holster, "what would they want with a bunch of refugees traveling on a decrepit starliner?"

As the packed-to-the-bulkheads tender pulled into docking position alongside the once magnificent luxury liner, Han suddenly realized what C-3PO had been trying to tell him back on Ord Mantell.

Of all ships, he said to himself as the vessel's faded and battle-scarred legend came into view. The *Queen of Empire.*

Originally owned and operated by Haj Shipping Lines, a company whose loyalty to the Empire and the Alliance had varied in response to which side had the most to offer, the *Queen* had been the vessel of choice for passengers traveling between Corellia and Gyndine—with numerous ports of call en route—and occasionally Rimward as far as Nar Hekka, in Hutt space.

Slightly larger than an Imperial Star Destroyer, the ship was capable of carrying tens of thousands, but instead had restricted its passenger list to a mere five thousand, so as to provide unparalleled comfort, exceptional service, and more diversions than anyone had a right to savor. Species-specific pools, spas, restaurants, shopping malls, climate zones, and exercise rooms, tonsorial parlors for the hirsute and buffing stations for the smooth-skinned, jizz lounges and null-g ballrooms, casinos, observation blisters, and amusement areas ... all on more decks than could possibly be explored on a single cruise. The plushest of her many nightclubs had been the Star Winds lounge, where fifteen-limbed Rughjas had played the finest in swing-bob, and affluent passengers had danced the margengai-glide till all hours.

In her heyday, the *Queen* had rivaled the older *Quamar Messenger* and the Mon Calamari starliner *Kuari Princess* and had been the template for newer vessels, such as the *Tinta Palette* and *Jewel of Churba*. But frequently the target of pirates, a magnet for meteors, and once stranded in hyperspace for five days, the *Queen* had fallen on hard times.

Han had never been aboard, but he had heard all about the ship from Lando, who had met Han's first love, Bria Tharen, aboard the *Queen*. Bria was by then a high-ranking member of the Corellian resistance, and Lando, his usual dapper self.

Han was still deep in recollection when he transferred to the liner, and it wasn't until he was aboard that he grasped just how far the *Queen* had fallen.

While he and a handful of others actually held tickets, the ship was overwhelmed with keelrunners, casualties of war, and refugees previously stranded on Ord Mantell and the *Wheel* and now on their way to various Colony and Core worlds, thanks in large part to Leia's efforts.

A babel of languages and a dizzying amalgam of smells, the *Queen*'s once grand ballrooms and lounges had become temporary camps, where folks of a hundred different species huddled inside makeshift tents and shelters, carefully safeguarding children, pets, or what little foodstuffs and belongings they possessed. Among them roamed guards and soldiers, settling disputes over deck space or alleged theft, or breaking up vicious fights born of plain and simple discrimination. Also circulating were droids, vendors, and hawkers—many protected by bodyguards—charging exorbitant prices for quick-prep meals, derma supplements, dubious pharmaceuticals, and tickets to the portable refreshers that lined some of the passageways.

Picking his way among everyone, Han followed deck routing lines to the sour-smelling, cramped compartment to which his ticket entitled him. Perching himself on the edge of the tiny, swaybacked bed, he considered his situation. The cabin space didn't bother him; Bilbringi was only two jumps distant, and the *Queen* was scheduled to arrive within three ship days. Once there—where Han had contacts and acquaintances—he would snoop around for Reck or other members of the Peace Brigade, and perhaps even get a lead on what had happened to victims of the Yuuzhan Vong attack on the *Jubilee Wheel*.

He dozed for a few moments and awoke ravenous—no surprise, in that he hadn't eaten anything since bar snacks in the Lady Fate Casino.

Ticketed passengers were supposed to be afforded exclusive privileges to both an upper-deck cafeteria and the only restaurant that hadn't been converted into living spaces for the refugees. But crowding had overtaxed whatever controls had once been in place, and the cafeteria had been set upon by near-starved passengers. By

the time Han arrived, only limited quantities of food remained and there wasn't a utensil to be found. It had
come down to using hands, claws, pincers, or whatever
foraging appendages nature had bestowed.

Han was assessing whether any of the grime on his
hands might be toxic when he remembered the survival tool Anakin had given him—the one Chewie had
made—which, remarkably, after all that Han had been
through on the *Wheel*, was still clipped to his belt. And
sure enough, the tool contained a fork attachment.

Han prized the three-tined utensil from its clever recess and edged into the crowd surrounding the buffet
table. Closing on the warming trays, he saw that only
one piece of nerf steak remained—an overdone, gristly
piece at that—but he wasn't about to pass it up. As he
reached forward and speared it, however, a talonlike
nail attached to a somewhat velvety, five-fingered hand
lanced the steak at the same instant.

Han whirled and found himself face-to-face with the
male Ryn in whose company he had escaped the *Wheel*.
The prehensile-tailed alien was sporting the same vi-
brantly colored culottes, vest, and jaunty beret.

"Ha!" the Ryn yapped in amused surprise. "I told you
I'd see you around!"

Han grimaced. "Around five years from now would
have been more to my liking."

"Ah, but you can't fight fate, my friend."

"I can try," Han snapped. "What are you doing here,
anyway?"

"Why, the same as you: traveling forward." He cut his
large eyes to the thin slab of meat. "So who claims the
prize?"

"I guess we share it," Han said in a rankled tone. "Providing you eat the half you stuck your fingernail into."

The Ryn laughed. "And folks say there are no honest beings about."

Han transferred the steak to an inexpertly washed plate, and the two of them found opposing seats at a nearby table, among a mixed group of Sullustans and Bimms.

"Droma," the Ryn said, extending a hand as he was sitting down.

"Roaky Laamu," Han told him, reluctantly shaking hands.

"I have to say, Roaky, you look a lot better than when I saw you last."

Han scratched at the rectangle of synthflesh Leia had applied to his forehead. "The marvel of bacta. Wish I could—"

"—say the same for you," Droma completed.

Han slapped the tabletop and leaned forward angrily. "You and I need to come to an arrangement. I don't know the trick to how you do it, but from now on you're going to keep my thoughts to yourself, understand?"

"Quite a challenge," Droma mused.

"That's *your* problem." Han stared at him for a moment. "Just how do you do it?"

"Why, haven't you heard that all Ryn are mind readers and fortune-tellers?" Droma asked facetiously.

"Yeah, and I'm a Jedi Knight."

Droma laughed. "Now, that would be a stretch."

Han frowned and used the survival tool's knife blade

to saw the steak in half—its blackened underside bearing the stamp of the provider, Nebula Consumables.

With obvious hesitation, Han forked a small portion into his mouth. Droma watched Han's face as he chewed— or tried to.

"Not what you expected?"

"I expected edible," Han mumbled around the piece.

"That bad?"

Droma borrowed the survival tool to saw a bite-size portion from his half.

Han pushed an empty saucer toward him. "You can spit your teeth in here."

Droma chewed for several moments before politely taking the piece into his cupped hand and dropping it under the table.

Han forced a breath. "Look, what do you say we try the restaurant—my treat."

Droma grinned. "I thought you'd never ask."

They left the cafeteria and walked a short distance along the promenade deck to a crowded dining room that had managed to retain some of the grandeur long surrendered by the rest of the *Queen*. As they were about to be seated, however, a Klaatooinian maître d' intervened.

"I'm sorry, sir," he told Han, "but we can't serve the . . . Ryn."

Han showed the heavy-lidded, long-jawed humanoid an incredulous look. "What, do you think you're working on the *Tinta Rainbow*? This is a refugee ship!"

The maître d' sniffed. "We still have our policies."

Han's nostrils flared and he cocked his arm back, only to have Droma restrain him.

"A fight won't change anything," Droma advised, all but hanging from Han's biceps.

"Except my mood," Han growled.

"But not our appetites."

Han lowered his arm and snatched a menu from a passing waiter. Scanning it, he jabbed his finger at a chef's specialty and thrust the menu into the maître d's long-fingered hands.

"Two of these—to go."

The Klaatooinian looked down his nose at Han, then hurried off, returning shortly with the requested items.

Han and Droma took the packaged meals to tattered deck chairs in the observation bay and ate without conversation as the *Queen* maneuvered out of Ord Mantell space, accruing velocity for the jump to lightspeed. Starlight shone on the badly damaged outer ring of the *Jubilee Wheel*. Han was determined to keep thoughts of Roa and Fasgo from his mind—at least until Bilbringi.

Sated, he leaned back in the chair and locked his hands behind his head. "Where are the Ryn from?" he asked while Droma was licking his fingers clean. "Originally, I mean."

Droma smoothed the ends of his white mustache. "A world in the Core, but even we Ryn don't know which one."

"Were you forced to leave?"

"There are two schools of thought. The first has us descended from a tribe of ten thousand musicians donated to a nearby world that was bereft of artists. The second has us descended from warriors deployed against an Inner Rim threat. Our language contains many military terms, such as our word for *non-Ryn*, which has linguistic ties to the word *civilian*."

"How'd so many of you wind up in the Corporate Sector?"

"We were essentially chased there by circumstance. After leaving the Core, the Ryn learned farming, metalworking, and other skills, but suspicion followed us everywhere. With forged documents of safe passage, we were allowed to settle on remote worlds in Corporate Sector space. It helped that our healing techniques, borrowed from many disparate groups, saved the life of an important Authority executive.

"Still, our nomadic ways, our fondness for secrecy, our lack of written records—all for the sake of self-preservation—persuaded others to believe us black mages or stealthy thieves. We were said to feast on living flesh, and in some sectors laws were enacted that made it legal to hunt, brand, or kill us. We were blamed for the crimes of others. Our native language was outlawed, and many of us were sold into slavery or made breeders for slave children."

Soberly, Han recalled the Ryn on the *Wheel* who had approached the *Happy Dagger*, and the pair that had approached him personally in the Bet's Off, regarding onward passage to the Core.

"How did you end up on the *Jubilee Wheel*?" he asked.

"I was among a caravan of Ryn ships that had left the Corporate Sector for the Lesser Plooriod Cluster when the Yuuzhan Vong pushed into the Ottega system and destroyed Ithor."

"You're a professional pilot?"

"A fair one," Droma said, "as well as a scout and all-around spacer."

"So what happened after Ithor?"

"Our ships were scattered, as were our families. I've been searching for my clanmates ever since, including a sister and several cousins."

"Tough," Han said.

Droma nodded. "But what about you, Roaky? You handle a ship as masterfully as a starfighter pilot—or a successful smuggler. What brings you out here?"

Han took a moment to collect his thoughts. "I'm more a mechanic than I am a pilot. Taking time off from normal life to figure some things out."

"So you, also, are trying to return to your family?" Droma said.

Han looked at him. "Maybe I am."

From the restaurant came the strains of "Smoky Dreams," a song that had been perfectly matched to Bria Tharen's whiskey contralto, and one she would often sing.

"The song reminds you of something," Droma said, observing Han cannily.

Han smiled without showing his teeth. "Good old days."

"How old?"

"Old enough to be good," Han told him.

TWENTY

His back to the room, Luke was standing at the wrap-around transparisteel window when Kyp Durron, Wurth Skidder, Cilghal, and the other Jedi he had asked to come to Coruscant filed in. The chamber occupied the top floor of the Ministry of Justice building, which while far from the tallest tower in the vicinity, nevertheless enjoyed majestic, panoramic views of the cityscape in all directions. Against the light of the sinking sun, the windows were darkly tinted, but not so impenetrable that the chamber wasn't bathed in the same reds and oranges that painted the sky.

Luke was seemingly absorbed in watching Coruscant's ceaseless traffic flow. By the time he turned from the window, all twenty Jedi Knights had entered and were taking seats at the round table or simply standing about, hoods lowered, waiting for Luke to explain why he'd asked them to come nearly halfway across the galaxy.

"The New Republic has two enemy defectors in custody," he announced without preamble. "One is a priestess, the other is apparently her mascot or companion. As a result of their supplying military intelligence that was at least in part responsible for the recent victory at Ord Mantell, the defectors are being brought to Coruscant for further debriefing."

"Now we're getting somewhere," Kyp Durron said above outpourings of surprise and excitement. "I knew there had to be some disaffected among the Yuuzhan Vong." He showed Luke an eager, thin-lipped smile. "When do we get a shot at debriefing them?"

"But it has to be subterfuge, doesn't it?" Cilghal said before Luke could respond. "Notwithstanding the alleged military intelligence." Her webbed hands were concealed in the opposite sleeves of her Jedi robe, and her bulbous eyes took in Luke and Kyp simultaneously.

Luke nodded as he moved to the table. "The New Republic is being cautious. If the defectors continue to supply intelligence that holds up, they'll be given more credence."

"They've agreed to provide more?" Wurth Skidder asked. He was the only one who wasn't wearing Jedi robes, though from the tousled look of his blond hair he might have passed the entire journey from Yavin 4 with the hood of his cloak raised.

"Conditionally."

Many of the Jedi traded glances, but no one spoke. Luke perched himself on the edge of the table, with one booted foot extended to the floor.

"They've requested a meeting with us."

The gray-haired and bearded Streen uttered a short laugh. "Exactly the sort of thing I expected." He regarded Luke. "Did they happen to say why they want to meet with us?"

Luke stood up and took a few steps toward the former Bespin miner. "They claim to have information about an illness Yuuzhan Vong agents introduced, long before the first worldships landed on Helska 4."

A shocked silence fell over the room.

"I won't try to fool any of you," Luke said after a moment. "With all my heart I want to believe it's the illness Mara has been suffering, but that remains to be seen."

"If it is the same," Cilghal said, still a bit stunned by the revelation, "dare we surmise that the Yuuzhan Vong *know* that Mara is ill?"

Luke tightened his lips and shook his head. "I don't think we should leap to that conclusion."

"Of course they know," Wurth said firmly. "What's more, I say they're using Mara to get to us the same way they got to her."

"You don't know that," Anakin said sharply. "The defectors have been scanned for just that sort of thing, and they'll be scanned again before we meet with them."

Nonplussed, Wurth sat back in his chair and stared at Luke. "Then you've already made up your mind to meet with them?"

Luke nodded once. "As an accommodation to the New Republic as much as anything else—a way of demonstrating to them that we can work together."

Several meaningful glances were exchanged.

"We can all appreciate that, Master," Ganner Rhysode said, "but if we're going to do this, let's do it for Mara and not for the New Republic. Personally, I couldn't care less about accommodating the military or the senate after all that's happened."

Murmurs of agreement filled the room. Luke waited for everyone to settle down, then said, "I'm going to propose that the defectors meet with Mara and me alone."

Jacen shot to his feet. "You *do* think it's a trap!"

Luke turned to him. "I don't know that it is or it isn't."

"Then let them meet with me or Streen or Kam Solusar," Jacen said. "Any one of us would be willing to risk our lives to help Mara."

Cilghal looked at Jacen and Luke, her broad slash of mouth slightly ajar. "Your nephew is correct, Master. If there is some risk, you and Mara are the last ones who should assume it."

Luke glanced around the room. "What are you suggesting, that all of us meet with them?"

"You can count me in," Kyp said. "I'd like nothing better than a few moments alone with a Yuuzhan Vong."

"Kyp speaks for me, as well," Wurth said.

Lowbacca brayed forcefully. Em Teedee, the miniaturized translator droid hovering near Lowie's shoulder on his own repulsorlift jets, supplied, "We're all for one. Together, we are stronger than the sum of our individual powers." Built by Chewbacca and programmed by C-3PO, Em Teedee spoke in the voice of the protocol droid, but absent his sometimes prissy inflection.

"I stand with Lowbacca," Streen said. "Whatever insights are to be gained about the Yuuzhan Vong will be shared by all of us."

"I, too," Tenel Ka added.

Luke clasped his hands behind his back and paced to the windows. The camaraderie heartened him. He thought back to the early years of the academy, and how his students had rallied to defeat the spirit of a dark Jedi who had sought to possess Yavin 4. Some of those in the room now had been there—Cilghal, Streen, even the kids. And some who had joined the fight were dead, as were Cray Mingla, Nichos Marr, Miko Reglia, Daeshara'cor . . .

Luke exhaled slowly, turned, and nodded. "I'll inform New Republic Intelligence of our decision. We'll meet with the defectors as soon as they arrive on Coruscant."

"One for the human," the dealer said, pressing a sabacc chip-card from the shoe.

An Ithorian card-bearer fitted with a paddle appendage where an arm should have been slid his wafer-thin device beneath the microcircuitry-embedded card and deposited it faceup in front of Han.

"Six of sabers," the dealer announced to the table.

Han calculated the total of the three cards he held and made a subtle waving motion with the forefinger and middle finger of his right hand, signaling the dealer that he would stand.

The dealer, a Bith whose opposable thumb and little fingers made for adroit card handling, looked to the Sullustan seated to Han's left for instructions. The heavy-jowled, jut-eared being rapped his fist once on the long table's nonskid surface and failed to repress a grin when a card flipped by the bearer's paddle turned out to be the face card Endurance.

The Bothan in the next seat folded, as did the diminutive Chadra-Fan alongside him. That left Han playing against the Sullustan, and to Han's right, an Ithorian and a Rodian—both of whom were unscrupulous vendors—the latter holding tightly to the two cards originally dealt to him, and with none on the table.

Han leaned back to show Droma his concealed cards: the Ace of coins, worth fifteen, and the one of staves—

recently altered by the sabacc randomizer from the Queen of Air and Darkness. With the six of sabers showing, the hand had a total value of twenty-two, a mere point away from a pure sabacc. He felt certain that the Sullustan wasn't holding more than twenty, despite the Endurance face card. The Ithorian's two table cards alone valued twelve, and from the way the alien had bet, Han doubted he held more than eighteen or nineteen. As for the Rodian, his two cards certainly totaled more than twenty but probably not more than twenty-two. A pure sabacc dealt to him earlier in the game had all but propelled him from his chair, and while he had greeted the present hand with excitement, there was nothing in his glassy, bulging eyes to suggest another instant win.

No one had fixed the value of any chip-cards by placing them in the interference field at the table's center.

Additional cards were refused all around, and final bets were placed. Unless the randomizer struck again, Han knew he had the pot.

The Sullustan called, and everyone showed their hands.

Han's instincts were right on the money, and he won his third straight pot. Under the wary and watchful gaze of a human pit boss with enhanced vision for spotting skifters—rigged chip-cards sneaked into the game—or players attempting to glimpse color reflections from ionization of the interference field, the bearer's paddle gathered the cards, and the banker assembled Han's winnings into neat stacks and slid them across the table.

The game was being conducted in the *Queen*'s sole extant gaming parlor, where a couple of uvide and jubilee wheels spun noisily in the background and a half-dozen Twi'lek women with tattooed head-tails moved about with trays of free drinks, transdermal drugs, and a host of smokable substances.

Curiously, Droma had ridiculed Han's decision to buy into the game—at the cost of almost all his credits—even when Han had justified it as a means of delaying the inevitable return to his filthy cabin, where Han had reluctantly passed the previous night and most of the day, and even the current win failed to disabuse the Ryn of disdain.

"An enterprise entirely lacking in depth," Droma commented as Han, with arrogant delight, made even neater stacks of his winnings. "And humans, owing perhaps to their evolutionary good fortune, seem more inclined to be taken in than any other species."

Han's retort was a smug snort, but he couldn't help recalling a similar sentiment he'd heard expressed more than twenty years earlier.

"Of all the races who gamble their well-being on uncertain returns—and there aren't many, statistically—the trait's most noticeable in humans, one of the most successful life-forms."

The speaker had been a Ruurian academic named Skynx, who had accompanied Han on the search for Xim the Despot's treasure.

"Laugh all you want," Han told Droma, "but I've been playing since I was fourteen, and sabacc once won me a ship, not to mention a planet."

"It's a fool's enterprise, nonetheless," Droma said.

Han smiled cavalierly. "I'll take a handful of luck to a cargo hold of wisdom any day."

The Bith loaded a new deck into the shoe and showed the palms of his hands—ritual assurance that he had nothing up his sleeves, as well as the signal for the start of a new round.

Traditional sabacc games pitted player against player in a contest to come closest to negative or positive twenty-three, without bombing out by breaking twenty-three or holding cards equal to zero. And while the *Queen*'s casino employed the standard four-suit, seventy-six-chip-card deck, randomizer, and interference field, the house not only demanded a buy-in price but withheld 20 percent of all pots—the entire pot if all players folded—half of which went into a special bank for rounds played against the house.

The *Queen* also had special rules governing pure sabacc hands. A positive twenty-three beat out negative twenty-three, but a two-card twenty-three beat out a three-card twenty-three, and no player was permitted to request more than three cards in addition to the two received on the deal.

The next round found Han with an initial value of fourteen, a twenty after one randomizer hit, but a thirteen after an unexpected second randomizer hit. Even so, he drew the five of coins and, through skillful bluffing, managed to keep three of his opponents betting until the call, when he raked in another pot.

The following round went much the same, though he wound up edging out the Sullustan by a mere point and winning with a fifteen. With his original buy-in stake, plus his winnings, Han had close to eight thousand credits stacked on the table.

"When they fold every time you bet a good hand, you play to their eyes," he bragged to Droma, just loudly enough to be heard.

He was about to ante up for another round when Droma called, "Bank!"

While Han's jaw was dropping, the pit boss hurried over to confer with the cashier, who shortly announced that Han needed 7800 credits to play the hand against the house.

Murder in his eyes, Han whirled on Droma. "Is that fright wig of yours growing down into your brain? If I lose, I'm cleaned out!"

Droma merely shrugged. "The randomizer is the only worthy opponent in this game. The randomizer is fate. Play against that if you want to impress me."

"Impress you?" Han echoed irascibly. "*Impress* you? Why you—"

"You called 'bank,' " the strapping pit boss reminded in a threatening tone. "Are you playing or not?"

Everyone at the table looked at Han, and a crowd of passengers began to gather round. To decline would not only be gutless but an insult to the players he had nearly cleaned out. He shoved the credits toward the center of the table.

"Bank," he grated.

As the Bith prized cards from the shoe, the passengers pressed closer to watch. Outside of tournaments, it was rare to see so many credits wagered on a single hand.

Han carefully lifted his two cards and forced them apart: twenty-one.

Almost immediately the randomizer struck, reducing the value to thirteen.

He threw the Commander of flasks, worth twelve, into the interference field—just short of another strike, which converted the one of coins into the Idiot, with a value of zero.

He asked for a card and drew the Evil One, valued at negative fifteen, leaving him with a total value of negative three. Whispered disappointment spread through the crowd.

Tension mounted as Han studied the shoe, glanced at the randomizer, then studied the shoe some more. When he announced that he would stand, the audience gasped in unison. A twelve in the interference field and a negative fifteen on the table; he was either an inspired player or a born loser.

The Bith turned over the house's two cards, the one of staves and the Commander of coins, for a total of thirteen. House rules required the dealer to draw a third card on a twelve or thirteen.

The Bith's hand went to the shoe and the crowd held its breath. A ranked card would put the house on the wrong side of twenty-three, and a face card could very well drop the house into the negative. Han appeared to have a fighting chance. A rivulet of sweat coursed down the side of his face and dripped from his jaw.

But when the bearer's paddle lifted the card, Han caught a glimpse of its reflection in the interference field.

The nine of sabers.

A twenty-two for the dealer.

Han's heart sunk.

In the same instant the randomizer struck for an unprecedented third time. Han's Evil One became the Mistress of staves, increasing his total to twenty-five! But then the Idiot transformed, as well—to the Queen of Air and Darkness, valued at negative two, for a total of twenty-three.

Pure sabacc.

Sitting tall in the chair once more, Han showed his hand. Wild applause erupted behind him. He had won again.

The banker shoved Han's winnings forward and closed the table. As the disheartened players left and the crowd dispersed—save for a Twi'lek woman trying desperately to attract Han's attention—Han counted out his initial buy-in stakes and pushed the hefty remainder to Droma.

"Here," he snarled, "buy yourself a new outfit—something that doesn't shout."

Droma grinned and swept the credits into his two-toned beret. "I know some folks on the lower decks who can use this."

Han showed him a gimlet stare. "You knew I'd win."

"I may have had a hunch," Droma allowed.

"So you're a player."

Droma shook his head. "But I am familiar with the cards. The Ryn invented them. The ranked and face cards, that is."

Han made a face. "This I gotta hear."

"Each card embodied certain spiritual principles," Droma went on. "In sum they were a training device for spiritual growth, you might say—but never meant to be used in a game of chance."

He reached across the table for one of the discarded decks. Fanning the deck in one hand, Droma rid it of the suit cards numbered one through eleven. The rest he spread in a semicircle on the tabletop.

"The ranked cards—Commander, Mistress, Master, and Ace—represented individuals of speci .c inclination, with the staves corresponding to spiritual enterprise, the flasks to emotional states, the sabers to mental pursuits, and the coins to material well-being. But regard the eight pairs of face cards and ask yourself why a game would include such titles as Balance, Endurance, Moderation, Demise."

Droma plucked the Master of staves from the semicircle and placed it in front of Han. "You," he said. "A dark-haired man of formidable strength and intuition, but often brash and self-absorbed. Despite his years, he charges boldly into every situation, regardless of the odds, sometimes banging his head on things. And yet he is at heart a seeker of knowledge."

"Hokey religions," Han said under his breath, but deliberately loud enough for Droma to hear.

Grinning, Droma leaned away from him, twirling the left tip of his mustache. "Think so? Let's see what we can see."

Leaving the Master of staves undisturbed, he gathered the rest of the ranked and face cards, shuffled them deftly, performed a one-handed cut, and set the abridged deck on the table. Peeling a card from the top of the pack, he placed it faceup below the Master of staves.

"The Master of flasks," Droma said. "A father figure, protector, or close friend. Loving, dedicated, loyal to a fault." He fingered another card from the pack, placed it on top of and perpendicular to the Master of flasks, and frowned. "Crossed by the Evil One. A harmful addiction in some cases, but more often a powerful enemy."

Han swallowed, but said nothing.

The third card—Demise—crossed Han's card in the same way. Han felt Droma's gaze on him.

"You lost a friend—a protector?" Droma asked.

Han put on his best sabacc face. "Go ahead, finish with your little divination."

Droma placed a card to the left of the Master of staves. "The Idiot. The start of a journey or quest, usually down an unknown path. A sometimes unsettling plunge into the unknown." The next card crowned the Master. "Moderation—but inverted. A craving for retribution or vengeance."

Han nodded and snorted. "You're good, you're really good. You watch and you pay close attention to what people say. That way you get a sense of who someone is or what someone's going through. Then you put it all in a nicely wrapped package"—he indicated the spread of cards—"and feed it right back. Just like your second-guessing what someone's about to say."

Droma made his face long in feigned astonishment. "I'm simply laying out cards."

Han gestured in dismissal. "You arranged the cards when you shuffled. Or maybe you're dealing seconds."

Droma lifted his hands to his shoulders and nodded to the deck. "Draw four cards in rapid succession and line them up alongside the Master of staves."

Han hesitated, then did so. But before Droma could speak, he jabbed his finger at the first of the quartet. "Don't tell me what it means, just tell me what the location stands for."

"Someone who might be affected by your actions."

Disquiet tugged at the corners of Han's mouth as he scrutinized the card. "The Commander of sabers," he said quietly. "Maybe a younger version of the Master. Headstrong, clever . . ."

"And brave," Droma added. "An able fighter."

Anakin? Han asked himself. He moved his finger to the next card.

"It occupies the place of unforeseen consequence or hidden danger," Droma supplied.

"The Queen of Air and Darkness," Han mused, examining her depiction for clues. "Could be a person hiding something. Or a delusion, maybe."

Droma nodded. "Something unrevealed." He indicated the next card in the line. "How best to proceed."

"Balance," Han said. "Being able to stay on your feet when the going gets rough and the ground around you's shaking."

"Adjustment to what life dishes out," Droma elaborated. "Persistence in the face of adversity. And spiritual power."

Han's finger fell on the final card. "The future?"

Droma rocked his head back and forth. "A likely outcome. In this case, what the Idiot may find."

Han scowled and regarded the card. "The Star. But upside down—inverted." He glanced at Droma. "Not all it could be. Less than a complete success."

Droma smiled with his eyes and nodded. "Congratulations, Roaky. Fortune has granted you a glimpse of its innermost designs."

TWENTY-ONE

Above a gibbous Obroa-skai, Harrar's faceted ship hung in the shadow of the most recently arrived of the Yuuzhan Vong's yorik coral battleships, under the command of Malik Carr. Where the one dazzled the eye, the other looked to have been cast fully formed from the churning bowels of some impossibly gargantuan volcano.

In the command center of the smaller vessel, Malik Carr, Nom Anor, Harrar, Commander Tla, and his chief tactician studied a holographic swirl of star systems given life by data fed to the war coordinator lodged in Obroa-skai's mutilated surface, and relayed to the faceted ship by signal villip. In dimly lighted recesses, attendants and acolytes stood still as statues.

"The auguries are encouraging," Commander Tla was telling his peer. "Our campaign proceeds apace. In addition, a group of captives fresh from Ord Mantell's orbital station is being assigned to a special project that may provide us with new insights into the species that dominate this galaxy."

Commander Malik Carr nodded in approval. "Warmaster Tsavong Lah will be pleased to learn." A tall male whose incised face and bare upper torso touted an illustrious military career, he wore a vibrant turban, which conformed closely to his elongated skull. His shoulders and hips bulged with newly acquired bone and cartilage, from which hung a resplendent command cloak. "Where do the auguries direct us next?"

Tactician Raff answered. "The environment is rich with targets, Commander Malik Carr." He instructed the signal villip to enlarge and enhance specific sectors within an area of space referred to by the New Republic as the Colonies. "In anticipation of our striking at the Core, the enemy has deployed its fleets at hyperspace egresses throughout this region. The worlds that lie along our side of the frontier—Borleias, Ralltiir, Kuat, and Commenor—all make for excellent staging areas for an eventual assault on Coruscant, the capital world."

"The auguries suggest caution, however," Harrar interjected.

The tactician concurred. "At this moment in the perpetuation, careful thought must be given to the battle plan. Advance too slowly and we provide the New Republic with an opportunity to initiate counterattacks along our flanks. Advance too quickly and we run the risk of encountering more resistance than we are prepared to overcome."

Malik Carr grunted. "Additional warships are forthcoming from Sernpidal. With those we will be able to engage and occupy the enemy on numerous fronts. At the same time, we may be able to discover a more subtle approach to Coruscant." He looked at Nom Anor. "What of these Hutt creatures I've been hearing about, Executor? Do they pose a threat?"

Nom Anor advanced a step. "I have had several meetings with Borga the Hutt—in my guise as intercessor, of course—and am delighted to report that the Hutts are more interested in reaching an accord than in going to war, even in defense of their territory. Their sector of space is extensive, and includes numerous worlds that can easily be remade to provide us with yorik coral and other resources, one of which they have already placed at our disposal. Thus, a brief detour into Hutt space would not be unwarranted. I have also tasked some of my agents to sow disinformation in advance of your arrival."

"Duly noted," the battleship commander said. "And what of the Jedi?"

Harrar vouchsafed a thin smile. "Their days may be numbered, as well. We have taken steps to provide the Jedi with a crisis, by infiltrating one of our own among them—Priestess Elan."

"We have even gone so far as to provide the New Republic with minor victories in the Meridian sector and at Ord Mantell to substantiate the peerless value of our operative," Commander Tla added.

Harrar intruded eagerly. "It is our belief that Elan is en route to a meeting with the Jedi even now."

The priest stopped himself when he saw a herald appear at the entry to the command center, bearing a villip in his folded arms. Approaching Nom Anor, the herald stroked the villip's ridge, inducing it to evert. Nom Anor gestured for one of his own dedicated villips to be brought forth, and watched as the transforming villip took on the aspect of one of his Yuuzhan Vong underlings.

"Executor," the subaltern's facsimile began, "a group of your agents—those enlisted in the Peace Brigade—have apparently taken it upon themselves to return something seemingly lost to us."

Nom Anor's eyes grew wide. "Not Elan," he said in false hope.

"She, Executor."

"What?" Harrar said in alarm. "What's this?"

"How is this possible?" Nom Anor asked. "The Peace Brigade was never made aware of Elan's feigned defection. What's more, you yourself informed me that the Peace Brigade was occupied in Hutt space."

"As they were, Executor—at least until they learned of Elan's defection and capture."

Nom Anor's face contorted in mortification. "From whom?"

"I have not been able to ascertain."

"This is ludicrous," Harrar shouted. "How do they plan to retrieve her?"

"Apparently they have been apprised of the means by which she is to be relocated to Coruscant."

Nom Anor's villip mirrored his rancorous expression. "Impossible. Even I had difficulty sorting through the New Republic's subterfuges. Even within the Intelligence division the route is a closely guarded secret."

"I know only that the Peace Brigade is planning to move against a passenger ship bound for Bilbringi," the subaltern said. "They have persuaded at least one of their immediate controllers to assist them. And they have a dovin basal in their possession."

"We must see to it that they are prevented from interfering." Harrar became angrier as he spoke. "At any cost."

Nom Anor induced his own villip to return to normal and dismissed the herald. Commanders Tla and Malik Carr were watching him and the priest closely.

"Is anything wrong, Executor?" Malik Carr asked at last, raising a faint eyebrow.

Nom Anor traded quick glances with Harrar. "A possible setback involving our operative," he conceded. Regaining control of his indignation, he gestured negatively and fixed his gaze on Malik Carr. "Nothing we can't handle. Though I may have need of your swiftest frigate, Commander."

"We're husband and wife," Showolter told the Askajian officer stationed at the most forward of the *Queen of Empire*'s starboard boarding gates. The starliner was in stationary orbit above the planet Vortex. "Recently displaced from Sernpidal."

"Where the moon came down?" the officer asked.

"Unfortunately, yes."

"What was it you folks called that moon? I remember hearing on the newsnet . . ."

"Tosi-karu."

"That was it." The stout near-human regarded Vergere. "Is . . . he with you?"

"She," Showolter amended. "Our servant."

The boarding officer nodded uncertainly, then returned the identity documents and tickets Showolter had provided. "Your stateroom is located on deck twenty-four, berthing space twelve. Welcome aboard, and safe journey."

Showolter took Elan's hand and led her and Vergere to the nearest bank of interdeck transfer tubes—broad cylinders that functioned like turbolifts, but without cars. Buoyed by repulsorlift fields, riders could ascend or descend as necessary, in lift tubes or drop shafts respectively.

The *Queen* was just waking from relative night, and clamorous throngs of refugees were lined up at the species-specific refreshers or searching for food. Droids rushed about performing tasks that were assumed to be beneath the dignity of living beings.

Despite the ease of the trip from Myrkr to Vortex and the smooth boarding, Showolter remained alert for signs that they were being watched or followed—by in-place NRI operatives or by unknowns. Vergere drew a few curious looks, but most folks were too preoccupied guarding their claims to deck space to take much interest in her. Still, Showolter knew that he wouldn't relax until his backup agents made contact.

The stateroom was more spacious than he had expected, with a sitting area of couch, table, and chairs, and four pull-down beds. Ushering the two defectors inside, Showolter checked the passageway before securing the door.

"Home sweet home," he said. "Until tomorrow, at least."

"What happens then?" Elan asked as she sat down on one of the platform beds.

"I'll tell you when the time comes."

She shook her head at him. "You still don't trust me, do you?"

"Nothing personal," he said. "Just following procedure."

"I'll bet you say that to all your defectors," Vergere offered from one of the other beds, atop which she roosted like an outsize avian.

Showolter set their luggage in a corner and made certain that the door to the adjoining suite was locked. He was about to make himself comfortable when someone knocked at the entry door.

Drawing his blaster from his shoulder holster, he positioned himself alongside the lock jamb. "What is it?"

"Cabin service," a resonant voice said in Corellian-accented Basic.

"We didn't request anything."

"Compliments of Captain Scaur," the man in the passageway replied. "He also invites you to be his guests at his table this evening."

"That can be arranged."

"I'll tell him you said so."

Showolter lowered his weapon and hit the hatch release. A tall, dark-haired, and dangerous-looking human entered, followed by a Rodian.

"I'm Darda," the man announced. "This is Capo."

Green, coarse-complected, and a bit hard on the human nose, Capo had a lithe grace and an easygoing air. Catching sight of Elan and Vergere, he drew his partner's attention to them.

"Where'd you come aboard?" Showolter asked.

Darda pivoted away from Elan to face him. "Right

here at Vortex. We were ahead of you in the boarding line."

Showolter grinned. "Yeah, I noticed you. Is it just you two?"

"Three more are already on board," Darda supplied. "Mingling with the refugees in steerage. They'll probably show themselves at dinner."

Showolter nodded. "Where's your cabin?"

Darda nodded his square chin at the passage door to the adjoining suite. "Right next to you."

"Convenient," Showolter remarked. "Someone at HQ actually did their homework." He glanced at Capo. "Where do you work out of, Capo?"

"Bilbringi," the Rodian said, pressing suction-cupped fingertips together.

Showolter's eyes returned to Darda. "You?"

"Lately out of Gamorr, but they're pulling me back to Coruscant after this op."

Showolter looked surprised. "Is that right? Who's your new boss?"

Darda had his mouth open to respond when another knock sounded at the door.

Showolter gestured for silence and raised his blaster once more. "What is it?"

"Cabin service," a human voice replied.

The three NRI operatives exchanged disconcerted glances. Showolter gestured Darda and Capo into the adjoining suite and motioned for Elan and Vergere to remain still. When the passage door closed behind Capo, Showolter moved to the entrance.

"We didn't request anything."

"Compliments of Captain Scaur. He also invites you to be his guests at his table this evening."

"That can be arranged."

"I'll tell him you said so."

With an economy of movement, Showolter slid his blaster under a pillow on the couch, arranged two chairs so that their backs were turned to the passage door, and opened the entry door. A muscular human male and a handsome Bothan female entered, introducing themselves as Jode Tee and Saiga Bre'lya.

Shrewdly, Showolter maneuvered them into the chairs and asked where they'd come aboard.

"We've been aboard since Ord Mantell," the Bothan said after she'd had a pure eyeful of Elan and Vergere.

"Is it just the two of you?"

"Two others were supposed to have come aboard at Anobis, but they haven't made contact yet."

"Where's your cabin?" Showolter asked Jode Tee.

"Ten doors down the passageway, starboard side."

"Convenient." Showolter sat on the couch, facing them, his hand closing slowly on the concealed blaster. "Where are you based?"

"Bilbringi," Jode Tee said.

"What about you, Saiga?"

"Ord Mantell."

The passage door began to open, revealing Darda with a blaster raised to his chin in a two-handed grip. Showolter made brief eye contact and laughed to cover any sounds the door might make in opening wide.

"So was that serious about dinner at the captain's table?" he asked.

"I wish," Saiga said, smiling.

Showolter brought the blaster out with cool efficiency and fired. The bolt flashed between Jode Tee and the Bothan, hitting Darda squarely in the chest. Darda flew back from the doorway as if kicked by a gundark, but managed to squeeze off one blast that caught Jode Tee in the back, propelling him onto the couch.

Showolter and Saiga hit the deck. At the same time, Vergere leapt from her bed to protect Elan, forcing her into a corner of the cabin and planting herself between the priestess and harm.

Capo slithered through the doorway on his belly, weapon extended in front of him and firing repeatedly. Blaster beams ricocheted sibilantly around the stateroom. Showolter rolled across the floor until he hit the corridor bulkhead. With nowhere to go, he risked a shot at the doorway, but by then Capo had moved. Showolter rolled back the way he came and managed to get to one knee, but Capo had him in his sights and fired. The blast found his left shoulder, just under the collarbone, and spun him completely around. The smell of burned cloth and seared flesh filled his nostrils. But even as he was falling, shots from the floor told him that Saiga had joined the fight.

A bloodcurdling scream rang out, followed by an agonizing moan. Showolter blinked his eyes open in time to see a wounded Capo dragging himself toward the front door of the adjacent suite, and Saiga—propelling herself backward on her rear—pressing a hand to the gaping hole a blaster bolt had opened in the center of her chest.

Showolter came to his feet and staggered into the adjoining cabin space, gun raised in one shaking hand. Capo was already halfway into the corridor, and all

Showolter's shot did was provide him with an impetus to hurry. Showolter stumbled to the door, but only to close and lock it. Wisps of smoke coiling from his charred shoulder, he wobbled back to his cabin.

His fingers found no pulse in Jode Tee's throat. Throwing Elan and Vergere a quick look, he crawled over to Saiga, who had propped herself against the entry door.

"Did you get him, Major?" she asked weakly.

Showolter shook his head.

"Who were they?"

"I don't know, but they had the code."

The Bothan's eyes widened. "Our code?"

"Same one I was given."

"Then how did you know we were on the level?"

"One of them claimed to be working out of Gamorr. I guess whoever supplied the code didn't know that we phased out that safe house a long while ago."

A pained groan escaped Saiga.

"Saiga," Showolter said sharply. "You said we have two more aboard."

Eyelids fluttering, she managed a nod.

"Who are they? How were you instructed to make contact? Saiga. Saiga!"

Her eyes rolled up into her head. A final breath rattled from her lungs and she died.

Showolter's eyes glazed over. He turned and sat unmoving on the floor.

"You're hurt," Elan said, close to his ear, in what sounded like genuine concern.

The *Queen* trembled innocently. "Lightspeed," Showolter slurred, mostly to himself. He tried to focus on Elan. "Got to get you out of here. Capo'll be coming back with reinforcements." He made a futile attempt at standing, then pointed to the luggage. "In my bag . . . painkillers and bandages."

Vergere was suddenly beside him, her slanted eyes brimming with tears. "Let me help you," she said.

Cupping her delicate hands, she held them to her eyes. Then she rubbed her moistened palms together and pressed them to Showolter's wound. He locked his teeth against intense but short-lived pain, then he took a long, shuddering breath.

"Better?" Vergere asked.

"Yes," he told her, plainly astonished.

"It's a temporary repair. You're going to need medical attention."

He nodded in understanding, pushed himself to his feet, and rearmed his blaster. Cautiously opening the door, he peered into the passageway.

"We're leaving," he said. "Our only chance is to locate my backup."

"But you don't know who you're looking for," Elan reminded.

Showolter nodded grimly. "I'm hoping they'll recognize me."

Elan offered her shoulder for support, and the three of them headed for the communal areas belowdecks.

TWENTY-TWO

Han emerged from the portable refresher like a man on his last legs, slamming the door behind him as if to prevent something horrible from escaping. "I'll bet anything some Gamorrean's been in there," he growled to Droma. "Can't stick to their own 'freshers. Have to foul ours."

"Is this your typical morning mood?" Droma asked.

Han glared at him. "No, but it's my mood when I don't get any sleep."

The Ryn made a sound of dismissal. "I didn't ask to share your cabin space. I was fine being in steerage."

Han stopped short in the passageway. "I don't mind sharing my cabin space. What I mind's your tail in my face half the night!"

Droma frowned. "We Ryn are compelled to alter our sleep positions frequently. We never sleep twice in the same spot."

"Next time I'll reserve the ballroom," Han said sarcastically. "Would that give you enough room?"

"We're a superstitious folk," Droma explained as they resumed walking. "We never eat three times from the same bowl, and we have many rituals regarding bodily fluids—"

Han's hands flew up. "I don't want to know about them." He glanced at Droma. "Why are you still on board, anyway? You told me you were getting off at Vortex."

Droma shrugged. "I decided I'd have better luck finding a ride to Ralltiir from Bilbringi."

"Yeah," Han said slowly. "But I thought you only had fare to Vortex."

Droma adopted a docile look. "The truth is, I kept just enough of what you won at the sabacc table to secure onward passage."

"A fine thing," Han snorted.

The Ryn's former pugnacity resurfaced. "You'd begrudge me a modest remuneration, even after I didn't charge you for the card reading?"

Han stopped again. "Charge me? You're the one who laid out the cards."

"I don't recall you telling me to desist."

"I was being polite."

"Impossible," Droma said. "You're incapable."

"Hey, if you knew the company I keep . . ."

Droma looked bemused. "Rich and famous customers in the ship repair business?"

"I . . . Ah, this is hopeless," Han said.

Shouldering the travel pack, he accelerated, figuring that the Ryn's short legs wouldn't allow him to keep up. Leaving Droma behind after twenty long strides, he quickly rounded a corner in the passageway, then another. Then, out of nowhere, powerful arms grabbed him from behind, holding him fast and whirling him around.

"Han!" his interdictor said, latching on to him for dear life. "I won't even try to imagine how Scaur talked you into this duty, but I'm sure glad to see you."

"Scaur?" Han said, then recognition dawned. "Showolter? What the—"

"They hit us in the cabin, Han. Agents working for the Yuuzhan Vong. Killed two of my people. I got one of them, but the other got away—a slippery-looking Rodian named Capo. He's probably got reinforcements aboard, and they're probably searching for us now. You've got to find a secure place to hide them."

Han followed Showolter's hand to Elan and Vergere. "What's so important—"

"They're Yuuzhan Vong," Showolter rasped. "Defectors."

Mouth falling open, Han gave them a closer look, then returned his attention to Showolter. "How'd you—"

"Is this your partner?" the NRI operative asked.

Han spun, found Droma standing behind him, and frowned. "He's—"

"Just until Bilbringi, Han," Showolter said with sudden frailty.

"Han?" Droma asked in mild surprise.

Showolter collapsed back against the corridor wall and slid to his rear, with Han following him down. "Backup personnel will meet you in Bilbringi. They'll handle the transfer from there." The NRI officer groaned in pain.

Han realized he had blood on his hands and cut his eyes to Showolter's shoulder. "You're hurt—"

Showolter shook his head. "Can't afford the time. Send a med, I'll be all right."

Han rose and grabbed hold of a passing Duros steward. "This man needs to be moved to sick bay," he said. "Immediately—got it?"

The steward's round head bobbed nervously. "Yes, sir, immediately."

Han sent him flying with a shove and bent down to support Showolter. "You have a weapon?"

Showolter looked up at him and nodded. "You need it?"

Han restrained Showolter's hand from going to his shoulder holster. "No, you do—in case they find you."

Showolter screwed his eyes shut against a wave of pain. "Get going, Han."

Han turned to the defectors. "You two are coming with me. Any trouble and I'll stick you in a locker for the rest of the voyage, understand?"

The woman bristled, but the little alien nodded. "We're in your hands."

Han raised his index finger. "Remember that."

They hadn't gone ten meters when he heard Droma ask, "Han?"

"My code name," Han said over his shoulder.

"You're an intelligence agent?"

Han came to a halt and whirled around. "Stay out of this, Droma. We're not playing cards now."

Droma tilted his head. "Where are you planning to hide them—in your cabin? I know this ship better than you do. The only safe place is down below, where you can lose them in the crowd."

Han mulled it over, then nodded curtly. "All right. Let's go."

They set out for the nearest turbolift and were just shy

of them when the *Queen* sustained an unexpected jolt, powerful enough to send Elan off her feet. While Droma helped her up, Han hastened to a nearby observation blister. In place of the purplish-white chaos of light-speed, local space was fracturing into elongating lines of light. Han watched the lines compress to pinpoints, only to disappear and elongate once more. Finally, the pinpoints spun and arranged themselves into a starfield. In the middle distance a large, heavily pitted planetoid was revealed by a distant red-orange sun.

"We've been decanted," he said, not without puzzlement.

Droma glanced at a time display on the corridor wall. "It's too soon for Bilbringi—"

Howling sirens silenced him, and the PA annunciators came alive.

"Attention, all passengers," someone began in standard Basic. "This is the captain speaking. We have been forcibly reverted to realspace by unknown raiders. On-board confederates of the raiders are already assaulting the bridge."

"Raiders," Han sniggered. "They're not raiders, they're after someone in particular."

"Are you sure?" Droma asked warily.

Han thought back to another time he'd been separated from Chewie and the *Falcon*, booking commercial passage aboard the luxury liner *Lady of Mindor* with Fiolla, a companion far more enjoyable than the Ryn beside him. That ship, too, had suffered a phony pirate attack—led by Fiolla's traitorous right-hand man, Magg.

"Pretty sure," Han deadpanned.

"It's my people!" Elan said, stricken with fear. "They've

brought a dovin basal to bear on the ship." She dug short nails into Han's biceps. "Please don't let them find us—*please*!"

"Our shields have been rendered useless," the captain continued, "and our pursuers are coming alongside to board. Distress calls have been dispatched. I'm certain that someone will come to our aid. But in the meantime I request that everyone remain calm. I repeat, I urge everyone to remain calm."

"The nerve of him," Leia said, venting to Luke and Mara as she paced the tile floor of their apartment on Coruscant. "Telling me I'm incapable of understanding his grief, then running off to who knows where."

"You can take the boy out of Corellia, but you can't take Corellia out of the boy," Mara remarked from the couch.

Luke smiled faintly. "Leia, this isn't the first time Han's done something like this. Remember when he and I went to Crseih Research Station?"

"That was different," Leia said, shaking her head. "All right, he might have been yearning for the good old days, but that trip was more about his resignation from the military." She took a seat opposite her brother and his wife. "What he's doing now has nothing to do with nostalgia or his feeling hemmed in by an honorific. It's all about Chewie."

"But that's natural," Mara offered carefully.

"The grief and confusion, yes," Leia said. "But I think he's bent on vengeance." She sighed with purpose. "An old friend came to see him—a man named Roa. And off they went to Ord Mantell. Why would they venture so close to enemy-held space unless Roa had information of some sort?"

"But of what sort?" Luke asked. "The Yuuzhan Vong directly responsible for what happened on Sernpidal are dead. Han helped see to that himself at Helska 4."

"Luke, if that was any consolation, he wouldn't be out there," Leia said.

Luke saw the truth of it. "Even so, Han's beyond doing anything rash."

Leia pinched her lower lip between her teeth.

"When Han and I first met, he had me convinced that he was as reckless as he pretends to be," Luke continued. "But Obi-Wan said something I'll never forget. He said that there was more to Han than met the eye, and that he had real substance beneath his callous front." He smiled in recollection and looked at Leia. "Obi-Wan also said that only a special person would have a Wookiee for a companion—and that not just any Wookiee would be found roving the galaxy in the company of someone like Han."

Leia smiled sadly. "You don't have to remind me that Han's special. But that's just the problem. He needs that kind of companionship. Chewie and Han, I don't know, they seemed to steady each other. Chewie kept Han in check." Forcing herself to brighten, she turned to Mara. "I'm sorry to unleash on you two. I haven't even asked how you are."

"I'm feeling a lot stronger," Mara said, and let it go at that.

Leia smiled to herself, thinking about how deeply she cared for Mara. She asked herself how she could ever have distrusted her. "I thought you would have returned to Yavin 4 by now," she said after a moment.

Luke and Mara traded secretive looks. "Have you been informed that a Yuuzhan Vong has defected?"

Leia gaped at him. "What? When?"

"Shortly before you left for Ord Mantell. She's being brought to Coruscant for further debriefing."

"That's great news." Leia's eyes lit up briefly, then she trained them on Luke. "Does the defector have something to do with your still being here?"

"She's asked to meet with some of us."

" 'Us' as in Jedi?" Leia straightened in her chair. "Don't tell me you've agreed to it."

"She claims to have information about an illness the Yuuzhan Vong brought to our galaxy," Mara answered.

Leia brought one hand to her mouth. "But, Mara—"

A familiar shriek emanated from the adjoining room, and C-3PO hurried into view, jerky movements reflecting his inner agitation. Behind him rolled R2-D2, razzing and squeaking in what was clearly derision.

"Oh, please don't deactivate me!" C-3PO whined. "It wasn't my fault! I was only trying to help!"

R2-D2 zithered something scornful.

"Oh, switch off, you little . . . *drink caddy*."

"Threepio, calm down," Leia said. "What's this all about?"

He swung to her. "It was just on the newsnet, Mistress Leia. The *Queen of Empire* has been set upon by raiders, Rimward of the Bilbringi system! A distress call was dispatched, but the ship is probably being boarded at this very moment!"

Luke showed Leia a quizzical look.

"A vessel transporting refugees from Ord Mantell to the Core," she explained. "Threepio, access the newsnet and see if you can learn anything more. It may be pirates rather than Yuuzhan Vong."

"But Master Solo!" C-3PO said.

Leia stared. "What about him?"

C-3PO threw his hands in the air. "He's aboard the ship!"

Leia shook her head as if she hadn't heard him correctly. "Threepio, I don't understand—"

"Oh, I shouldn't have listened to him. But when he repeated the very same words you had used earlier, I was certain that my decision was justified."

"What words?"

"That sometimes it's better not to know what others are thinking. That sometimes it's less painful *not* to know the truth. You yourself said so, mistress."

R2-D2 whistled in sarcasm.

"Be still!" C-3PO said, hopelessly flustered.

"But what does all that have to do with Han being aboard the *Queen of Empire*?" Leia asked.

"Master Han asked me to arrange for his passage, and I did so by impersonating you, Mistress Leia—your vocal patterns, at any rate. And as to why I never made mention of Master Han's whereabouts, that was because you never once asked me directly if I had knowledge to that effect. Master Solo promised to arrange for my memories to be stored, in the event of my deactivation. That way I might be able to practice detachment—"

"Threepio!" Leia cut him off. "I'm certain you're not fully to blame—not when it concerns Han. But be honest with me now, why was he going to Bilbringi?"

"I know nothing of his reasons, Mistress."

R2-D2 rotated his domed head in a full circle, chirping and chittering, in a mix of rebuke and concern.

Leia narrowed her eyes at her brother. "So Han wouldn't do anything rash, huh?"

"Threepio," Luke said, "you said that the ship issued a distress call?"

"According to the newsnet reports, yes, Master Luke."

Luke looked at Leia. "Help is probably on the way."

Leia shook her head in anger. "Who's going to care enough about the lives of a few thousand refugees—especially if they've fallen into Yuuzhan Vong hands?"

"We could go," Luke said.

Mara threw him a dubious glance. "Even if we used the Namadii Corridor, we'd never make it in time."

Leia shot to her feet. "You're forgetting one thing. We'll be flying the fastest hunk of junk in the galaxy!"

TWENTY-THREE

"You mustn't let them find us!" Elan wailed into Han's ear as they threaded and shouldered their way through a mixed-species mob jamming the passageway.

Han angled his head just enough to throw her a warning look. "Either you pipe down or I turn you over to them myself!"

Elan's eyes became hooded.

Han snorted in response. "That the best you can do?"

"You'd do well to fear me," she told him.

"Save the threats for someone who cares, sweetheart. I'm only doing this because Showolter took a blaster beam for you, which means he thinks you're pretty important."

"More important than you know."

"We'll see about that. But right now you're my charge and you'll do as I say, got it?"

She allowed a defiant nod.

The captain's request for calm notwithstanding, disorder reigned. Reports of raiders were seldom greeted with enthusiasm, but the fact that most of the *Queen*'s passengers had experienced the Yuuzhan Vong firsthand had only made matters worse. Most were searching out places of concealment in utility lockers, ventilation shafts, cargo containers, and the narrow closets of lower deck cabins. As a consequence, crowds of passengers and crewmembers swarmed the corridors and clogged the interdeck transfer chutes. Many had made frantic dashes for escape-pod bays only to find them locked down; others had stormed the upper decks only to be repelled by armed contingents of ship's officers and vendors. Clearly intent on ignoring the time-proven dictum that surrender was the best survival strategy against pirates, the *Queen*'s refugees had turned the starliner into a seething catacomb.

In spite of everything, Han and company had succeeded in making their way to the docking bay deck, where if nothing else, the crowd was more dispersed and acquiescent. The worst that could happen, Han had told himself, is that he would end up in the same fix as Roa and Fasgo.

From a portside blister it was possible to observe the approach of the raiders' ship, from relatively below and slightly aft of the starliner. Running lights suggested a long, cylindrically shaped vessel, equivalent in size to an old Blockade Runner.

As it maneuvered within range of the *Queen*'s outboard illumination arrays, Han saw—much to his initial bafflement—that the ship was in fact an old Corellian corvette, though heavily modified and anodized a non-reflective black. In addition to the standard aft and ventral turbolaser batteries, the vessel's barrel-shaped bow boasted side-mounted Taim & Bak H9 cannons, and the dome that usually supported the communications array had been elongated to house either a formidable interdiction field generator—or the Yuuzhan Vong dovin basal that had tugged the *Queen* from hyperspace.

A trio of twenty-year-old *Martial*-class shuttles dropped from a retrofitted launch bay in the corvette's belly and made for the *Queen*'s own ventral docking bay deck. As the corvette's steering thrusters fired to bring her into alignment with the liner's portside airlock, Han got a good look at the starboard side, where just aft of the cockpit module the matte hull was emblazoned with the clasped-hands insignia of the Peace Brigade.

The words of Big Bunji's Aqualish lieutenant rushed to mind. *They have an operation planned for Bilbringi.*

Reck! Han said to himself in astonishment.

The Peace Brigade was after the defectors. Reck might already be aboard the *Queen*, he thought. With luck the mercenary would turn out to be the one Showolter claimed to have killed.

"Why are we standing here?" Elan asked anxiously. "The agent who escaped will be searching for us."

"That isn't a Yuuzhan Vong ship," Han told her.

"But that is," Droma said, pointing.

Han followed the Ryn's thin, velvety finger. High up in the blister, starlight glinting off a curve of scabrous surface, a flattened oval of yorik coral was paralleling the corvette, as if waiting in the wings. Fear laddered up Han's back as he recalled going to guns with similar Yuuzhan Vong at Dubrillion and Helska months earlier.

He turned to Elan. "I take back what I said. You must be pretty important for them to send a warship."

"As important to my people as I am to yours," she answered in a rush, without a trace of arrogance. "I have vital information for your Jedi Knights."

Han's brows knitted in interest. "Concerning what?"

"An illness my people introduced."

Before he could stop himself, Han had taken her roughly by the shoulders. "You're serious about this?"

She nodded, seemingly unruffled by the pressure of his hands. "I am against the use of bacterial weapons. Such a tactic demeans the Yuuzhan Vong."

Han tightened his grip and held her gaze. "Don't toy with me, sister. I was at Sernpidal and Dubrillion. I know exactly what you people are capable of, and a little thing like disease wouldn't rattle the Yuuzhan Vong conscience for a moment."

She raised her head haughtily. "It prompted me to secrete myself in an escape pod and allow myself to be captured by your forces."

Han looked over at the woman's wondrous companion. "And you?"

Vergere regarded him calmly. "I am with her."

Han let go of Elan and jerked a thumb toward Droma. "Yeah, well, he's with me and that doesn't say a whole lot."

"I couldn't have put it more delicately," Droma muttered.

Vergere looked at Droma, then Han. "I'm Elan's familiar. Where she goes, I follow."

Han ran his hand down his face. Out of nowhere another choice had been forced on him. By remaining on the *Queen* he might be able to finish the business with Reck, as Roa had put it. But if Elan was who she claimed to be, her safe conduct to Coruscant could mean a cure for Mara's illness.

He blew out his breath. Reck would have to wait.

"Maybe you are worth the effort after all," he said at last. "Which means we should be thinking about getting you some different clothes." He glanced at Droma. "Think you could rustle up new outfits for these two?"

Droma rocked his head from side to side. "Provided that they're not particular about size or fashion."

"They can't afford to be." Han paused to study Elan in earnest. "Is that the real you or are you wearing one of those living body sheaths?"

"I am adorned with an ooglith masquer."

Han nodded. "Well, a Yuuzhan Vong in a masquer fooled the members of the ExGal team on Belkadan. Let's see if it works as well with the Peace Brigade."

The *Queen* shuddered concussively as the corvette fastened herself alongside.

"The raiders will hook up with the survivors of the team that hit Showolter and begin a deck-by-deck search," Han said, his nose all but pressed to the transparisteel bubble. "They might sweep with sensors or dose the ship with obah or some other disabling gas." He whirled from the view. "We need to move fast."

"Where to?" Droma asked.

"The docking bay. Our only hope is to make off with one of their own ships."

A hatchet-faced Peace Brigade member met Reck Desh and his heavily armed escort as they emerged from the docking bay. Reck was outfitted with only a hand blaster, but his riot-helmeted cadre carried stun batons, stun nets, flechette launchers, and other antipersonnel weapons. By Reck's side marched the Yuuzhan Vong overseer he'd persuaded to join them in the retrieval operation, cloaked to conceal the telltale markings of his kind.

"Bridge is secured?" Reck asked as he brought everyone to a halt.

His confederate nodded. "But we've got problems. Which do you want to hear about first?"

Reck glanced around. "Where's Darda? Has he got them?"

"Darda's dead. The Rodian took a beam, too, but he'll live. Capo being the only one who's seen the defectors, we had him patched up. He's waiting for you in sick bay."

Sudden blood mottled Reck's face. "The two of them tried to take on the Intelligence team?"

"There were only three agents. Capo swears that two of them are dead, and the third is badly wounded. Besides, Darda insisted on it."

"And Capo listened to him," Reck grated. "I'll deal with him later."

"This was supposed to be in and out," the hulking human to Reck's left said. "There isn't time to search the entire ship. I say we abort."

Two of the other men grumbled agreement.

"Stow it!" Reck told them. "What else?" he asked the bearer of bad news.

"A Yuuzhan Vong ship has shown up."

"What?" Reck stared in disbelief, then swung to the Yuuzhan Vong among them.

The enemy operative nodded. "I was compelled to

reveal the nature of this operation to my superiors. It's likely that the ship has been sent to support us."

Reck gestured broadly and furiously. "That ship's going to draw New Republic forces into this! They've got too much to worry about to bother with chasing pirates. But with the Yuuzhan Vong involved—"

"Maybe the ship can buy us the time we need to flush out the defectors," the sharp-featured messenger said. "Even if New Republic forces do show. So long as we're the ones to return the defectors, nothing's changed, right?"

Reck tugged at his jewel-studded lower lip for a moment, then nodded. "Time the passengers knew the score."

The messenger pointed to a comlink on the bulkhead. "We can tie into the public address system."

Reck took the comlink in hand while one of his men fiddled with the channel selector. The man nodded when he found the proper channel, and Reck switched on the handheld device.

"Attention, all passengers," he began in Basic. "Just to set all of you at ease, we have no designs on hijacking, piracy, or turning you over to the Yuuzhan Vong. We're looking for two passengers in particular—a human-looking female and a nonhuman female, probably in the company of a wounded human male. If they want to come forward and save everyone a lot of grief, they should report to the bridge. If anyone has information on their whereabouts and is interested in collecting a substantial reward, they should also come to the bridge.

"If no one comes forward and we're forced to conduct a deck-by-deck search, we're going to go hard on every-

one, and you just might end up in enemy hands after all."
Reck paused briefly. "Oh, and a note to the two we're
searching for: we have ways of identifying you. If you
think you can hide or lose yourself in the crowd, think
again."

An ovoid of yorik coral, nubbed with cone-shaped
projectile launchers and propelled by a dovin basal of the
highest caliber, Commander Malik Carr's personal ship
was the swiftest vessel in his flotilla. From the bridge,
Nom Anor addressed villips consciousness-joined to the
commander and Harrar. His view through the crystalline
viewport took in not only the Peace Brigade's gunship
and the *Queen*, but also several cratered planetoids and
the distant sun beyond them, all in near syzygy.

"I have my agents under surveillance," Nom Anor updated. "The capabilities of the dovin basal aboard the
gunship have been neutralized, and I have commanded
our own dovin basal to prevent the gunship from sepa-
rating from the starliner. Should the Peace Brigade succeed in locating Elan, any attempt at embarkation will
fail."

"That corvette may carry fighters that will be able to
launch," Harrar's villip relayed with a grimace.

"Three vessels have already done so and have docked
aboard the liner. I will utilize our dovin basal to thwart
their return to the gunship."

"House a dovin basal in a remote to accomplish both
tasks and prepare to withdraw," Commander Malik
Carr's villip relayed. "By the time your agents discover
what has happened, New Republic ships will have come
to the liner's rescue."

Harrar's villip spoke. "No doubt your misguided operatives are aware of our presence. When they realize that they are unable to launch, they will wonder why you aren't coming to their assistance and they may attempt contact."

"Let them wonder," Nom Anor snapped. "I'm only interested in persuading the New Republic to conclude that the actions of the Peace Brigade are simply another attempt on our part to retrieve Elan."

He was interrupted by his second on the bridge, fists snapped to opposite shoulders in apology for the intrusion.

"A ship emerging from hyperspace, Executor." The subaltern pointed out the viewport in the direction of the nearby primary. "Our signal villip identifies it as a New Republic cruiser-carrier."

Nom Anor addressed the villips. "The arrival of that vessel should simplify matters. As suggested, I will position the dovin basal in a remote. The Peace Brigade will attempt to flee and be apprehended, and Elan will remain in custody."

He swung to the bridge officer. "Make ready to engage the enemy's starfighters, as well. You may disapprove of this, Subaltern, but you're going to have to make it appear as if you were chased off. You have my word that your losses will not be held against you."

TWENTY-FOUR

Still recovering from the bruising it had taken at the battle of Ord Mantell, the cruiser-carrier *Thurse* winked into realspace at the Rimward edge of the Bilbringi system, X-wings tumbling from her launch bays like bedevilers from an agitated nest. Between the cruiser and the distant blip that authenticators had recognized as a Yuuzhan Vong warship floated the *Queen of Empire*, with what appeared to be a seasoned corvette nursing at one of the starliner's airlocks.

Apex of the fighter formation that gradually assumed shape, Wing Commander Kol Eyttyn chinned the helmet switch that opened the command net.

"*Thurse*, we have visual on the Yuuzhan Vong ship. Low-profile coral oval. Looks to be frigate class or thereabouts. Reminds me of the stones I'd skim across water in the carefree days of my youth."

"Let's see that it doesn't come skimming this way, Commander," the voice of the cruiser-carrier's captain said in his left ear.

"That's affirmative."

Screen chatter from the R2 unit socketed behind the cockpit canopy told him that short-range scans had picked up a flock of Yuuzhan Vong fighters—skips. Eyttyn chinned open the tactical net.

"Blips are enemy vessels, coralskipper designation," he told the pilots of the gathered squadrons. "Enable countermeasures and deflector shields. Inertial compensators to maximum boost. Keep in mind we're sacrificing laser yield for increased bursts. That means mixing it up at close quarters, so listen to your group leaders and stick to your wingmates."

Eyttyn called on the life-maintenance system controls to expand the starfighter's inertial compensator field. While the volume of protection afforded by the enhanced field had been determined to be sufficient for tricking the compensator into treating Yuuzhan Vong–created gravitic anomalies like any others, the field could be overwhelmed by large dovin basals or a confluence of singularities, such as might easily be fashioned by three or more skips.

The same held true for the sensor database package developed in the wake of engagements in the Outer Rim. While the retrofitted tracking adjunct augmented a pilot's ability to target coralskippers, substantial variations in the size and shape of the fighters limited the effectiveness of the array. As ever, an X-wing was only as good as its pilot and droid.

Eyttyn increased the gain on the sensors and, with his thumb, flicked weapons control to lasers, quadding them up so all four would fire with a single squeeze of the stick's trigger.

"Red and Green Squadrons will lay back to deal with assaults directed at the *Thurse*. Blue will form up behind me to take the fight to the command ship. All other squadrons will break on my command."

Eyttyn tightened his seat harness and waited for the droid to affirm that the coralskipper swarm was within range; then he flipped a switch that locked the X-wing's S-foils in attack position and gave the word to engage.

Almost immediately the coralskippers opened fire with their volcano-like guns, loosing a storm of fiery projectiles. The opposing sides met in a dizzying contest of feints, rolls, and loops, punctuated by torrents of laserfire and streams of deadly plasma. The tactical net grew cacophonous with warnings, exuberant outbursts, and shrill cries for help.

"Blue Four, skip locking onto your six."

"Thanks for the heads up, Three. I think I can shake him."

"I've got your flank, Four."

"Blue Eight, can you give me a fix on Blue Ten?"

"Negative, Ten. Things are fast and furious just now."

"Watch your starboard, Five. Three skips angling in!"

"Scissor right, Five, they're on you!"

"I can't shake them! Shields down to 30 percent!"

"Hold tight, Five. I'm on my way!"

Though loud in his right ear, Eyttyn ignored what cries he could. For Blue Squadron it was going to be a matter of avoiding hits and conserving firepower. While individually piloted, the yorik coral fighters were thought to answer at least in part to organic elements aboard the command vessels—what the enemy called yammosks, or war coordinators—like the droid ships of old. Eyttyn knew better than to expect that Blue Squadron could take out the ship, even with proton torpedoes, but as

New Republic forces had proved time and again, distraction was often enough to sow turmoil among the coralskipper pilots and slow the responses of their craft.

Yuuzhan Vong fliers relied less on evasive tactics than on the capabilities of their shield-nullifying dovin basals, in any case. As he maneuvered through the swarm, Eyttyn could feel the influence of that macabre, biogenetically hatched technology tugging at the X-wing's shields with invisible fingers. The R2 unit could feel the tug, as well, and signaled its dismay with flurries of translated code that scrolled across the cockpit display screen.

Another thing to ignore, Eyttyn told himself.

With two skips closing on him, he rolled the X-wing up on its stabilizers and veered away to starboard. In the same instant, his wingmate peeled away in an abrupt bank, then dived to rejoin Eyttyn on the original approach vector. Another pair of coralskippers swooped beneath him, but only one came about in pursuit and was easily evaded.

Eyttyn glanced at his range finder. Already the frigate was growing larger in his canopy, but it had yet to open fire, and probably wouldn't until Blue Squadron began their runs against it.

Off to Eyttyn's left, Blue Four began to wobble under the influence of two skips that had fastened themselves to the X-wing's tail. Eyttyn's wingmate dropped back to loose a burst at one of the craft, but it refused to take the bait. Hoping that Blue Four's lead pursuer might cut across his own path, Eyttyn decreased velocity, but the coralskipper pilot divined Eyttyn's tactic and was in and out of his sights in a flash.

In a dazzling display of evasive maneuvers, Blue Three

broke from the pack to speed to his wingmate's aid. Halfway there, however, destructive projectiles sought and found him, blowing the X-wing to pieces.

The two coralskippers chasing Blue Four accelerated, settled into kill position, and opened fire. Caught by an ellipsis of blazing missiles, Blue Four vanished in a roiling of crimson fire and white-hot gas.

Eyttyn summoned his remaining ships into a weaving, mutually protective circle. Laser bolts from Blues Eight and Nine sheared off chunks of an encroaching skip; crippled, the ship spiraled off to port and exploded.

Not a moment later, Blue Six made a kill, but soon found himself trapped at the center of intense return fire. Shields pilfered, the X-wing sustained hit after hit, splitting into four pieces before disappearing from sight.

Eyttyn glanced at his primary monitor. Bright red damage icons peppered the screen. "Stay with your wingmates," he warned over the net. "Conserve fire until we're in the pocket."

He snap-rolled to bring one Yuuzhan Vong killer under his weapons. With a belly-up slew to starboard, he seized the coralskipper in his sights and tightened his middle finger on the stick's auxiliary trigger button. With the X-wing's lasers cycling more rapidly than they would have in single-fire mode, each bolt burned with a scarlet intensity that belied its reduced strength. Dazzled by the task of distinguishing the heavier, more lethal bolts from the hail of essentially harmless bolts loosed by the quadded lasers, the skip's dovin basal failed, and a packet of Eyttyn's energy darts found their mark.

The coralskipper cracked apart like pumice and disappeared.

Blue Six avenged, Eyttyn raced through the Yuuzhan Vong's debris cloud of glowing motes to close on another coralskipper. A sustained, convergent burst of flickers from the X-wing's wingtips caught the enemy unprepared, destroying him, as well.

With Blue Squadron down to nine fighters, Eyttyn formed everyone up into a trailing wedge. But no sooner had they closed on the frigate than they instantly became targets of its craterlike gun ports. Another X-wing was annihilated, then another, although by then Eyttyn was in position to make a strafing run. Jinking to port, he paid out a pair of proton torpedoes, only to watch in utter stupefaction as the scintillating spheres soared away into empty space.

He had grown accustomed to seeing laser beams and torpedoes swallowed by gravitic anomalies, but this was something different. It was as if the enemy ship itself had disappeared.

He glanced frantically around the canopy, thinking that he had somehow become disoriented and that the frigate was actually above him. Star-swept darkness met his gaze in all directions. Data scrolls from the R2 were telling him that the Yuuzhan Vong ship had moved, but the droid was obviously mistaken. No vessel could move that quickly—even when making microjumps.

"Where'd the blasted thing go?" he asked over the net.

"Don't know, Commander," Blue Two responded. "I was right on your Six when it disappeared—in a blink."

"Cloaking device?" Blue Eleven suggested.

"Well, it vanished like it was cloaked," Eyttyn said, "but I figure we'd still pick up residual gravitic traces from a ship that massive."

"Hyperspace," Blue Ten interjected.

"Not without taking me with it," Eyttyn told him. "It's—"

"Commander," Blue Two cut him off. "I've located it."

Eyttyn aimed the X-wing's scopes at the coordinates Blue Two supplied, and sure enough, the frigate was there—two thousand kilometers away.

Blue Eleven offered a stunned whistle. "That ship jumped two thousand clicks in a split second."

Eyttyn forced a breath and tightened his grip on the controls. "Adjust course," he ordered. "If it's a game of tag they want, it's a game of tag they'll get."

The *Millennium Falcon* burst into realspace on the far side of Bilbringi's profusion of orbital habitats and heavily mined planetoids. Leia and Luke had the forward seats, with Mara behind Luke in the chair normally assigned to a communications officer and C-3PO in the navigator's chair. R2-D2 had planted himself at the rear of the cockpit, with his grasping arm clamped to a slender conduit.

In the fan-shaped viewport, the *Queen of Empire* was well off to starboard. Rimward, local space was a pyrotechnic welter of laser beams, radiant projectiles, fusial thrusters, and blossoming explosions.

"Unidentified Corellian freighter," an incensed voice barked over the comm, "this is Captain Jorlen of the New Republic cruiser-carrier *Thurse*. You've jumped into a combat zone. I suggest you hold fast or return to wherever you came from."

"Captain Jorlen," Leia said, "this is Ambassador Organa Solo."

"Ambassador, what in blazes are you doing here?" The captain sounded surprised, though hardly cheered. "And when is that husband of yours going to get around to installing an authorized transponder?"

"I'll ask him when I see him, Captain. He's aboard the *Queen of Empire*. We've come to lend a hand, if you'll have our help."

"Negative, Ambassador. I request you hold your position. We've got a Yuuzhan Vong frigate jumping all over the arena. For all we know, it'll be in your lap next."

"Acknowledged, Captain, we'll stay put. For now," Leia added under her breath. "Have the raiders issued demands of any sort?"

"We've had no contact with them," Jorlen said impatiently. "We assume they've come for the passengers themselves—to supply the Yuuzhan Vong with sacrifices."

"Then why the Yuuzhan Vong warship, Captain?"

"Why, indeed," Jorlen mused.

"Something's out there," Luke said, pointing away from both the starliner and the ongoing firefight.

At first Leia wasn't sure whether he'd sensed something through the Force or merely observed it, but when she followed his finger she saw what he was referring to and called up an enhanced view on the console display. The screen showed a blunt-nosed object reminiscent of a yorik coral fighter but clearly reinforced by some sort of burnished black armor.

"Disabled ship?" Mara suggested.

"Could be," Luke said, staring not at the screen but out the viewport. "But I'm sensing something else . . ."

"A space mine?"

Luke shook his head. "A void."

Leia and Mara reached out with the Force, verifying the emptiness that had drawn Luke's attention. Luke was about to speak when the comm board came alive once more.

"Ambassador Solo," Jorlen updated, "we've just been hailed by the *Queen of Empire*. The raiders have issued an ultimatum. Unless all New Republic forces move off, they're going to begin expelling passengers out the airlocks."

"Oh, my!" C-3PO said in trepidation.

R2-D2 twittered, then whimpered.

Leia's eyes clouded over with alarm. "What was your response, Captain?"

Jorlen took a moment to answer. "It's contrary to New Republic policy to bargain with pirates, Ambassador. I'm sorry that your husband is aboard, but the fight goes on. More to the point, if the raiders have in fact come for captives, their threat is an empty one, since the *Queen*'s passengers are already marked for death."

"That's hardly a relief, Captain."

"My apologies, Ambassador. But there'll be no negotiations while that Yuuzhan Vong ship is present."

"Then we'll have to do something about that."

No sooner did Leia sign off when Luke said, "Whatever that object is, it's abetting the coralskippers in some way."

"A war coordinator?" Leia ventured.

He tore his eyes from the viewport to regard his sister. "A dovin basal."

Leia adopted a determined expression and centered herself over the controls. "Living. But not for long."

*   *   *

With concussive explosions rocking the *Queen*, Han peeked around the corner of a corridor at a hatch that opened on the docking bay. Guarding the way were two men armed with blasters and stun nets. Han considered bringing out his blaster, which was still secreted in his travel pack, but then recalled that the power pack had yet to be replenished.

"No good," he told Droma and the recostumed Yuuzhan Vong, "they've sealed off every approach." Withdrawing, he pressed his back to the bulkhead and glanced left and right. "We need a hole to hide in. With all that's going on outside, it won't be long before the Peace Brigade surrenders or attempts an escape."

He led them to a bank of drop shafts and cautiously peered over the edge of one of them. Far below was the floor of a cargo hold.

"In case you haven't noticed," Droma said, "the shafts have been deactivated."

"So we find some shock cord," Han said. "It's only, what, fifty meters or so to the bottom?"

Droma looked skeptical. "Might as well be from here to Coruscant."

The sound of approaching footsteps put a quick end to the dilemma. Slinking away from the drop shafts, the four of them entered an intersecting passageway, where they were greeted by the sound of yet more footsteps, along with a chorus of piqued voices. They hurried around another corner, searching high and low for a place to hide.

Determined footsteps to their left grew louder, and not a moment later the owners of the piqued voices strode into view. Han's eyes roamed over the raiders. Even after all the years, Reck Desh was recognizable by his cocky gait and full sleeve of tattoos. With him walked five examples of well-armed Peace Brigade thuggery and a spindly miscreant who would have made a perfect Yuuzhan Vong, if in fact he wasn't one, disguised by an oversize cloak.

Reck stationed one of his men at the intersection of the corridors and moved on.

Han felt his blood rush and heard his heart pounding in his ears. He thought about Chewie, and about Lwyll, Roa, and Fasgo. The travel pack slid from his hand onto the floor, and he immediately squatted down and pulled out his empty blaster.

Droma watched him with mounting concern. "I thought the idea was to steal a shuttle and get off ship."

"That can wait," Han grumbled. "This is personal."

"Personal?" Droma whispered harshly. "I feel compelled to mention that your weapon—"

"Save it for someone who cares," Han interrupted.

He regarded the blaster, compressing his lips in anger, then forced a breath and stood up.

"What is he doing?" Elan asked Droma worriedly.

Droma shrugged resignedly. "He has this need for confrontation, even when unnecessary."

Han swung to them. "Find yourselves someplace to hide. I'll be back for you."

Cautiously and with the useless blaster raised, Han moved toward the intersection Reck and company had passed through. The man Reck had left behind remained oblivious to Han's presence until he felt the business end of the blaster touch the side of his neck.

"Not a sound," Han warned.

The man tensed and swallowed audibly.

Han's right hand closed on the raider's blaster. "I'm relieving you of your weapon, soldier."

The man nodded. "It's your party, pal."

Han grinned. "You catch on fast."

"What now?"

Han pressed the muzzle of the loaded blaster against the man's back and took hold of his own weapon by the barrel, raising it over his head. "This might hurt a bit," he said.

The man turned ever so slightly. "What might—"

Han brought the grip of the blaster down hard on the back of the raider's neck, crumpling him to the deck. Then he set out in the direction Reck had taken. Approaching another intersection, he could hear voices ahead. Pressed to the wall, he lowered himself somewhat, and peered around the corner. Reck and the possible Yuuzhan Vong were only ten meters away. With no plan in mind, other than to finish things with Reck, Han started around the corner. At the same time, however, he heard something behind him and swung to the sound. A thickset human in spacer garb had a Tenloss disruptor rifle trained on him.

Han dived to the right, getting off one shot as he did. The raider fired back but also missed. Han caught a glimpse of Reck turning toward him as he disappeared into another corridor and straight into the blaster sights of two more Peace Brigaders. He jinked to the left, firing blindly, then launched himself feetfirst at the larger of the pair. The raider grunted in pain and tumbled backward, losing his weapon. But Han hit the floor harder than he had planned to and lost most of his wind. By the time he had scrambled to a crouch, the smaller raider was all over him, along with the one with the Tenloss.

Han swung wildly, struggling for all it was worth, but it didn't take long for them to pin him, flat on his face with the right foot of the largest raider planted on the back of his neck.

With a skewed view of the corridor, Han watched Reck and the rangy miscreant hurry onto the scene.

"All right, hero," the big raider said, "get up."

The pressure on his neck eased, and Han expelled his breath. He tasted blood in his mouth and was suddenly aware of a throbbing pain in his right hand. As he was pushing himself to his feet another raider showed up, escorting Droma, Elan, and Vergere at blasterpoint.

"I found these three running scared," he reported to Reck.

"We were just searching for a 'fresher," Han heard Droma say in a good-natured way. "They're never around when you need them."

Reck advanced a couple of steps and swept his eyes over everyone. Much to Han's surprise, Reck didn't appear to recognize him, but perhaps only because he was too busy scrutinizing Droma.

"You're a . . . Ryn?" Reck ventured.

Droma bowed slightly. "The impossible-to-find item on every scavenger hunt list."

Reck ignored the remark, squinted at Vergere, and shook his head. "I haven't a clue."

Vergere adopted a bashful expression. "I get that a lot."

Reck moved down the line and gazed curiously at Elan. Shortly, a knowing smile began to pull at the corners of his mouth. He turned and waved a signal to his rail-thin confederate.

From a sturdy carry case the lanky man set at his feet, he extracted—by the scruff of its bristly neck—a nasty-tempered, sharp-toothed creature that looked like the offspring of a ng'ok and a quillarat. Han heard Elan's sharp intake of breath and saw her eyes widen as the creature's handler let the thing get a whiff of her. All at once a layer of skin seemed to peel back from Elan's nose, cheeks, and neck and withdraw into the collar of the blouse Droma had found for her. Bulging as it rushed down her body, the layer of skin flowed out the hem of her skirt and down her bare legs to mass on the floor and slither off for safety, revealing Elan in all her tattooed splendor.

Out of the corner of his eye, Han saw Droma's jaw drop in unabashed wonder.

"Got'cha," Reck said, beaming.

Two men stepped in to take charge of Elan. At the same time, the creature who had sniffed out the ooglith masquer leapt snarling from its handler's arms and went after the living sheath with a vengeance, snatching it with its razor-sharp teeth and shaking it around as if it were a slab of meat. The Yuuzhan Vong followed, grabbed hold of the creature, and shoved it and the shredded flesh-garment back into the carry case.

Reck couldn't have been more pleased.

"That's the thing about ooglith masquers," he said to newly decorticated Elan, "they're as easy to intimidate as . . ."

Reck's words trailed off as his gaze settled on Han. Then he, too, went a bit wide-eyed, in a manner that mixed pleasant surprise with sudden disquiet.

"Han?" he said. "Han, it is you, right? Grayer, heavier, but, son of a gun, same off-kilter mouth and lady-killer looks."

"Hello, Reck."

Reck grinned broadly and gestured to Han's chin. "I don't remember that scar."

"I could have had it fixed, Reck, but it reminds me that my past was real."

Reck looked confused for a moment, then laughed as if he meant it. "Han Solo." Shaking his head back and forth, he swung to his comrades. "Can you believe this? Han Solo." By the time he came full circle, however, the smile had been replaced by a look of vexation. "Figures they'd put you in charge of these two."

"That isn't exactly the way it happened, Reck."

"I'm sure." He gestured to the Yuuzhan Vong's carry case. "What do you think of the unmasker?"

"I'll say this much, you don't make many mistakes."

Reck snorted. "Hey, they don't let me."

"Have you taken a look outside, Reck? How far do you think you're going to get?"

"I only need to get as far as that Yuuzhan Vong ship."

"If I were you, I'd start rethinking my loyalties."

"Loyalties?" Reck said in exaggerated dismay. "What's loyalty worth on the open market?" He laughed again, mordantly this time. "Guys like you break me up, Han. Profiteers without the guts to change sides suddenly calling themselves patriots. I *know* who's coming out on top in this one, and I'll do whatever I have to, to live happily ever after."

"You're talking treason, Reck."

"I speak it fluently, friend."

Han fought down an urge to throw his stiffened fingers into Reck's windpipe. "Remember Chewbacca?"

"The Wookiee? Sure I do. Best of the best."

Han swallowed. "Your new employers killed him. Pulled a moon down on him."

Reck's eyebrows arched. "The Wook was at Sernpidal?" He puffed out his breath and shook his head back and forth. "I'm sorry to hear that, Han—honest. But I had nothing to do with that op."

"What about the op on Atzerri, Reck? That's where Roa's wife, Lwyll, died because of what the Peace Brigade set in motion."

"Roa's wife?" Reck blinked, then began to shake his head in protest. "That op wasn't supposed to end like it did."

Han's eyes bored into him. "Does that make it easier to swallow?"

Reck frowned. "A man has to work."

Han lunged for him, barely managing to wrap his hands around Reck's neck before someone knocked him to the deck.

"I don't mind a turncoat, Reck," Han said, gazing up as he got to his feet, "but I draw the line at second-rate ones. You're going to give mercenaries a bad name."

Reck's rejoinder was a sneer. He pulled out his personal comlink and thumbed it on. "We've got them," he said into the pickup. "We'll be heading back to the ship momentarily."

"Won't do you much good," a brittle voice replied from the unit. "We can't detach from the airlock. All systems, even sublight and repulsors, are down. No response at all from the dovin basal. It's like the thing's gone into stasis."

Reck swung to the unmasker's handler, who looked mystified.

"Have you attempted to contact the Yuuzhan Vong ship?" Reck said into the comlink.

"No response."

Reck cursed. "All right," he said after a moment. "I'll take her to them in my shuttle."

The man at the other end of the link laughed. "It's doomsday out here, Reck. You'll be lucky to clear the launch bay without getting yourself wasted."

"Are the weapons operating?"

"Affirmative."

"Then you just clear a path for me. The New Republic's not going to interfere while we're holding several thousand hostages. Once I make the Yuuzhan Vong ship, I'll see to it that the rest of you are brought over."

Reck switched off the comlink. He had his mouth open to say something to Han when another Peace Brigade contingent arrived on the scene, making haste for the docking bay. Supported by two of them was a wounded Rodian who had to be Capo.

"You people are supposed to be on the bridge," Reck bellowed.

"This is your operation, Reck," the largest among them answered. "You want to stay and feed refugees to the vacuum, that's your business. But we're out of here."

The man who had discovered Han and Droma started to raise his disruptor rifle, but Reck restrained him.

"Knock it off. Fighting among ourselves isn't going to do any good. We'll pack the shuttles and convoy for the Yuuzhan Vong ship."

Han smirked. "Proverbial droch in the ointment, huh, Reck?"

Reck gestured two of the men to take charge of Vergere, then he turned to Han. "You know, I'm less worried about interference from those starfighters than I am about interference from you."

He drew his blaster and ordered Han to move to the nearest drop shaft. Droma followed silently. At the blaster's insistence, Han backed himself to the edge of the tube, then he held his hand over it.

"Not much of a breeze," he thought to point out.

Reck grinned. "You always were a funny guy, Han."

Han shrugged. "You know what they say about a punch line being the best revenge."

Reck considered it. "If we'd met somewhere else, we could be sharing ice-cold Gizers right now. But I can't have you trying to follow us or talking to your New Republic friends. You've got way too much good fortune on your side. You always did."

"Seem's my luck's run out," Han and Droma said at the same time.

Reck looked from one to the other, then laughed shortly. "You two make quite a pair. Too bad I've got to split you up." He lifted the blaster's barrel. "Down you go, Han. Next stop, the cargo hold."

Han gulped. "Come on, Reck, you don't need to do this. For old times' sake."

"Oh, but I do, old friend." Again, he motioned with the blaster. "Be a good sport. Don't make me shoot you."

Han tightened the straps of his travel pack, thinking that it might somehow cushion his fall. Then he squared his shoulders and blew out his breath. Narrowing his eyes at Reck, he took a backward step into the abyss.

Droma let out an anguished shriek and went rigid with shock.

TWENTY-FIVE

Relayed to Obroa-skai by signal villip, the fierce fighting at the Rimward edge of the Bilbringi system unfolded in real time for commanders Malik Carr and Tla, tactician Raff, and Harrar, aboard the priest's faceted starship.

"The Peace Brigade gunship has made several attempts at communication," a villip of Nom Anor reported, "but we have refused all appeals to render aid."

Behind him in the signal villip's visual field, outside the frigate's observation bay, light streaked and flashed in the black of space. Every so often a snub-nosed fighter would pass close to the bay, discharging blinding globes of encapsulated energy. Most were immediately gobbled up by singularities, but some detonated against the ship with trembling force, crazing the villip feed with undulating lines of interference or suspending it altogether.

"With due respect, Commander Malik Carr," Tla said, "I find it irksome to have to abandon allies—even though they wrongly took it on themselves to redeem Executor Nom Anor's infiltrators. More, I dislike having our forces leap about to avoid engaging the enemy directly."

Harrar placed himself in full view of the issuing villip.

"Are you concerned that some may judge your actions cowardly?" he asked Nom Anor.

"Knowing that my actions are for a greater cause, no, I am not concerned."

Tla glowered. "Your opinions matter not, Executor."

Commander Malik Carr watched Tla for a moment, then turned to face the transmitting villip. "Would you surrender your command to assuage Commander Tla's concerns, Executor?"

Nom Anor ridiculed the idea. "Even I know better than to exchange a lesser indignity for a greater one."

From somewhere outside the confines of the visual field, the subaltern in command of the frigate bridge spoke. "Executor, an enemy ship has targeted the dovin basal we housed in a keeper. Thus far the dovin basal has been unsuccessful at repelling the attack. It reacts as if dazed."

"Show us that ship," Nom Anor ordered.

The receiving villip on Harrar's vessel relayed an image of a gray-white saucer-shaped vessel with protruding mandibles and armaments of extraordinary firepower.

Nom Anor's villip looked to the tactician. "You've studied the villip images of our previous battles with New Republic forces. Do you recognize this ship?"

Raff's enhanced brain went to work on it. Finally, he nodded. "The ship was present at Helska," he announced to those in the command center as well as to those aboard the frigate. "It was remembered by the villip beacons left in place by Prefect Da'gara."

"At Helska," Malik Carr said in surprise. "Jedi?" he asked Nom Anor. "Could they have grasped your intent?"

Nom Anor shook his head firmly. "Unlikely. And if in

fact they are Jedi pilots, they're too focused on confusing the dovin basal and prevailing in this insignificant contest to realize what they're doing.

"Subaltern," he continued, "do nothing to protect the remote dovin basal. Should that ship succeed in destroying it, you will instruct our coralskipper pilots to behave as if thrown into sudden disarray."

Tactician Raff spoke up. "I would point out that the destruction of the dovin basal will allow the smaller ships that boarded the starliner to launch—"

"The dovin basal has been destroyed," the subaltern updated.

The villip field showed those aboard Harrar's ship the saucer-shaped ship up on its side, streaking away from the annihilated remote.

"Three shuttles have left the starliner," the subaltern reported to Nom Anor. "Two are disappearing behind the passenger vessel, bearing toward the planet. One is vectoring for our current position."

"It would appear that the Peace Brigade has reclaimed Elan," Commander Malik Carr said flatly, breaking the silence that fell over the command center. "I suspect they're attempting to bring her home."

"Their gunship is still held fast to the liner," Nom Anor countered. "They could be hoping for sanctuary, and nothing more."

Commander Tla was unsuccessful at concealing his self-satisfaction.

"Exercise discretion," Harrar said at last, "but hold the shuttle at bay."

"And if Priestess Elan is indeed aboard?" Malik Carr asked.

Harrar glanced at Nom Anor's villip, who answered for the priest. "Elan will know what to do."

Droma was still wailing when Han finally hauled himself hand over hand up the Ryn's tail and swung panting to the deck, a safe distance from the edge of the deactivated drop shaft.

Droma immediately fell to all fours and began crawling around, weeping in pain.

Han caught his breath and went to his side. "Must be something I can do to help."

"Yes," Droma said, scowling at him through tears, "learn to fall more gracefully. Learn to fall brilliantly."

Han dropped into a sitting position, with his hands resting on his raised knees. "Easy for someone with a tail to say." He let a moment pass, then he grinned. "You saved my neck, Droma. I won't forget this."

Droma snorted. "I couldn't very well let you fall. As you said, you're too well-known to die."

"You'd better believe it." Clapping him on the back, Han helped him to his feet. "Come on, we might still be able to catch them."

Droma exhaled in exasperation. "You never give up, do you?"

Han threw a smile over his shoulder. "Thanks to you I've got my second wind."

"I'll know better next time," Droma muttered.

With the Ryn hobbling after, Han raced down the passageway for the hatch to the docking bay. But even from a distance it was clear that the hatch-release mechanism had been rendered inoperative by a well-aimed blaster bolt.

Han palmed the release pad anyway, then turned to Droma, frowning. "Reck doesn't miss a trick."

They raced back down the passageway and through a series of right-angle turns that brought them to another hatch—also fused by blasterfire. It was the same at every hatch that accessed the docking bay from that part of the *Queen*. But by the time they had circled back to the first hatch, the passageway was thick with the astringent smell of molten plasteel, and a neat half circle had been burned through the hatch.

"Hull cutter," Han said excitedly.

He and Droma fell back as the cutter completed its work. Moments later a massive disk of alloy dropped from the hatch with a resounding boom and rolled a few meters down the passageway, gyrating like a coin before it ultimately settled to the floor. Through wisps of white smoke agitated by the pressure differential surged a dozen New Republic elite forces in black helmets and A/KT combat jumpsuits, carrying BlasTech E-15A rifles and grenade launchers.

Han and Droma ducked into a recess as the soldiers stormed down the passageway, seemingly unaware that most of the Peace Brigade had already abandoned ship. Han motioned Droma through the circular breach in the hatch. In the spacious pressurized bay beyond sat the sleek assault craft that had brought the troopers aboard, along with two X-wings.

One of the starfighter pilots was just climbing from the cockpit when Han ran up to him to ask if he'd seen any ships leaving the bay.

The pilot took off his helmet and shook his long hair out of his face. "Word is that three shuttles launched, but

I didn't see any of them." The pilot gave Han and Droma a distrustful look. "Who are you two?"

Han was considering just whose name he should drop to facilitate commandeering a fighter when another ship nosed through the docking bay's transparent force field and surrendered itself to the grasp of the starliner's artificial gravity.

It took Han a moment to accept that it really was the *Falcon*.

Droma guffawed in derision. "Will you look what the *Queen* dragged in."

Han whirled on him, brows beetled and mouth an elongated O. "Hey, that's my ship you're talking about."

Droma looked from Han to the *Falcon* and back again. "Your ship?"

Without bothering to explain, Han hastened for the landing zone while the *Falcon* was settling down on her broad disks of landing gear. He was waiting at the foot of the starboard ramp when Luke, Mara, and Leia appeared. Behind them came R2-D2 and C-3PO, who on seeing Han, raised his arms and nearly took a tumble in his haste to reach him.

"Thank the maker you're alive!" the droid exclaimed. "I don't know what I might have done had my actions contributed to your demise!" He turned to his counterpart. "You see, Artoo, no matter how great the odds, there is always a chance of beating them."

Leia's face lit up. She tried to run to Han's arms, but he deftly avoided contact.

"Did you spot any departing shuttles when you were coming in?" he asked.

She shook her head. "We—"

"Leia, meet Droma," he said in a rush, dragging the Ryn between them. "Droma: my wife, Leia."

Leia blinked. "Droma? Who—"

"The corvette," Han said to Luke. "Is it away?"

"No, Han—"

"Reck must be headed for the Yuuzhan Vong ship," Han said, shooting Droma a look.

"Reck?" Leia asked.

"Peace Brigade," Han said, as if one word. "They reclaimed the defectors."

Luke regarded him with intense interest. "Defectors?"

Han turned to him and a fragile-looking Mara, clenching his fists in recall of what Elan had said about a Yuuzhan Vong–introduced illness.

"No time to explain." He raced up the ramp.

Droma glanced at Leia. "Nice to meet you," he said, then dashed up the ramp, stiff tail shaking behind him.

Luke looked at Leia in puzzlement. "Han, wait," he started to say, when Leia laid a restraining hand on his arm.

"No, Luke, let him go." She gazed up the ramp as Han and his accomplice were vanishing from view. "I've a feeling he needs this."

Han let momentum carry him into the outrigger cockpit and clear into the pilot's seat. He was flipping switches and toggles when Droma entered.

"You familiar with YT-1300s?" Han asked over his shoulder, both hands in ceaseless motion.

"Our caravan from the Corporate Sector included several 1300s—though that wasn't something we bragged about."

Han scowled and gestured to the copilot's seat. "Strap in, scratch coat. This one's something to brag about."

Droma edged uncertainly between the rear chairs and settled into the outsize chair to Han's right. "You'd have to be a person of considerable dimensions to fill this seat," he said.

Han stopped what he was doing to look at Droma. And for a brief moment he had a vision of Chewbacca. Sitting tall in the seat, the Wookiee had a grin on his face and his big paws clasped behind his shaggy head. His black-tipped, cinnamon fur shone as if freshly shampooed and his teeth gleamed. He turned toward Han and boomed his delight in an earsplitting yowl, then woofed with laughter that reverberated throughout the ship.

Han's chest filled with a tight warmth and his eyes brimmed with tears. He had to swallow to find his voice.

"You can say that again," he muttered, swinging toward the viewport.

Droma assessed the cockpit as the *Falcon* powered up and repulsors moved her toward the hold's magnetic transparency and the starfield beyond. "I thought you said you ran with a wealthy crowd."

Han snorted a laugh and jerked his thumb over his shoulder. "That guy in the robe back there—that was Luke Skywalker."

Droma looked impressed. "The Jedi Skywalker?"

"One and the same. My wife is Leia Organa."

Droma scratched his head. "So your real name is Han Organa?"

"*Solo*," Han growled in annoyance. "Han Solo." When Droma just stared at him, he added, "You're saying you haven't heard of me?"

"I may have," Droma allowed. "But we Ryn meet so many people."

Han loosed a long exhale and concentrated on the business at hand. Local space was still frenetic with war craft and fire, but the real fighting had moved far afield of the starliner, out toward where an ovoid Yuuzhan Vong ship was defending itself against an onslaught of laser beams and proton torpedoes.

In the time it had taken Leia to dock the *Falcon*, the Peace Brigade's corvette had managed to disengage from the *Queen* and just now was trading shots with a quartet of X-wings in a race for the far side of the largest of the nearby planetoids. Closer to the planetoid, over which a New Republic cruiser-carrier hung like a lightsaber, starfighters and coralskippers were matched in a tumultuous battle.

"Set the friend-or-foe authenticator to scan for Sienar Fleet Systems *Martial*-class shuttles," Han directed Droma while he increased power to the *Falcon*'s drive.

Droma located the authenticator and initiated a scan. "Found one," he reported almost immediately. "Making for the Yuuzhan Vong ship."

Han compressed his lips. In the heat of battle the New Republic pilots hadn't recognized the shuttle as an enemy. "That would be Reck," he said.

"We'll never catch him."

Han threw him a sidelong glance. "Don't be fooled by age, partner."

Despite the high setting of the inertial compensator, the *Falcon*'s sudden increase in velocity nearly pinned Droma to the seatback. His rakish cap flew from his head and his eyes opened wide in astonishment. He loosed a raucous cry.

"Yee-ha, what a ship! What a beauty!"

Han merely grinned. "When you catch your breath, tell me about that shuttle."

"Still closing on the enemy vessel," Droma said through his thrill.

"Come on, come on," Han urged his ship.

Unexpectedly, the comm board crackled to life. "*Millennium Falcon*, this is the *Thurse*. Ambassador, I thought I asked you to keep out of this."

"Ambassador Organa Solo is presently aboard the *Queen*," Han said toward the console's audio pickup.

"Is that you, Han? It's Mak Jorlen."

"Mak!"

"What are doing out there, Han?"

"Chasing down a shuttle that has something the New Republic needs. Mak, once I grab it, I might need support on the way back in."

"Affirmative, *Millennium Falcon*. And, Han, welcome back to the cause. Now I know we've got a fighting chance."

Han felt Droma's eyes on him.

"This gets more and more curious," Droma said.

Han enabled the autotracking fire controller for the *Falcon*'s aft warship-rated quad laser. Bracketing the fleeing shuttle in the display's targeting reticle, he moved his right hand to the trigger joystick.

He was about to fire when, without warning, the *Falcon* seemed to plunge through a gravitic anomaly. Han barely had time to hit the reverse thrusters to keep the ship from pouncing on its quarry in the worst of ways.

In fact, though, the shuttle had slowed drastically and was all but drifting in space. "It's like it hit a repulsor field," Han said as he made rapid adjustments to the controls.

Droma nodded. "She looks dead."

When the distance between the *Falcon* and the shuttle had decreased to a few kilometers, Han unfastened his seat harness and stood up.

"Take over," he told Droma. "Maneuver us alongside. Use the tractor beam if you need to. I'll ready the portside grapple and cofferdam."

"You're planning to board?" Droma blurted, gawking at him. "The Yuuzhan Vong must know what it's carrying. What if that ship draws a bead on us?"

Han glanced out the viewport. Still some distance away and illuminated by brilliant spherical explosions, the frigate sat at the center of a swirling firefight.

"Guess I'll have to work fast," Han said, and rushed from the cockpit.

On the bridge of the Yuuzhan Vong frigate, Nom Anor studied the villip's enhanced view of the droop-winged shuttle the onboard dovin basal had repulsed and evidently traumatized. The same saucer-shaped ship that had destroyed the remote dovin basal had linked itself to the drifting shuttle, and those aboard—whether or not Jedi—were surely in the process of reclaiming the priestess the Peace Brigade had reclaimed earlier.

With the decimation the coralskippers were undergoing and the pounding Commander Malik Carr's personal ship was taking, Nom Anor found it challenging to fix his attention on a single aspect of the battle. But as

Harrar had made abundantly clear, there was no more significant aspect than the recapture of Ela...

To the subaltern, he said, "Allow the New Republic ship a few moments with the shuttle before giving chase. We must convince them without overtaking them. By then, our coralskippers will have been all but annihilated and our final jump from this farce will at least appear credible."

He glanced out the viewport at the maelstrom. "All glory to you warriors," he sent quietly to the coralskipper pilots.

Suited up for EVA and armed with a blaster rifle, Han floated through the extensible vapor-tight tube that magnetically linked the *Falcon*'s portside docking arm to the shuttle's starboard airlock. Making use of the cofferdam's rigid-ring handholds, Han propelled himself along.

He stopped at the shuttle's hatch to communicate with Droma over the helmet comlink a final time. "Any reply?"

"Nothing," Droma told him once more. "The shuttle must have taken a hit without our noticing. Keep your suit tight."

"Yeah, thanks," Han said.

He switched off the rifle's safety, brought a gloved hand to the external hatch release, and moved into the shuttle's airlock. Once the hatch had resealed and the airlock had cycled, he raised the rifle to his midsection and hit the internal hatch release.

No one met him at the door.

"I'm inside," he relayed to Droma. "Pressure, gravity,

and atmosphere are all operative. I'm going into the passenger compartment first."

Opening the hatch, he stepped inside. A grainy black substance, which crunched underfoot, covered the deck plates and nearly every horizontal surface. Han stooped to take a pinch between his gloved fingers and bring it to the helmet's faceplate. "Some kind of black stuff all over the place," he said into the comlink. "Like tiny nut husks or something."

"Any sign of Reck?"

Han moved down the aisle and gave a start as he came to the forward row of seats. Slumped there were three of Reck's comrades, their faces hideously contorted and their shirts soaked with blood that had cascaded from eyes, ears, and noses.

"What is it?" Droma asked in anxious response to Han's brief outcry.

"Three dead—from I don't even know what. Massive blood vessel ruptures, it looks like."

"You're certain the shuttle didn't depressurize?"

"Even if it did, this is like nothing I've ever seen." Han glanced at the open forward hatch. "I'm moving into the cockpit."

Inside he found the same black grit, as well as Reck, Capo, and the one Han thought to be a Yuuzhan Vong— all dead and similarly drenched in blood. Open and overturned on the floor was the case the enemy agent had carried. Close by lay the body of the vicious creature that had sent Elan's ooglith masquer into a panic.

"Reck's dead," Han said into the comlink. "They're all dead."

"The females, too?"

"No sign of them. Unless they're in cargo."

Han took one last look at Reck. "Down you go," he said, mostly to himself.

He walked back through the passenger compartment to the rear hold and hit the hatch release. "Found them," he told Droma, even before the hatch had pocketed itself.

On a large square of deck grating lay Elan and Vergere, unconscious but otherwise unharmed. The hold was free of black husks. Han put his arm under Elan's narrow shoulders and gently lifted her. Her intense blue eyes blinked open, then went wide in fright. She flailed in his arms, her sudden movements causing Vergere to stir, as well.

"It's me—Han!" he said through the EVA suit's external speaker.

Elan began to relax. "They drugged us," she said groggily, then glanced around in confused apprehension. "Where are they? What happened? Why are you wearing a space suit?"

He helped her to her feet and slowly led her into the passenger compartment. Her foot had scarcely touched the black grit when she gasped and stood petrified.

"*Bo'tous!*" she said, in what Han assumed was Yuuzhan Vong. "A bioweapon—an airborne blood agent!"

"This black stuff is *bo*—whatever?"

Elan shook her head. "What you see is the aftermath of bo'tous—a harmless residue." She gestured to the forward seats. "What they inhaled killed them."

Vergere stepped from the cargo hold and stifled a scream.

"Everyone but you two are dead," Han said.

Elan stared at him in bewilderment. "But who did this?"

"That's what I'd like to know. Could the Peace Brigade have been carrying some of that . . . stuff?"

"Yes, possibly. They had a dovin basal and an unmasker. They might have had *bo'tous*, as well." She looked at Han. "Perhaps they planned to use it on passengers aboard the starliner."

"Why didn't it affect you?"

"On launch from the *Queen of Empire*, they sealed us into the compartment where you found us." She held his gaze. "We Yuuzhan Vong are immune, in any case."

Han nodded noncommittally and activated the comlink. "Droma, meet me in the docking arm. I'm bringing them aboard."

"You'd better be quick about it," Droma replied rapidly. "That warship's headed right for us!"

TWENTY-SIX

With missiles from the Yuuzhan Vong frigate slamming against her shields and detonating to all sides, the *Millennium Falcon* raced back toward the still-immobile starliner. Beams from the *Thurse*'s main batteries lashed blue light at the frigate, but to no apparent effect.

"You're telling me it jumped that far in a second?" Han yelled at Droma while he fought to stabilize his ship.

"That's exactly what I'm telling you! One second it was there, the next it was practically right on top of us!"

Han's hands flew across the cockpit console. "Angle the rear deflectors! If we can't outrun them, we can at least try to stay in one piece!" He looked over his shoulder at Elan and Vergere. "Get to the acceleration couch in the forward hold!"

Droma waited until they had disappeared to say, "Vergere's not an extragalactic, Han. I don't know the species, but I have seen her type before."

Han glanced at him. "What are you telling me? That she's an impostor?"

"I'm not sure. Maybe only that those two don't add up."

"You don't trust them?"

"Do you?"

Han considered his answer, then shook his head.

"Something's been nagging at me. Why would the Yuuzhan Vong send a warship to back up the Peace Brigade? If they knew Elan was aboard the *Queen*, they would have done the job themselves. And another thing: even if some Yuuzhan Vong bioweapon escaped aboard the shuttle, that doesn't explain the shuttle's decelerating the way it did."

"Unless the Yuuzhan Vong deliberately slowed it down."

Han made his lips a thin line. "Exactly what I was thinking. You remember Reck's man reporting that the corvette was glitched—that they couldn't disengage from the *Queen*?"

Droma nodded. "The corvette pulled the *Queen* from hyperspace, but suddenly was unable to break away from her."

"Which could happen if the Yuuzhan Vong tasked the dovin basal aboard the corvette to hold fast to the *Queen*."

The *Falcon* shook as a projectile caught up with her. Han and Droma flinched, but dozens more missiles streaked past the ship to port and starboard.

"I'm tempted to see what happens if we stop taking evasive action."

"Not too tempted, I hope," Droma said worriedly.

Han growled. "I've gone up against the Yuuzhan Vong ships before. They just don't miss this often. It's like they're doing everything they can to convince us they want their property back—"

"When they actually want Elan and Vergere to remain where they are."

Han rubbed his jaw. "But why the ruse?"

"Something unrevealed," Droma said l adingly. "The Queen of Air and Darkness."

Han scowled. "I don't put any stock in card games."

Droma shrugged. "Watching you play sabacc, I would have thought otherwise."

Han fell silent for a moment, then reached for his pack and located his holstered blaster. Getting to his feet, he buckled the holster around his hips and fastened the thigh grip.

"Take over," he told Droma.

He hurried to the forward hold, where Elan and Vergere were seated side by side on the acceleration couch.

"Can you outspeed the warship?" Elan asked in a way that was meant to sound guileless.

"Probably not," he told her. "But I think your people will make us think we did."

She looked at him questioningly.

"I mean that I'm beginning to think they don't want you back. That this whole thing—your defection, maybe even this battle—is part of some elaborate scheme your superiors cooked up."

"You don't care that I have important information for the Jedi?" she said in a scurrilous but composed voice.

Wrestling with uncertainty, Han paced the hold. "I don't know what to think." He came to a halt and regarded the two of them. "I suppose I could take you back to the *Queen* and let Jedi Master Skywalker decide."

"Yes," Elan said hurriedly, "you must at least do that."

Han heard her. But what struck him was the look of

shocked recognition that played briefly over Vergere's exotic features.

"You're right," he said at last. "I guess I'm just being overly suspicious."

He turned, as if to head to the cockpit, then stopped and said, "That creature that shredded your ooglith masquer aboard the *Queen*—does it respond only to a Yuuzhan Vong handler or will it adapt to anyone?"

"Only a Yuuzhan Vong," Elan said.

Han saw her stiffen, if ever so slightly. "You said the Yuuzhan Vong are immune to that bioweapon that got loose aboard the shuttle."

Face tightened with hatred, she nodded.

And Han grinned.

"You just remembered that I found the handler dead in the cockpit—a *Yuuzhan Vong* handler. You loosed that bioweapon from the safety of the cargo hold. When the toxin had dispersed enough, you came out and tipped over the handler's carry case, knowing it would draw my attention. You were never drugged. That was all part of the act."

Han's smile straightened and he cocked his head toward the *Falcon*'s starboard ring corridor. "Droma! Take us about. Steer a course for the Yuuzhan Vong ship!"

Though muted by distance, Droma's "What?" teemed with disbelief.

"You heard me. Unless I'm seriously mistaken, they won't fire on us." Drawing his blaster, he ordered Elan and Vergere to rise from the couch. "I'm not taking any chances with you two."

"You're making a big mistake," Elan said.

"It wouldn't be the first time, sister. Stand up and get moving."

He gestured them into the portside ring corridor and marched them aft to the *Falcon*'s noisy rear compartment. Scrunched between the deck and the exhaust conduits of the bellowing power core, and to either side of an access shaft that had once contained a freight elevator, were the ship's escape pods.

Roomy, state-of-the-art spheroids in keeping with the *Falcon*'s status as a family vehicle, the pods were launched through ventral hatches by explosive separator charges, and featured such amenities as padded g-couches; a sophisticated sensor, communications, and flight-control suite; an automatically activated distress beacon; maneuvering jets; soft-landing coils; and enough rations and survival gear to keep two or three people equipped for a good while.

Han considered confining the bogus defectors in one of the pods, but quickly changed his mind. For all he knew, they had some way of poisoning the *Falcon* the way they had Reck's shuttle.

He approached one of the portside pods and slammed his hand on the hatch release stud. When the broad, circular hatch had irised open, Han motioned to it. "You're going back where you belong, ladies, marked 'returned to sender.' "

He waved the blaster, and Elan climbed nimbly into the pod. Vergere was about to follow when Elan suddenly brushed her aside, grabbed hold of Han, and tugged him headfirst into the sphere. Slamming him into the curved hull, she backed toward the still-open hatch, her mouth an intentional rictus of retaliation.

Han shook his head in an attempt to uncross his eyes. He raised the blaster and squeezed the trigger, only to realize that it was depleted. Staring at the useless thing, he felt his jaw drop.

"Careless," Elan said as she continued to sidle toward the hatch. "But don't worry, I'll gladly put you out of your misery."

"Huh?" he asked dizzily.

She grinned malevolently. "One breath for you, one left for the Jedi. Breathe deeply, *Han*."

Crouched to spring through the hatch, she forced an interminable exhale. Then, whirling about, she leapt for the hatch. But the *Falcon*, dodging fire, slewed acutely to starboard and the hatch irised shut. Dumped onto his back, Han again got the wind knocked out of him. At the same time, Elan hit the closing hatch and rebounded.

Bug-eyed with fear, she scrambled to her feet and tried desperately to force the hatch open. She balled her hands and pounded on the porthole with all her might. Expertly, she side-kicked it, then threw her weight against the hatch repeatedly, but it refused to budge.

Dumbfounded and still unable to catch his breath, Han heard a voice say, *Poisoned air*—though he couldn't be sure just whose voice he was hearing, or indeed if it was actually a voice or a thought that had come to him in response to what he'd observed on the shuttle.

As if on its own, his hand seized the survival tool clipped to his belt. Fumbling frantically with the compressed oxygen feature, he finally managed to shove the twin-tanked device to his lips and bite down on the spatulate mouthpiece to start the oxygen flowing. Through the pod porthole, he caught a brief glimpse of Vergere, but he couldn't tell if she was attempting to open the hatch or secure it further.

Elan swung away from the hatch in dread, her lips pressed tightly together and her face a blotchy red. Staring at Han, she made a grab for him, but he sidestepped and tripped her in the process. Collapsing to her hands and knees, she threw a baleful look over her shoulder, cursing Han with every cell in her body, then inhaled hoarsely.

Her body went rigid. A sudden cough sent blood fountaining from her mouth. From eyes, ears, and nose it poured as she lifted her head and howled in anguish. Mouth twisted around the lifesaving inhaler, Han backed away, pressing himself to the curved wall and averting his gaze. Spots formed before his eyes, and he thought he might pass out. Then the spots began to precipitate and scurry madly around the pod.

The black residue of Elan's toxic exhalation crawling all over him, he staggered for the hatch and hammered the release stud with the heel of his hand. Wild-eyed he hastened to the pod's comlink, only to find it dead, owing perhaps to a Yuuzhan Vong projectile that had penetrated the *Falcon*'s weakened shields. He brushed frantically at the tiny life-forms and crushed dozens at a time with stomps of his feet.

A warning tone sounded from the survival tool. He was fast running out of air. Eyes bulging from his head, he slammed his fists against the padded hatch and porthole. He was down to recycling his last breath when the hatch suddenly irised open, and he pitched headfirst to the floor of the rear hold.

Gulping air, he looked up to see Droma standing over him.

"What made you come back here?" Han asked between breaths.

"A feeling," Droma told him.

Han gestured weakly to the pod. "The bugs . . ."

Droma caught sight of Elan's bloodied corpse and momentarily froze. Then he quickly resealed the hatch and began killing escapees with his hands and feet. Shortly, some of the few remaining critters began to expire on their own, transforming into featherweight husks.

Han propped himself against the bulkhead and wiped sweat from his forehead. "That's two I owe you."

"I'll add it to your tab," Droma said, panting.

A ship-rattling explosion brought Han fully alert. "Where's Vergere?"

Droma glanced down the ring corridor and shook his head.

"Get back to the cockpit," Han said. "I'll find her."

Another powerful strike sent the *Falcon* on edge, and out of the starboard ring corridor flew Elan's familiar, crashing into Han just as he was getting to his feet. The collision sent him careening against the sealed escape pod and the hatch release stud. The hatch irised open once more and a few last critters leapt through the door and found purchase on the front of Han's shirt. Stuttering a phobic cry, he whisked them away, then turned his attention to Vergere, who had planted herself in the center of the hold, arms at her sides and her reverse-articulated legs tensed for action.

"Don't make this hard on yourself," Han warned.

Another projectile found the ship, rocking it to its ribs. Droma's voice wailed from an intercom annunciator in the bulkhead. "Han, you sure the Yuuzhan Vong don't want them back? They're being awfully convincing!"

Han kept his gaze on Vergere and adopted a combat stance. "They're gonna have to settle for half," he mumbled.

Vergere brought out her right hand to show Han a drinking bulb she had obviously grabbed from the galley. Squeezing the bulb, she suddenly brought it to her right eye as if to suction brimming tears.

Han hurled himself at her, but Vergere executed an agile leap that carried her out of reach, then another that front-flipped her straight into the escape pod. Han made a lunge for the pod, but an evasive maneuver by Droma set the ship on edge once more, and Han went sailing past the pod and a quarter of the way down the portside ring corridor. By the time he regained his balance and had stumbled back to the rear hold, Vergere was already arming the pod's separator charges. Han reached through the hatch for her, only to have his hands deflected.

"Thank you, Han Solo, for giving me the chance to return to my own kind," she told him. Without warning, she tossed the filled bulb at him. "See that this reaches the Jedi."

Reflexively, Han caught the bulb, then tossed it aside. He threw himself at the closing hatch, but not in time. The pod's launch warning system came to life with flashing light and metered sound.

Han beat a fast retreat into the rear hold and flattened himself to the deck grating as the pod launched with a concussive thump that made his ears pop.

"Blast!" he screamed, yanking himself upright.

Rushing to the cockpit, he found Droma still steering a slalom course directly for the Yuuzhan Vong frigate.

"The other way, the other way!" Han screamed, heaving himself into the pilot's seat.

"Make up your mind!" Droma yelled back.

Han took the controls and threw the *Falcon* into an ascending loop, hoping to catch sight of the launched escape pod on the downward curve. For a moment he had the sphere in the ship's tracking reticle, but he lost it just as quickly as a Yuuzhan Vong missile streaked across the *Falcon*'s bow.

The flaming projectile appeared to lock on to the pod like a predator hot on a blood scent. A blinding explosion forced Han to glance away, and when he looked back the pod was gone. A second later, however, he thought he glimpsed it out of the corner of his eye, plunging toward the night side of a heavily cratered planetoid. Then again, it was possible that the frigate's dovin basal had already captured the pod and brought it on board.

An agitated voice issued from the communications console. "Han, what the blazes are you doing? I thought you wanted cover fire."

"We do, we do!" Han told Mak Jorlen. "Punch it, Droma!"

The *Falcon* banked sharply, barrel-rolled to evade a slew of projectiles, and sped toward the *Thurse*. With the field clear, the cruiser-carrier opened up with all batteries, stunning the Yuuzhan Vong ship with ion cannon and turbolaser fire. A few remaining battleworthy coralskippers attempted to launch suicide runs at the *Thurse*, but were instantly pulverized. Defenseless, the frigate abandoned pursuit of the *Falcon*. Then, streaking away, it made an abrupt jump to lightspeed.

Han leveled out the ship and Droma cut her speed. He and the Ryn collapsed in their seats, as if someone had just let the air out of them.

"Is it over?" Droma asked after a moment.

Han nodded. "For the time being."

Droma glanced at Han and uttered a short laugh. "You know, I could almost believe you've been doing this sort of thing all your life."

Han pushed himself upright in the chair and favored him with a roguish grin. "What makes you think I haven't?"

TWENTY-SEVEN

Removed from the frenzied tempo of lofty Coruscant, deep in a vertical slice of the city-world known colloquially as the Abyss, a mixed-species dozen sat nervously at a long table in a windowless and otherwise secure chamber. The chamber resided at the heart of the entombed headquarters of the New Republic's Intelligence division and was accessible to upper-echelon officers only. In a sterile realm of artificial illumination and sunlight purloined by shafts and mirrors, the big-leafed shrub lodged in a corner of the chamber stood out like a chance oasis, and so had been given the name Mirage.

Separate conversations came to an abrupt halt when an entry-granted tone sounded from the door and Director Dif Scaur stamped into the room, a sheaf of durasheet documents and optical prints under one arm and a gunmetal-gray modified protocol droid trailing in his wake. Everyone was standing by the time he reached the head of the table, but the obvious attempt at deference only deepened his scowl and he motioned brusquely for everyone to be seated. A former admiral with the Fourth Fleet, Scaur was tall and gaunt, with watery blue eyes and a pronounced widow's peak.

"I've been in meetings with Defense Force command staff all morning," he began on a sullen note, "and the advisory council is expecting a full report later this afternoon. So the sooner we get this done the better."

Scaur glanced angrily at his deputy director of operations. "Colonel Kalenda, since you've been attached to this fiasco from the beginning, I'd like you to start by telling me which parts of Han Solo's report can be considered fact and which parts can be dismissed as owing to an obvious case of space giddiness. Frankly, I'm not even clear on how the defectors wound up in his hands to begin with."

Belindi Kalenda stirred in her chair. "Sir, after Major Showolter and his support team were ambushed by members of the Peace Brigade, Showolter and the defectors went in search of backup elements known to be aboard the *Queen of Empire*. When the major spotted Solo, he assumed that Solo was part of the operation—"

"When has Han Solo ever worked with this agency?"

Kalenda cleared her throat. "Well, sir, I did recruit his help during the Centerpoint Station crisis."

Scaur's nostrils flared. "That was seven years ago, Colonel."

Kalenda returned the look. "Major Showolter was in bad shape, sir."

The director's expression softened. "How is he doing?"

"He took a nasty burn to the upper chest, but he's coming along."

Scaur nodded and glanced around the table. "My condolences to any of you who worked with officers Jode Tee and Saiga Bre'lya, or with Dr. Yintal of Fleet Intel. Their deaths and the deaths of Showolter's backup agents, who were apparently tortured into revealing the countersign, add tragedy to this calamity." He turned to Kalenda once more. "So the defectors became the property of Solo, who then proceeded to surrender them to the Peace Brigade."

"The Peace Brigade had a means of identifying the one called Elan. They took her and her companion, Vergere, aboard their shuttle and were attempting to reach a Yuuzhan Vong warship when the entire crew was apparently poisoned by Elan."

"By Elan's exhalations, I take it."

"Yes, sir. Solo retrieved her and Vergere, but was then convinced that both were part of an intricate plan to assassinate as many Jedi as possible. As you know, they had requested to meet with the Jedi to furnish details about an illness released by Yuuzhan Vong agents. We have since ascertained that Elan may have been referring to a molecular malady that has claimed some one hundred lives this past year—though just what the Jedi have to do with the malady is presently unknown.

"In any case, Solo considered the enticement to be part of the plot and was preparing to eject the defectors from his ship when he himself almost fell victim to Elan—to Elan's exhalations, that is. Sir."

Scaur stared at her for a long moment before replying. "On what basis did Solo determine them to be assassins rather than political fugitives?"

"As I say, sir, Solo became convinced that Elan had killed the members of the Peace Brigade to prevent them from returning her to the Yuuzhan Vong. The residue we collected from the Peace Brigade's shuttle matches that found aboard Solo's ship. Autopsies conducted on the men—including a Yuuzhan Vong operative—revealed that they died of hemorrhagic shock, induced by an inhaled vesicant toxin—a blood agent—of an unknown type."

Scaur located Solo's report from among the documents he had brought with him, scanned it, then tapped it with the back of his fingertips. "Solo claims that what you refer to as residue was actually alive at one point. He describes the creatures as some sort of mites that appeared out of thin air."

Kalenda compressed her lips. "Sir, I won't pretend to understand the nature of the toxin or the mechanics of its delivery. I know only that Solo was clearly meant to die."

"And instead, this Elan succumbed to the toxin herself."

"Presumably. Inside an escape pod, which Elan's companion subsequently employed to make her escape."

"Do we know what became of the pod?"

"Not yet. We conducted a search of the planetoid, but nothing turned up. While it's possible the pod is there somewhere, lodged in some crevasse or cave, it could just as easily have been recovered by the enemy frigate or destroyed during the firefight between the frigate and the cruiser-carrier *Thurse*."

"I still don't understand why Solo had to take it upon himself to send them back," Scaur grumbled. "No, belay that. Knowing Solo as I do, those actions are entirely consistent with his brash character."

"In defense of Solo's actions, sir, he was being pursued by an enemy warship."

"Yes, but the enemy obviously didn't want the defectors returned."

"Solo was convinced that Elan had already killed once and would do so again—perhaps even kill him to safeguard her secret, which in fact she attempted to do. Had Solo died and had Elan been brought into our midst, who knows what she might have done. In addition, sir, this defection has been suspect from the start. The commander of the cruiser *Soothfast* will attest to that."

Scaur nodded at Kalenda. "Granted, Colonel. Assuming for the moment that Solo's actions were justified, the New Republic's success in the Meridian sector must be reassessed, along with the victory at Ord Mantell." He shook his head regretfully. "We should have allowed military intelligence to handle this. Do you realize how this makes us look?"

"Sir?" Kalenda asked.

"The command staff is convinced that we bumbled the job. Despite the fact that Elan posed a threat, much could have been gained from having her in custody. What's more, it's apparent that someone with top secret clearance apprised the Peace Brigade of the plans to relocate Elan to Coruscant."

Scaur extracted another durasheet document from the sheaf and glanced at it. "Six members of military intelligence, fourteen in-house officers, the half-dozen senators who make up the Security and Intelligence Council . . . Someone leaked the information—either directly to the Peace Brigade or to a third party who did so." He looked around the table. "Do any of these individuals appear a likely source for a leak of this magnitude?"

"All of them had access to the same information," Kalenda supplied. "But whoever it was not only made contact with the Peace Brigade, but also managed to slice into our network and discontinue surveillance on the group. Traces of that slicing are still being analyzed."

"All well and good," Scaur pronounced, "but the real question to ask is whether we have a traitor in our midst or a mole—an enemy agent?"

"Someone wearing an ooglith masquer?" a Mon Calamari officer asked from the far end of the table.

"Not necessarily. The Yuuzhan Vong probably bought the services of the Peace Brigade. The same could hold true for whoever passed the information on to them. Members of the New Republic government could be in collusion with the enemy."

"But returning Elan to the Yuuzhan Vong ran counter to the entire plan," the Bothan deputy director of intelligence thought to point out.

Scaur plucked at his lower lip. "It's possible our traitor wasn't aware of the plan, only of the defection. Our seeming win at Ord Mantell convinced the traitor that Elan needed to be retrieved before further harm was done."

"Could have been someone testing the waters," Kalenda mused. "Reaching out to the Peace Brigade, without having any affiliation with the Yuuzhan Vong."

"Perhaps the Peace Brigade had something on the traitor," a human officer suggested. "The traitor may have been erasing a debt."

Scaur put his elbows on the table. "Did we get anything from the captured Peace Brigade members?"

"Two of thirteen we have in custody maintain that the only person who had contact with the traitor was Reck Desh, who died aboard the Peace Brigade shuttle. They claim that the initial contact was made by comlink, and that the only meeting between Desh and the source took place on Kuat, where Desh apparently met with a telbun."

Scaur grimaced. "A telbun?"

"The telbun could have been an intermediary for the one we're actually looking for," Kalenda said.

Scaur snorted. "So what you're really telling me is that we're without leads."

Kalenda nodded. "Thanks to Elan, Reck Desh took his secret to the grave."

In lofty Coruscant—though not so high up that the skyscraping spires, obelisks, and towers of the nucleus didn't defy perspective and boggle the mind—the Mon Calamari Jedi Cilghal, the Ithorian healer Tomla El, and the Ho'Din physician Ism Oolos waited expectantly for the MD-1 technician to complete its analysis of the tears Vergere had allegedly shed into a drink bulb aboard the *Millennium Falcon*.

Shortly, the vaguely humanlike droid projected the results as animated holograms of the liquid's chemical composition and its interaction with cells scraped from the inside of Mara Jade Skywalker's cheek.

"The chemical structure reflects what might be expected from tears," Tomla El said, leaning forward on his great buttressed feet, "but we've no way of determining whether they are indeed characteristic of Vergere's species."

"Yes, but look here," Oolos said excitedly, gesturing to the interaction hologram. "See how the substance is being drawn into the cells, almost as if being sponged up. And look how the cell reacts! Like an infusion of nutrient!"

Taller than a Wookiee, though rail-thin, Oolos had a broad, lipless mouth and a serpentine crown of stubby tresses, brilliant with red and violet scales. Like Tomla El, he wore a long white coat, which set the pair apart from Cilghal, whose homespun tunic and trousers were the color of fine sand.

"I'm encouraged," Oolos said to the laboratory's other two occupants. "Come, see for yourselves."

Hand in hand, Luke and Mara stepped closer to the droid's holographic projections and made a pretense of regarding them with the same scientific captivation demonstrated by the Ithorian and the Ho'Din. Luke was keenly aware that one of Cilghal's bulbous eyes was trained on Mara rather than on the displays.

Tomla El turned his sinuous head toward Luke and said out of both mouths, "I'm uneasy."

Everyone waited for him to continue.

"The priestess Elan was a weapon, dispatched by the Yuuzhan Vong to assassinate the Jedi. Why think that Vergere wasn't an accomplice, equally involved? Han Solo obviously believed that she was, or he wouldn't have sought to return her to the enemy."

"Han wasn't sure about Vergere," Cilghal said, answering for Luke.

"Why would Elan be harboring a deadly toxin, while her own familiar harbored an antidote to Mara's illness?"

"Perhaps Vergere was not what she seemed," Luke said, "even to Elan." He paused briefly, then added, "Han admits that he was tempted to destroy the drink bulb, until he began to think about what Vergere said to him before she jettisoned in the escape pod. She thanked him for giving her the chance to return to her own people."

"Naturally," Tomla El said, in a kind of lilting stereo. "The Yuuzhan Vong."

"But Han said that earlier Vergere had reacted to hearing my name. And Droma claimed that he once encountered a member of Vergere's species in the Corporate Sector."

"That means little," Tomla El argued. "Yuuzhan Vong agents infiltrated our galaxy as far back as fifty standard years. Vergere's species could be an extragalactic client race of the Yuuzhan Vong."

"Tomla El is correct about one thing," Oolos said, turning from the holograms. "We can't be sure this ostensible gift isn't part of a plan to instill us with false confidence and inadvertently do greater harm to Mara."

All eyes fell on her. As wan as she had become over the course of only a few weeks, she continued to reveal boundless grit and defiance. "I'm finding it pretty hard to swallow that the Yuuzhan Vong would go to all this trouble to kill one Jedi—namely, me—when Elan was out to assassinate all of us."

Oolos told the MD droid to deactivate the holograms; then he spent a moment in deep contemplation. "We should proceed cautiously." He looked at the drinking bulb. "We don't even know whether the liquid is supposed to be injected, ingested, or applied."

"We do have a clue," Luke said. "Vergere used her tears to mend a blaster wound suffered by an intelligence officer aboard the *Queen of Empire*. She applied them by hand."

"Topically," Oolos clarified.

Cilghal studied him with one eye. "But Mara's illness isn't topical, it's systemic."

All at once Luke called the bulb to his hand with the Force. Inverting it, he brought it to his mouth, prepared to squeeze a drop onto his tongue. But Mara just as quickly snatched it from him and took a few drops into her own mouth before Luke could stop her.

"Mara!" Oolos and Tomla El said in unison.

But Mara wasn't in distress. She inhaled sharply, then opened her eyes wide. "Oh, Luke," she said, as if in awe. "I can't explain exactly how I feel, but it's like water after days of going without it." She looked at her hands—first the palms, then the backs—and touched her face. "My fingers and my face are tingling."

Gently, Luke took the bulb from her and squeezed a drop onto his tongue. "I don't feel anything," he said after a moment.

Mara took the bulb back and held it close to her heart. "There's no reason you should feel anything."

Luke looked his wife in the eye. "Mara, there's one more thing you need to hear: Showolter said that the healing effect was temporary. Vergere told him as much when she came to his aid. He was already going into shock when he found Han."

"That doesn't mean it will work that way on me," Mara said firmly. "Besides, at this point, I'll accept temporary." She forced a breath and took Luke's hand in hers. "You have to let me do this, Luke. I know that you and Cilghal have been trying to heal me through the Force, and I know that I haven't made it easy for you by withdrawing into myself. But this illness has been part of me for over a year now. It's been my challenge, and I've fought it every way I know how. But it's winning, Luke. It's winning."

She lifted the bulb to eye level. "If this makes things worse, then I'll just have to fight even harder. But everything in me tells me that won't happen. Do you understand?"

"At least let us monitor you," Tomla El advised. "If something begins to go wrong, there are steps we may be able to take."

"No," Luke said, holding Mara's gaze. "We'll do this Mara's way."

She gave his hand a squeeze, then moved to a nearby countertop and carefully dribbled some of the tears into her cupped right hand. Before she could bring the transparent liquid to her lips or face, however, it vanished.

"My hand absorbed it," she said in amazement, showing her palm.

Oolos approached, looking down at her from his towering height. "Mara, at least tell us what you're feeling."

She took a stuttering breath. "I'm not sure. Lightheaded, flushed. Everything is suddenly so bright—" She gave a start. "It's triggering something inside me! I can—"

Mara's arms and legs began to tremble. She put her head back, as if fighting for breath. She might have fallen if Luke had not hurried to her side.

"Quickly, Luke, convey her to the table," Oolos said.

Luke carried her to the diagnostic table and set her down on her back. Eyes tightly shut, Mara groaned and hugged her trembling torso.

"We'll have readouts momentarily," Tomla El said from the table's control console.

Luke's eyes didn't move from Mara. "Mara," Luke whispered, close to her ear. "Mara . . ."

She groaned once more and then gave a start, staring wide-eyed at Luke. "I don't know," she said, her voice a raspy whisper. "I can't explain what I'm feeling. Did I make the wrong choice, my love?" Her expression became imploring. "Look at me, Luke. Look at me . . ."

Her voice trailed off and she lapsed into a state of semiconsciousness. Luke searched for encouragement in the eyes of Cilghal, Tomla El, and Oolos, but found none. He returned his gaze to Mara and reached for her in the Force.

As he did, the spastic movements of her limbs began to subside and her entire countenance began to change. Her face relaxed and tears leaked from the outside corners of her eyes. Luke's face grew warm, and his eyes grew moist with relief and vigilant joy.

Mara's eyes blinked open and she smiled weakly. "I think it's working," she said softly, wetting her lips with her tongue. She closed her eyes once more, as if luxuriating in what she was experiencing. "I can feel it coursing through me. It's as if every cell in my body were being bathed in light." She groped blindly for Luke's hand and drew it to her breast. "I think I'm healing, Luke. I'm sure I'm healing."

"Oh, Mara," Cilghal said tearfully, coming to the table to lay her webbed hand on Mara's shoulder.

Luke caught sight of the skeptical glances exchanged by Tomla El and Oolos, but he said nothing. Rather, he looked again at Mara through the Force and found her luminous.

A smile of unabashed delight split his face. He put his arm under his wife's shoulders and gently lifted her into his embrace. Her arms encircled his neck, and she clung to him, crying quietly and joyously.

"We have our victory," Luke whispered.

TWENTY-EIGHT

Leia hurried through the apartment's front entry onto the skyway balcony. But as eager as she was to give Han and Anakin the good news about Mara, she restrained herself from intruding on their conversation.

"The thing I still can't figure out," Han was saying, "is what put it in my head that Elan's breath was deadly. It was like I heard a voice warning me. That's when I grabbed the multitool."

Gazing out across the city canyon, Han had one foot up on the balcony railing and the survival tool in his right hand. His travel pack sat at his feet. When a long moment had elapsed and Anakin still hadn't responded, Han turned to him and loosed a short laugh.

"Thanks."

Anakin's brooding look changed to one of perplexity. "For what, Dad?"

"For not telling me that I was hearing Chewie through the Force."

Anakin smiled. "Yeah, like I'd even think about saying that to you."

Han raised his index finger. "And don't even think about telling your uncle, either. All I need is for Luke to hear that I'm hearing voices. This is strictly between you and me and the stair pillar, got it?" He turned slightly in Leia's direction. "No offense, sweetheart."

Leia showed him a blatantly counterfeit smile. "Better the stair pillar than the tread, *sweetheart*."

Han nodded smugly, stood up, and approached Anakin. "Anyway, I just wanted to say thanks for showing up at Roa's ship that day." He proffered the survival tool. "If it wasn't for this . . . well, you know all about that."

"Thank Chewie," Anakin said. "He made it."

Han shook his head. "I've already thanked Chewie. This is something between you and me." He grasped Anakin by the shoulders and tugged him into a tight embrace.

Leia thought her heart might break. Her hand flew to her mouth and she fought back tears.

Han moved Anakin away, but he kept his hands on his son's shoulders. "I'm sorry for what I said and the way I've been acting since Chewie died, Anakin. We did everything we could have done at Sernpidal, and Chewie knew that. We both know who's responsible for his dying. But I don't want vengeance prompting you to do anything foolish, you understand? You and Jacen and Jaina are more important to me than you'll ever know."

Anakin nodded and almost grinned. He and Han embraced once more.

"I've gotta get going," Anakin said after a moment. "Uncle Luke is expecting me back on Yavin 4."

"One thing before you leave," Leia said, smiling. "Vergere's gift seems to be working." She cut her eyes to Han. "I just heard from Luke that Mara is stronger than she's been in months. Whatever the tears contain, they're taking a lot out of her, but Oolos and Tomla El are hopeful that Mara will be in full remission in a few weeks."

The three of them fell into a brief, gleeful embrace, which Anakin broke.

"First the Yuuzhan Vong poison Mara, then they send an assassin against us," he said bitterly. "I'll remember what you said about vengeance, Dad, but they've made this war personal."

Leia's eyes clouded over with misgiving, and she gave Anakin another hug and a kiss on the cheek. "Take care of yourself."

"Hey, kid," Han shouted as Anakin was heading for the skyway bridge. "Any chance that Lowbacca's become so busy with Jedi stuff that he and Waroo have forgotten about the life debt?"

"Not when I spoke to him last."

"Blast," Han muttered. "I guess I'm going to have to deal with this sooner or later." He glanced at Leia and smiled. "So Vergere was on the level, after all." He gave his head an incredulous shake. "It's funny the way things work out. You go in search of one thing and end up finding something else. If I didn't know better, I'd think it was the Force at work."

Leia kept quiet.

Han narrowed his eyes and nodded. "Wookiees have an expression, that the real quarry of every hunt is the unexpected. But I guess you tend to forget that when you've been out of the game for a long while."

Leia heard something different and troublesome in his tone. She indicated his travel pack. "That hasn't left your side since you got back," she said, as casually as she could. "Are you going to unpack or are you planning to have it stuffed and mounted?"

Han moved for the pack. "No use in unpacking just yet."

Leia folded her arms under her breasts. "I guess I should have seen this coming. Then you're not really home."

"I've been home too much lately." He grinned at her. "I figured you must be getting tired of seeing me hanging around."

Leia didn't move. "Don't try to turn this around, Han."

He gestured to himself. "Who's trying to turn anything around? I'm only saying that I've got a few things that need doing."

"Such as?"

"Such as finding Roa, for starters. And helping Droma locate his clanmates. He saved my skin, you know—twice."

Leia launched a sardonic laugh to the sky. "Don't tell me you owe Droma a life debt. This is too much, Han—even for you."

His brow furrowed. "You can't expect me to just forget about Roa or leave Droma hanging."

She took a step toward him. "Do Wookiees have anything to say about taking senseless risks? Not a moment ago I stood here listening to you caution Anakin against doing anything foolish, and now you tell me you're going off after Roa and Droma's missing clanmates. Make up your mind which way you want it to be, Han."

"What's wrong with having it both ways?"

Leia snorted. "Relapse complete. Say hello to your former self, Han."

"Relapse, nothing. This is the same me you married, sweetheart. Besides, you're one to talk. While I was moping around here, you were on Dantooine, in Imperial Remnant space, all over the place, taking exactly the same kind of risks."

"Are you saying that if I give up helping refugees, you'll give up your fling with the past?"

"*My* fling?" he said. "What do you call what you're doing?"

Leia started to say something but changed her mind and began again. "The New Republic is in a tough spot, Han. I could use your help."

He held up his hands. "I've heard that before."

"And you've usually listened."

Han paced to the railing and back, avoiding her gaze. "In a way I'm already helping you out. I mean, with Droma's family being refugees and all . . ."

Leia fell silent for a moment. As relieved as she was to see him finally emerging from grief, she couldn't help but sense that he was intent on starting over, as he had done all his life—from abandoned kid to Imperial officer, and from smuggler to Rebel leader—always re-creating himself. From what little she knew of Droma from their few encounters, he seemed cut from the same cloth. For all Droma's concerns about his scattered clanmates, he was a drifter and a rogue at heart, addicted to adventure.

Leia watched Han pace the edge of the balcony. "I don't know how you've done it for so long," she said finally.

He stopped to look at her. "Done what?"

"Raise a family. Walk so far from the edge."

"That was just my 'fling' with stability." He tried out his grin, but it didn't work. "Look, I'm just leaving, okay? I've got obligations."

"What about your obligations to us?"

"This has nothing to do with us."

"Oh, no?" She advanced on him. "I learned a long time ago that you couldn't be bound by anyone's preconceived ideas of who you should be. And I'll admit I love that about you. But keep one thing in mind: I'm not Malla, Han. I won't have you dropping by here once a year, using our home as a base for your escapades."

Han curled his upper lip. "You're way off the mark."

She smiled faintly. "I suppose we'll just have to see about that."

Han frowned sadly, then put his arms around her. "Trust me."

She leaned away to show him a dubious look. "I've heard that before."

He raised her hand and kissed the palm. "Tuck that in your pocket for later on."

Scooping up his pack, he made for the sky bridge without looking back.

Elsewhere in the Solo apartment, C-3PO and R2-D2 were just concluding data upgrades that had obliged them to plug into the HoloNet and newsnet feeds. The 3-D images still shone from the HoloNet projectors, but the two droids were paying more attention to their own internal circuitry than to the displays.

"Events couldn't possibly have worked out better," C-3PO was telling his squat counterpart. "Mistress Mara is well on her way to recovery, Master Han has returned home, and the Yuuzhan Vong have suffered a major setback. I couldn't be more content if I'd just emerged from a refurbishing bath at an exclusive oil spa."

R2-D2 rotated his hemispherical head and intoned a series of discomfiting chitters and modulating whistles.

C-3PO gazed at him for a moment. "What do you mean, I need to have my neural processor overhauled? What do you know of events that I don't?"

R2-D2 fluted a reply.

"Master Han has not returned home?"

The astromech droid mewled and directed C-3PO's attention to a display screen fed by the front entry security cam. The screen showed Master Han crossing the sky bridge in the direction of a public transportation balcony, and Mistress Leia, with the fingertips of one hand to her mouth, watching him leave.

"Oh, dear, you're right. But perhaps he's only going on an errand."

R2-D2 warbled truculently.

"Well, how should I know why he has his travel pack with him or why Mistress Leia appears dismayed? I'm certain there's a reasonable explanation."

R2-D2 loosed a lengthy and haughty chirrup.

"What's that you say? The New Republic was tricked into thinking it was victorious at Ord Mantell?" C-3PO adopted an akimbo posture. "I don't know where you're receiving your information, but I suggest you pay closer attention to what's going on around you, and stop spending so much time plugged into the HoloNet."

R2-D2 rotated his head to the newsnet hologram, where real-time images beamed in from a Mid Rim world showed droids of all variety hurrying to escape a riotous mob bent on destroying them.

"Oh, my," C-3PO said in distress, then immediately adopted a peeved tone of voice. "I see that you continue to excel at presenting the worst side of things. But I have some news for those gloomy sensors of yours: No matter what you may choose to parade before my photoreceptors, you will never again hear me express concerns about deactivation."

R2-D2's zither approximated a derisive laugh.

"Well, of course you wouldn't understand what I'm talking about, because you have no awareness that fears of deactivation are the result of unhealthy aspirations for uninterrupted activation. With a bit of detachment, even you will find that all fears disappear."

R2-D2 razzed.

"You just watch your language, you barrel of bits! And so what if I am beginning to think like a human being. You say that as if it was something negative."

R2-D2 hooted and toodled in rebuke.

"Oh, so you're going to remind me of all this when we're both being melted down for spare parts, are you? What makes you think you'll be in any position to remind anyone of anything? And just you try, in any case. I'll have you know that Master Han has promised to store all my memories, so that in the event of the destruction of my metal body, my thoughts and memories could simply be transferred to another—perhaps even to a newer model of the protocol series with the SyntheTech AAA-2 verbobrain."

R2-D2 issued a razz, the meaning of which was beyond dispute, and rolled off toward the doorway.

"Put a restraining bolt where?" C-3PO said in shock. "Why, I've a good mind to forewarn Master Luke that your circuitry is irreparably glitched. Go ahead, roll out on me," he said to the astromech's back. "See where it gets you. You'll soon return, wanting to learn all I know about becoming a real person."

A sudden flutter brought a quick end to C-3PO's tirade, and he tilted his head in consternation. Folks of all manner had frequently characterized him as priggish, fretful, and faultfinding, but his newfound insights into the nature of existence appeared to have boosted those personality traits, as well. If awareness could be achieved only at the expense of logic and dispassion, it might not be such a desirable state after all.

"Why, it's no wonder sentients wage war on one another," he said aloud as he hurried out the door after R2-D2.

TWENTY-NINE

Harrar rued the day he had been sent to Obroa-skai. Still recovering from the pummeling Yuuzhan Vong warships had inflicted weeks earlier, the planet sat framed in the command center hull transparency of the priest's black jewel of a ship, enshrouded by gray clouds, as if too traumatized to so much as rotate. Harrar was constrained to suffer the view while he sought to offer explanation for the probable failure of his and Nom Anor's plan.

"At this point, Excellency, we do not know for certain whether Elan and Vergere are in captivity or missing in action."

"Or dead," Commander Tla said from behind him.

Harrar was left to wonder how accurately his dedicated villip rendered his pained grimace for those at the receiving end of the communiqué—namely the high priest Jakan, father of Elan, chief of their domain, and adviser to Supreme Overlord Shimrra; Nas Choka, supreme commander of the flagship of the Yuuzhan Vong fleet; and Prefect Drathul, administrator of the worldship *Harla*. Consciousness-linked villips of the three rested in outsize eggcuplike holders positioned between Harrar and the view he found so abhorrent. It was Jakan who responded to Tla's utterance.

"Why do you include death in Harrar's list of possible outcomes, Commander?" While spectacular to behold, the villip scarcely did justice to the high priest's fully re-shaped and transfigured visage, with its nub of nose and deeply set eyes.

Tla turned to one of the transmitting villips. "Despite our firing on it, the New Republic ship carrying Elan and Vergere was racing *toward* our vessel, clearly intent on returning the priestess. The infidels in command must have divined that we had restrained the shuttle, and as well that Elan had exterminated the crew. At the last moment before it altered course and fled, the ship jettisoned an escape pod, but Nom Anor failed to retrieve it."

Nom Anor worked his jaw but offered no apology.

"Then you did attempt to retrieve it?" Jakan asked.

"I did, Excellency," Nom Anor allowed.

"Even in the knowledge that by doing so you would have doomed Harrar's plan to failure?"

Nom Anor glanced briefly at the priest, then nodded.

Supreme Commander Choka's villip spoke, summoning Commander Tla and his scrawny tactician forward. Choka's facial tattoos lent him gravity; his trace of mustache and merest wisp of beard, a noble demeanor.

"As I understand it, Commander, your part in this was to arrange for New Republic victories, to ensure that Elan was well appraised." Choka's decurved eyes—above large bluish sacs—fell on the tactician. "But at what expense to us?"

"It was a costly enterprise, Supreme Commander,"

Tactician Raff began. "Many coralskippers were sacrificed, and several small warships were destroyed. Were our resources replete, the losses would be insignificant. But Belkadan and Sernpidal are overtaxed and resupply has slowed. To continue to guarantee adequate defense for the fleet, we will need to cannibalize some of our larger ships to reinforce the coralskipper battle groups, or divert from the invasion corridor and replenish by preparing new worlds for yorik coral production."

Raff gestured to Nom Anor. "Executor Nom Anor has assured us that we will receive a warm reception in a nearby sector known as Hutt space, as the reigning species—the Hutts—have no wish to engage us in warfare."

"Nom Anor assures," Choka said contemptuously. "Continue, tactician."

The tactician inclined his head. "Lastly, the New Republic military has deployed its fleets to protect the Core, or perhaps in the aim of mounting a counteroffense. I remain confident that we could repulse an attack, but I am obligated to report that they are learning slowly how to dupe our dovin basals and frustrate our weapons."

"There will be no cannibalizing of ships," Choka ordered gruffly. "I will be arriving soon from our shipyard at Sernpidal with a young yammosk and additional forces. In the meantime, the fleet will divert to Hutt space, under the leadership of Commander Malik Carr."

Malik Carr stepped forward and offered salute.

"Commander Tla and Eminence Harrar are hereby recalled to the Outer Rim."

Tla and Harrar said nothing.

Attention turned to the third villip, consciousness-joined to Prefect Drathul. "I would speak privately with Executor Nom Anor," Drathul said.

When everyone else had filed from the command center, the prefect's wide and broad-browed face took on a minatory look. "Precisely what occurred, Executor?"

Nom Anor gestured in dismissal. "The blame lies with Harrar and Elan. They had no knack for improvisation."

"Were the Jedi involved in thwarting us?"

"They may have had a hand in it."

Drathul's villip nodded. "Word has reached my ear that some of your agents were responsible."

"They were trying to protect our interests, nothing more."

Drathul considered it. "For your sake, Executor, I hope so. After the Praetorite's disaster in the Helska system, Warmaster Tsavong Lah will brook no further failures on your part."

Nom Anor nodded. "I understand, Prefect. I have a new plan in mind, which I intend to launch once the fleet has been relocated to Hutt space."

"Do not disappoint me."

"You have my word. What's more, we may have found a potential ally on Coruscant. Someone as yet unknown—though highly placed in the New Republic military or intelligence divisions—reached out to us through my agents."

"Interesting," Prefect Drathul allowed. "Learn the identity of this one."

"I will do so."

"One final question, Executor. Have we under-estimated these infidels?"

Nom Anor scoffed. "Only their blind good fortune."

*   *   *

"We were lucky," Droma called down to Han from the roof of the *Falcon*. "Some minor scoring around the aft heat exhaust vents, but nothing a bit of plasteel and paint won't remedy."

"We don't have the time for that," Han said from the floor of Docking Bay 3733. "Besides, I like her scratched and imperfect."

The *Falcon* sat on its hard stand, umbilicaled to diagnostic monitors, pressurizers, and tanks of coolant and liquid metal fuel. They had spent more than two days going over the ship, inside and out, making repairs where necessary and generally tidying up. Droma had shown himself to be an able mechanic, although slightly better at intuitive problem solving than he was with hydrospanners or macrofusers.

"Come to think of it, a paint job might not be such a bad idea," Han said a moment later. "After what happened in the Bilbringi system, opticals of the *Falcon* are probably plastered inside every Yuuzhan Vong warship and coralskipper."

"Provided the paint job turns out better than your beard."

Han frowned and grabbed hold of his chin. "You want to talk about follicle disasters, if those mustachios of yours get any longer, you'll be tripping on them."

Droma climbed down off the roof and jumped nimbly to the floor. Han tossed him a rag and watched as Droma cleaned his hands, then used the bristly edges of his hands to clean his velvety fur.

Aware of Han's gaze, Droma paused. "What?" he asked.

Han concealed a grin. "Nothing. How 'bout you unhook the outboard power feeds while I take care of the refueling lines?"

Droma shrugged. "Fine with me."

"Then I guess we're all set."

Droma studied him for a moment. "Will Leia be coming by to see you off?"

"I don't think so."

"A pity. I wanted to tell her good-bye."

"Next time," Han said, then quickly added, "Not that there's likely to be a next time."

"Well, then, tell her good-bye for me—the next time you see her."

Han scowled. "All I'm saying is that I don't want you making yourself too comfortable in the copilot's chair."

"I know better than to do that."

"I'm just trying to make clear that this isn't a permanent arrangement. You and me, I mean. It's just till we find your family."

Droma smiled faintly. "What happened to the tab I was running for you?"

"Look, chum, humans don't believe in life debts. When somebody does us a favor, we return it and the slate's wiped clean. I help you locate your clanmates, then we both go our separate ways, understand?"

"As opposed to what—my flying around the galaxy with you in this relic?"

Han sniffed. "You weren't saying that when we went after Reck."

"I was just being polite. I had you figured for the type who'd be sensitive about his ship."

"Sure you did."

They fell into an awkward silence, which Droma

broke. "I'll see to the power feeds." He had started for the stern when Han called out to him.

"Hey, Droma. We'll find your sister, you know." Han allowed a grin. "Even if we have to search half the galaxy."

THE COMPLETE
NEW JEDI ORDER SERIES

WWW.READSTARWARS.COM

Published by Del Rey/LucasBooks • Available wherever books are sold